The
Necklace

By Carla Kelly

CAMEL
PRESS
Kenmore, WA

CAMEL PRESS

A Camel Press book published by Epicenter Press

Epicenter Press
6524 NE 181st St. Suite 2
Kenmore, WA 98028.
www.Epicenterpress.com
www.Coffeetownpress.com
www.Camelpress.com

For more information go to: www.camelpress.com
www.carlakellyauthor.com

This is a work of fiction. Names, characters, places, brands, media, and incidents are the product of the author's imagination or are used fictitiously.

The Necklace
Copyright © 2021 by Carla Kelly

ISBN: 9781603813549 (trade paper)
ISBN: 9781603813778 (ebook)

Printed in the United States of America

To Martha Abell, who had faith in this story. Thanks, Marty.
And to my editor, Jennifer McCord, who did, too.

Books by Carla Kelly

FICTION

Daughter of Fortune
Summer Campaign
Miss Chartley's Guided Tour
Marian's Christmas Wish
Mrs. McVinnie's London Season
Libby's London Merchant
Miss Grimsley's Oxford Career
Miss Billings Treads the Boards
Miss Milton Speaks Her Mind
Miss Wittier Makes a List
Mrs. Drew Plays Her Hand
Reforming Lord Ragsdale
The Lady's Companion
With This Ring
One Good Turn
The Wedding Journey
Here's to the Ladies: Stories of the Frontier Army
Beau Crusoe
Marrying the Captain
The Surgeon's Lady
Marrying the Royal Marine
The Admiral's Penniless Bride
Borrowed Light
Enduring Light
Coming Home for Christmas: The Holiday Stories
Regency Christmas Gifts
Season's Regency Greetings
Marriage of Mercy
My Loving Vigil Keeping
Double Cross
Marco and the Devil's Bargain
Paloma and the Horse Traders
Star in the Meadow
Unlikely Master Genius
Unlikely Spy Catchers
Safe Passage
Softly Falling
One Step Enough
Courting Carrie in Wonderland
A Regency Royal Navy Christmas
Unlikely Heroes
A Hopeful Christmas

I Told Thee, Soul

I told thee, soul, that joy and woe,

Were but a gust, a passing dew.

I told thee so, I told thee so,

And oh, my soul, the tale was true.

Canción, Middle Ages

In 711 A.D., the kingdoms of Visigothic Spain suffered a Moorish invasion from North Africa, fueled by the desire for conquest in the name of Allah, and by the prospect of wealth and land. The Spaniards were overwhelmed and driven far to the north in their peninsula. During the next five hundred years, they slowly reclaimed their land in what later became known as the Reconquest.

By 1211, the Christian frontier was guarded by a thin line of fortresses south of Toledo, where Spanish warlords fought savagely to maintain control of their hard-won lands wrested from the Almohades, other warriors who followed the Moorish conquerors.

To wage war, the Spaniards needed soldiers, horses, weapons, supplies. Centuries of battle had drained their resources. Sometimes the only way to fill empty coffers was to marry well, even below one's station. And if the bride was the daughter of a herring merchant from The Low Countries, or Netherlands? Money is money and war doesn't care.

Prologue

When he read the letter from his cousin King Alfonso, that royal part of his otherwise-ordinary family tree, Santiago Gonzalez de la Victoria understood it as a document from a scheming relative to a susceptible relative. Who else but a landless man of some ambition would consider marrying a herring merchant's daughter from the Netherlands for her dowry?

Santiago nearly burned the letter before Manolo read it, or Engracia, who could not read, pelted him for more information. Like him, his brother and sister-in-law had watched the arrival of the courier. Letters were rare.

Here at Las Claves, on the remote *frontera* they shared unwillingly with the Almohades, latest invaders from North Africa, news of a letter traveled fast. For all he knew, the people who farmed Manolo's land and tended his flocks wondered what the king had to say. Maybe even Yussef el Ghalib – Almohad and his worst enemy – wanted to know.

Santiago read the letter to Manolo, after his crippled brother made himself comfortable, then waited. Thin and wasted he may have been from a lifetime of pain – Santiago's fault, according to Juana, miserable servant and curse – Manolo commanded the estate. Santiago was his younger brother.

"Santiago, such a dowry will buy you an army to add to Alfonso's, and the armies of our Leon and Aragon cousins," Manolo said. "We know the caliphate of the Almohades is weakening. Caliph Muhammad al-Nasir commands less and less respect from his own Almohad warriors. Another army from this dowry could mean all the difference."

Then came the clinching argument: "You would possess land of your own to the south, and the chance to prosper, once the land is Spain's entirely.

3

Even more, armies mean Spain will be Christian from the Pyrenees to Gibraltar."

"Suppose I don't like her?" Santiago asked, since they had come this far. For a moment – *solo un momento* – he envied Manolo of his wife. Manolo's marriage to a merchant's daughter, and *her* vulgar dowry had come in time to bolster the dwindling fortunes of Las Claves. His envy quickly passed. Engracia loved his brother. And what's more, Engracia was ample of bosom but small of brain.

He didn't know what else to say, so Manolo filled in the silence. "Have you a better idea how to raise an army?"

No, he did not.

"I will do it." Santiago said the words quickly, to make them go away. "How bad can this be?"

After the harvest, Santiago sent his letter of agreement north to Valladolid with Antonio Baltierra, a man he trusted as no other. Santiago also sent along Father Bendicio, a timid priest whose paltry virtues included skill with languages, and a possible flair for negotiation.

Antonio returned two months later, ragged and bearded. He handed over King Alfonso's reply, with the news that the king had dispatched Father Bendicio, in the company of Father Domitius, to Vlissingen, prosperous port in the Netherlands.

In his letter, King Alfonso assured Santiago that the two priests – Domitius was a lawyer – were equal to the task of dealing with a simple herring merchant with pretentions. "'Here is the copy of the document I sent,'" Santiago read aloud to Manolo and Engracia. "'You will have your army, courtesy of my agreement to a Dutch monopoly in Spanish ports of cod, herring and eels. And a wife, of course.'"

Santiago looked up from the document. "Manolo, here we are in the Year of Our Lord 1210. It lacks one year of five hundred years since the Moors conquered Spain."

He handed the letter to Manolo, who read it with a smile. "You have a year's reprieve, brother," Manolo said. "Father Bendicio will remain in Vlissingen, teaching this woman our language." He looked closer. "In the spring of 1211, she will arrive at the northern port of Santander with the dowry and we will buy an army."

"I hope you will like her," Engracia said.

The brothers smiled at each other. Did that matter?

"What is her name?" Engracia asked.

Manolo handed back the document and Santiago turned the pages until he found a name. "I cannot even pronounce it. How would *you* say it?"

"I have no idea."

"H-a-n-n-e-k-e A-a-r-d-e-m-a," Santiago spelled. He shrugged. "I do not know. Perhaps Ana?"

As he stared at the document, Santiago knew he had made a mistake. "It's a devil's bargain," he said softly, so Manolo couldn't hear. "What was I thinking?"

Chapter One

All romantic notions aside – Hanneke Aardema had few – marrying a cousin of the king of Castile and Leon seemed precisely what a man as ambitious as her father might attempt. Why hadn't she suspected he might do something like this?

The daughter of a Netherlands herring merchant, Hanneke had assumed that Papa would bring home a catch for *her* someday in the form of another merchant, or possibly an up and coming fisherman such as he had been.

Mama had assured her of that. "Listen, my love," she had said a few years earlier, when Hanneke became a woman. "If I know your father, he will trot out three or four sons of equally rich merchants. He will let you choose."

As it turned out, Antje Aardema didn't know Hans Aardema as well as she thought. The trouble came when Papa, once the most amiable of men, became ambitious, pretentious, and secretive. To Hanneke's surprise and then her consternation, no sons of wealthy merchants came around. When she turned sixteen, people began to talk.

"Mama, I'm becoming the subject of gossip," Hanneke said one morning. "'What is wrong with the herring merchant's daughter? Does no man want her?' people are saying."

"I regret to tell you that Papa is ambitious," Mama had managed to say between coughs that produced an alarming amount of blood each time. "He told me in confidence that he has his eye on Spain, and a monopoly on trade."

"How can that possibly affect me?"

"I don't know," Mama whispered, exhausted and ready to die.

When Mama perished within the month, Hanneke had no trouble stuffing Mama's uncertainty into a dark corner of her mind. There was a household to manage, even though she had been running it since Mama's illness began. Maybe Papa would forget about a marriage.

He did not forget. Hans Aardema also did not squander more than two months as a widower. Soon another Mevrouw Aardema slept in Mama's bed, counted the silver spoons and scolded the servants. This new wife usurped Hanneke's household reign, an efficient takeover that allowed Hans Aardema to resume his search for a way to turn his only living child into a useful commodity.

Letters went here and there. In late winter of 1210, two black-robed Spanish priests came to their brick manor in Vlissingen, the most prosperous port in the Netherlands.

In passable Dutch, Father Bendicio introduced himself as a priest from Las Claves, a fortress-castle on the line dividing Christian Castile from Moslem Al-Andalus. Father Domitius proclaimed himself a lawyer from the court of King Alfonso of Castile. Uneasy, Hanneke noted the fleeting but triumphant glance between husband and second wife, and knew her life was going to change.

How, she wasn't certain. After one day with the door closed, followed by the priests storming out, and then another similar day, she began to relax. She knew how stubborn Papa could be in the pursuit of more ships and fisherman. How could bartering away a daughter be any different?

To her dismay, after a week of threats, and angry letters back and forth, the priests returned, looking as determined as Papa. It ended with smiles all around, except for hers.

Her stepmother summoned Hanneke from her room, where she had been attempting to unsnarl a ball of yarn. Mevrouw Aardema pushed her into Papa's office and closed the door.

In silence, both priests walked around her. She had seen Papa do that when he bought draft horses to pull his fish wagons, and it unnerved her.

"She is so short," Father Domitius said, in heavily accented Dutch.

"She is almost seventeen," Papa said. "She will grow."

"She looks fragile," Father Bendicio said. "And so old."

"Strong as an ox."

The Spaniards withdrew to talk in low tones, darting critical glances her way until she found herself edging closer to Papa, even though he was the author of her misery. At least she knew him.

With a put-upon sigh, the lawyer strode across the room and bowed to Hans Aardema. "Very well."

Papa clapped his hands, his face nearly angelic with the same smile Hanneke recognized from word of a good catch, when his fleet of herring boats made port. Hans Aardema, king of salted fish, was a happy man.

"I am rich!" he had exclaimed, after ushering out the priests, who would return tomorrow with documents to sign. He pulled Hanneke close. "You will become the bride of someone the king is related to, a cousin, I think." He thumped his chest. "You are looking at the proud possessor of a monopoly – what they call a *privilegio* - in salted fish for every port of Spain not controlled by the Muslims. I am a wealthy man."

"Papa, you already were," Hanneke said. She might have been a cricket chirping on the hearth, for all the attention he paid her.

Could she cajole some sense into him? "Papa, couldn't I choose from one of the sons of your wealthy friends?" she asked. "After all, if I am to go to Spain, you will never see your only child again."

Did she touch a sympathetic nerve? No. Papa laughed until he had to wipe his eyes. "*Choose?* Since when is that done? Write me a letter now and then. That will suffice."

She left the room in silence. Papa's laughter followed her.

Now, six months later, she stood on the deck of a filthy Spanish scow, bumbling toward Spain, blown two leagues backward for every four leagues forward, or so it seemed. When the vessel took on water, that meant endless weeks in Caen among the less-than-accommodating French.

Their Spanish sea captain raged and sputtered, and French shipbuilders ignored him, declaring, "Your problem is not our problem." They even had the nerve to laugh at the priest when Father Bendicio explained that King Alfonso expected them a month ago. Shamed, Father Bendicio scurried below, while Hanneke turned away, heartily tired of everyone.

Finally, the wretched vessel ventured away from the French coast as June arrived. She stared down at the water. Spring had turned to summer. She was seventeen now, truly old. She had just fled to the deck, weary of one more language lesson. Did the priest have to continue them on the ship?

It was partly her fault, which she acknowledged as she rested her elbows on the railing. Before Father Bendicio had begun his tutelage in Castilian, she knew she possessed a flair for languages. She had pretended ignorance, forcing the priest from Las Claves to sink to humiliating depths as he tried to teach her Castilian and blamed himself when she pretended ignorance. Hans Aardema had scolded the prissy fellow for being a poor teacher.

That was unkind of me, she thought, not for the first time. *It is something a powerless person does, though.* Father Bendicio had tried so hard. She would never have admitted that the language of Spain was easier than French and interested her.

"There you are."

Hanneke did not turn from her contemplation of the water. "I cannot go far."

Now was the time for her revenge, one or two sentences in flawless Castilian. "Father, do you think the time will ever come when I speak your language as well as you? I would fear to disappoint King Alfonso."

When he blinked in surprise, started to speak, then looked away, she knew his humiliation should weigh on her conscience. Should.

"Hanneke, you surprise me," he said finally, all the hurt evident.

"Sometimes I surprise myself," she said, happy to watch her triumph.

What she saw made her regret her smallness of soul. She saw the dismay in his eyes, he who had tried so hard to teach her. Even on this voyage, when seasickness rendered him pale and unable to eat, he had doggedly persisted with the hated lessons. She saw in his eyes the awareness that she had been toying with him.

Better to change the subject. "How much longer, Father?"

"How much longer?" he echoed, quietly and humbly. What a prickly thing a conscience was. She writhed inside at her mistreatment of this priest she had decided to hate, simply because he was Spanish and she disliked where fate was taking her. Was her heart so small?

Poor man, why do I torment him? she asked herself. "You look ill. You should go below," she said in her kindest voice, one she hadn't used with him before.

"I am not a man for hard times," he admitted, and left her at the railing.

Dismayed with herself, she couldn't go below, where the air stank of rotten things, and the smell of unwashed bodies, hers included. She looked around at the crates lashed to the deck, each of them holding some portion of her dowry, beyond the sizeable stash of gold coins Father Bendicio had hidden somewhere. The crates held everything from finely woven fabric to candlesticks, to beautiful blue and white pottery from Delft. There was even Dutch cheese, the best in the world.

She sat on one of the crates and drew her knees up to her chest, thinking about vulgar excess and a salt fish monopoly, and the morning they sailed from Vlissingen. Papa had surprised her by taking her hand and declaring, "You are so much like me."

"Never," she declared, her heart breaking.

"You might not want to admit it," he said, "but we are both resourceful and brave. Maybe even shrewd."

She had tried one more time. "Papa, all I wanted was a choice in my fate. A husband lasts a long time."

To his credit, he had not laughed. She thought she saw a moment of contrition, but it passed soon enough, because he was still Hans Aardema, shrewd dealer in fish and now the possessor of a *privilegio*, little stamp for each invoice and keg that proclaimed he was the sole distributor of salted herring to the crowns of Castile and Leon.

He had whispered to her, "Don't hate me forever for my ambition."

"Do I hate you, Papa?" she asked now, as she sat on the crate. "You could have been nicer." She faced into the wind. "So could I."

Chapter Two

Hanneke left her perch on the crate and walked around the deck before going below. She nodded to the sailors squatting on their haunches around their small fire in the box of sand, roasting bits of meat.

She had feared the crew at first, but learned they were only little people like herself, eager to return home to Spain, in their case. They had stories to tell of a voyage to England, then to the wealthy German cities and then to Vlissingen to take a woman and her dowry to their home port of Santander.

Father Bendicio had warned her not to listen to their coarse talk. She didn't know some of their words, but she heard mostly longing for home and family. She did not long for home. She feared what waited, ready to pounce on her, in this place which would be her home until she died.

As much as she didn't want to, she remembered Father Bendicio's patient lessons on the sad history of Spain, overrun by Moors from North Africa five hundred years ago, conquering with the zeal of men ready to spread the religion of Mohammed, and find wealth among the prosperous kingdoms of the Visigoths. In Bendicio's opinion, these Moors – succeeded by Almoravides and now Almohades – had long overstayed their welcome.

He had told her candidly that her dowry would purchase soldiers and weapons to aid in the reclaiming of Christian lands. "The time is now," he had said one evening in Vlissingen as she listened unwillingly.

She returned to her favorite place to watch the water – endless water, as if land had disappeared forever. *What will I get out of this?* she asked herself. She had no answer, beyond the obvious one: nothing.

Hanneke felt none the wiser in the morning, when she woke to the sound of the cabin boy by the mast, singing his morning hymn to God. She put her hands behind her head, enjoying his clear voice.

He hadn't finished the hymn when another voice broke in, sounding high and far away, coming from the top of the mast. "*Tierra! España!*"

Hanneke hurried into her dress, the one she had worn for the entire voyage, because there was nowhere private to wash. She was as dirty as the crew, but she poked at the wrinkles and stains, wishing them gone.

On deck, all she saw was a gray outline that disappeared and reappeared as the ship wallowed on, as ungainly as a floating wheel of cheese. So that gray lump was Spain?

Night still found them far from shore, teased by contrary winds that had plagued them for the entire voyage. She stayed on deck in the shadows, listening as the sailors recited the Our Father. After the Ave and Credo, the ship's boy cleared his throat and faced the captain, his father, for the nightly ritual. "Amen. God give us a good night and good sailing. May the ship make a good passage, Sir Captain, Master, and good company."

To Hanneke's delight, the boy bowed in her direction at "good company." She nodded to him in turn and earned an ear-to-ear grin.

"*Salve regina, mater misericordia*," he sang, as the sailors joined in. Hanneke sang, too – O *padre, o dolcis Virgo Mater* – holding out the final notes, teasing them over the water and letting them drop in the sea.

She watched, envious, as the captain put his arm around his son. *Will you ever put your arm around me, Santiago?* she asked the waves. *Be good to me. I might be much more than a dowry.*

A bump woke her at daybreak, as if the ship finally blundered into the dock. She would have been on deck sooner, if she hadn't paused in front of her scrap of a mirror and noticed the carnage. With a sigh, she brushed her long black hair and braided it, wishing it were cleaner. After glance at her fingernails, she found a broom straw and quickly cleaned them. Her dress was hopeless.

She tapped on Father Bendicio's door. She heard mumbling inside, papers rattling, and waited.

"We've docked," she said when he opened the door. "I'm going on deck. Will Santiago meet the ship?"

"Unlikely," he said. "We are long overdue, at least six weeks. Why would he?"

She hadn't thought of that. Even a suitor eager for wealth could grow irritated at waiting. She realized with a pang that she had never asked the priest about him. "Father, what does he look like?"

"He's tall and blond with blue eyes, a true Castilian," Father Bendicio said, not hiding his impatience. "Don't ask me anything else. I have to pack." He reconsidered. "What else…what else," he muttered. "If he comes, he will be riding a gray stallion."

There was no one on horseback at the dock. She perched on a crate closer to the railing, surprised when the ship's cat took a silent leap and landed beside her, purring and rubbing against her. "Now, at the end of the voyage, you decide to make my acquaintance?" she asked. She petted it absently and scanned the dock for a man on a gray horse.

When she decided it might be better if he didn't appear, she noticed a boy wrapped in a man-sized apron, squatting at the end of the dock, watching the sailors at work. She thought of her younger self, watching sailing boats return to Vlissingen with her father's ship in the lead.

Because a basket rested on its side beside him, she wondered if he had been sent by a cook to bring back fish. Hanneke hoped the supposed cook wasn't in a hurry for fish; the boy was oblivious.

Her smile faded as three horsemen rode up behind him. Uneasy, she hopped off the crate and walked to the railing, shading her eyes against the early morning sunlight. One, two, three – two white horses and a black one. She let out her breath in relief; no Santiago.

Two of them were obviously warriors, although none wore chain mail. One was dressed much better than his *compadres*, and two were blonde, with some resemblance between them. The third man was darker, with hair more the color of her own, but an olive cast to his skin. Of the three men, he alone seemed to notice her. He raised his hand in greeting. She raised hers, then put it down quickly.

As she watched in dismay, Regal Dresser edged his horse closer. Other Blonde and Dark Man looked at each other as Regal Dresser nudged his horse directly behind the boy, who turned, threw up his hands and lost his balance.

Angry, Hanneke grabbed a rock from a ballast box beside her and threw it at Regal Dresser. The stone struck Other Blonde, who jerked back on his horse's reins. The sudden motion upset Regal Dresser's horse, who threw him into the water, knocking the boy in, too.

As Other Blonde flashed her a murderous glance and fought to subdue his mount, Hanneke saw to her horror that his horse was more than white.

Aghast at what she has caused, Hanneke ran down the gangplank and tugged at a tow rope dangling in the water. Since the boy was closer, she held it out to him first as she knelt on the dock.

The boy hauled himself up as Dark Man dismounted and held out his hand for the man still thrashing in the water. The sailors laughed, none of them offering assistance.

His horse under control now, Other Blonde dismounted, shouldered past Dark Man and reached for Hanneke. Before he could touch her, both Dark Man and the sodden boy stepped between them. "Don't, Santiago," Dark Man warned. "Enrique had bad intentions."

Santiago? What have I done? Hanneke thought, her fear confirmed.

"Let me at her," Regal Dresser said, as he tried to squeeze between them.

The boy took a firm stand. "Here I am, sire. Strike me instead."

The one called Enrique cuffed the boy back into the water, his gloved hand making a cracking sound against the boy's neck as he plunged into the water again before Hanneke could reach him.

"No more, sire," Dark Man said. "Move aside, little one."

She did as he said, only to be grabbed by Santiago, who lifted her off her feet. "Someone should whip you, *puta*," he hissed.

She swallowed, terrified, and looked at the man she knew was her future husband. "I didn't mean...he...that man was going to push the boy..." she stammered.

"Let her go, Santiago," Dark Man said. "You know your cousin was up to mischief." He gave the floundering boy a hand up. "Boy, hurry back to the kitchen. Wings on your feet."

The boy ran, leaving her between two agitated men – one wet, both angry – and Dark Man trying not to smile. Uncertain, afraid, she stood still as Enrique walked around her, sniffing with every step.

"Santiago, I smell herring," he said.

Before she could stop him, he lifted her gown and petticoat. "No scales."

"That will do, my cousin," Santiago said. He pulled down Hanneke's dress and pushed her toward the ship. "Go."

She backed up to the gangplank. "Truly I am sorry, *señores*," she said, when she was out of reach.

"You should be," Santiago said, his voice calmer. "If your father is captain of this scow, *puta*, tell him to keep you far from Spain."

Santiago walked Enrique to their horses. They rode away without a backward glance. She turned to the man remaining on the dock, the one who seemed more amused than irritated.

"I didn't want that man to hurt the boy," she said. "I'm sorry."

He shrugged and she saw no animosity. "He will recover. You can return to...to..."

"Vlissingen," she said, wishing she could do that. Now.

"You can tell your children someday how you nearly drowned the next king of Spain and threw a stone at the warhorse of Santiago Gonzalez."

She gasped at this information given so casually. "And you, señor? Please don't be someone important."

"Hardly," he said with a laugh. "Antonio Baltierra, *a su servicio.*"

She ran up the gangplank and into Father Bendicio's room. He looked up in annoyance from the document in front of him. Hanneke sank onto a stool and stared at him. "What now?" he asked, clearly out of patience.

She couldn't keep the panic from her voice. "I did a terrible thing."

Chapter Three

Hanneke took a deep breath and told Father Bendicio everything. He put down his quill and pushed the papers aside, his face pale.

"You are certain it was Santiago? And Enrique?" His silence unnerved her.

"Why did you not tell me how light his gray horse is?"

"Gray is gray. Don't blame me for your stupidity."

She flinched at that, but he was right. "He thinks I am the captain's daughter. What does *puta* mean?"

"We are *not* off to a good start," was all he said. He sighed again; Father Bendicio had an amazing repertory of sighs.

Muttering to himself in Latin, Bendicio took a final look at what she knew was the marriage document, sighed yet again, and stuffed it in a leather holder. He looked long and hard at the large strongbox containing Hans Aardema's renowned dried herring, cod and hake, turned into gold pieces. He collared two sailors to carry the heavy box and follow them.

Carrying her one paltry satchel, Hanneke hurried to keep up, only to find herself stumbling like a drunken person. One of the sailors assured her that she would walk straight soon, once her head realized she was no longer on a wallowing old scow. "We have been nearly three months at sea," he reminded her, but not unkindly. "Twice as long as we thought."

Father Bendicio glared at her. When he fell down from the same affliction, the sailors laughed. No one liked the priest.

It wasn't far to the Abbey of the Holy Bodies, as strange a name as Hanneke had ever heard, but this was Spain. Father Bendicio rang the bell and a monk ushered them inside. She wanted to ask where the palace was, but thought better of it when she heard angry voices behind a closed

17

door off the main hall, stark and painted white. The statues of two saints, perhaps those holy bodies, glared at her.

The door swung open, and there stood Santiago Gonzalez. He stared at her, then looked at Father Bendicio. "Surely not," he said, after a long pause that made Hanneke's stomach start to ache. "Please no."

"Señor, I..." she began, not sure whether she should remain silent, or kneel, or prostrate herself in abject apology before this man she was going to marry. "I'm sorry," she whispered, then compounded her felony by saying, "I had no idea who that bully was."

She saw the anger in his eyes, the dismay, the hurt, and her own eyes welled with tears. She discovered a sudden fascination with the tiles in the floor, wishing they would open and swallow her. When she found the courage to look into Santiago's face, she took heart. He seemed to be regarding her now with something she could only call appraisal. She looked at the tiles again, even more uncertain.

"Señorita, I have a question."

He spoke slowly, making certain she understood him. She looked up.

"If...if you had known Enrique, the other rider, was a son of Alfonso Rey – King Alfonso – would you not have thrown that stone?"

Other black-robed men had joined him in the hall, one of them the lawyer-priest she remembered from Vlissingen. There was another man, thin to emaciation, dressed in black with an ornate surcoat of gold lace.

"Well?" He sounded brusque but not unkind, or so she hoped. She would have given the world for an ally just then, and there was none in sight. If it took a lifetime, she knew she would have to coax courage out of its hiding place in her heart.

She gave him the truest answer. "I still would have thrown the stone, señor. He was ready to push the kitchen boy into the water and that was wrong."

She couldn't take back her words. She stood there, hands folded at her waist, her gaze meeting his.

"I should have stopped him," Santiago said. "You are right." He bowed to the man in the doorway. "Cousin, she may be dirty and little, but she is honest."

Hanneke opened her mouth and stared, wide-eyed, at the man in the doorway. He smiled at her and gestured, so she lowered herself into a graceful curtsy. *I'm dirty but I can bow*, she thought, as she came up out of a bow of obeisance she had practiced for weeks in Vlissingen.

Santiago took her arm. "I know you would like to refresh yourself, but we need to do business. Come inside. Let us see this final marriage document. Father Domitius said he left it with Father Bendicio."

This is business, Hanneke reminded herself silently. *I stink and my hair is greasy, but all eyes are on the strongbox. If I had three eyes and two noses, it wouldn't matter.*

The king returned to a modest-enough throne at the end of the long table and everyone sat. When Hanneke looked around, Alfonso pointed to a cushion.

"On the floor?" she asked. Her face grew warm when the men chuckled.

"It is the tradition for women to sit closer to the ground than men." King Alfonso shrugged. "I suppose the Moors brought this custom with them five hundred years ago. Sit."

She sank down on the pillow and arranged her pathetic dress around her. She worked up her courage and looked around the room, pleased to see Antonio the Dark Man sitting in the window. He had been kind at the dock, and she needed kindness.

Alfonso nodded to Father Bendicio, who took the marriage document she had been forced to sign from its holder. She felt her worries begin again when she saw how pale he was. What was wrong?

"Sire, these are the dowry arrangements from Hans Aardema," the priest said. He glanced at Father Domitius. "There was an additional stipulation after you left."

The other priest's eyes narrowed but he said nothing. Father Bendicio seemed to have trouble breathing. "Look here, the merchant and his daughter signed their names."

"You can read and write?" Alfonso asked.

"Sí," she whispered, frightened because Bendicio looked anything but reassuring.

"Perhaps, sire, you should read it through again," Bendicio said.

"Is that necessary?" the king asked. "Didn't we state our terms before you and Father Domitius left for the Netherlands?"

Bendicio gulped. "Sire, Hans Aardema was a hard bargainer." He knelt beside the king's chair. "Please, sire, I did my best."

The king gestured, and Bendicio handed him the document. He read it, nodding, tracing his finger down the words. He stopped at the signatures. "What is this?" he asked, jabbing the parchment with his finger.

Bendicio let out a huge breath. Alarmed, Hanneke raised up to see for herself. After their signatures, she saw more writing she knew hadn't been there when she signed. *Papa, what have you done?* she asked herself, as the king read it again, looked at the ceiling and laughed.

"The old rascal!" he murmured, then pushed the document toward Santiago. "Read there, my cousin, the lines *after* the signatures. We have been diddled by a fisherman."

Santiago leaped up from his stool and read it, standing by the king. With an oath, his eyes widened. He whirled to face Bendicio. "What foolishness is this?" he demanded.

"He would not yield to reason," the priest managed to choke out.

"I rather think he was looking out for the welfare of his daughter," the king replied.

The sudden silence in the room pressed down on Hanneke. She heard sea birds in the harbor and a child singing somewhere, and the sound of people breathing, which reminded her to breathe. She held out her hand for the document.

With an oath, Santiago rolled it up and slapped it in her hand. She recoiled in fright. Her hands trembled as she unrolled it and read the addition after her signature.

"Read it out loud," Santiago demanded.

She cleared her throat in a room where silence reigned. She read it silently first and felt the blood drain from her face.

"Out. Loud." Santiago spoke distinctly, but this time it was not a thoughtful kindness.

"Santiago…" Alfonso cautioned.

The writing wasn't going to magically change or disappear. "'N…n… not until Hanneke Maria Aardema and Santiago Gonzalez de la Victoria have been married for one year will said husband be at liberty to disburse any of the funds of said described dowry as he chooses.'"

She shivered. How could a room be so cold suddenly?

"Read on," Santiago said, his expression neutral, his eyes boring into hers.

Unnerved, she continued. "'an…and should my daughter die before that year is up, the dowry will return to me in its entirety, with interest.'"

That was not the end. Too frightened to look at anyone, she stared at the document and noticed a small arrow. She turned over the parchment and read silently.

"There is more?" Alfonso asked.

She nodded, wondering about men and ambition.

"Well?" he coaxed. "It can't be worse."

"I suppose it isn't, sire," she told Alfonso. "Not for a man, at least."

"Read it and be done," Santiago said, resigned.

She took a deep breath and another, wondering how many deep breaths she would have to take in Spain to navigate her life. "'Should Santiago Gonzalez de la Victoria die before the year is out, the dowry will go to the next man who marries her.'"

"That is logical," the king said, then joked, "Watch your back, cousin. This woman is a prize."

No, I am a person, she thought. "I'm not quite done, sire," she managed.

"How could it possibly get worse?" Santiago murmured.

Some demon drove her on, or perhaps a guardian angel. "'If she survives everyone, the dowry is hers.'" A spark of something she didn't recognize yet made her slap down the document on the table and step back, her face calm.

Santiago perched on the table in front of the king, which made the others in the room whisper to each other. Some men even laughed. "Cousin, what do I do? How can I raise an army when all I have is a promise? The fisherman might as well have put sand in that strongbox and offal in the crates!"

"It's only a year," Hanneke said.

He rose and towered over her. "Only a year! *Dios mio!* For five hundred miserable years we have been pushing back the Moorish dogs inch by inch to Africa!"

"Santiago, don't frighten her," Alfonso said.

He ignored Alfonso. "The Almohades and their miserable caliphate have been weakening. If we could have raised an army this winter, we could have pushed them out! We were so close!"

He shouted those last words in her face. She gazed back with all the serenity she could muster, yielding nothing.

"Not one more word that you will regret, Santiago," Alfonso ordered. "I speak as your king and not your cousin."

Santiago softened his voice. "If we do not have an army by next spring, it might be too late. You know that as well as I, sire. El Ghalib will marshal his forces – God, I hate that man – and he will push us back to... to the caves of Cavadonga!"

"He forced me to sign. I didn't know. I had no choice," Hanneke said, determined not to show fear. Out of the corner of her eye, she saw Antonio nodding to her from his window seat.

"Stop." Alfonso stepped between Santiago and Hanneke. "Marry her this afternoon, Santiago. Take the dowry to the Jews in Toledo. You can make a deal with them. It remains for Ana to stay alive." He chuckled. "And you, apparently, or someone else gets the dowry."

"Or the Dutch woman herself," someone added.

"The Levis will charge cruel interest," Santiago shot back to his king and cousin.

"So they will, but you will have your army," Alfonso countered. "You are not alone in gathering troops. We are all in this together, I would remind you."

The king rose and stood beside Hanneke, to her relief, because her courage was draining fast. "We have waited here too long, child, and I am busy. Marry this noisy man quickly." He touched her shoulder. "You may be small, but I would never underestimate you."

You are busy. Santiago is angry. I am a dowry, she thought, all courage gone, done in, somehow, by Alfonso's tiny kindness. She stifled her tears and straightened her back. "Please, sire, may I have a bath and a clean gown at least before the wedding?"

The king nodded. "Santiago, arrange that. Santiago?"

Santiago was gone, the door wide open. The king looked around. "We'll find someone to..."

"I'll help her."

Antonio was on his feet and gesturing to her. She walked toward him, humiliated but determined.

"It's a small moment in God's eyes, little one," he whispered to her. He looked closer, and she wondered what he saw. "I believe you are equal to this small thing. I will be your friend."

Chapter Four

"**S**antiago is usually better than this," Antonio said as he walked her down another corridor and stopped. "We have been waiting here in Santander for weeks now, spring has come and gone, and he is anxious to get back to Las Claves."

Go ahead and say it, she thought. *Anxious to get my dowry and raise an army.* She knew she should say something, but nothing came to mind. All she wanted to do was open a door and have the room magically turn into Vlissingen, with the raucous noise of seabirds, the chill of the North Sea and the odor of fish.

No such thing happened. Beyond the door was a chamber with white walls, an ebony cross, a travel chest and a bed. The smell of leather, and armor stowed in one corner proclaimed it as Santiago's room. She hesitated to enter.

Antonio pushed her forward gently. "Look over there," he said, pointing her toward a wooden tub. "I told you he was better than that."

She sighed to see steam rising from a bath, with soap and a towel on the floor beside it. She sniffed the air. "Is that lemon?"

"Yes. I wouldn't have thought you knew lemons," he said.

She dabbled her hand in the water. Perfect. All it lacked was her sitting in it, which would happen as soon as Antonio left. "One winter, fishermen from the south brought my father a lemon. We passed it from hand to hand and sniffed it." The memory made her smile. "Papa took a bite out of it, made a face, and threw it in the fireplace."

"Nothing quite prepares you for that first lemon," he commented.

"Perhaps not, but I wanted the lemon," she assured Antonio. "After everyone was asleep, I took it from the ashes, wiped it off, and tucked it under my pillow."

"I know where there are vast groves of lemons and oranges," Antonio said.

"Around here?" she asked, interested.

"No, alas. In the land of the Almohades, to the south of Las Claves," he said, "land that El Ghalib controls." She heard the wistfulness in his voice. "With an army, we can push them back beyond the groves and south into the sea."

"It always comes back to the army," she said.

"It must, until we regain our country," he told her. "But here is a bath, and time is passing."

He turned to leave her at the same time a thin woman with deeply etched frown lines burst through the open door and pointed at her. Hanneke instinctively stepped closer to Antonio.

"Here she is! Santiago, here she is."

She wanted him to be some other Santiago, but no, it was the same man who had stormed out of the king's presence. He nodded to Antonio and spoke over Hanneke's head. "The wedding is in one hour. This is Juana. She will help you." He backed out of the room with Antonio and closed the door.

Who was this woman? Should she curtsy? Hanneke looked her over and decided no, but what now?

Juana clapped her hands impatiently. "One hour! Get in that tub. Must I wash you?"

"No. Leave me alone," Hanneke said, not caring how she sounded. *Leave me alone to figure out how I can escape a high-walled monastery and vanish into a crowd of Spaniards. And while I am at it, teach me to fly.*

"Hurry," Juana said, as she shut the door.

Hanneke hurried from her dirty dress and filthier shift and sank into the water. She washed her hair three times, breathing in the tang of lemons, then scrubbed until she was clean.

She considered the feeling as a wise lesson, hopefully the first of many. The pleasure of cleanliness was a simple one, a small thing she had never considered before the voyage to Spain. Although certain her future husband was unaware, she decided Santiago Gonzalez had given her a wedding gift of low expectations, one that would suit her well, all things considered.

Mindful of time passing, she stepped out of the tub and wrapped a towel around her, wondering what to wear. She was reaching for her old dress when the door opened without a knock and Juana returned, Santiago behind her, dressed in a dark blue tunic with a scarlet surcoat, the color of royalty. No one else could afford those dyes. However unwilling, he looked like a man ready for a wedding.

She felt her face grow hot, not wishing anyone's scrutiny as she stood there wrapped in a towel, her hair in tangles. All she could do was plunge ahead.

"I have clothes somewhere. Everything is in crates. I don't know what to do." She spoke quietly, her eyes lowered.

"Juana, you could have told her to look in the chest," he said.

From lowered eyes, Hanneke watched them glare at each other, and wondered if Juana was angry at everyone, or only a select few. Hanneke already knew the woman had no patience.

Hanneke said nothing until Juana picked up her discarded clothing and shook it, her face a mask of revulsion. Hanneke swallowed down tears of shame when Juana held out her stained shift, and demanded, "Tell me it is not your time of the month."

Hanneke sobbed out loud and reached for the garment Juana held just out of reach. "Please," she begged, ashamed, as she stood in front of Santiago, her head down. "There was no place to wash or bathe."

"Disgraceful," Juana muttered.

"That's enough!" Santiago exclaimed. He grabbed the shift from Juana, who stepped back, alarm replacing scorn. "How dare you treat this woman so shamefully? Get out."

She heard the door slam, and turned away, ready to sink into the tiles underfoot. So far this was the single worst day of her life, and she wasn't even married yet. "Forgive me."

"It's not your fault," he told her. "We can burn these." He opened the chest. "It is our custom for the groom to provide the clothes. Take a look."

She did as he said because she had no choice. Besides, she was getting cold, wearing a towel, with her hair heavy and wet on her back.

He looked from her to the chest and back again. For the first time since his angry outburst, she felt something from him besides ill will. He almost looked amused.

"We have a problem. My brother Manolo assured me that all women of the Netherlands are tall and fat, and you are neither. Find something that fits, if you can." He looked toward the door. "Do you need Juana?"

"No, no," she said hastily. "I will manage."

He managed a self-deprecating sort of grin. "Wise of you."

"Who is she?" she asked, brave enough to ask him because of his smile.

She watched a range of emotions cross his expressive face. "She is the devil."

Wearing a green linen dress that only stayed on her body because of a leather belt, her thick hair braided but still damp, Hanneke was married an hour later by the bishop of Santander. Her shoes fit because they were her own, scuffed, but covered by the too-long dress, with its graceful sleeves she had to tug back during the ceremony. At least she had found a silk scarf to match the deep green of the dress, and a circlet to hold it in place on her head.

There were few people attending the ceremony, but there was the kitchen boy, looking none the worse for wear after two dousings at the dock. Enrique was conspicuously absent, probably still sulking over his ruined finery.

Bless that kitchen boy. As she had hurried toward the chapel in Father Bendicio's wake, he ran up to her, holding out a piece of cheese. "I found this," he said, which made her laugh, even as she reached for it, famished. "No, I did find it." He pulled out a hunk of bread from his doublet. "Hiding behind this piece of bread."

She ate it quickly, brushing off crumbs, ignoring Father Bendicio's frown. "I'm hungry," she told him. "It has been hours."

He hurried ahead. "We're going to be late," he warned her.

Did it matter? This day had been one blunder after another. "Go ahead and tell him I'm dawdling," she said, out of patience with the man. "This boy will be my escort. By the way, what is your name?"

"Pablo," he said.

"Pablo what?"

"Just Pablo. I am to escort you? I'm not very clean," he said.

"It doesn't matter. This is just a business transaction," Hanneke explained, thinking of her father haggling for fish, declaring what he would pay, slapping his forehead, cursing, stalking away, then allowing himself to be cajoled back to the bargaining table. She almost smiled to think what would happen if she carried on like that before the bishop of Santander.

"I thought it was a wedding," Pablo said.

"It is."

The sun had nearly left the sky by the time the bishop finished his business of yoking her forever to a man she did not know. When the rings were exchanged and she had pledged fealty, obedience and devotion, the bishop declared them married.

Santiago helped her to her feet and held her hand. The bishop placed his ringed hand over theirs and looked at Santiago. He leaned close and spoke softly to him. "Santiago Gonzalez de la Victoria, I give you a wife, not a servant. Treat her well."

They knelt next to King Alfonso, pledging more fealty and obedience, then followed him to the monastery's refectory. With a shrug, the king apologized for the spartan dining hall. "My hall in Valladolid is much grander, as you know, Santiago, but here we are in Santander and I am at the mercy of cousins." He clapped his hands. "The food is good, and so is the music, my dears."

The food could have been gall and wormwood, but the king was right about the music. "He is playing an *oud*, one of our pleasant gifts from the Moors," Alfonso told her, when Santiago had nothing to say. "His daughter keeps time with *palillos*, another gift from you-know-who." He chuckled and looked at the musician's daughter, who shuffled her feet in time to the rhythm. "She would like to dance for you, but I reminded them both that this is still a monastery."

Hanneke ate, grateful for a full meal. Santiago and Antonio sat by her briefly, but they were soon gathered in a corner talking earnestly to men about their age.

King Alfonso leaned closer. "What can I do with a cousin who recruits fighters during his wedding banquet?"

The king also looked eager to be away. He finally rose and gestured to his cousin and the men in the corner. "Come, come, gentlemen. Santiago, let me grant this lovely wife of yours a gift."

Give me the gift of wings, and I will fly away, she thought.

"What would you have from me, my dear?"

"Sire, I don't understand," she told him, uncomfortable with the attention focused on her.

"Since you are now my relative, I will grant a wish, if it is within my power. What would you like?"

A dress that fits, she thought. "I don't need anything, sire."

"There must be something," Alfonso insisted. "Santiago, did you find the perfect wife, one who expects nothing?"

He did, she thought, at the same time she heard a loud crash near the door. Hands flew to swords, but it was only Pablo standing among goblets and plates he had dropped. Hanneke left the table and helped him put the dishes back on the tray.

She looked into the boy's kind eyes, a boy as powerless as she was, and knew what to ask. "Sire, I would have Pablo come with me to Las Claves."

When Alfonso laughed, everyone joined in. She wanted to sink through the tiles. Could the day get any worse? She glanced at Santiago; it would get worse. "Yes, sire, Pablo. I want a friend."

"Most brides as for jewels." He conferred with the abbot seated beside him, who nodded. "Very well, Ana. The abbot says he will free Pablo from his service. Go with Señora Gonzalez, lad."

The boy in the too-large apron came to her side. "Señora, I will be by your side from now until I die."

She kissed his head. "I doubt it will come to that. Pack your things and I will see you tomorrow morning."

"My things?"

"Your possessions, Pablo."

"I have none." He grinned and fled back to the kitchen, stopping in the door to bow awkwardly.

Alfonso clapped his hands together. "My charge was easily dispatched. Good night to you all. Santiago, do your duty."

Her new husband bowed and took her by the arm. They left the refectory to the applause and laughter of the guests.

Now it had come to this. She walked silently beside him to their room. She felt powerless, helpless, and frightened, far from resourceful and brave.

Santiago closed the door and unbelted his sword with a sigh. "I am always happy to take that off." He looked at her for a long moment.

What could she do? Nothing. Who would come to her aid? No one. In silence, she took off the braided belt, which meant her too-large dress slid down to her ankles. Her *camisa* large enough for three women slid down next.

She stepped out of them and stood naked. She yearned to shield herself, but what good would that do? She put her hands to her sides and waited.

"Is this the worst day of your life?" he asked, surprising her.

"Yes," she replied, thinking, *Go ahead and make it worse. It is your right. The king called it your duty.*

When he said nothing, she grabbed her courage before it darted out of reach. "Santiago, is this the worst day of *your* life?"

"Not even slightly."

Hanneke felt her heart go out to him in a way she had never anticipated. She watched as he opened the chest of women's clothes, looking through it as a man would, as if afraid something would leap out and snarl at him. He found a nightdress, the pretty one of silk she had admired earlier, even as it terrified her.

He handed it to her. "Wear this. I am not going to ruin your entire day, Ana. I am not that heartless."

She did as he said. He chuckled when the cursed thing slid off her shoulders like the other garments. His laugh stuffed the heart back in her body.

"Ana, *where* are your clothes?" he asked, sounding more amused than not.

"Somewhere in a crate with the dowry goods."

"We'll find it in the morning."

He turned away, stripped and found a nightshirt. He had wide shoulders, capable looking. He indicated the bed. "Lie down. Sleep. I am a second son with no prospects, except that I now have your dowry. I made a mercenary decision. War is why I did it. All I know is war. When I have peace and time and land of my own, we shall see."

He pulled her closer and touched his forehead to hers. "Calm yourself. You may hate me at times, but know this: I am always between you and any door. You are safe with me."

Chapter Five

Hanneke woke several times during the night, once to wonder who snored so lightly beside her. Papa had been a noisy engine, heard through doors and down the hall. She woke up the second time to discover that this husband of hers hogged the blankets. Just as well; the air was warm, a night in June.

She thought of his promise to keep between her and a door. Did he mean she could never escape him, or that she would always be safe? *Which is it?* she asked herself, then admitted she knew Santiago not at all.

"Up, up, sleepy woman," woke her too soon. "We're riding in one hour."

Startled awake, she pulled the blanket close, a gesture not lost on her husband. "I have a bad habit," he told her. "You can always yank it back."

Oh, no. She thought of last night, when Pablo dropped the dishes and every man reached for his sword. No, no sudden moves.

Still sleepy, she watched him dress. "Up, up," he said again. "I will find your crate of clothing and have Pablo bring it to you. Do you have a garment for riding?"

"I have never been on a horse," she admitted.

She dreaded the irritation on his face at her honest declaration, then realized how tired she was of apologizing. "I can learn to ride."

He turned at the door and appraised her in that intense way of his. Did the man never rest? "This will not be an easy journey from here to Las Claves, which is far to the south. The morning fog here in Santander will burn away too soon, and the heat will command every league of our journey. I will have no time for complaints from you about things I cannot change."

"You will not even know I am here." She did not add, *I wish I weren't.*

"You will never disobey my decisions. Never."

"No," she murmured. After the door closed, she added, "I know a threat when I hear one."

In a matter of minutes, Pablo and Juana lugged in her chest of clothing. After assuring them she needed no help, she fished in the bottom of her chest and pulled out a gown of gray wool, and its darker surcoat, one she already knew could hide a multitude of stains and dirt. Perfect. She nodded at her trusty shifts and sturdy shoes. Nothing in her wardrobe would dare slide off her shoulders. *My own clothes*, she thought in triumph. *Me.*

She added a veil and Mama's circlet of woven fabric, wishing it still boasted Mama's scent. No matter. Her simple headgear kept a little of her homesickness at bay.

She sniffed hot bread and sausage, but nearly walked past the refectory, too shy to make herself known. She opened the door instead, telling herself that if she feared Castilians, she would starve and die. She curtsied to King Alfonso then joined Antonio on the bench, gratified to sit by someone who didn't frighten her.

He passed the sausage and bread to her. "Your husband tells me you have never ridden before."

"Never," she replied, determined not to apologize. "Remember, I am a fishmonger's ordinary daughter."

"I doubt you are ordinary at anything," he said, and speared another sausage for her plate. "Eat more. Journeys like this lack everything except heat and trouble."

She finished her sausage and was buttering another slice of bread when Santiago entered the refectory, searching for her. He gestured to her. "I have been summoned," she said.

"*We* have been summoned. I told him I would find you, and here we are eating like sensible folk, instead of worrying about what will go wrong."

He helped her over the bench, then walked beside Santiago as she hurried to keep up. She was joined by Pablo and Juana, who looked her over carefully with a smirk.

"Your color is good. You're not clinging to the wall. He must not have ridden you too hard last night," Juana said, making no effort to lower her voice.

Santiago looked back in annoyance, his lips set in a tight line, as Hanneke felt her face grow hot. The soldiers around them laughed.

Hanneke looked away. These were the men in Santiago's employ. She had to journey with them, and here she was, an object of ridicule already.

She already knew her expectations were nonexistent. As everyone hurried toward the courtyard, she slowed down. There was nowhere to turn, no safe place where she could gather her courage, take a deep breath and try again. She stopped, and noticed Pablo, quiet but at her side.

"I wish I could do you a real service and stop Juana," Pablo said. She heard all his distress.

"This is but a small moment in God's eyes," she reminded him. "Isn't that what you told me?"

"*I* told you that."

She turned to see Antonio, noting again his olive skin and his eyes so slightly slanted. He did not look like the other men, which told her he had his own story. She wanted to hear it, but now she would do as she was told.

"Juana will go too far someday," was all Antonio said. He gestured to the courtyard. "See there, Ana? Your husband found you a real treasure."

She followed Antonio into the courtyard, seeing only a white mule. "It looks huge," she said, unwilling to move closer.

"Any smaller and she would be a colt drinking mother's milk. Her name is Blanca."

"I am going to die."

Antonio laughed. "No one ever died on a mule this well-mannered and little."

"You don't know that."

"Well, no, but trust me."

"Do I have a choice?"

"Who does?" Antonio said cheerfully. "Up you get."

With no warning, he grabbed her around the waist and threw her on top of Blanca, who remained in place, unperturbed. Terrified, Hanneke grabbed the nearest thing she could reach, Antonio's helmet.

"There is nothing to it, Ana," he assured her, as he straightened his helmet. "Put your right leg over the saddle brace."

Antonio wasn't a man she wanted to disappoint. "Like this?"

"Perfect. Now tuck your left leg close on the lower brace. There now."

She wanted to object, but there sat Santiago on his gray horse that looked more white than gray. "Perhaps I will not die atop this monster," she conceded.

"Perhaps you will not," Antonio agreed. "When you want to move, give her a little kick."

"I wouldn't dare!"

"You will," he assured her. "To stop, pull back evenly. Turn left or right like this. There now. Pablo will stay close to you, won't you, sir knight?"

Pablo sidled his mule alongside hers. "We are going to have an adventure," he confided. "I never had adventures in the kitchen."

She thought about that. "I never had an adventure in the kitchen, either."

She wiggled carefully, trying to find a comfortable spot, but there was none.

To her relief, Blanca seemed content to stay above the confusion of an army preparing to move, paying no mind to more unruly mules. She looked back at Hanneke, as though apologizing for those coarser equines. Hanneke took a chance and patted the mule's neck.

"One moment."

She looked toward the monastery and saw the king on the steps. He walked down to Santiago, who bowed from his saddle, then gestured to Hanneke to come.

Hoping for the best, she dug her heels into Blanca's flanks. Beyond a reproachful glance, the white mule obeyed. Holding her breath, Hanneke pulled back on the reins when they reached the church steps. Blanca stopped, to Hanneke's surprise and relief.

The king moved toward Santiago first. "Come to me in Valladolid this winter," he said. "Tell me how your recruiting is prospering. We will plan our next move." He stepped back. "There will be victory this time."

Santiago crossed himself. Alfonso turned to Hanneke and patted Blanca. "She will treat you well, Señora Gonzalez. She has carried my good wife Alionora many miles."

"The queen's mule?" Hanneke asked. "Sire, please thank her for me."

"I had to do better than a mere kitchen boy as your granted wish," he said with a smile. He waved off Santiago. "I have a few words for your wife."

After Santiago left, King Alfonso came closer to Blanca. "You seem to be a woman of some intelligence."

She said nothing, feeling anything but smart.

"It is this: There are times when events are larger than people. This is such a time." Alfonso placed his hand over hers. "The caliphate – the government – of the Almohades has visible cracks in it. We have seen the caliphs grow soft in recent years. Your husband will exploit these cracks."

"I have heard people speak of the Almohades," she said, waiting to know more but unsure who to ask. She glanced at Santiago, who looked impatient to leave, but not willing to cross his powerful cousin.

King Alfonso saw her look. "My cousin is too impatient, but I am king."

Hanneke smiled at that, charmed by this man.

"The Moors were first, and Berber tribesmen from North Africa," he said, "all filled with the zeal of a new religion. Wave after wave of invaders followed, the last the Almohades." He shrugged. "Granted these Muslims – followers of the Prophet Mohammed – came with gifts, too, which they generously shared with us: beautiful architecture, healing medicines, music, something called algebra." He looked away. "But as much as they think otherwise, this is not their land." His voice hardened. "The Almohades dealt me a cruel defeat fifteen years ago, but they are weakening."

"And you need my dowry," Hanneke added.

"We do," he said without hesitation. "Five hundred years of warfare is expensive." He patted her hand. "We are realistic, single-minded people."

Hanneke nodded. "I have noticed that already." She leaned closer to the king. "These are momentous times for you, sire."

"They are, indeed, the sort of events *cancioneros* will sing about in centuries to come." He lifted her hand to his lips and kissed it. "Here is what they never sing about – Some of us will be swept away, others ruined and embittered." He looked beyond her. "I pray you will not be one of those winnowed out, an innocent dragged into this to suit our purposes."

"If I am?" she asked. He frightened her.

"The sin be on our heads." He looked toward Santiago. "He is a good man, your husband, but he is a warrior above all." He released her hand. "Go with God, my child. Forgive us, if you can."

Chapter Six

They began their journey south from the misty coast of northern Spain to distant Las Claves, how distant she had no idea. Santiago led the way with his soldiers, Antonio Baltierra among them. Hanneke followed with Father Bendicio at her side, and Pablo and Juana behind. The dowry came next, everything securely tied to mules and draft horses, the strongbox well-guarded in the center. More soldiers brought up the rear, led by a one-eyed giant of a man with a face scarred both by battle and smallpox. As she looked back, he grinned at her, showing gaps where teeth should have been. She shuddered.

The fog burned away long before mid-day as they moved south into heat she never could have imagined. Her wool dress clung to her like a misdeed. The soldiers removed their helmets and fastened them to their saddles, which made Santiago frown. Soon enough, he sighed and followed suit.

She wanted to appreciate the scenery, but all she saw was a tired land blasted by the heat of only mid- June. She didn't want to think about the punishing heat of July and August. She noted mountains in the distance, crags, rocks, flinty soil and wondered why anyone lived here. The contrast with her own green and well-watered homeland was stark.

Antonio assured her that Blanca had a smooth glide of a walk, but nothing was smooth enough for a beginner. She wanted to ask Santiago to let her rest – hadn't he assured her she could? – but she hadn't the courage. She clung to the pommel and endured.

When the sun was directly overhead, her lord, master, and man with an iron backside called a halt. Hanneke eyed the distance from her saddle to the ground and shook her head. *I will sit here until I die*, she thought.

"*Dama*?"

Wretched, miserable and drenching wet, she looked down at Antonio. He had the nerve to smile at her and hold out his arms. Why was he so happy? Didn't he know pain either?

At least he wasn't Santiago, the impatient one. "How do I get off this beast?"

"Lift your right leg over the pommel and lean down. I'll catch you. You're not that far off the ground, you know."

She gasped as she lifted her leg, wondering when it fell asleep, or if it even belonged to her body anymore.

"Lean forward. Trust me."

She did as he said. He caught her handily, and held her up until some feeling returned to her leg.

"You could have requested that we stop," he said.

"I wouldn't dare. Santiago told me not to be a nuisance. You may let me go."

He did as she insisted, and she promptly fell to her knees. Antonio picked her up, carried her to the one tree on the entire plain, then propped her against it. "I'll get your husband." She watched him walked away, his shoulders shaking.

Did these men of Spain have no manners? Embarrassed, she turned her head when the men dismounted and relieved themselves in plain sight. In a panic she looked around, wondering about privacy for her own relief. Nothing.

Juana was the other woman in the company. Hanneke watched, dismayed to see her squat by her mule, spreading her skirt around her. *I can't do that*, Hanneke thought, in utter horror.

Here came Santiago. Why did these men have to look so spry after six hours in the saddle?

He uncorked a leather flash and held it out to her. "Drink."

She took a sip. The water was warm and tasted like cow, but it was wet. She took another sip before returning it.

He pushed it back. "Drink some more. That wasn't enough."

She knew better than to argue and did as he said. He took it from her this time, shook it, and handed it back. "More."

Hanneke eyes welled with tears. "Not until I... I..." *Why don't you understand what I need*, she thought, exasperated, then realized she was being foolish. "Sire, I can't squat like Juana."

"You can," he said, with some spirit. "Every man here knows what women look like. Well, perhaps not Father Bendicio."

"This isn't how I do things," she said softly, taking a chance.

He opened his mouth to say something, probably to scold her, or make fun of her, or exert his prerogative as leader, then seemed to change his mind. "I'll be back."

Too shy to look at anyone, Hanneke managed to stand up straight. She took one halting step, and another, wishing the earth would swallow her. When it didn't, she took another step and another.

"Here."

Santiago carried a blanket over his arm. "I've ordered Juana to hold out this blanket. Get behind it and do your business." His tone changed, and she almost heard the man who told her last night that he would always sleep between her and the door. "She will do this every time we stop." His expression hardened. "I told her to make no rude comments, but I cannot guarantee that. I wish I could."

He held out the blanket to the servant, who snatched it from him. She shook out the blanket and raised it. "Do your business, fancy lady," she mocked. "Be quick."

Squatting was beyond her, but Hanneke did the best she could, her relief enormous. When she finished, she limped back to Blanca and leaned against her mule until Santiago lifted her into the saddle and mounted his own horse.

She thought he would ride ahead. When he looked at her closely, Hanneke held her breath, wondering what she had done now. *I know I didn't complain, not really*, she told herself. To her utter amazement, he took the reins from her and tugged Blanca after him. It was an easy matter then to close her eyes and grasp the pommel.

"Thank you," she said.

"I should have done this sooner, Ana."

It was a small kindness, a simple act that filled her heart with peace. Maybe this was another lesson: Appreciate small things formerly taken for granted. *I am now Hanneke Gonzalez, the woman of small things*, she told herself.

They camped that night beside a feeble stream. The men in the company took the horses and mules to water, but it was a slow business, since there wasn't much water. The ugly scarred soldier with an eye and teeth missing raised a tent for her, as Pablo helped.

"Your name is Carlos?" Hanneke asked.

"*Si, dama*," he said. "Santiago told me to help you. Juana will bring some bedding and you will lie down."

Everyone orders me around, Hanneke thought, but she decided she didn't mind, not when she was ready to drop. "I don't mean to be trouble."

"No trouble," he said cheerfully. He gestured at the men around him, who were putting up their own tents, and lighting small fires. "We can do this in our sleep, and it is not our first time on horseback."

"When will I start to feel better?" she asked, drawn to this man because she felt his sympathy.

"By the time we reach Toledo."

"Is that far?"

He nodded, then must have noticed her evident dismay. "Maybe sooner. Are you tough?"

She considered his question, happy to have someone to talk to, after the long silence of the day. "I think I have to be."

"You do." He touched his hand to his forehead. "God keep you, *dama*."

Juana was less charitable. She carried in an armful of blankets and a pillow, dropped them and left without a word.

Hanneke shook her head over the servant, wondering if there was any way to placate Juana for whatever misdemeanors she had committed. Unable to think of anything, she arranged the blankets, lay down and was asleep in minutes.

She woke with a start because Santiago knelt beside her, watching her, or perhaps trying to decide if waking her was a good idea. She sat up, aware that she ached everywhere, from the top of her sunburned head to her legs, where she had gripped the saddle so hard, hoping not to fall off and further disgrace herself. The pain in her legs and rump were beyond description.

"It's never easy the first time," he told her as he set down a bowl.

When she didn't reach for it, he inched it closer. "You haven't eaten all day. Why didn't you say something?"

"I wasn't certain how often people ate on the march," she said honestly. "I didn't want to ask for something out of turn."

He looked away from her. "I haven't taken good care of you."

"You're busy with everything."

"It's no excuse. Call me to account when I deserve it."

Not I, she thought, as she pulled the bowl closer, sniffing the meat. There was no spoon, and she didn't want to use her hands, still uncertain about customs among these morose and taciturn people.

Santiago pulled out a loaf of bread he had tucked under his arm and broke off a piece, dipping it in the stew. "Here you are."

She ate it, and he handed her another piece of bread for the sop. After the second dip, she shook her head.

"That's not enough, Ana." In went the bread in the bowl and again he held it out. "When there is food, you eat. When there isn't, you starve."

Next came the wineskin and a handful of dates. He seemed disinclined to leave, and she did have a question.

"Sire, that man with the scars. What happened to him?"

"Carlos?" Santiago took a long pull on the wineskin. He wiped his mouth with the back of his hand. "Did he frighten you?"

"A little," she replied. "No, a lot."

Santiago grinned, then grew serious. "That's what happens when El Ghalib wants to leave a calling card." He settled back. "It was years ago, when that enemy of mine killed my father. Ambushed him on one of the mountain passes near Las Claves. Carlos was much younger then. El Ghalib peeled the skin back on Carlos's cheeks and cut him free to let me know who had done the foul deed."

Hanneke shuddered. "Others have mentioned that name. What kind of monster is this?"

"Why, Ana, Yussef el Ghalib is my favorite neighbor to the south of Las Claves," Santiago said. "I doubt he was more than fifteen years old when he killed my father. Do you understand what I am up against and why I need an army?"

She nodded, deeply uneasy. "Carlos could have died from that."

"Many have."

Chapter Seven

They traveled through high plains and rolling hills and reached Valladolid a few days later, a heavily walled city where the gatekeepers were beginning to close the massive gates as they rode up. After a heated discussion, the gatekeeper allowed them through.

"This is my king and cousin's actual residence," Santiago said, after another glare directed at the gatekeeper. "He remained near Santander, where it is cooler."

As Hanneke rode through behind Santiago – by the end of each day as a matter of course, he led her mule now – she heard whisperings about campfires on the surrounding plains.

She had seen those, too, but knew better than to ask about them, not with Santiago looking more wary and preoccupied each night. She had mentioned her fears to Father Bendicio, who mouthed the words, "El Ghalib." She also noticed that the soldiers were wearing their chain mail and helmets, even though the days were sun-soaked.

The night before Valladolid, she gathered her courage to ask permission to walk down to the little rivulet grandiosely called a *rio*. Santiago came with her, even though she knew he had other things to do.

"I will just be down that incline," she said. "I needn't take your time."

"I am coming, too."

She couldn't say no. She couldn't tell him that she wanted a moment away from everyone to wet her sunburned face to cool it, run a cloth up her legs for comfort from the chafing, and a moment to sit and think. She contented herself with washing her face as he sat above her on the bank.

"I would have been safe," she said, grumpy enough to argue when she finished what little she could do.

40

He gave her that wry smile which seemed to be coin of the realm with Spaniards, and held out his hand to help her up.

"The Gonzalez family has an interesting crest," he told her. "It is a crest born during our great retreat north centuries ago: *Nullus credite*, Trust No One."

"That is sad."

"That is Spain."

But this was Valladolid, a city most proper, according to Father Bendicio, who had told her more about the architecture of Islam and their conquerors. To her eyes, it was a middling city with a picked-over appearance, as if weary of warfare. Some of the buildings had that Moorish look Father Bendicio explained, with tracery in stone that looked almost lace-like. By now, she needed no one to tell her that Valladolid had changed hands many times in five hundred years of conquest.

She was familiar with the flinty soil, rocks and desert that seemed to comprise so much of the dry land they traveled through. Although she did not miss the smell of fish that permeated the very walls in Vlissingen, she longed for rain and the shade of trees and grass she had taken for granted in her homeland. Did it ever rain here? Apparently not in June. Or was it July? Time had little meaning to someone trying to stay in the saddle and not irritate anyone.

She found herself preoccupied with the furnace that was Spain. Valladolid's stone buildings threw back shimmering heat that nearly vibrated in the plaza. She blinked her eyes from the overpowering weight of the sun's rays and wished for winter.

Not a moment too soon, Santiago raised his hand and they stopped. There was no shade anywhere, but she saw a stout little man peek around a door, then hurry toward them.

She heard Santiago's sigh and saw Antonio's grin. Antonio leaned closer to her and whispered, "I think Santiago would rather face El Ghalib than Señor Palacios."

"Who is...," she prompted.

"The father of Engracia, your new sister-in-law."

She watched in surprise and then amusement when the shorter man grabbed her husband in a fierce embrace that nearly toppled him, caught off balance. She held her breath when Santiago reached for his sword, a reflex she had seen before when he was startled.

"*Dios*, he must be tempted," Antonio joked. "Let me help you down so you can placate everyone."

"Do I do that?" she asked him, surprised.

"More than you know, I think."

In a moment she was beside Santiago with a curtsy. "You must be Señor Palacios," she said, and braced herself for the same treatment.

The little man was as round as he was short, with a wispy beard and bald head covered with sweat. He let go of Santiago and beamed at her.

His rotundity was deceiving, Hanneke discovered. He clapped hands on her arms and lifted her off the ground, to Antonio's further amusement. "Santiago, you lucky man!" he proclaimed. "You fortunate one!" He set her down. "Consider this your house, wife of Santiago. Engracia will be so happy."

He pulled her toward the door, talking all the while. "Stay a month until the weather cools, especially with Engracia in her present condition."

The house reeked of burned olive oil and pungent perfume that failed to mask household odors. Flies clotted the windows and crawled over the food on the table. Señor Palacios waved his arms. The flies rose, then settled on the table again.

"Urraca, my rib, my flesh! We have guests! Engracia, show yourself!"

Santiago looked down at the floor to hide his smile. He glanced at Hanneke and rolled his eyes. A woman as tall as Señor Palacios was short, as angular as he was round, launched herself into the room.

Does no one in this household move slowly? Hanneke wondered, as the woman hugged Santiago, her eyes on Hanneke.

"Santiago, you did not tell us she would be so pretty."

Santiago stepped back from Urraca's embrace. "I didn't know."

"She is little." Señora Palacios waved her arms around, too, and the flies rose and fell. "Not at all like my Engracia. Surely you do not mean to take my darling daughter from me?"

Santiago set his lips in that familiar thin line. "That was our agreement."

"Mama, you know Santiago does not like to be teased. He is not a Palacios."

Hanneke looked past Urraca to the doorway where a lovely woman stood. Hanneke glanced from Señor Palacios to Urraca, wondering how such beauty had come from this odd couple. Engracia Palacios Gonzalez was tall, with red hair that peeked out from under her lace cap. She was with child, but so graceful, as she hurried to Santiago.

He kissed her cheek, but she had eyes for Hanneke. "Brother, you have brought me a sister. Come, sister, tell me what you think of this great, tall fellow?"

A man I barely know, Hanneke thought. *Still, he doesn't mind leading my mule when I tire.* "I think he is a good man," she said shyly.

"I know he is," Engracia said, her eyes kind. She clapped her hands together. "Here we stand in all this heat. Let us find you a soft bed, sister. Perhaps some water to wash in?"

"*Sí, por favor.*"

Engracia pressed her advantage. "Please stay a few days, unless Santiago means to carry us off like an Almohad raiding party."

"We must return to Las Claves," Santiago reminded her. "That was my condition."

Urraca burst into tears and Señor Palacios hurried to calm her, even as he pleaded with Santiago. "Take pity on us, *señor*! We cannot bear to lose our treasure."

"But I…"

"What is the rush?"

Who was this new voice of objection, ganging up on her husband? Hanneke watched another tall redhead enter the room. He could have been Engracia's twin; perhaps he was.

Whoever he was, this man knew how to command a room. Hanneke watched his entrance, a grand sort of strut, as if he knew how good he looked and how fine his clothes. She lowered her eyes when he turned to look at her, because it was an all-encompassing glance, the kind that saw through her dress. *I don't know you, but I don't like you*, she thought.

"Ana, let me introduce Felipe Palacios, Engracia's brother," Santiago said. "*Señor*, this is my wife, Ana Aardema Gonzalez."

"*Dios mio*, you have outdone yourself," Felipe said. "The honor is mine."

Ana edged closer to Santiago, trying not to be obvious, and then not caring. *Nullus credite.* Trust no one. She bowed, relieved when her husband rested his hand on her shoulder. Maybe he felt as she did.

"Really, Santiago, must you leave so soon?" Felipe asked.

"I must. We will be gone by morning," he said, then turned to Engracia. "Sister, please find a comfortable bed for Ana. This journey is a trial to her."

Engracia gestured and she followed, after a backward glance at Santiago, which she hoped registered at least a portion of her gratitude.

Señor Palacios began his protests before they were out of the room. She pitied her husband because he must stay and listen.

"Is Juana with you?" Engracia asked as they entered a chamber at the back of the house.

"As always," Hanneke said, then checked herself. Perhaps Engracia liked the servant. "I mean, yes."

"I will send her with a tub for you, and I will find salve for your sunburn." She sighed. "Papa will argue, Mama will cry. Poor Santiago! I would like to stay longer, too, but I promised Manolo I would not argue and cry."

"Santiago is a man with many responsibilities," Hanneke said. "Please, not Juana. All I need is a basin of water. Maybe a little soap."

"Very well," Engracia said. "Lie down. Rest. I must finish packing." She rolled her eyes. "Santiago will snarl when he sees how much I am taking, and I haven't even told him about Jawhara."

When the door closed, Hanneke lay down and closed her eyes, relieved to be in a quiet place with no donkeys braying, no swords rattling, no dust swirling. The heat didn't go away, but she felt a breeze through the open window.

She tried to sleep, but she heard voices outside. Curious, she went to the window and saw Santiago, Antonio, Carlos and other horsemen standing in the corral below. She settled herself on the window ledge, watching as they gestured toward the distant hills. Santiago took out his knife and drew in the dirt, as the men gathered closer. She thought it was a crude map.

He pointed, they nodded. After a few minutes, they dispersed. By now, there was a servant at her door with a welcome basin of water and soap. She stripped and cleaned herself as best she could, then crawled into bed.

The room was dark when she woke up, aware someone was in the room.

"I am glad you saved me a little water."

She sat up in bed, aware of her nakedness. She heard clothes drop and then more water splash into the basin. She lay down, wondering if tonight was the night when her husband decided to claim what was his, bought and paid for. It was inevitable.

He had other ideas. He flopped down on the bed, with his feet dangling over the edge.

"You could sleep," she suggested.

"I could, but I dare not." He sat up. "Here. This is for you from Engracia."

He held a dress and shift. "They don't fit her, and I am certain they are too long, but you will be cooler, Ana. That wool dress must be purgatory."

"I will thank her in the morning."

"You can thank her tonight." He sighed and rose, putting on his same dirty clothes while she got as far as the linen shift, much cooler than her own. "We are riding tonight." He stopped and cocked his head toward the door. "*Ay de mi*, Urraca is wailing and pleading, and Engracia is in tears. God, how their racket chafes me! Thank you, Ana, for not behaving that way."

I wouldn't dare.

"There is Felipe, too. I despise the man. Imagine this: He wanted to know all about your dowry, then had the effrontery to demand to know what would become of it if I died in battle."

She stared at him, as amazed as he was.

"He wanted to know if you would return to the Low Countries, or if someone else would control your dowry."

They regarded each other, and Hanneke spoke first. "I think I would rather not spend any longer in this house than an hour or two."

"Wise of you," he said then laughed. "If he kills me, run."

"Santiago, that is *not* funny," she said firmly.

"It is, actually," he assured her. "In addition to being a greedy man, he's a notable coward. He will never kill anyone." He thought a moment. "He would send others, though. Stay away from him."

He sat in the window after he dressed, but not for long, because his attention seemed to focus on the hills.

"Fires," she said, sitting beside him. "We saw those last night and the night before. Is it people who came after the gates were closed?"

"*They* are why the gates are always closed at night," he said, pulling her closer. She thought it was an unconscious gesture.

Ana thought she knew who it might be. "You call them Almohades," she said, working to keep her voice calm, even though she felt the fear, too.

"I do, indeed. I wondered how long it would take for word to get out that Santiago Gonzalez is carrying a fortune to Toledo. Or trying to."

"But who would tell…"

He shrugged. "Everyone. No one. The wind. That is Spain. We will leave as soon as we can, a few at a time, and then assemble in another place. I want you to ride with me."

"I am afraid," she admitted.

Her husband surprised her. Would she ever come to know him? "I am afraid, too."

Chapter Eight

When Hanneke heard Urraca's by now familiar wails coming closer to their room, she pointed Santiago to the bed. "At least lie down for a few minutes, husband. I will see if I can get rid of her."

"Señora Gonzalez, that is worth more than you can imagine to me," he said as he lay down. "Good luck."

"What should I tell her?"

"Have Engracia packed and waiting in the hall in one hour."

How do I console the inconsolable? Hanneke thought, wondering why she had offered.

She watched her husband, his arm over his eyes. In an amazingly short time, she heard his deep breathing. Here was a man who took things as they came. She decided she had better learn from him. Right now, in fact. She closed the door behind her and faced Engracia's mother.

"I must speak to Santiago," Urraca demanded, and tried to force herself past Hanneke.

"No, you may not. He must get some sleep before we ride out tonight."

"You cannot stop me!"

"I will."

"He cannot tear my child away from me!"

Try a different tack, Hanneke, she told herself. *Papa always says that if the wind changes, the ship must tack.* "He does not wish to tear her away, señora, but think how much better it will be for Engracia in her present state to travel when it is cooler. Traveling at night is a kindness."

Urrace stopped wailing and wiped her nose on her long sleeve. "How thoughtful of him. I hadn't considered that."

Better you not even have a hint there are Almohades and campfires,

Hanneke thought. The mere idea terrified her, too, but not as much as Santiago's displeasure, or even his need to sleep.

She patted Urraca's shoulder. "Help Engracia finish her packing. Remember. One hour."

Urraca went down the stairs, and Hanneke took a deep breath.

"Bravo, wife of Santiago," she heard from the shadows.

Felipe Palacios stepped into view, a bare outline by the light of a few candles.

He bowed to her. "You are a brave woman, to handle my mother so adroitly."

She wished him elsewhere. "I am a good wife," she said simply, aware that she stood with bare feet and in a shift. With as must dignity as she could muster, she entered her room and leaned against the door until she heard his footsteps recede down the hall.

"Who was that?" Santiago whispered.

She started in surprise. "I thought you were asleep."

"Who can sleep with such a racket?"

"It was Felipe. I do not trust him either," she admitted.

"It appears you have already adopted the Gonzalez family credo. *Nullis credito*. Dress yourself. That shift will never work when we have to ride tonight."

She laughed and he joined in. The homely sound reminded her for a small moment of her father and mother in good times, before Mama took ill. It warmed her heart. Maybe things would be different in Las Claves.

Leaving Valladolid was less difficult than Hanneke envisioned. There was one complication, though, perhaps a minor one.

Urraca must have told Engracia that Santiago was riding in the cool of night for her advantage, Hanneke's little tale. When he helped her onto her horse, Engracia kissed Santiago's cheek and thanked him for his thoughtfulness.

He took it in stride. "Anything for you, my sister," he said, then managed a sidelong glance at Hanneke that made her turn away to keep from laughing.

His smile vanished as Urraca resumed her wailing and scolding. Even Señor Palacios started to sniff, too, which meant that Engracia was in tears soon enough. Hanneke remembered infant twins in the house next door in Vlissingen – one would cry, then the other would join in, for no discernible reason.

She gave her husband a nod of approval as he gently shepherded both Palacios away from their daughter. He gave them each a kiss and promised a visit next year. "You can dote on your new grandchild to your heart's content," he assured them.

"Thank you for not being a monumental pain in my ass," he whispered to Hanneke as he helped her into the saddle.

"You told me not to complain," she reminded him.

"I did, didn't I?" he replied with a slight smile. "Who knew I had any power over women?"

I could tell you I am now the mistress of small things, but why ruin a good moment?

As Urraca and Señor Palacios moved back, Urraca still weeping, but more softly now, Santiago motioned the others closer. "We will leave a few at a time through a side gate that Señor Palacios has made known to me. When the moon is lower, we will gather at the junction of the Esgueva and Pisuerga. Father Bendicio, you will keep Engr..."

At the sound of someone running, his hand went immediately to his sword. It was half out of the scabbard when a woman stepped forward, out of breath. With a glance at Santiago, she sidled toward Engracia.

"Wait," he commanded, and she kept moving. He said something harsh and guttural in Arabic, and she stopped.

He rode between the woman and Engracia, forcing her back with his horse. "She thinks to ride with us? Surely not," he said to Engracia.

"Santiago, she is my new servant, given to me by my brother. Please."

"I will not allow it. Never."

Hanneke saw Engracia's lips quiver. "Surely there can be no harm from Jawhara. Please, brother, I beg of you." Her head went down and she cried, her tears added upon by Urraca, who threw herself into her husband's arms and sobbed.

Those thin lips. That muscle in the cheek moving. Hanneke leaned back, waiting for the explosion, then relaxed, knowing it wouldn't come in front of all these people. Something strange happened to her; she pitied Santiago Gonzalez.

"Engracia..." More tears. How much could a man take? "*Dios*, I can see you will leave me no peace if I do not allow this," he said, the words wrung out of him. He forced a laugh. "Don't get any ideas, wife," Santiago told her.

On the contrary, she thought. *You have my sympathy.* She looked from Jawhara to Engracia and knew it was going to be a long journey to Toledo.

"Juana, pull her up behind you," he said. "Let us be off before everyone in Valladolid knows our business."

They moved out a few at a time, traveling through quiet, narrow streets where no one stirred. Santiago took Hanneke's reins and kept her close. "We'll gather at the river and head for those low hills," he told her. "We'll hug them for protection."

The air was still cool. Hanneke raised her face to the slight breeze, knowing it would turn oven-hot when the sun rose. She silently thanked Engracia for the gift of a linen dress and shift, much better than Dutch wool. Small things.

At the river, Santiago explained the plan of riding deep into the mountains tonight to avoid the raiders, the plan she had seen drawn in the dirt below her window. She looked around the circle of men, not one of them soft, with the exception of Father Bendicio. Even little Pablo looked filled with purpose. *My true knight*, she thought.

"*Hay preguntas?*" Santiago asked. "If no questions, let us move."

He put his hand out to stop Antonio, and the man reined in.

"Antonio, I give you a charge," Santiago said. "In the event of trouble, you will take Ana's reins and pull her to the mule train." He sat back. "As I think of it, she is in your care from now on." He put his hand to his lips and gestured to Hanneke, then moved ahead.

"I hope I am not a burden," she said to Antonio.

"Fall in behind me and ride beside Engracia." He held up his hand and leaned close enough to whisper, "I know! I know! Take pity on us men, *dama.*"

"You already rule," she said, easy enough in his company to complain a little, but not enough to get her in trouble.

"Not us," he replied. He gestured with his head. "Second sons don't rule, and neither do cast-offs like me. We have no choice."

"Cast-offs?" *No choice like me? Surely not.*

"Bendicio will tell you more, when he gets bored. Ride now, and shh."

They rode all night, stopping once to relieve themselves and stretch.

Since it was dark, Hanneke didn't bother with a blanket. Some of the soldiers lay down and slept during the brief pause. They woke without a sound when Santiago walked among them.

Hanneke watched her husband of less than a week. He was tireless, his back straight as he rode, head tipped to one side, as if listening to the very ground. He said nothing, but he was constantly looking about him, riding ahead, or dropping back until he was a distant, solitary figure on the plain that rose toward hills.

When Antonio dropped back to trade places with him, Santiago rode beside her. He reached out several times in the night to touch her leg. It startled her at first, but she decided he was making sure she was awake. She could think of no other reason.

Engracia had long since fallen asleep, cradled in Father Bendicio's arms. Pablo sang softly to himself, the same tune over and over, until Santiago ordered him to shut up. Juana maintained her angry silence, probably irritated that Engracia's servant rode behind her, but then, Juana never needed a reason. As for Jawhara, she sat ramrod straight, as if afraid to lean against Juana. Jawhara looked about her, too, much like Santiago. As her own thoughts began to blur together, Hanneke wondered why.

When morning was only a suggestion, Hanneke started to sag. When she shook her head to clear her brain, she struggled to stay on the mule's back.

Before she could pull herself erect again, Santiago lifted her onto his own horse. "Stubborn, stubborn woman," he said, his mouth close to her ear.

She closed her eyes. After a moment's hesitation, she leaned against her husband. He dropped back, and through a haze of sleep, Hanneke listened as he conversed with Father Bendicio.

"Perhaps I was wrong, Father. No one follows us. It seems there was nothing to fear after all."

Content with that news, Hanneke drifted into deeper sleep, her husband's arms strong about her.

She woke with the sunrise, but it wasn't the light that made her open her eyes and look around. It was the smell of smoke, and something more. She sniffed the early morning breeze. She saw the entire company bunched closer together now, moving slower and then stopping.

For one fanciful moment, she thought it was smoke from the sun. She shaded her eyes with her hand, wondering as she did so why Santiago had suddenly stiffened in the saddle. His sword came out of its scabbard quietly and he rested it across her lap. He leaned forward, his face close to hers and looked.

He gasped. "*Dios mio*. He was in front of us all the time!"

Chapter Nine

The smell grew stronger. Hanneke sucked in her breath as she
remembered such smoke when plague struck Vlissingen. She was
young, but who can forget corpses stacked in the street and the smell
of burning bodies?

Santiago called for his soldiers and they came up quickly, Antonio
leading them. "Let us go forward slowly," he said.

The smoke increased as they walked their horses, but she saw no village.
The unforgettable odor of burning flesh increased and she coughed.

It was then that Santiago realized she was with them. "*Mierda!*" he
swore. He looked behind him, but the mule train was no longer visible
through the smoke. She looked, too, wondering where Father Bendicio
and Engracia were. He took the sword from her lap and shifted in his
saddle. "Hang on. I'm putting you behind me. Wrap your hands through
my belt and don't let go, no matter what happens."

He pulled her around until she sat behind him. She tugged at her dress,
but it would not cover her legs as she straddled the big war horse now.

"Don't squirm," he said. "Hang on."

She put her hands through his sword belt. Her vision was blurry from
the smoke, but she saw a village, or what was left of it.

From the mill near the river to the small church, where the roof
suddenly collapsed in a shower of sparks, she doubted it had ever been
more than a place to stop when there was nothing else nearby. Hanneke
clung tighter to Santiago's belt, putting her face against the surcoat that
covered his chain mail.

Lances ready, swords drawn, they rode slowly through the burning
village. The small huts were already reduced to ashes and curious smoking

mounds she recognized immediately. The small ones brought more tears to eyes already streaming from the smoke.

There were no signs of life as they traversed the village. No dogs barked, no mules brayed. She was starting to breathe easier when they left the village and came to the threshing floor.

Santiago sucked in his breath. He pulled Hanneke's fingers from his belt and dismounted with great effort, as if he weighed five times more. He walked to the threshing floor and stood there, looking down. He walked from body to body, then raised his arms and wailed.

Hanneke leaped off his horse and ran to him. The paved stones of the threshing floor were gluey with blood and chaff from wheat already winnowed before the raiders struck. She looked down and put her hand to her mouth.

They had once been women, flung like dolls to the threshing floor in a terrible winnowing. Hanneke clutched Santiago's arm, dizzy and disoriented, as if she stared from a great distance.

One of the bodies stirred. Not knowing how she got there, Hanneke found herself on her knees, cradling the head and shoulders of a woman covered in blood and chaff. Hanneke looked into the glazing eyes of someone her own age.

Santiago knelt next to her, running his fingers lightly over the girl's cheeks that hung in bloody tatters. Her dress was bunched around her waist. Hanneke looked away, horrified at the damage.

"Can…can she tell us who did this?" Hanneke's voice didn't sound like her own. She pulled the girl's dress down.

"She cannot talk." Gently, he opened her mouth. "She has no tongue. I know who did this. I already told you about him, the man who killed my father, and who nearly killed Carlos. This abomination is his signature."

Speechless herself, Hanneke looked away, but that was only worse. A woman lay just beyond them, her skirt ripped entirely away, her arms outstretched as she reached in the rictus of death for a baby folded in impossible directions.

"Yussef el Ghalib did this," Santiago said softly, as if trying not to disturb the dead and soon-to-die. "I was not wrong. He has come up from the south. He must know about your dowry."

He stood up, removed his belt and pulled off his surcoat, covering mother and baby. "This would kill Engracia."

The girl in her arms trembled violently, then died, her eyes never wavering from Hanneke's face. Shocked Hanneke made a sign of the cross in blood on what remained of the girl's forehead, then ran her hands down to close her eyes.

They wouldn't close. Hanneke tried again. The eyed remained open and staring at horror beyond anyone's vision. She looked closer. The eyelids had been pared away.

Don't leave me alone here, she thought in panic. Santiago stood with Antonio on the edge of the threshing floor. "Santiago, I need you," she managed to say, before great sobs tore through her body.

He was at her side in a moment, taking the body from her lap and lowering it to the floor. He pulled up the woman's apron to shield the perpetually staring eyes.

Hanneke struggled to rise. Her wonderful linen dress had acted as a wick on the threshing floor and was soaked in blood. She held her arms out to Santiago. He lifted her to her feet, put his arm around her waist, and half-led, half-dragged her to the edge of the floor, where he sat her down, facing out. He sat, too, and held her close.

"Why did you get off my horse?" he asked, when her shivering stopped.

"You cried out."

"Engracia would have run the other way. Bendicio, too. You did not. Why not?"

"I thought you needed me."

His expression turned contemplative. "I think I do." He gestured over his shoulder. "You see what we are up against, fighting such an enemy."

She nodded. She had no energy, but she knew there was much to do. "I can walk."

He walked her toward the mule train, where the drivers were coming toward them with shovels and hoes. "Can you stand?"

She nodded and he let go of her, but not before giving her a homely pat on her hip, and whispering, "We must bury these women. Later we will talk."

He followed his men back to the threshing floor, but not before pointing some of them with shovels toward smoldering mounds. She stood there a moment longer, remembering King Alfonso's words to her on the steps of the church in faraway, more-civilized Santander.

She turned to contemplate the innocents swept away. "Pray God I will not be numbered among the winnowed," she whispered. "Not me. Not mine."

She dreaded to see Juana coming toward her, but there was no animosity this time. The servant sat her down in the circle of the dowry wagons and rummaged for another dress. Hanneke slowly unlaced her bodice. She wanted water to wash her bloody hands, but there was none.

Juana returned with a dark wool dress. "It was all I could find quickly."

Hanneke stripped off her dress, ignoring what muleteers remained there. Her shift was deep in blood, too, but Juana hadn't found a clean one. At least the dark dress wouldn't show blood from the shift underneath.

She sat down, hearing Engracia sobbing somewhere behind her, but too shocked to do anything except tell herself that Jawhara could comfort her; that's what servants were for.

But Jawhara still sat on Juana's mule, looking steadily to the south. *What is she doing?* Hanneke asked herself, before she closed her eyes.

"Ana, Ana."

Someone flicked water in her face and she opened her eyes. Santiago set a bucket beside her and handed her a shirt fragment burned around the edges. She didn't want to think where it had come from, but she dipped it in the bucket, grateful.

"We found a well. Even El Ghalib cannot burn water, although he would if he could. Hurry."

The water felt good on her face, and then her arms and legs as she raised her skirt with no embarrassment and scrubbed them. Whatever standards she had brought with her from Vlissingen had sloughed away in Spain.

Santiago helped her stand, steadying her until she nodded that she could manage. She saw Engracia, her face white and terrified, already on horseback, and Juana, with the servant Jawhara behind her again. Pablo was stowing away the shovels in the dowry wagon.

"We buried them by the threshing floor," Santiago told her as he washed his face and hands. He pulled on his surcoat again, the one he had removed to cover the mother and child. She turned away, unable to look at the rusty stains.

He put his hands on her shoulders and spoke to her alone. "We are too far away to return to Valladolid. We are going to ride all night and tomorrow through those mountains. We're going to skirt the towns and stay high. Can you do it?"

She knew there was only one answer, so she nodded.

"One of my soldiers is from that village…"

"…poor, poor man," she whispered.

"I know." He pointed toward the rising hills. "He tells me of a shepherd's path through those hills."

She stared where he pointed. "Hills? Those are mountains."

He smiled for the first time all day. "Maybe to you Low Country people who live below the level of the sea. Hills now. They'll turn into mountains soon enough."

"If you say so."

"Skeptic," he said mildly. Then his expression changed, becoming the thin-lipped, intense-eyed man who married her. "If we can shake El Ghalib, we won't be that far from Toledo. I can get more soldiers there for the rest of our journey, and we'll travel faster without the dowry."

She said nothing. Did he expect her to argue?

"Ana?"

"It's a wonderful plan. Words fail me," she said, then regretted her flippancy.

She looked at him, afraid, then remarkably not afraid. Could there be anything worse than the threshing floor? "Certainly I will follow."

To her relief, he pulled her close. She had never put her arms around him, but she did now, holding him closer.

Chapter Ten

As much as she knew that the threshing floor would remain lodged permanently in her mind and heart, Hanneke felt a reluctance to leave the place. They were heading toward what her husband called hills but still crossing the broad plain, with not even a bush large enough to piss behind, and for certain no protection from raiders who thought to return.

Or who might even be watching them now. One could think that, looking at Jawhara, who continued to stare toward the south, as though waiting for the Almohades to return and smite them, too.

Antonio ordered the servant back onto Juana's mule, which suited neither woman. "God spare me from disagreeable females," he muttered as he passed Hanneke. "Not present company," he said. "You are wiser than they."

"I don't feel wiser, and certainly not braver," Hanneke admitted.

"You hide it well, *dama*."

But Jawhara, *dios mio*. Her face set in a scowl, she leaped off Juana's mule. Pablo dismounted and grabbed her as she fought him.

Hanneke heard the thunder of a horse behind her. Santiago rode down on the pair of them, lifting Pablo off his feet, then turning his big gray to knock down Jawhara, who drew herself into a ball.

He set Pablo down carefully enough. "Is there not enough worry without a childish fight?" he asked.

Pablo never took his eyes off Santiago. "Señor, it is Jawhara. She wants to leave us."

"And you thought to keep her here?" Santiago asked, his voice calmer. He glared at the servant, who shrank away this time and ran toward Engracia. He pointed at Jawhara. "Engracia, if there is one more sound out of her, I will kill her. I told you I did not want Almohad trash along."

Engracia began to wail, adding her tears to Jawhara's. With an oath that even made the teamsters gape, Juana leaped off her mule and slapped Jawhara, then bent her arm back until she cried out. Fierce in her wrath, Juana gestured to Pablo to mount his mule. When he was in the saddle, she forced Jawhara up behind him.

"Engracia, control your servant," Santiago ordered. "No more of this."

His sister-in-law glared at him out of mutinous eyes. "I will tell Manolo what you have done. Don't think that I won't."

"I know you will," he replied, sounding so weary. "I don't care."

He turned toward Hanneke. "Try to keep them in line. I cannot deal with Engracia. I do not dare."

"I don't understand any of this," she whispered for his ears only.

"Talk to my worthless priest," was all he said, as he spurred his horse to the front of the procession, shouting at everyone to pull in close and be prepared to ride.

They led out in their usual order, moving fast, everyone intent on the hills ahead, the soldiers with their heads on a continuous swivel. Hanneke thought they might slow down when they reached the foothills, but no one slowed down.

They stopped briefly when Engracia started to sway in the saddle, but only long enough for Antonio to carry her to Carlos, he of the scarred face and few teeth. In mere moments, they were moving again.

Hanneke found herself riding beside Father Bendicio, who looked vaguely comical, with his black robes hiked up and his legs so pale and spindly. She remembered Santiago's words.

"How long have you known him?" she asked. She wondered why she had not asked him more during their lengthy time together before Spain. She reminded herself that she *had* asked; Bendicio had only given her vague answers.

"Known him? All my life. He and I are the same age, at least I think I am twenty-four," he told her.

"You do not know?"

"I was hidden in an oven and found by Santiago's father," he said, and gestured over his shoulder. "It was a village much like that one. My parents were killed by Almohades. I was raised at Las Claves."

Since he seemed willing to talk, she rode closer. "Tell me about my husband. How long has he been a warrior?"

He changed his mind and said nothing. When the silence grew, she dug her heels into her mule's side and rode ahead, angry at his silence, into a dusk filled with heat possessing fangs and claws.

She looked around, surprised to see Santiago riding so close to her.

"You're supposed to ride back there," he said. "Women never listen to me."

It seemed so funny that she wanted to laugh. He handed her his leather water pouch, his *bota*. She took a deep drink, but not too deep.

"Can you keep going?"

She handed back the *bota*. "I have a choice?"

He shook his head. "No choice."

"Then why ask?"

"Las Claves will fit you like a glove," he said finally. "Las Claves offers no choice, either."

The first horse dropped as they reached the mountains. "It begins," Santiago said, as they halted. "Fernan, get your gear off that worm meat. Diego, give Fernan your horse, and you take Ana's mule, because you're the lightest man I have. Help her down. Ana, ride with Bendicio. You hardly weigh anything."

She did as he said. With efficiency borne of years of practice, two soldiers on horseback roped the dead animal and dragged it off the trail. Antonio dismounted long enough to help her in front of the priest. He patted her leg, then looked around as if to make sure Santiago hadn't seen such a liberty.

"My apology. I am tired," he said simply. "Ride on."

Wasting no time, they filed past the dead horse. Hanneke hesitated to lean back against the priest until he touched her shoulder and pulled her back. Riding astride was easier, with her dress around her knees.

"Forgive me for my reluctance to speak earlier," Bendicio said. "Does anyone care to remember a time when they were less than adequate?"

"Father, you would be describing me at any moment since we tied up at the dock in Santander."

"Hardly," he murmured, which pleased her. "You have a surprising facility with Castilian."

"I like languages and I was unfair to you," she said honestly. "Father, do not evade my question."

"Santiago killed his first Moor in battle when he was barely thirteen. I was his squire, *his escudero*."

"So young," she said, sad for the man.

"We were surprised and outnumbered and rode into battle with Santiago's father, I behind them on my mule."

"Were you afraid?"

"Terrified. I sobbed until Señor Gonzalez threatened to kill me."

After her afternoon at the threshing floor, Hanneke could nearly see the conflict in her mind: a sudden attack from nowhere, blinding smoke, shouts, horses milling about.

"How did…"

"…he kill the Moor? He jabbed him with a lance. It broke and then they were unhorsed. Santiago could barely lift that heavy sword, but he didn't quit slashing away until the Moor stopped moving."

"*God behoede ons*," she exclaimed in Dutch. She must have spoken too loud, because she got a reprimand from Antonio behind her. "*Silencio!*"

Bendicio sighed. "I thought he would never finish that bloody business, hacking and weeping." The priest cleared his throat and his tone changed. "Mind you, I saw this from a distance as I ran away. I was a poor excuse for an *escudero*. This was when I discovered all my desires were centered on a priestly vocation."

"Then?"

"Soon I was on my way to a monastery in Salamanca, and Santiago was condemned to the courtyard for sword practice until his hands were bloody blisters. By the time I returned, the blisters were callouses and he never cried again."

"Poor, poor child."

"That is not all. I suppose I must share what came before."

Hanneke waited for him to continue, but he was silent again. "You can't stop there," she said.

"I will tell you the rest later, when the moon is high, and we are trying to stay awake."

The moon did not rise until after midnight, and still they climbed higher, picking their way along a path overgrown with weeds and skinny bushes. Groggy with sleep, Hanneke clung to the saddle's pommel as Bendicio's mule picked its way carefully among the stones. She held her breath every time it seemed to stumble, imagining herself plummeting to her death.

Another horse dropped, struggling and trying to rise with no success, almost as if it knew its fate. On Santiago's quiet orders, the animal was dragged to the edge and pushed off. Hanneke covered her ears as it shrieked as it fell.

She blinked back her tears. "Father, couldn't they have killed it first?"

"No, my child," he replied, speaking slowly, as if sifting the words through his tired brain. "That would leave blood on the stones for others to follow."

Santiago rode beside them then, touching Hanneke's leg and giving her a shake. "Stay awake. Soon the path will divide. If El Ghalib does not know we have come this far, we may get your dowry to Toledo after all."

By all means, get the dowry to safety.

When Santiago resumed his place in the line of march, Bendicio looked back. "Have you seen Juana or Pablo?"

Hanneke shook her head, remembering that in some faraway place Santiago had told her to watch out for Engracia. Without thinking, she slid to the ground. "I will catch up," she told Bendicio. His head tipped forward and he slept. The mule moved on anyway.

Unsure, she started back down the trail, saying nothing. She nodded to Carlos when she passed him holding Engracia. He reached out to stop her, but she hurried on, worried now, wondering if Juana and Pablo were in trouble. She heard Carlos leave the line, and sighed. Trust the evil-looking man to tattle to Santiago.

She made herself small just off the path and watched the muleteers move past with her dowry. She edged onto a small boulder that was still warm from the day's scorching. More soldiers followed the baggage, some as silent as Bendicio, other chatting softly with each other. Maybe they didn't even see her.

She watched in silence, then drifted into her own dream, as the corpses from the threshing floor rose before her, women and babies. One by one, they fell to the ground then disappeared. Hanneke sobbed out loud and continued down the trail.

She found them around a bend in the trail. Pablo gave her a relieved smile, as if she could do something for him. Juana scowled at her and grabbed her arm. "See if you can hurry that useless *puta*," she hissed. "Jawhara says she is tired, or that her feet hurt, or that nature calls."

"You speak Arabic?" Hanneke asked.

"We all do," Juana said, looking at her as if she were not too bright. "How is Engracia?"

"She is asleep in the arms of Carlos," Hanneke said. "I wouldn't worry."

"*You* might not worry. Suppose my lady wakes up, takes fright, and her baby ends up looking like that scarred man!"

"Juana, that is perfect nonsense."

More scowls, more oaths. Juana beat her tired mule and forced it to stumble ahead over the rocks. "You get Jawhara then! I wash my hands of this."

More worried than ever, Hanneke turned to Pablo. He pointed down the trail. "There she is. I do not know what she is doing by holding back."

Hanneke stared where he pointed, and there she was, moving slowly among the rocks, always looking back. "Come, Pablo. There are two of us. We can do this."

They took Jawhara by the arms and dragged her up the path. She resisted, then must have seen the futility of it all. Cowed and silent, she walked between them, her head down. Pablo swung into the saddle and Hanneke helped her up, even though the servant struck her.

Santiago and Juana waited for them, silent. He grabbed Jawhara's hair, speaking low in Arabic, shaking her for emphasis. He cowed her into silence, but all the hate was there as the servant stared back.

"I don't trust you," he said in Spanish. "I would kill you here, except for Engracia."

"You don't dare," Juana taunted him.

Hanneke sucked in her breath and watched them exchange long looks of hatred. Santiago's hand went to the dagger at his side, slowly pulling it from its sheath. Only then did Juana look away. *What did I just see?* Hanneke asked herself in horror.

"No, she said softly. "Please, husband."

The spell was broken. Santiago sheathed his dagger and Juana rode ahead. Santiago hesitated, then followed.

"Here, Ana."

She turned around, her heart still in her throat, but it was only Father Bendicio, holding out his hand to her. Fear made her nimble. She stepped in his stirrup and sat in front again, wondering if she had imagined all that venom between servant and master.

But who was servant? Who was master?

Chapter Eleven

"I must know what is going on between my husband and Juana," Hanneke demanded, keeping her voice low.

"In a moment," the priest said. "This is where the trail divides and there is Santiago, our good shepherd, motioning to us."

Antonio had assumed the lead, ready to relinquish it when Santiago took his place, and fell back to the rear, as they had done all through this night journey. *One would think they are brothers*, Hanneke thought, feeling an unwarranted sense of security. *Two good shepherds*.

"Tell me now," she ordered. "Why does this obviously strong man let a mere servant taunt him? What is she to him?"

"The better question is, 'What is he to her?' That is what you need to know."

She waited. He had to speak, if only for her piece of mind.

"Tell no one."

She opened her mouth to assure him as Santiago trotted past them on the new trail. "We will rest just ahead," he said as he passed, and the priest fell silent.

They paused in a small clearing only slightly less rocky than the path itself. Hanneke slid off Bendicio's mule and walked on stiff legs to the edge of the path. The air was thick with dust and already strong with the odor of sweating bodies, animal and human. *This is what exhaustion smells like*, she thought.

Carlos deposited Engracia on a blanket Juana spread out, the servant making soothing sounds as she wiped the dust from Engracia's face. Jawhara crouched close by, trying to hide herself behind Pablo. She made herself even smaller when Santiago looked her way.

Santiago gave his *bota* to Juana. "There is only a drop," he said. "Make sure Engracia understands I am holding nothing back from her." He turned to Hanneke. "I have no more."

"No matter," she said. "I only want to lie down."

He scraped away smaller pebbles, coughing when the dust rose. "Lie down."

She did as he ordered, arranging her dusty skirt that smelled of blood from her shift underneath, and rested her head on her arm. With a sigh, Santiago sat down beside her. Her eyes were closing when he pulled her closer until her head rested on his thigh.

"We can't stop more than an hour, or at least until that star moves closer to the tree," he told her. "If El Ghalib is following, I think he is far back. If he is ahead of us, we must come out of the mountains where he doesn't suspect."

He looked up when Antonio knelt by them on one knee. "Did you do it?"

"To perfection. After you passed, ten of us brushed away your tracks. We took the other fork and went far enough to fool him, then cut across."

Santiago nodded, and patted Hanneke. "You'll probably demand that I pay you more, when this journey is done."

They both chuckled, which told Hanneke that they had this conversation before. She smiled to herself and closed her eyes.

She slept, despite the rocks and heat, her head pillowed on her husband's leg. It seemed no more than a moment before he touched her shoulder. The moon had risen, its light flowing around the warriors who slept close by. She was conscious of overwhelming exhaustion and thirst.

"You cried in your sleep," Santiago whispered as he righted her and stood up. He knelt by her again. "I think we still see the threshing floor." He looked into the distance. "Pray God we can raise a bigger army and end such murder."

She glanced farther down the clearing to the mules carrying her dowry. *Maybe I have this wrong*, she thought. *Peace will bring threshing floors where women can laugh and work and not die. You are right, King Alfonso. I am now part of a great endeavor.*

The thought gave her the energy to rise and pat Pablo's shoulder, in imitation of her husband, who walked among his followers. She started to pat Jawhara, but the servant was already awake, her eyes pools of darkness in the moonlight. She wanted to tell the servant not to be afraid, but she knew no Arabic.

She took another look at the woman's face and saw something instead of fear: a certain calculation. *Are you measuring me?* Hanneke asked herself, startled. *Are you measuring all of us? Why?*

She wanted to say something to her husband, but decided against it. What could she tell him? That Jawhara had something on her mind?

As they climbed steadily toward the summit of the mountain pass, she rode with Father Bendicio. "Father? Are you awake?"

"One of us had better be," he answered, his voice muffled, as his chin rested in the heavy folds of his habit.

"Tell me more, please."

He did not hesitate this time. "Old Señor Gonzalez would tell it when he was deep in drink, which was often enough. I speak of El Ghalib's father now, a man equally bloodthirsty. It is not a pretty story."

"I think Spain has no pretty stories. What is one more to me?"

"As I have heard it - this was before I was rescued – Santiago was two and Manolo – Manuel – was three. Juana was young, like Jawhara over there, who seems to be listening to every word I say. How curious. She speaks no Castilian."

"Forget her," Hanneke insisted. "Tell me."

"Las Claves was on fire. They delayed too long in leaving, probably because Santiago's mother was killed." He shuddered. "Those who remember it say they can still hear the old señor wailing when he found her body, abused like those women on the threshing floor."

"*Vreselijk, vreselijk,*" Hanneke murmured, crossing herself.

"As the story goes, he ordered Juana to carry the boys to safety. She tucked a child under each arm and made for the river. The men remained behind to cover the retreat, but before Señor Gonzalez sent her off, he begged her to get through with Manolo, even if it meant leaving Santiago behind, because he was younger."

"What a thing to say!"

"This is a land of hard choices. People say Manolo is the image of his mother."

They had reached the summit and were starting down, her husband leading. All the horsemen wore their helmets. She forced her attention back to the priest, even though she didn't want to know any more.

"You can imagine the rest. The smoke, the heat, the noise, the confusion." He shuddered. "And that peculiar sound the Almohades make as they ride into battle. Who can blame Juana for what happened?"

"Santiago?" She could barely say his name.

"She couldn't run fast with both children so she left one behind in a gap in the rock. Covered him with a blanket. She thought she left Santiago."

"It was Manolo," Hanneke finished, when the priest could not. Cold prickles overruled the sweat running down her neck.

"They tell me that when she reached the river and noticed her mistake, it took four men to hold her back. When Señor Gonzalez and the rear guard arrived, he nearly beat her to death for her error."

"Dear God," Hanneke whispered.

"God was otherwise engaged that night. Later, maybe a day or two, they were joined by knights from Calatrava, and fought their way back to Las Claves."

"What of…of Manolo?" Hanneke asked, almost not wanting to know.

"El Ghalib's father found him, slit the muscles in one leg, and hung him by his heels from a tree. No one knows why he was still alive, except that the Gonzalez family is amazingly resilient."

She heard the click of Father Bendicio's rosary. "A curious thing is revenge," he told her. "When Juana hadn't the grace to die from the beating, Señor Gonzalez made her tend his motherless sons., reminding her constantly of her terrible mistake. And Santiago? He was raised knowing that he should have died. Juana somehow blames him for her confusion. Him!"

Hanneke sighed, astounded at such cruelty. "He was just a baby."

"I doubt Señor Gonzalez said more than ten words to Santiago during his childhood. The boy had no friend or ally except Manolo. They have always been close, oddly enough."

The beads clicked more rapidly. "So it was, until that moment when we faced the Almohades. Even Señor Gonzalez could not withhold his pleasure when Santiago killed that poor heathen." He silenced the beads. "Do you understand your husband a little better?"

It was a lesson he never forgot, or was allowed to forget, she thought, appalled but understanding. "Santiago knew killing Moors or… or… Almohades pleased his father. He cannot stop, can he?"

"Here endeth the lesson," Father Bendicio said.

Poor man. Hanneke looked ahead at her husband, who rode beside Antonio, their heads together. Engracia, still slept, riding with Carlos, Juana close by. Pablo sat alone on his mule, his chin to his chest, asleep. Jawhara was gone.

Alert now, Hanneke weighed her own fear against greater harm. "Stop, Father. I must look for Jawhara."

"No, Ana."

"I must."

She slid off the mule and hurried back down the narrow trail. To her enormous relief, Jawhara stood at the side of the path. She turned quickly when she heard Hanneke.

Hanneke tugged the servant back to Pablo's mule. When the servant was mounted, and the recipient of Hanneke's most fierce glare, Hanneke retraced her steps to where she found Jawhara, wondering why she was there. She reached the spot when Santiago rode up behind her.

Before she could express her deep misgivings about Jawhara, he grabbed her arm and yanked her into his saddle. "This is no time to run away," he said. "Have you no brains?"

"But Jawhara… I'm…"

"Not one more word. My patience has run out."

He won't listen to me, she thought, humiliated more than worried. She could be fair, though. Mama always used to say women had a sense about things, but what man wants to hear that?

He set her down none too gently beside Bendicio's mule. "Watch her!" he demanded. "Must I do everything?"

Embarrassed, Hanneke kept her head down, trying not to hear the low laughter of the soldiers at her expense. She was so thirsty she knew she would never swallow again, but this was no time to complain. Would this journey never end?

She was almost asleep when she heard a sound that she knew even then would remain with her the rest of her life: a warbling, sustained cry from many throats. The hair rose on the back of her neck, this strange sound that interrupted the quiet of early dawn. Then, "Allahu akbaru" screamed at them from all sides, surrounding them.

She knew.

Chapter Twelve

Santiago's soldiers slammed down their helmet visors and drew their swords, almost in one motion. The warble became a yodeling wail that echoed in the narrow pass and crashed in from all directions, and no direction.

As the soldiers formed themselves into a line of defense, the muleteers yanked their terrified animals into a tight knot. The mules bumped into each other and bit whatever was handy.

Heard for centuries in this subjugated land, the war cry of Mohammed's followers grew louder. Hanneke covered her ears and leaned against her mule, shutting her eyes.

Santiago raced toward them. "Run!" he shouted. He pointed down the slope with his sword. Behind his helmet, his eyes were alive with defiance and tenacity. She had seen eyes like that once before on a caged wolf. Hunters had brought the beast from Saxony and stored it in her father's warehouse until it was too starved and weak to resist.

The priest leaped off his mule, tugging Hanneke with him. Carlos handed the sobbing Engracia to Bendicio, who dragged her off the trail. The priest motioned for Pablo and Hanneke to follow. They scrambled down the rocky slope, raising a cloud of dust, slipping and sliding until they crouched under an outcropping of stone.

Hanneke closed her eyes and hugged the earth, feeling the hoof beats of the enemy's horses through her body. Her sides heaved from running, and there was a funny taste of rust in her mouth.

The wailing of the Almohades joined with the centuries-old cry of "Santiago! España!" and the clang of sword against scimitar. Hanneke held Engracia's hand tight against her breast while Pablo burrowed into her side, trying to dig them both into the mountain. Hanneke stroked his hair with her free hand.

They hugged the slope and listened to the battle. Shrieking horses and shouting warriors welded into one awful clamor that grew louder until there was nothing else in the world except war.

The fight raged along the trail above them like a great wounded animal, lurching and falling, then rising again, more desperate, more vengeful. A horse and rider tumbled down the slope right by them, the rider small and swathed in turban and robe. Hypnotized, Hanneke watched as the warrior and horse sailed off the slope, separating at last, and falling to the valley floor.

They huddled together, arms around each other, mud-smeared now from tears and sweat. Hanneke wiped Pablo's dirty face with the hem of her dress.

He sniffed her dress. "It smells bloody."

She raised the hem, seeing again her bloody shift, a relic of the threshing floor and burning village. Pablo sniffed again.

"Jawhara smells like that," he said. "I noticed it all day yesterday and last night. She smells like your dress. I do not understand."

"Nor do I, Pablo," Hanneke said. "What are you saying?"

"I wish I knew." He looked around. "Where *is* Jawhara? Did we leave her behind, Father Bendicio?"

"We had no time to account for everyone, my son."

Hanneke covered her bloody shift and stared at the valley floor to distract herself. It didn't work, but she saw a great river in the distance and longed for it. She looked up the slope and wondered who would come down first, one of the warriors swathed in blue or her husband.

"I don't want any of this." She spoke into the hillside, where no one could hear her. "Papa, surely you didn't want this for me. Even you are not heartless."

The sound of battle faded and stopped, but it wasn't until the sun was directly overhead that they heard someone coming toward them. Engracia made animal noises deep in her throat and clutched her belly. Hanneke pulled Pablo close.

The footsteps grew louder than stopped in a cloud of dust, as if the person was too weary to take another step. When he started walking again, rocks and pebbles dislodged by his passage rained down on them. Pablo sneezed. Hanneke held her breath and closed her eyes.

"Bendicio? Ana?" The words were low and cautious.

Father Bendicio got to his knees and looked upward. "We are here and well, Santiago, *deo volente.*"

Santiago balanced himself on the slope, then knelt beside Engracia. "Is she well?" he asked Juana.

"Yes, señor, she is well," the servant replied. "It's a good thing for you."

Little pinpoints of light seemed to dance in his eyes. He stared at Juana until she had the grace to lower her own gaze. "Come."

As they struggled up the slope, Hanneke looked behind her, wondering how they had managed to scramble down in the first place and avoid the fate of the Almohad rider.

Santiago stopped them below the edge of the trail. "Engracia, you and Juana remain here."

"It is scarcely comfortable," the priest chided, which brought a sharp look from Santiago.

"We have to move some of the bodies. Do as I say."

Santiago reached the trail first and held out his hand for her. She couldn't help the fear in her eyes, which softened his own. "It won't get better with waiting, Ana," he told her, but she heard the kindness. "I need your help."

The dead were everywhere. She put her sleeve to her nose, but there was no escaping the smell of blood and loose bowels. In her terror she reached for Santiago. He circled her with his arms. "El Ghalib's soldiers," he said, "and too many of mine, God damn his eyes."

From the shelter of her husband's arms, she tried to find a view without bodies, but there was none. The Spaniards walked among their fallen enemies. She gasped when one soldier brushed past them, carrying two heads by their bloody hair. Holding her breath, she watched as he tied the heads to his saddle and grinned at her.

A few sharp words from Santiago, and the man led his horse away, only to disclose a row of wounded men lying by the path. One of them was Diego, the lighter man chosen to ride her mule, which stood close by, her dainty head down, as if she had failed him, too. Diego looked at her, pleading for help, an expression of great disbelief on his face.

She started toward him as he vomited a gout of blood and toppled over, dead, exposing the great hole that had been his stomach. His own face expressionless, Santiago picked up Diego and carried him toward the mule train. As if in a trance, Hanneke followed. Pablo joined her, grabbing her hand and staying close.

Several of the mules were dead, the dowry goods they carried jumbled from the packing and strewn on the ground. Bright-colored bolts of cloth mingled with spices and broken crockery. She stared at the mess of her dowry, trampled by mules and stained with their blood.

Pablo's hand tightened his hand in hers as he raised their hands and pointed. "Look. Jawhara."

Engracia's servant crouched in the middle of the mules, her eyes darting here and there like minnows in a quiet pond. As she saw Hanneke, Jawhara rose and backed away from her, clutching something under her dress. When she turned to run, Santiago handed Diego to a soldier, and clubbed her with the blunt edge of his sword. She dropped without a sound.

"How can you?" Hanneke asked. She knelt by the unconscious servant, brushing her tangle of hair off her face.

"I have never trusted her."

"I didn't trust her either," she said. "I wanted to say something to you back down the trail."

He pulled up the unconscious woman's dress. "Let's see what she was trying to hide from us."

Hanneke watched in amazement as Santiago unrolled her own dress, the bloody one from the threshing room floor. "I left that behind," she said. "I do not understand."

Pablo leaned closer and sniffed. "That is why she smelled so bloody."

Santiago shook out the dress. The fabric hung in strips, as if someone had been tearing it to pieces. Hanneke watched with growing uneasiness as dangerous lights played in his eyes. He knelt by Jawhara, turned her over and shook her. The girl dangled in his arms, unconscious. He dropped her back in the dust and gestured for Antonio.

He held out the dress. "Ride as far back down the trail as you think prudent and see if you can find any scraps of this dress. Take Pablo along. He can pick up scraps. I want to know where you find them."

The men looked in each other eyes until Antonio directed his gaze to Jawhara. "Were we betrayed?"

"We will know when you return."

Santiago walked him to his horse, Pablo following. "Watch Jawhara," he told Hanneke over his shoulder.

Hanneke sat by Jawhara, chafing at her uselessness. When she couldn't stand another moment alone with her fears, she told Juana to watch, and turned her attention to the soldiers who were carrying their dead comrades to burial, except she saw no shovels.

They took the bodies to a clearing a little way from the press of mules and horses. As she watched in disbelief, they removed all valuables and lay six bodies side by side, and then the remaining five on top. When they were symmetrical in death, another soldier started a fire. He wrapped cloth from her dowry around a stout tree branch someone else had broken off and trimmed. He set the improvised torch in the flames, turning it over and over.

"No," Hanneke said softly. "Please no."

Santiago took the torch from the soldier, holding it until other men had stuffed dry grass among and over the bodies. Bendicio joined her, praying out loud, as Santiago walked slowly around the corpses, touching off the grass.

"Why?" she asked Bendicio.

Strange how a young man could look suddenly old. "If we bury them, El Ghalib will only dig them up again. That is why."

The flames caught the grass, devouring the corpses like a starving animal, licking and murmuring and biting deeper. Thick black smoke rolled off the flaming pyre. The heat from the flames and the sun caused the air to undulate. As she watched in horror, the bodies seemed to move, made restless by the fire.

In tears, Hanneke ran to the edge of the trail. She tripped and sprawled in the dust, then picked herself up and ran back down the slope where she had huddled earlier. Covering her nose with her dress, she tried to mask the odor of flesh on fire. She cried until she slept, exhausted.

Chapter Thirteen

When she woke, Hanneke knew she was not alone. For one absurd moment, she wanted the man sitting there to be Antonio, who seemed more of a calm presence. What nonsense.

Pablo knelt a little distance from her. "Pablo?"

He said nothing. She touched his shoulder and he started to weep, this cheerful knight of hers who took life as it came. "Pablo?"

He grasped her hand on his shoulder. "I want to go back to the kitchen at the monastery."

"Where they beat you when you dropped things?" This was not her Pablo, her true knight.

She remembered his errand with Antonio. "Is Antonio well?"

He nodded.

"Then what?"

When he turned around, she saw disbelief in his eyes. "What did you find, Pablo? Tell me."

The words tumbled out. "I found scraps on every twig and bush, by every rock!"

"She betrayed us." Hanneke shook the dust off her dress, a futile attempt. "We knew she was doing something. We might have stopped her."

"No one listens to us," he said, and she heard her practical knight returning. He grabbed her hands. "I didn't like her, *dama*, but what terrible things they are doing to her now! I don't care if the cook beats me. I want to go back."

Hanneke looked up the slope, where shadows lengthened. "Come, Pablo."

He shook his head and refused to move. "My priest told me never to look on evil, if I could help it. No."

74

Should I? she asked herself, fearful. She hurried up the slope, willing her feet to move forward, even as her mind begged her to stay where she was.

She paused near the top, hungry, thirsty and dizzy. She looked over the valley far below, peaceful in late afternoon. She doubted any of the inhabitants in distant villages had any idea what had happened there in the mountain pass.

If Jawhara hadn't screamed, she would have returned to Pablo. She held her breath, listening to the scream carry on and on until it died in a whimper. She forced herself to walk to the path, where Juana, Engracia and Father Bendicio crouched.

The priest grabbed her skirt. "Before God and all his saints, stay here with us."

They sat staring out at the valley, Engracia's hands over her ears, Juana frowning so deeply that her eyebrows met, Bendicio clicking his beads as if it meant something to him. She looked toward the commotion to Santiago, who sat by the still-smoldering pyre. She looked closer and saw Jawhara.

"Bendicio, what is he doing?" she whispered, even as Jawhara screamed again, writhing in his lap. One of the soldiers held her down.

"Remember that she is a traitor and an enemy to God," the priest said. The words came from him as if part of a recitation he had memorized.

"No one should be in such pain, no matter what," she replied and walked toward the pyre. Her face must have looked deceivingly calm, because the soldiers parted before her without a word.

She stared down at what was left of Jawhara's face as her mind took her back to the threshing floor, and the woman with strips of skin dangling, no eyelids and no tongue. How could he do this?

Santiago ignored her presence. "Have you nothing more to admit, *puta*?" he asked, so calm, almost serene. Hanneke shuddered.

When Jawhara said nothing, but only moaned and tried to twist away, he pressed his hand to her forehead and peeled another layer of skin off her cheek, this one exposing the bone beneath.

"Stop!" Hanneke cried, digging her fingers into his shoulder. He slapped her hand away and she sank to the ground beside him, unable to stay on her feet.

Jawhara opened her eyes. "Ana, Ana, please help me," she begged, in perfect Castilian.

It was all a lie. Jawhara had understood everything they said and betrayed them. But this? "Santiago, I beg you to stop."

Santiago wiped his knife on Jawhara's hair. "This whore betrayed us. She left bits of your dress all the way down the mountain, messages for El Ghalib. Eleven of my men are dead because of this one, and you think I should stop?"

She put her hand on his arm and he shook it away. "She should die, but not this way. No one should die this way."

"Then explain what you saw on the threshing floor," he said, taunting her now. She sucked in her breath as he touched the knife to her cheek.

"You are no better than El Ghalib, if you do this."

He shoved her away, and returned her attention to the servant in his lap. He raised the knife again, then lowered it. He moved out from under the servant and got to his feet, his surcoat covered with blood. "That will do. Men, she is yours. Remember this: I want her alive when El Ghalib finds her."

He held out his hand to Hanneke, but she moved to sit by Jawhara. He touched her shoulder. "Stay then, but you will not like what happens." He turned away.

"Leave, Ana," Antonio said. "It is the men's turn."

Why had she thought Antonio was different? Some demon drove her on. "What will *you* do?"

Antonio's eyes did not waver from her face. "Me? Nothing. I don't stand in line to punish women." He reached for her, but she moved closer to Jawhara. "Unlike you, I know why he does this. Come away."

Hanneke did not move, even as one of the soldiers ripped away what remained of Jawhara's dress and two other pinioned her arms. She looked away, sickened.

"Don't do this," she begged.

Someone laughed. Hanneke tried to grab Jawhara, but her hands were slippery with the servant's blood. The circle of men parted and Santiago broke through, grabbing her around the waist and hauling her away, and she struggled and tried to bite his arm. When she dug her fingernails into his leg, he slapped her until her ears rang.

He plopped her down and clapped his hands on her shoulders as she tried to leap up. "Stay here," he ordered. "Don't move."

He mounted his horse bareback and started down the trail toward the valley. She leaped to her feet and ran to him. "How can you do this thing? How can you allow your men to have her like that?"

He slid off his horse and grabbed her face, holding it tight between his hands, looking deep in her eyes. "You are young," he said slowly and clearly, so there would be no mistake. "You do not understand us. Stop."

When she tried to speak, he grabbed her chin and tightened her grip. "Not another word. I don't want to see you for the rest of this night. Stay far away from me."

He shoved her down and mounted his horse again. She covered her ears to shut out the sounds of Jawhara's whimpers now and the coarse laughter, powerless to do anything but sit there as another woman suffered.

No one came near her, not even Bendicio, and certainly not Juana. Hanneke drew herself into a little ball and wrapped her arms around her knees, trying to free her mind of every thought and emotion of the days since she married the angry man who could torture a woman and summon his men like wolves to a meal.

Santiago returned as merciful darkness claimed the endless day. The men were still grouped around Jawhara, using her again and again. Antonio stood to one side, his eyes on Hanneke, as if afraid she would make a sudden move.

Ignoring her, Santiago dismounted and walked toward Antonio. "We will move down the trail. I see no sign of El Ghalib. Call the men off."

Antonio spoke quietly to the men by the pyre, which no longer burned. They moved away, talking among themselves, laughing. Hanneke pressed her lips tight. She had said enough.

"Is she alive?" Santiago asked Antonio.

"Parts of her. She will live until El Ghalib finds her, if that is your intent."

"Come along then, you women and Bendicio," Santiago ordered.

Numb in her soul, Hanneke moved to obey, but her eyes went to Jawhara. The servant lay naked next to the ashes of Santiago's men. As her husband watched, she walked to the mule train, searching the ground until she found a piece of brocade. She knew the fabric, woven in Delft. She shook it out and started toward Jawhara.

"What are you doing?" Santiago demanded.

"Very little."

He grabbed at the fabric but she resisted. "This is still my dowry!" she insisted, startled at her own ferocity. Santiago held up his hands to ward her off.

She covered Jawhara's broken body, bending down to smooth the hair from her dull eyes. The servant tried to speak. Hanneke leaned closer, appalled by the odor.

"Kill me. Please."

"I dare not," Hanneke whispered back.

"Please." Jawhara turned her head with some effort to allow blood to drain from her mouth. "Please."

Santiago called to her. Without a word, Hanneke mounted her mule, and followed Bendicio and Engracia, with Juana and Pablo behind. Her true knight glanced back at her, pleading with his eyes. Juana cuffed him, so he turned around.

For my sins, Hanneke thought, *for my sins, God forgive me.*

Chapter Fourteen

Silence stood sentry over the camp that night, after Santiago growled at Juana for complaining about no water. He sat with his soldiers, ignoring Hanneke. She kept herself apart from them all, humiliated at her rough treatment by her husband, but even more devastated by Jawhara, an evil woman to be sure, begging for death. Carrying a blanket, Santiago came to her as the camp grew silent. He dropped it beside her and left without a word.

She couldn't sleep, not with Jawhara suffering up the trail. *She is probably already dead*, competed with *Someone should check*. She knew what she wanted to do was folly, but the thought wouldn't go away.

One thought remained: *You are being ignored. What harm can come from checking? No one will know.* There was one other thought, the kind one, that she had learned years ago from her mother. Mevrouw Aardema's kindness took them to fishmonger's huts when there was a new baby, or to deathbeds, to sit in silence, do dishes, fold clothes, or tend little ones until other arrangements could be made. As she stared at cold stars overhead, Hanneke knew how deeply such little deeds of mercy were part of her.

What would she find in the clearing by the funeral pyre? She looked around, silent and watchful, for a knife. *Fine, Hanneke, fine*, she scolded herself. *Tap someone and ask to borrow a knife. When he asks what for, you can say you have dirt under your fingernails – which you do – and you want to clean them. They will believe you.* Discouraged, she lay down again.

You probably couldn't kill anyone, came next. She closed her eyes. Sleep didn't come. She looked around, knowing she had to try.

She saw a knife, then another and another, all resting in a pile. Other jumbled possessions told her these were the puny effects of those who died in the ambush.

After debating whether it was noisier to crawl or simply walk, she rose and picked up a dagger. No one stirred. She skirted around the mules and horses, stopping when they whinnied, her heart in her mouth. Nothing.

She knew there would be guards placed, because her husband was nobody's fool. To her amazing good fortune, the guard closest to her rested his hand against his cheek, asleep.

Thinking quickly, she cleared her throat. He rubbed his eyes and stood up, looking to see if any of his *compadres* were awake to see his shame and tattle.

"I didn't mean to frighten you," she whispered. "You must be exhausted. What a day this has been."

He nodded. "Thank the Blessed Virgin my watch ends soon. Why are you about, Señora Gonzalez?"

"I...well... you know," she mumbled.

"Be quick about it."

"I shall. Thank you."

She remained at the edge of the campsite, watching the sentry return to sleep. When the guard changed soon, no one would know she had been there at all.

She hurried down the trail. Somewhere a dog howled, and then another. She faltered, then grasped the dagger tighter and ran.

The moonlight in the clearing cast a soft light on the unburied Moslem warriors, nosed over by wild dogs who growled at her, but ran off. She heard them pacing back and forth, impatient to return to the clearing, but afraid of her.

Jawhara lay where the soldiers had left her. The brocade had been pulled some distance away, and Hanneke wondered if the dogs had already done her work for her. She shuddered at the thought of animals tearing into living flesh. She retrieved the dirty brocade, arranged it around Jawhara, and knelt beside her.

Hanneke gently touched her shoulder, surprised to find her still warm. Jawhara moved, uttering a low moan that seemed to come from the earth itself.

"Here I am, Jawhara," she whispered, even though they were the only quick among the dead.

Jawhara opened her eyes slowly, as if a cosmic hand weighed down her eyelids with stones. She tried to speak, but no words came out. Her face was mottled with dried blood. After great effort, she nodded.

Steeling herself, Hanneke pulled back the brocade until Jawhara's breasts were exposed. She patted the servant's shoulder, trying to reassure them both. Jawhara closed her eyes. "*Allah akbaru*," she managed to say.

Hanneke raised the dagger above her head and brought the weapon down, plunging it deep into Jawhara's breast. The servant stiffened, then uttered a sigh that went on and on. Her head drooped to one side, and she died.

Spent of all energy, Hanneke sat beside the body until several dogs rushed from the shadows. She stood up and they darted away, but not so far this time. She heard the yip of hungry puppies.

Devastated and sick at heart, Hanneke hurried from the clearing, half expecting the charred soldiers to rise from their warm bed and stumble after her, or for the Almohad warriors to reassemble themselves and follow her, too. She tuned to see dogs quarreling among themselves over the choicest bits, then ran.

Watching the sky for signs of morning light, Hanneke walked back to camp. The new sentry touched his hand to his head, none the wiser. She had succeeded.

As soon as she lay down and covered herself, Santiago stepped from the shadows, yanked away her blanket, and jerked her to her feet. She looked around in terror, as other men stepped from the shadows after him.

"Where have you been?"

There was nowhere to turn or run. Everyone was awake and watching her like the hungry dogs at the other clearing. She couldn't even back up; Santiago had pressed himself against her. He was so calm, so dangerous. She held her breath.

"Antonio, ride back. Tell me what you find. Hurry."

Antonio mounted his black horse and Santiago walked with him to the edge of the clearing, where he sat, his back to her.

He must have heard her shift her feet. "Stand where you are," he ordered, still so calm. "Pablo, no closer."

She stood there, her head bowed, as the whole of her life passed by, taking her right to this place again, this unfamiliar, unkind land. *He will kill me*, she thought. Hopefully he would not turn her over to his soldiers first, but who knew what an angry man would do with a disobedient wife? Hadn't he told her their first night together, to obey him always? She had agreed.

Surely he couldn't kill her. She had to be alive a year from her wedding, so the dowry would be officially his. She clasped her hands together, then put them to her face and let the tears flow silently. Death would be better than this, but she wasn't allowed to die.

Silence prevailed as the sun rose. No one seemed to breathe. Even the mules abandoned their usual ode-to-dawn brays. Songbirds trilled a few notes and stopped, as if caught in some misdemeanor.

When Santiago rose to his feet, she knew Antonio had returned.

He rode slowly, bending out of the saddle, his eyes on the ground. Never taking his eyes from the ground, he skirted around the camp, staying away from the animals, keeping to the edge of the clearing.

He was tracking her. She could go nowhere so she didn't try. His horse walked through her blanket and stopped. Antonio straightened up in the saddle, looking down at her from a great height, his face troubled.

Is this how it ends? Hanneke thought in horror. *I am only seventeen.*

Antonio spoke over his shoulder. "Santiago, *por favor*. Ask your wife to show us her feet."

"Do as he says, wife."

Hanneke took a deep breath and raised her dress to her knees. Her bare feet were the color of the funeral pyre.

Still speaking only to Antonio, Santiago asked in that calm voice. "Tell us what you found in the clearing."

"I found a dead woman stabbed through the heart with this dagger."

He pulled out the death weapon and dropped it at her feet.

"Who would do such a thing? Do you know, Ana?" Santiago asked.

Silence. Even the leaves had quit rustling in the trees. The sound of his gauntleted hand against her cheek broke the silence. "Do you know?" he roared.

Before she spoke, she thought of King Alfonso's words in distant Santander. Some would be winnowed out. She knew he meant her, but *this* soon?

Tired of everything – the fear, the hunger, the thirst, the sun, the dirt, the thought of one more day in Spain – Hanneke took a deep breath and another. She breathed in and out, knowing that breathing was over for her soon. Santiago would find a way to keep the dowry, whether she was dead or alive.

She dropped to her knees and held out her hands. "I killed her. No one, not even a traitor, should die that way. I do not excuse myself. Do with me what you will."

Hands still extended – For mercy? For pity? – Hanneke bowed her head.

She heard his sword leave the scabbard. Life was short; hers was over. From a great distance, she heard Antonio shout, "No!"

An eon passed until she heard the sword slam back in its scabbard. No one moved, then Santiago's boot in her back forced her down to the dirt as he pushed hard. She wanted to cry out, but something inside her refused to yield.

"You will ride behind the muleteers and your precious dowry," he said, still so calm. "Do you understand?"

She nodded. He walked away.

Chapter Fifteen

No one helped her to her feet. No one offered her bread and cheese. One of the teamsters was kind enough to saddle her mule. She looked around to thank whoever it was, but no one looked at her. The furnace of the sun on her aching back and against her raw cheek became Hanneke's traveling companions, since no one was allowed near as they left the mountains and returned to the high plains.

Her pretty white mule, the one given to her by King Alfonso himself, seemed to feel the shame, too, there at the back of the baggage train. She plodded, head down, looking neither right nor left, as mule and rider ate dust.

Hanneke sneezed over and over from the dust, but no one gave her a handkerchief. Her dress served that purpose. When they stopped for a break, no one provided a discreet blanket. She was forced to squat by her mule, tears of shame leaving tracks down her cheeks as she made water. She wanted something to drink, but knew better than to ask. She would only have been ignored, because that was the rule of the day, perhaps for the rest of her life. She had provided a terrible kindness to a suffering enemy, and this was her reward.

The endless dust churned up by horses and mules made every breath a struggle. She took increasingly shallow breaths until she grew lightheaded, and clung to Blanca to stay in the saddle.

When she thought she could not remain upright another moment, the caravan stopped. Soldiers dismounted. Santiago helped Engracia to the ground and Juana clucked around her, shading her with a blanket. Bendicio spoke to Santiago, but he shook his head before the priest finished speaking. Hanneke looked away, ashamed. She ran her finger around her dusty lips, feeling each crack and crusty spot. She wanted to touch her back, but she could not raise her arms.

Pablo slid off his mule and started back toward her, looking around to see if Santiago was watching.

"No. Don't," she warned.

He came to her quickly, and helped her off the mule. She leaned on him and he helped her sit down.

"I have no water, but there is this," he said, his voice low. He handed her a dried grape. "If you put roll it around in your mouth, it might help."

She did as he said. Gradually the grape became moist. She gave Pablo a gentle nudge. "Better go. He will beat you."

He shook his head. "I have been beaten before. I do not care."

"I care. Go now, my true knight."

Somehow she mounted her mule again. The dried grape had moistened her lips and she was grateful. She sat there as the soldiers and muleteers moved out, then took her place in the rear.

Her hand went to her cheek, where Santiago had slapped her. *Pablo, I too have been beaten, and I don't care either*, she thought. The idea was almost liberating, although she could never have explained that to a rational being.

Spain, why is your sun so merciless? she asked the landscape as her brains began to cook. On a better day, she might have appreciated the great plain of Castile, high and windy, heavy with the fragrance of late summer grass and harvest. Here on the valley floor, grass bent to the wind.

Closing her mind to the threshing floor, Hanneke watched women cutting and stacking the grain, working efficiently. They bundled the sheaves and leaned them upright at the end of each row.

She watched with idle interest as Antonio rode toward the harvesters. He leaned out of the saddle and spoke to one of the women. When he left them, he carried something. Hanneke closed her eyes against the heat.

She heard a horse approaching the mule train and opened her eyes, ready to look away. Antonio rode beside her. She remembered the look in his eyes when he tracked her steps around the camp, and leaned away from him, fearful.

"Here." He handed her a straw hat with a wide brim. "It cost me an Almohad's dagger."

When she did not take it, fearing a trap, he set it in her lap. "Put it on, señora, before you become silly with the heat."

"My back hurts too much to raise my arms," she said. "Thank you anyway for your kindness." She wished he would go away.

He took the hat from her lap and placed it on her head, leaning toward her until their knees touched, to tie it under her chin.

"The harvesters had no extra water to share, or I would have brought you some."

"I don't expect any," she said. "Please don't put yourself in danger on my behalf."

He looked toward Santiago, who watched them. "He doesn't own me but he gave me an order last night. I... I am truly sorry for what happened."

They rode together in silence, Hanneke terrified that Santiago might blame her for Antonio's attendance upon her. *Please go*, she thought. To her relief, he nodded to her, put spurs to his horse, and left her alone in the dust once more.

Camp that night was a subdued affair, with no teasing or joking, as she had heard on other nights. After another soul-sapping squat beside her mule, she found a spot away from everyone and sat down, leaning forward with her elbows on her knees, trying to relieve the pain in her back.

"Here."

She looked up in surprise. She had not expected any food, least of all a plate from Santiago himself. "Thank you," she said. "I didn't ask for food, so please don't blame anyone."

What could he say to that? She looked down at the plate of meat, pleasantly surprised that he had bothered, then deeply aware that she had not one single expectation left in her whole body. Not one. The girl from the Netherlands who had whined about having no choice seemed foolish and far away.

After he left, she tried to eat, but all she really wanted was water or maybe a little wine. She set the uneaten food on the ground and went a little distance from the mules, never looking at anyone. A few swipes of the ground cleared away the pebbles. She sat there until dark, then managed to remove her hat and pull her surcoat over her head. She gasped from the pain, then rolled the garment and tucked it under her neck as she lay down.

There. That wasn't too bad. She arranged her dress as best she could, then set the precious straw hat beside her. She knew she should say her nightly prayers, but she had nothing to say to the Lord God Almighty, Great Ruler of the Universe, anyway.

Hanneke woke at first light. The straw hat was there, but someone had covered her with a light cloak. She sniffed the fabric, wondering why Santiago had bothered. Still, it was nice of him.

The uneaten food was gone, but there was a leather wineskin in its place. She grabbed it, grateful beyond measure. Looking around to make sure it didn't belong to anyone, she drank deep, then sighed. She glanced up to see Santiago watching her. She set the wineskin away from her, afraid she had drunk more than allowed.

Her back didn't hurt so much, so she smoothed her hair down, wishing for a comb. Putting on her surcoat was agony, so she quickly followed it with the hat, counting one long pain better than two separate ones. She touched her cheek, happy to find it not so hot this morning. All in all, she couldn't complain. She thought a moment. "I am *La Dama de Cosas Pequeñas*," she said softly, "The Lady of Small Things."

Chapter Sixteen

They passed more harvesters this day, and even found a stream. She waited until everyone finished, troubling no one. She had spent a pleasant day thinking of Vlissingen and Christmas, and Mama when she was still healthy. She looked around for other sights think about when she ran out of pleasant Low Country memories.

The great plain of Castile stretched before her, but the land seemed less harsh. Villages grouped near stone castles, the air no longer filled with dust. She admired the windmills, smiling because they creaked the same as windmills at home. She missed the lap of water on Vlissingen's docks. Water would be good.

The hostility toward her seemed to lessen from the muleteers. One of them even picked up her hat when she dropped it while fanning herself. She thanked him, she, the queen of all she surveyed from the dusty rear of the dowry train.

As the sky darkened, they came at last to a river, wide and flowing leisurely in that way of water in late summer. She noticed that the soldiers sat up straighter.

"It is the Tajo," one of the muleteers said, speaking in Hanneke's direction, and almost looking at her. "The day after tomorrow, Toledo."

The bank was steep in spots, but there were shallow places to cross. If she fell off her mule, she could swim, so it didn't matter. Maybe she could stand in the shade of the trees for a while, if they camped here. At least there was water to drink, all she wanted.

She stayed close to the river while tents went up among the trees. The horsemen and muleteers took their animals down to the water, then hobbled them to graze above the bank. Hanneke sat and watched the animals, pleased to see her white mule cropping grass.

Pablo joined her for the first time in two days, sitting close to her. She put her arm around his shoulders and hugged him. "Why are you here?" she asked, keeping her voice low.

"I wanted to be," he said simply. He handed her a pear. "Antonio gave this to me for you."

"How kind," she said, and ate it with pleasure. "Pablo, do you think you could find me some soap?"

"Soap?"

"Yes, my true knight. What a shame to waste all this water."

He grinned. "I can steal some from Engracia."

"Be careful," she warned.

He was careful. "It's all I could find quickly," he said in apology when he returned, out of breath.

She took the sliver from him, inclining her head in his direction. "A lady never had a more noble knight."

The muleteers were busy about their cooking fires. Santiago and Antonio stood together in the distance, pointing toward the hills to the north. Hanneke walked to the water's edge and took off her shoes, the sand so soft and inviting.

A short walk along the bank led to a quiet bend in the river, where she was out of sight of everyone. The Tajo had carved a sandy stretch of beach, with the high bank above. The water barely rippled. Minnows nibbled at her toes, which made her laugh.

She removed her surcoat and carried it into the water, dipping the bloody thing, then scouring it with handfuls of sand. She rinsed, scrubbed some more, then rinsed again, spreading the garment on a hot boulder a short distance above the water where the trees met the sand.

In the water again, she untied her bodice and let her dress fall to her knees. Balancing against the current, she stepped out of her dress and washed it, too.

She debated a long moment about her camisa. The dried blood from the threshing floor had turned a rusty brown and she wanted to remove what stains she could. She glanced in the direction of the camp, hidden by the trees and the bank, wondering if she dared. She reminded herself that no one cared enough to look for her, and peeled off her camisa. Naked now, she hurried into the deeper water and scrubbed the filthy garment. After it went onto a patch of grass, she hurried back into the river.

The water was warm and surprisingly deep. She sank to her shoulders after only a few steps, then swam to the middle of the river, clutching the soap. She ducked her head under and washed her hair. Her face was next and then her soft parts. A handful of sand sufficed for the less tender places. She sniffed and pronounced herself good, or at least better.

She put her sunburned face in the water and blew bubbles, then floated on her back, admiring the setting sun through the leaves overhead. After another rinse, she swam to shore, looking for a spot where she could sit on a rock with her body partly out of the water.

To her shock, Santiago sat on the bank above her, his sword across his lap, his helmet by his side. His bare feet dangled over the edge.

"You should have told someone where you were going," he called, looking down at her.

She nearly covered her breasts with her arms, but saw the folly of that. He knew what she looked like. "No one talks to me, señor," she said, wishing he would go away.

He did not. Hanneke came quickly out of the water. She dried herself with her dress then put on her camisa, ignoring him. She walked down the little beach until she was out of his sight. Her surcoat was nearly dry on the boulder. She reached for it, then froze.

"Señora."

A man stood in the deepening shadow close to the water. He was tall, but not as tall as Santiago, and dressed like the Almohad warriors she had seen only days before. She knew – just how, escaped her – that this was El Ghalib.

Her eyes on him, she slowly took the surcoat in her arms, holding it in front of her as puny protection.

"Señora," he said again. He came closer. She did not move.

He was close enough now for her to see indigo tattoos on his chin. Something else about him caught and held her. She had seen that face before, where, she could not say.

"Do not scream."

"I had not thought of screaming," she said truthfully.

He smiled at her words and squatted a little distance from her, but out of Santiago's sight. "You know who I am?" he asked in excellent Castilian.

She sat down, too. What was the point in running? "El Ghalib?"

"Yussef El Ghalib. You are the wife of my worst enemy."

There was an awkward silence; this was no ordinary conversation. El Ghalib fingered the pebbles at his feet. "I do not wish to appear indelicate, señora, but I could not help noticing a bruise on your back."

She nearly asked him what else he could not help noticing, but she bit back sharp words. She saw sorrow in his eyes, and she had no desire, oddly enough, to wound this man further.

"It doesn't hurt much."

"Again, I do not wish to appear indelicate, but I was watching your camp when…when… Santiago treated you poorly." He looked down at the pebbles. "I followed you from the funeral pyre."

She gasped, then looked around, unwilling to be overheard. "Why didn't you kill me? You saw what I did."

"I saw."

He was silent, struggling with some emotion Hanneke did not understand. Impulsively, she touched his hand.

He took her fingers in his and kissed her palm. "Thank you."

He wept. Hanneke averted her eyes to allow him some privacy in his grief, then turned for a long look. Suddenly, she knew. She moved closer.

"Jawhara?"

"My sister." He took a moment to collect himself. "She thought she would be my spy. She insisted. We had heard about a dowry, and a forthcoming visit to Valladolid. With another's help, she presented herself to the wife of Manolo Gonzalez as a servant."

Another's help. "Felipe," she said. "Engracia's brother? What is he to you?"

He waved away her questions. "It is of no importance to you, wife of my enemy." He seemed to rethink his words; perhaps he thought them rude. "Let me say that the border between Moslem and Christian is sometimes fluid."

Hanneke wondered how far she would get if she ran. She reminded herself that she had no expectations, and settled her mind. "I hope you will kill me quickly," she said, not taking her eyes from his.

"You do not understand, señora," he said. "I *thank* you. I arrived in that clearing just before you, but I could not bring myself to kill her, not my sister. I knew she needed to die as soon as possible. My sorrow is that you were punished for my weakness."

Hanneke bowed her head, surprisingly aware of her strength, she who counted the least to the man sitting on the bank above the Tajo. "I would do it again. No woman should have suffered the way she suffered."

"I saw that, too," he said quietly, and leaned his head against hers for a brief moment.

They moved away when Santiago's voice came from upriver. "Ana! Come back. Now."

"I come, husband," she called. "I must go, El Ghalib, if you will let me."

"I will, but one moment, please."

He lifted a chain from around his neck and held it out to her. "Take this necklace. If you ever have need, send this to me through that boy who worships you. You will find a way." He smiled. "You are resourceful and brave."

"My father said that about me once," she told him. "I didn't believe him."

"You should. It is true."

She took the necklace, admired the delicate links, and put it over her head.

"Very good. Farewell, señora. We may meet again or not. We will leave it in Allah's hands." He gestured gracefully with his hand to his head, his chest, and out. "I am going to the bank. If I can surprise your husband, I will kill him. If not, who knows? Remember this: He is my enemy."

Chapter Seventeen

He was gone before Hanneke could say anything, not that a man bent on bloodshed would have listened; she knew that much. She ran back to the spot where she had last seen Santiago.

He still sat there, his sword in his lap. She opened her mouth to warn him at the same moment he wrenched his head around and leaped to his feet, his sword raised above his head like a staff. After the initial blow, he grasped his sword by the grip and parried El Ghalib's advance, stepping back to scoop on his helmet and slam down the visor.

Hanneke ran into the water and waded out far enough to see around the curving bank. The soldiers in the distance were busy at their campfires. She shouted, but no one looked up. Why should they? She was nothing.

She struggled back to shore, watching in horror as El Ghalib struck a massive blow that glanced off Santiago's helmet before it struck dirt and bounced from the Almohad's grasp. Her husband dropped to his knees, the helmet off kilter so he could not see out of the eye openings.

El Ghalib's sword fell to a small ledge below them, but he could not find it. He looked back at Santiago, who regained his feet, even though he was now sightless, his sword still in his hand, but moving oddly, because he had no idea where his enemy stood.

"Oh, please, no," Hanneke begged, clasping her hands in supplication. "Please stop. Don't kill him."

El Ghalib turned to stare at her.

"You of all people," he said. "You?"

He was right. She could say nothing and Santiago would die. The same compassion that governed her actions with Jawhara took over her heart, lessons in kindness learned from her mother. "No," she mouthed.

With a great scream, El Ghalib grabbed the back of Santiago's tunic and threw him into the river.

Santiago plunged in headfirst and Hanneke swam toward him. She looked up at El Ghalib with all the thanks she could muster in a glance. She knew he would not help. El Ghalib had struck a strange bargain with her, one that had nothing to do with Santiago.

Santiago bobbed to the surface, his helmet still off kilter. He held out his hands as he went under, weighed down by his chain mail, blind inside his helmet. He had fallen into the deeper channel, and she swam toward him, grateful she had nothing on but her shift to weight her down.

He broke the surface so close to her that she screamed in fright. She grabbed him, tugging with all her strength at his helmet. It would not budge. Santiago's weight pulled them both under.

She took a deep breath before the water closed over them and did not lose her grip on his helmet. As he thrashed around, blind, she felt around the helmet until she found a latch. It was jammed, but as they sank deeper, the latch broke and the helmet opened.

Wishing he were more helpful, she found the strength to tug him toward the surface, where she wrenched off the helmet, scraping his cheek until the blood came, but freeing him.

"I can't swim!" he gasped, and went under again.

She took another deep breath and grabbed his hair. He flailed about in her grasp and pulled her under with him. Desperate, she felt his tunic until she touched his dagger. Yanking it from its sheath, she slammed the hilt against his temple. He sank without a murmur.

She broke the surface for another breath of air, and there was Pablo, running toward her on the bank, waving his arms. "I cannot swim!" he shouted, but he waded into the Tajo anyway.

She dove once more and grabbed Santiago's hair, wishing it weren't so short. She couldn't bring him to the surface, but she towed him underwater toward the shallower edge, and reached the surface to see Antonio, wearing only his small clothes, leap into the water and swim toward them.

He hefted Santiago higher, getting his face out of the water. Between them, they towed Santiago toward the bank, Pablo reaching out. Hanneke treaded water, exhausted.

Once Antonio and Pablo had pulled Santiago from the river, Antonio went back into the water for Hanneke, grabbing her around the waist and swimming with her against his body. He heaved her onto the sand and she collapsed beside Santiago.

Antonio grabbed her hair and pulled her around to face him. He let go of her when he was satisfied that she was breathing, then pulled Santiago on his side. Water drained from his mouth, but he did not open his eyes. Antonio pounded Santiago's back until he began to gag and cough. He breathed in gasps that gradually slowed, even as water continued to pour from his mouth.

"Dear God, where is Ana?" he managed at last.

"Right beside you," Antonio said. He sat back on the sand and let his breathing slow, as well. "She saved your life."

Still on his side, Santiago felt behind him until he touched Hanneke's thigh. She heard a sigh of relief. He flopped onto his back and looked at her. "So she did," he said. "So she did."

Hanneke raised herself up on one elbow at the same time Antonio looked down at his near nakedness. "Pablo, my clothes," he said, and caught the bundle, putting on his surcoat. He chuckled because the sides were open, then shrugged.

"I fought El Ghalib," Santiago said. "Did you see him, Ana?"

"Yes, I saw him." Hanneke said nothing more. She sat up and tugged down her shift, feeling as bare as Antonio. "Pablo, my dress is just around the bend."

He hurried to retrieve it as Carlos and other soldiers ran toward them. Santiago tried to sit up and fell back. "I fought El Ghalib. He threw me in the river. Help me up." Carlos stared at him. "Yes, yes! He threw me in the river. Why he did not kill me I cannot imagine," Santiago said impatiently. "Help me up!"

Santiago blinked his eyes several times when he was on his feet, then retched up more of the Tajo. "I should learn to swim," he said to no one.

Hanneke watched him sway and nearly fall, until Carlos grasped him more firmly. He started to walk, then turned back and knelt beside her. He looked into her eyes and she saw only gratitude. He touched her hair gently, so unlike the angry man of several days ago. "*Chiquita*, thank you."

She nodded, too tired to say anything, and wondering about *chiquita*. In one of his endless language lessons, hadn't Father Bendico told her that *ita* or *ito* on the end of a noun meant affection? And what was *chica*? Perhaps she had misheard him. At least he wasn't angry at the moment.

Carlos and the others led him away and she remained on the sandy beach with Antonio and Pablo, who held out her dress. With his help, she pulled it on, too tired to do up the bodice, too tired to do anything except sit there. And where was her surcoat?

"Can you walk, señora?" Antonio asked, holding out his hand. He had found his clothes and put them on, except for his chain mail, which he handed to Pablo.

She shook her head. "Leave me. I'll come in a moment."

"Oh, no!" Over her protests, he picked her up and settled her against him. "*Dama*, you weigh nothing. How in the world did you manage to drag Santiago out of the channel?"

"I don't know." She touched the little necklace, wondered about enemies, and closed her eyes.

It was dark when she woke. She was lying on a pallet with a sheet and blanket, a far cry from her bed of shame by the mules. She sniffed her nightgown, grateful Engracia had felt enough kindness to share. She burrowed deeper into the pallet, then turned over.

Santiago lay beside her, close enough to touch, had she wanted to. She didn't. Still, it was nice to know he had thanked her for saving his life. Maybe in the morning he would let her ride closer to the front; even a little closer would help. She was tired of breathing dust in and out, running her tongue over gritty teeth, and feeling everyone's rancor because she had committed an awful act of mercy. A little less unkindness would be enough.

He looked so peaceful, breathing evenly. She closed her eyes, ready to return to sleep.

"Please forgive me," he said.

Hanneke had somehow wormed her way close to her husband, her head on his bare chest, his arm around her shoulder. Maybe there was water in her ears. She couldn't have heard him correctly.

"For what?" she asked, honestly curious. Did he mean his anger over Papa's terms in the dowry, the awful wedding, his utter disregard for her safety, the heat, the thirst, her harsh kindness to Jawhara?

"Name it. I am guilty," he said. "Did ever a husband make a worse beginning?"

"I doubt it," she told him honestly, and felt his little laugh more than heard it.

"Listen to me, please."

She wanted to return to sleep rather than carry on a midnight conversation. Better hear him out so she could sleep. "I'm listening."

"Would you try to forgive me?" he asked.

She considered his question, not of a mind to trust him. He had told her on their wedding night that his whole life was war. After the threshing floor, she understood. She knew there would be no peace in this land until either the Almohads or the Spaniards were vanquished. Her dowry was a means to an end, and she came along with it.

"Does it matter whether I forgive you or not?"

She winced at the sound of that, but she knew in her heart that her treatment of the past few days had given her more strength than weakness.

"It matters to me."

He said it quietly at the same time he ran his hand down her arm, which felt, not merely comforting, but something more exciting. Maybe she wasn't as tired as she thought.

She fingered El Ghalib's necklace, wondering if she should tell him what had happened on the bank of the Tajo. Was the necklace going to mean more trouble or less? No, it was her secret to keep, at least for now.

"Ana?"

She couldn't answer him; it wasn't in her. His hand moved to her breast, then to her stomach, and she liked the feeling. She would change the subject.

"What does" – gracious God, something was happening to her voice. He was so distracting. She cleared her throat as his hand went lower and he moved closer. "What does *chiquita* mean? I don't know the word."

"Someone small with a big heart, like you."

That was all he said for many minutes. She forgave him.

Chapter Eighteen

is space on the pallet was empty when Hanneke woke up, but still warm. She moved into his warm spot and stretched, alert to her body as never before.

There was no one to talk to about how she felt. She knew Engracia was not bright. Juana was unpleasant and evil. Perhaps some quiet evening in the autumn, she and Santiago could sit close together, she might talk about what she had discovered last night about herself. Quite possibly she didn't know even part of what had happened when he took her, except that despite all her uncertainties, she wanted to love this man.

Maybe someday, she thought, as she washed and dressed. Sooner would be better, she knew, considering that she never had a choice in the matter. It would be better not to forget that she was the lady of small things only.

She fingered the necklace, thinking through what little conversation passed between them last night. After he sighed out his satisfaction against her body, and surprised her by keeping her close, he asked, "Why did El Ghalib not kill me? I wish I understood. It would have been so easy."

Almost of its own volition, her hand went to the necklace, then dropped away quickly. "Perhaps this is a mystery known only to God," she had said, then changed the subject by moving closer, knowing that the less he thought about the inexplicable El Ghalib, the better for her.

She reconsidered the turmoil inside her body, touched now in places she had only imagined. The tumult of her life since the ship docked at Santander, schooled her to not show anything beyond a bland face. Women were to be used; she knew that, but all the same, she felt different. She decided she liked the feeling.

Why should she feel shy to join the others? To her further amazement, there was no overlooking the shyness on Santiago's face when she left the tent and looked about, hoping for food. His lingering glance suggested that today she wouldn't have to wait until everyone else had eaten and pray there was enough. Whether that translated to a better place in the line of march was debatable. Food first.

Something else came before, also unexpected, something to store up in her heart. As she walked to the cooking fire, hopeful, Santiago took her hand and tucked her close. She wasn't brave enough to look at him, so she glanced around, surprised to see the entire company waiting, expectant.

She felt the blood drain from her face as she wondered what she had done this time. Was she wrong? Surely not, especially since he had whispered *chiquita* to her several times during the night.

"Listen to me, men," he said, not raising his voice, his face calm. He never raised his voice with his men. "Please know that I have apologized to my wife for my inexcusable treatment of her, this woman who is my wife and not my servant."

They looked at each other; she hoped he did not mistake her stunned look for revulsion. "We'll tell the bishop of Santander that I was listening when he said that," he said quietly, as if to her alone.

He returned his attention to his soldiers and employees, to all who had made this journey so far. "I pledge to you I will be a better leader. Forgive me, Ana."

She nodded, too shy to speak. He looked at his men with a smile. "*Amigos*, always marry a woman who can swim."

The company joined in his laughter. Delighted, Hanneke laughed. She noticed Antonio standing beside Pablo, laughing with the others. He touched his hand to his heart and bowed to them both.

But wariness is something that lingers, Hanneke discovered. Santiago said nothing more to her as they broke camp, so she took her usual place in the rear with the dowry and other baggage. She put her straw hat on, pleased that she could sit on her mule for hours now, happy to have eaten breakfast, and willing to tolerate what came her way. She touched her necklace, wondered where El Ghalib was, and hoped there would be a soft bed for her in Toledo.

"Ride with me, Ana."

She looked around in surprise, embarrassed to be caught daydreaming by her husband, who probably never whiled away his time thinking about small things.

"You're certain?"

He shrugged. "If you prefer to ride with Engracia and be bored to death, or suffer a frosty glare from Juana, I won't detain you."

Was he teasing her? She looked into his eyes and saw something more than the usual hard expression. "If you insist," she said, keeping her tone light. "I'll try to manage without idle chatter."

He glanced at Engracia. "I insist."

"Thank you," she said. "I didn't really want to swallow any more dust. Could Pablo ride closer to the front, too?"

He nodded. "He can ride beside Father Bendicio. I'm sorry, Ana. You probably have more Castilian dust coating your lungs than someone born here."

"*Pulmones*? That is not a word I am familiar with."

He looked around, then came closer on his big horse and touched one breast, hefting it a little. "Where you get your air. What also helps make you so pretty."

She blushed.

The battle-tested army of Santiago Gonzalez entered Toledo when the sun was high overhead, beating down on men and beasts foolish enough to be out of doors.

Her white mule from King Alfonso seemed as relieved to be safe again as she was, and proved it by keeping up with Santiago's war horse. Or perhaps, just perhaps, Santiago had slowed the march to make an easier journey. He looked back at Engracia often, as if measuring her exhaustion. His own face turned grim when he intercepted Juana's look of bald loathing. *It's not my husband's fault that Engracia insisted in coming along*, Hanneke thought. *Stop, Juana. Leave him alone.*

Father Bendicio rode beside Engracia, but Pablo stayed near her, looking about as they passed through the gate into the old city. "What do you think of this place, *dama*?" he asked her.

"I have never seen anything like it," she replied, admiring the architecture of Islam, with airy porticos and elaborate carvings on walls, oddly shaped windows and soaring arches. She pointed to a massive fortress on the city's highest point. "What is that?"

"The Alcázar," Santiago said. "Some say the Romans built the first fort. It has traded hands in recent years – Moors, Castilians, Berbers, Almoravides, Castilians, Almohades next, until more than a century ago." She heard his quiet satisfaction. "Now it is in our possession and will remain so."

Hanneke saw the resolution on his face. *He means it*, she thought, and felt a tug at her heart, a timely reminder that this was now her land, too, whether anyone knew it yet. Did she?

He leaned over to touch her thigh. "As much as I know that Toledo means I am closer to home, now begins the difficult part of our journey."

Hanneke stared at him in amazement. After all they had been through, *now* was the difficult part? Unmindful of her mule, she allowed it to bump into Santiago's war horse, whose ears went back. Santiago expertly steered his mount away as she gaped at him.

"*Now* comes the hard part?" she couldn't help asking. "*Now*?"

He laughed when she frowned at him. "Yes, now, *chiquita*. Now I must deal with the Jewish bankers. I would almost rather fight El Ghalib again."

"Don't say that." She reached for the necklace, then lowered her hand. "It frightens me."

"I, as well," he admitted. "Antonio, what should I do to make this bargaining session remotely palatable?"

Antonio moved closer. "Take Ana with you."

"God in heaven, why?" Santiago asked. "This is a man's business."

It's my dowry, Hanneke thought, irritated. *Isn't that enough reason?*

"She's shrewd, and she looks better than you do," Antonio said.

"No doubt, friend. Put her in a pretty dress?" Santiago turned his attention to Hanneke. "And wash her face. Comb her hair. I believe you are onto something, Antonio."

"Even the Jews will not resist a pretty face," Antonio said. His face reddened. He rode ahead.

Santiago watched him, his expression inscrutable. "I believe you have an admirer, wife. Should I watch my step around Antonio Baltierra?"

Hanneke watched Antonio, too. "He is a friend," she said quietly. "We saved your life together."

"That's no answer," he said.

Wary, she glanced his way, relieved to see his smile. He smiled back. She had no other answer.

Chapter Nineteen

Not far from the cathedral, Santiago stopped at an inn on a quiet street, its rooms opening onto a garden with flowers and a fountain. Hanneke helped Engracia lie down and tugged off her shoes, dismayed to see her feet swollen.

"I wish I had not begged Manolo to let me make this journey," Engracia said, as Juana loosened her dress.

"Why did you?" Hanneke asked.

"Las Claves is so isolated, so lonely sometimes. No one laughs," her sister-in-law said. She gave the servant a sidelong glance. "And there is occasional meanness."

I believe that, Hanneke thought. *It doesn't take a wizard skilled in divination.* She watched as Juana passed a damp cloth over Engracia's face, murmuring and scolding.

"Don't stand there like a lump," Juana said to her, when Engracia's eyes closed. "Look in the trunk for a dress to charm the Jews. I will hem it. Do something."

It was the wedding trunk with the clothes that did not fit, jumbled into Engracia's room by mistake. The green wool dress on top suited her. She had worn it for her wedding. "This one."

"I should think you would want to forget," Juana said, as Hanneke pulled out the dress. "Such a wedding."

"It was my wedding," Hanneke said. "Don't be disagreeable, Juana. It's hot, I'm anxious about the bankers, and you know I am deadly with a dagger. Come to my chamber with your needle and thread, if you dare." *Think about that, you witch.*

She paused at the balcony to watch small birds dipping and bobbing in the fountain below. She smiled as they ruffled their feathers, and wished for the cool waters of the Rio Tajo.

In her chamber, Santiago and Antonio sat on the bed, their heads together, deep in discussion. She stood a moment, noting the contrast of her husband's blond hair with Antonio's dark hair. Now that she had seen El Ghalib up close, she wondered about Antonio Baltierra's origin. Perhaps if he was bored enough someday, he might tell her.

Santiago looked up as she stood there. "I can wait outside," she murmured. She asked herself if there would ever be a time when she didn't hesitate to bother him. She had learned Spanish from Father Bendicio, and wariness from Santiago.

"No. Come in. Antonio and I were discussing how many soldiers we can find between now and Christ's Mass." He stared into the distance and she saw his lips tighten. "And wondering how much interest the bankers will charge to mortgage your dowry."

"But I thought…"

"I cannot spend it? There is nothing in your father's cursed contract that says I cannot mortgage it and make a reckoning after a year of marriage. I will get my money and I will get my soldiers, even if it costs me my soul."

She crossed herself. "Please don't say that."

"My soul is a small matter, compared to the larger matter of our independence from the caliphs."

"Not to me." *I mean that*, she thought.

"Then you are more generous than most." He looked to the door. "Here is Juana with needle and thread."

"I will see to the men and their lodging," Antonio said.

"They've probably already scattered to the whorehouses." Santiago laughed. "You can, too."

Hanneke felt her face grow hot. There was nowhere to look but down at the dress in her hands.

"You know I do not stand in line for women," was all Antonio said before he left the room, closing the door with a decisive click.

"Should I apologize?" Santiago asked, after a moment's reflection.

"Probably," Hanneke replied. Mama had told her once that men were simple creatures. She was wrong. This man she was yoked to until death was a man of light and shadow. He was also fixed in his purposed and determined, which were not flaws to be repented of, unless taken to extremes. She has seen him in battle. She thought of last night, so tender. She didn't understand him. Would she ever?

"Have a care this enterprise does not consume you, husband," she said without thinking.

He gave her a sharp look, narrowing his eyes. He could strike her, but she didn't care. She knew she was powerless and small and too young for the enormity of the battle before them.

I will not look away, she thought, as serenity filled her heart. With no hesitation, she touched her husband's face. To her gratification, he turned his head and kissed her palm. *I think we could make something of ourselves, if this enterprise does not consume us.*

Juana cleared her throat and Santiago stepped back. "This dress will not hem itself," the servant announced.

"Then get to it."

Would the day never cool off? Why had she thought a wool dress was the best idea? At least she wouldn't trip over it, as she had in the chapel, thanks to a deeper hem. She tried to overrule Juana's insistence on her matron's cap, but the servant would have none of it. "How can you impress anyone, especially a banker, if you cannot follow custom?" Juana snapped. She placed the cap on Hanneke's head. "No more of this nonsense. One would think you wanted to ruin this entire attempt."

"I would never do that," Hanneke said, weighing each word. "It's this heat."

"You can cool off in the winter, when the wind cuts through everything and sometimes it snows," Juana told her. "Remember your duty."

My duty, Hanneke thought. *My duty is to look charming enough to strike a better bargain for my dowry, which is going to end in misery and death for some.* She sat on the bed, unwilling to wish for something better because there was nothing better, not now and not later.

Santiago came for her too soon. "Are you ready to face the lions?"

"No," she answered honestly, "but I know I must strike you a good bargain."

"If all goes well, things will be different in a few years, and we will have precious time," he said. "Come, wife."

He ushered her out the door, into the full heat of a Toledo afternoon, the siesta over, and people in the streets again. Women swept doorsteps;

children ran alongside those on horseback, offering oranges and sweetmeats for a price; Muslims wrapped from head to foot squatted by the wall, looking at everything and nothing. The scent of fruit competed with odors that seemed to crawl from ancient walls, odors that made her cover her nose with her hand.

They passed a grand and curious building that looked more Muslim than Christian, where swarms of beggars crouched on the steps, then rose like locusts when horsemen passed. Hanneke noticed priests at the entrance and shook her head in confusion.

Antonio must have noticed. "You will see this in Spain," he told her. "When Toledo was reconquered, an earlier King Alfonso turned this into the cathedral." He shrugged. "We live in a half-Muslim, half-Christian world."

The blind, the lame, the confused surrounded them, lurching and hopping, exposing their wounds for sympathy, holding out their hands for coins, some mumbling, others pleading with their eyes only.

Antonio unsheathed his sword.

"Don't hurt anyone," she pleaded.

"I won't, but we must get through." Using the flat of his sword, Antonio kept the beggars at bay.

"The children, Santiago, the children."

The little ones crowded as close as they dared, some naked and sunburned, others covered with rags masquerading as doublets and tunics, each one clamoring for attention.

A young mother stepped in front of Santiago's horse and he reined in sharply. Shriveled and scalded by the sun, her baby sucked at her breast that hung like an empty sack.

"Milk from dry udders," he murmured. "How sad is Spain."

He motioned the woman back. She bared her teeth at him, muttered something low in her throat, and vanished into the crowd.

As they left the plaza, Hanneke turned to watch the beggars as they slowly drifted back to the cathedral steps to roost again and wait to show others their misery.

Antonio sheathed his sword. "Santiago, I see these pitiful people and I think of old soldiers. Do you?"

"Always. One-armed, one-legged. Better to die in battle than to have to fight each day for food." Santiago shrugged. "What good is a one-armed man on the frontier?"

Antonio nodded, then crossed himself.

They rode through the stultifying heat until they came to another gate and wall within the walled city. When Santiago sighed, Antonio leaned forward to get Hanneke's attention, his eyes merry.

"*Dama*, I have never seen your husband cower in battle, but here he is before La Judería, the Jewish quarter, in agony as if from a mortal wound." He leaned back to regard Santiago with some sympathy. "Will it be so bad, friend?"

Santiago shrugged. "Don Levi admires pretty women. He married one, and he appreciates beauty." He gave a little bow. "Thank you for being so lovely, *esposa mia*."

What could she do about that, except blush, which made Santiago give his low, nighttime laugh.

"Here we are. Courage." Santiago dismounted before a tall, narrow house no different from the other houses on what looked like the ghetto's main thoroughfare. With a glance around to make sure no Jews lurked on the street to see him, he crossed himself, then knocked.

Antonio helped Hanneke from her mule. "That cap becomes you."

Still rosy from Santiago's compliment, she knew she wasn't any redder than before. "Juana insisted. She said I must be a proper Spanish matron. Oh, dear. That sounds so old."

"A worthy custom, señora," he said. "It should ward off the riff raff and remind the rest of us." It was his turn to blush. "I mean...well..."

He was spared further explanation when the door swung open and a servant beckoned the three of them inside. Hanneke followed her husband into the cool interior, her ears immediately tuned to the gurgle of bubbling water and bird mutter.

She admired the green courtyard inside the house, wondering what it told her about the character of Spain: reserved on the outside, with the sweetness within. She glanced at her husband, thinking of last night, wanting more of his intimacy. She tried to move closer and say something - what, she wasn't certain - but he was staring down at the leather case she knew contained the document he found so pernicious, Hans Aardema's cleverly worded marriage document.

She looked at it, too, and saw it for what it was - a parchment dealing in death. The idea took her breath away.

She spoke so softly that no one heard her. "Don't."

The servant left them on the patio. Hanneke moved toward the blue-tiled fountain and rainbow-colored parrots, perching on wooden stands and grousing to each other, their beaks touching.

"Look at the old gossips," she said, fascinated. She slowly put out her hand. Someone behind her reached out and gently swatted her fingers.

"*Nein, baheft froy*, they are not gossips but watch dogs. Have a care, or you will never point again."

Hanneke put her hands behind her back like a small girl. Santiago laughed and looked around. "David Levi. So we both live to see each other again?"

There stood the shortest man Hanneke had ever seen. His voice, low and deep, in no way matched his frame. He was dressed in black, with a gold necklace looping down the front of his long robe, where it roped into his belt. She saw a smaller necklace inside it. He did not look old, but glints of gray appeared here and there in his long beard. Curley ringlets framing his face danced as he nodded to Hanneke.

She returned his gaze as he cocked his head to one side. "Santiago, she is beautiful. May you have many fair sons and dark daughters. She will bring you good luck."

"I need it."

"*Claro*," Don Levi gestured down the hall. "Come with me. We in Toledo have heard of your recent troubles."

"From whom, may I ask?"

The banker shrugged. "A word here, a word there. Who can say? Join me, you three."

Antonio waved them off. "I would rather watch the birds fight," he said, grinning at them. "Ah, the peaceful life of a man with no land and no prospects: I have all the fun and none of the worries."

Hanneke and Santiago followed the banker from the patio into a chamber lined with books on shelves far too high for the little man to reach, except with a moveable ladder.

Santiago seated himself where Don Levi gestured. Hanneke look around for a cushion. Instead, the money lender pointed toward a stool and bowed slightly, his hand to his chest.

"Señora, my wife does not think ladies should be lower than men. Is this not right? Adam without Eve would be a dull dog indeed. Please be seated."

Hanneke perched on the stool, arranging her skirt around her, fascinated by Don Levi. He walked to his desk, with its little steps to his chair. "You wonder how we know, Señor Gonzalez? Only yesterday, the watchmen saw an Almohad army circling Toledo and heading south. Many horses had no riders. I would venture that it was El Ghalib." He coughed politely into his hand, his eyes merry. "But how is a poor Jew to know?"

"You know everything you need to know, don't you, Don Levi," Santiago said, and it wasn't a question.

"I know enough." He tilted his head back, regarding Santiago through partly closed eyes. "I also know of certain marriage papers."

Santiago took the parchment from its leather case and slapped it in Don Levi's hand. Sitting at his desk, the little man read the document at least twice through, then looked up. "Your father loved you more than most," he told Hanneke.

"That marriage contract is the devil's bargain," Santiago burst out. Hanneke heard all the frustration and winced.

"It isn't," Don Levi contradicted. "How did this herring merchant know what thieves' den his daughter would find herself in?"

"All he knows is herring, senor," Hanneke said.

"It is enough, apparently." The banker bowed to her. "And you, Santiago Gonzalez, are here to talk about an army."

"I need one. I need it now, not a year from now."

"You shall have one." Don Levi clapped his hands. "To work! We will probably shout at each other, and storm and rage, before we part as friends." He turned to Hanneke. "Should we not spare your wife this ugly scene?"

"She is stronger than she looks."

Don Levi nodded. "Of that I have no doubt. Other stories have reached us."

Hanneke looked from one man to the other, mystified. She turned her attention to the banker, and then, to her further mystification, to his smaller necklace.

A master goldsmith with enormous patience and skill had braided and soldered each tiny link. Only with great force of will and sudden fear could she keep from touching her own Almohad necklace, the links smaller, to be sure, but equally intricate, the work of the same artisan.

How did you get your necklace, Don Levi? she asked herself with great unease. *What bargain did you make?*

Chapter Twenty

Unnerved, Hanneke headed for the door. "Before the estimable Señor Baltierra drags you away, please wait a moment in the patio," Don Levi said. "Someone else would like to meet you."

"Very well," she said, anxious to leave. "Thank you."

"For what? For an army that will take your husband away? For more bloodshed? That is what you are buying." He shrugged, his hands out. "If God wills it, you are also buying the peace that follows war."

"That is what I hope," she said. "Peace."

"And land. Don't forget land," Santiago interjected.

Don Levi contemplated the warrior sitting by his desk. "How could I forget the ambitions of a second son? Yes, land." He touched her hand. "I will strike you a bargain worthy of your dreams and his. Go with God."

She turned toward the patio, admiring it through Moorish columns, but eager to leave. Antonio sat on the lip of the fountain. She watched the same two birds preening each other's feathers now and chuckling, as if over some huge joke.

"They seem to have sorted out their quarrel. They have been making up." He looked beyond her. "And the banker and the warrior are dealing in death."

She touched her necklace. "In Santander, King Alfonso said this venture is bigger than all of us. I am afraid."

She knew Santiago might not understand, but Antonio nodded. "So should we all be, warriors, women and children. El Ghalib is no respecter of persons."

A door opened and a woman taller than Don Levi stood there. She nodded to Antonio, her eyes lively. "Antonio! You do not grace our home often enough." He bowed. "Who is this who fits so tidily by your side?"

Hanneke blushed, but her companion seemed equal to the blunder. "She is Ana Gonzalez, the wife of Santiago, Señora Levi."

The woman held out her arms and embraced Ana with a pat on the back and a kiss on her cheek. "I am Raquel Levi. Welcome to my house, which is now yours, should you ever need it." She looked around Hanneke to Antonio. "I will borrow her a moment. Come with me, Ana."

She led Hanneke up a shallow flight of stairs, ushering her into a room where a servant sat, mending socks. Señora Levi crossed to a crib by the window.

"This is our son. He occupies me totally when he thinks he is hungry."

Hanneke touched the sleeping baby's curly hair, twisting a curl around her finger and watching it spring back. The baby stretched, extending small fists, then sighing back to sleep again.

"We all have a stake in your army, Ana. It may build us a safer world. When you have little ones of your own, you will dream of such a world, too."

Raquel took her hand and led her back to Antonio, who still watched the water. Raquel whispered, "Truly good men are scarce, Ana, but he is one of them." She spoke so he could hear, as they came closer. "Take care of her, Antonio."

"I was given that charge after we left Valladolid, *dama*, and I do not take it lightly. Go with God, you and your household."

Antonio paused outside the house and tossed another coin to the urchin he had already paid to watch their horses and mule. "Stay here, *muchacho*, and tell the blond man who comes out that we are going to the main city gate. Come, Ana."

He helped Hanneke onto her mule. "I should ask you. Let it be your choice. We can return to the inn, or I can show you something by the gate."

"The gate, please, no matter how hot the afternoon. If I am back at the inn, then I must listen to Engracia complain of her swollen ankles."

He swung into his saddle. "But Engracia whines so prettily. She sighs, sniffles, then cries some more."

They rode slowly through La Judería, then out the gate of Toledo. The sun had turned the world white hot and smoldering.

They topped the little rise and looked down on the Tajo, winding its way through the valley in the gorge it had cut through centuries, maybe millennia, of meandering. The sun turned the water gold and it sparkled like a molten necklace.

"I like it best at night when the moon is full," he said, "or just after rain. No wonder Moors and Christians fought over this city."

She looked across the water as it rippled and whitened over rocks, then flowed smooth, heading west. She turned toward Antonio. "This is silly of me, but during the first few days of our journey, I tried to stand looking west and north, as if I could imagine myself by salt water again, or home."

"And now?"

"Now I am more practical, maybe like you Castilians. Here I am, and here I must remain."

He laughed. "We are practical? There is another side to we Castilians, one I think you felt at your wedding dinner."

"You were watching me?" she asked, surprised.

He didn't seem embarrassed by her question. "I was. We will agree the day did not start out well. Maybe I worried."

"No, señor, it did not begin well." If he wasn't embarrassed to speak of personal matters then why should she be? "What is this other side you speak of?"

"You'll see."

They rode slowly back through a different gate of Toledo. As they dismounted, she saw the usual hangers-about that any city seemed to accumulate: beggars, traders, tax collectors, young people.

"Listen."

To what, she nearly asked, and then she heard it – great gusts of sound, punctuated by hands clapping rhythmically but just off the beat. The rhythm surged over her, and she hurried inside the gate, Antonio following and leading their mounts.

One small girl whirled and stomped to the sound of an *oud* and clicking bones. Unmindful of the crowd growing around her, the child raised her hands above her head and twirled. Her patched skirt flared out from her thin body, then wrapped around her legs when she changed direction suddenly. Her eyes closed, she threw her head back and sang, the tune sad and exultant at the same time.

When the jarring note ended and resolved, the child sank to the ground, her sides heaving. Antonio handed her a coin and spoke to her. She got to her feet in one smooth motion and nodded to the equally youthful musician. Shaking the dust off her skirts, she approached Hanneke and held out her hand.

Hanneke turned to Antonio, a question in her eyes. "She wants you to dance with her," he said.

Hanneke took her hand. The boy strummed his guitar and watched Hanneke's first attempt. He smiled, then slowed his tune. Hanneke tried to imitate the steps of her partner in the dusty dress. She beckoned Antonio with her eyes and he joined her, holding her other hand and dancing as the boy picked out a faster tune and begin to sing.

The child joined him, pitching her song to the empty sky, giving herself to the melody. Hanneke let the beautiful blending of voices soak into her like rain on dry ground. She closed her eyes and danced until she was filled with the pleasure of it.

She opened her eyes when the girl's hand turned into Santiago's. She laughed in delight and danced between the two warriors, one tall and blond, the other nearly as tall, but dark.

The music ended, and the three of them stood there holding hands. "The scamp who watched my horse told me where I might find you," Santiago said. He raised Hanneke's hand to his lips and kissed it. "If we are cast out and left destitute by El Ghalib, we can at least dance for our supper."

In pleasant accord, they traveled down the side streets to the inn's corral, where Santiago's soldiers had staked out their tents. A few men guarded the dowry, but the rest were nowhere in sight.

"The business is accomplished," Santiago said. Hanneke heard the quiet triumph in his words. "I will have my army. Tomorrow we take the dowry to Don Levi's underground storehouse. Antonio, find the men by morning. Take Pablo to help you."

"I would never take such a tender soul as Pablo, where I will find your soldiers," Antonio said with a shake of his head. "They are rubbing their stomachs raw on all the whores in Toledo. *Perdóneme*, Ana, but it is the truth. *Adios* for now."

Dinner was an awkward business. Engracia sniffed and made sad comments to the ceiling about leaving Toledo so soon. Juana muttered about Manolo's probable anxiety at seeing his wife so worn down, and Pablo spilled his soup.

Santiago bore it in silence. Hanneke marveled that he could tolerate their nagging, and wondered what life was really like for him at Las Claves. Her head began to ache from their complaints.

Engracia dabbed at her eyes all through dinner. "Some people think they have all the power," Juana muttered, "when all they are is second sons and never should have..."

Santiago stood up in awful silence. He pointed his finger at Juana. "Someday there will be an end to this," he said, choosing his words carefully. "I do not know how it will end, but it will end, Juana."

He set down his wine cup. "Listen, you two. We leave tomorrow. Don't complain to me about the Almohades." His voice, so low, frightened Hanneke more than shouts. "I can do nothing about your discomfort. What I can do is get you safely back to Las Claves. I will be months in the saddle this winter, trying to raise an army so we aren't burned out of our beds next spring."

He turned on his heel and left the silent room. Hanneke did not hesitate to follow him down the stairs and into the night.

"Wait, Santiago," she called. "Please wait."

He slowed. The grief on his face broke her heart.

"Please," was all she said.

With no hesitation, he tucked her arm into his and started walking, but slower this time. Soon they were strolling almost leisurely, as if they were a burgher and his Dutch wife out for an evening with no cares.

As they walked, he kissed her hand as he had done earlier. "Thank you for not complaining at any moment on this journey."

She was wise enough not to mention that in Santander, he had ordered her not to complain.

"Why haven't you railed against me? I believe - I am certain - you have been more put upon than those two harpies."

Hard lessons, nothing more, she wanted to tell him, but it was true: she was wiser. He nudged her shoulder, and the intimate gesture made her smile.

The gates were still open. They walked through them toward one of the campfires where she heard the same haunting music of this afternoon. His arm around her waist now, they stopped to listen.

"When I was a child, I wanted to run away with the gypsies," he said.

She laughed, not wanting the disturb the peace. "And I wanted to go to sea and fish for cod and herring - anything to avoid embroidery." She watched his eyes. "*I* am not much of a seamstress, and *you* cannot run away."

That earned her a ruffle of her hair, and then a sigh. "No, I cannot. You cannot. I have the money for an army. Don Levi made me a loan - a good one and I thank you, wife - against that time when your entire dowry is in my control. I must cover Castile, Asturias and Leon - maybe Navarre - convincing soldiers, felons and younger sons to join me. I will promise them land, water, sheep, cattle, women, anything, to join the attack against the Almohades in spring. My thanks will be land of my own for me, for you, for our children."

He had never said so much to her before. It was as if darkness freed him to speak his mind. "That is my goal." He looked toward the campfires "*Oye.* This is what I like best about Toledo."

They sat on the ground as a woman sang to the darkness around her, her voice uncluttered by any accompaniment. Her song was long and stretched fine, her voice full of warbles and ripples like the majestic Rio Tajo. Hanneke thought of beggars and dancing girls, Raquel Levi's dreams for her baby, and Juana's implacable hatred. She wanted to ask Santiago about his contradictory country, but she said nothing, too shy.

"So sad are the songs of Spain," he told her.

"What does she sing of?"

He cuddled her close. "Love and sorrow, joy and woe. In Spain, they are companions."

"Will she ever sing of happy things?" Hanneke asked.

"Yes, but they will sound sad. That is the way we are, Ana. Come now. The lamplighters are out and soon the gates will close. Let us leave the night to such as these."

She was not afraid to sleep beside Santiago Gonzalez this night in Toledo. She reached for him first.

Chapter Twenty-one

Santiago Gonzalez and his little army left Toledo by noon, after seeing the dowry safely stored in Don Levi's underground vaults, protected constantly by ferocious dogs and guards that Hanneke knew her husband would like to recruit for the coming season of war. Still wary, she waited to take her place at the head of the army until Santiago gestured to her.

Antonio had gathered mercenaries – a hard, silent lot – from the whorehouses of Toledo, men at loose ends and eager to fill saddles emptied by El Ghalib in the mountain pass. Assembled and ready, they rode south from the safety of Toledo's walls, unburdened now by the dowry, every man looking to the right and left continuously.

The first attack came near dusk, after they had pitched their tents by one of the streams that flowed into the Tajo. Hanneke had removed her shoes and was sitting with her feet in the water when she heard the warbling war cry and felt the thunder of horses.

Santiago's men ran toward the picketed horses. Engracia screamed and screamed as Juana dragged her to the river, pushing her down beside Hanneke. "Do not move!" Juana hissed.

Hanneke put her arms around Engracia, shielding her body with her own. They made themselves small as the Almohades raided through the camp, scattering supplies, knocking down tents, and challenging the soldiers briefly as they guarded the horses.

The raid ended almost as soon as it began, no one injured except a wounded horse, puncture with many arrows, that tried to rise. A soldier killed it quickly and walked back to camp. Others searched for arrows to add to their depleted quivers.

Hanneke dusted off Engracia's dress and set her cap on straight. Her sister-in-law babbled about dangers until Hanneke wanted to slap her. Instead, she crooned to her, reminding her that soon they would be safe at Las Claves.

After a meal of barely cooked goat, Santiago knelt by Hanneke and his sister-in-law. "We will not use the tents tonight."

The fear returned to Engracia. "The soldiers have put up the tents, brother," she said, her lips quivering.

"So they have. There they'll stay. You, Ana, and Pablo will sleep by the river. The Almohades will come again. Don't look so terrified, little mother! Antonio or I will be close."

Engracia sniffled, but she did not cry. Santiago sat by them, his bow across his lap, arrows lined up near to hand. Engracia lay on her side, propped up on one elbow.

"Do you know what I am going to do, Santiago, when we reach Las Claves?"

"What will you do?" He sounded absentminded, staring into the gathering darkness.

"I will go to bed, pull the covers over my face, and know I am safe."

"Engracia, you are a goose," he said, and Hanneke heard his affection. "What about you, Ana?"

"I think Engracia's idea has enough merit to try," she said honestly. "I hope I never see another Almohad."

"With luck, you won't." He leaned closer. "I'll be there with you, under those covers," he whispered in her ear, then kissed her cheek.

She slept well, but woke when Santiago left and Antonio sat in his place.

"Antonio?" she asked, rubbing her eyes.

"Go to sleep," came his quiet reply. "I am here."

In silence this time, the raiders swept down just before dawn, sneaking almost to within sight of the horses. Alert, Hanneke watched as Antonio rose to his knees, an arrow nocked and ready. She tried to rise, but he patted her down.

She saw nothing but vague shadows, and then a tent burst into flames. She put her hand on Engracia as Antonio stood and fired one arrow after another at targets she could not see. His face was calm in the glare of the fire.

The enemy left two dead men behind. Santiago cut off their heads. He picked up one by the hair and tossed it to Carlos. "For our collection. This one, too."

Hanneke looked away, wondering what he meant, wondering why she wasn't as horrified as she would have been a month ago.. *You have seen too much*, she told herself.

They traveled fast that day though dry land as before, dotted now and then with trees. Hanneke wanted to rest under each one, but she did not complain, remembering her husband's pride in her. Even Engracia and Juana were more subdued, especially after Santiago gave them a fierce stare when they complained.

Even in the heat and glare, Hanneke knew better than to wish for sundown, because she knew the Almohades would try again.

El Ghalib struck as soon as shadows lengthened. Antonio pulled Hanneke from her mule and sat her down. He rode after Santiago, who had grabbed up a lance from one of his dismounted soldiers.

They returned in only a few minutes, the lance bloody. Hanneke held her breath, but this time there was no head dangling from Santiago's saddle. She sighed with relief, then pitched forward and fainted.

Her faint lasted no more than a few seconds. Through an odd fog, she saw Santiago drop the lance and dismount. He carried her into the shade of a tree, then set her down. Her head seemed filled with little drums, all of them beating a different rhythm. She wanted to close her eyes and wish them away, but Santiago looked so worried.

"Really, husband, I am well," she said, wishing her voice did not sound so far from her ears.

"Lie still. I have spent so much time worrying about Engracia that I have ignored you."

And to think I wanted that at one time, she thought, glad he was beside her, even if briefly. She knew someone or something would soon demand his attention. She did have a question, even as she did sound like a querulous child.

"Are we almost there? Tell me we will see Las Claves soon, even if it is a lie."

"No need to lie." He sat her up and made her drink from a flask Antonio handed him. "We will be there by noon tomorrow. I had thought to ride all night, but no, better we arrive tomorrow, for Engracia and for you."

Her tiny moment with Santiago ended when one of his men called to him. "I am coming." Still he knelt beside her. "What is it Ana? The heat?" He wiped the sweat from her face. "Or is it just too much?"

He didn't wait for an answer, which was just as well, because she couldn't explain. She was content to rest against the tree and watch the soldiers set up camp. High above, a hawk wheeled on the air currents. She wanted to join it, anything to be done with this journey. She closed her eyes.

When she woke, Antonio sat beside her, his back to her, his sword in his lap. He leaned slightly forward, no relaxation in him. Without thinking, she touched his back. He tensed, and then gave a short laugh, as if embarrassed to be surprised.

"Antonio, you should have wakened me," she chided, but gently. "I would have moved closer to camp."

"Santiago ordered me to do that, but you were sleeping so peacefully I could not." He gestured with his sword. "I've been watching the hawk. There is a family of really stupid field mice."

"Growing smaller in number by the minute?"

"How wise you are. Shall we go, before the hawk starts to eye us?"

She let him help her to her feet, surprised at her dizziness. She hoped it did not show, but the look on his face suggested he was watching her more closely than the hawk spied on the field mice.

She fell asleep right after their meager meal of wheat mush, curling up right by the fire, her head pillowed on her arm. When she woke in the morning, she lay close to Engracia in a small ravine. As she lay there, half awake, half asleep, she felt horses again, even more horses than before. She scrambled to her knees, then yanked the back of Pablo's tunic as he stood there watching someone she could not see. "Get down!"

He shook his head and pointed. "Come look! See this."

"There is no danger?" she asked, her heart beating so loud she knew she would see it jumping about in her breast if she looked.

"No. Over there."

She stood up, relieved to see Santiago's soldiers watching, too, their swords loose in their hands. Santiago and Antonio were already riding bareback toward an army of men in white surcoats with red Greek crosses embroidered on them.

Who are you? she wanted to ask, wishing she weren't so disheveled, hoping she didn't stink as bad as her traveling companions.

Father Bendicio stood like all the rest, gaping at an army not worn down by fierce winds, Moslem attacks, or exhaustion. "Praise to God," he said. "El Ghalib will not attack us now."

"Father," she called, "who are these men?"

"These are the Knights of Calatrava," Father Bendicio said. "They are a military order of the Cistercians."

"Calatrava? We do not have those in the Low Countries," Hanneke said.

"Neither do you have Moors, Berbers, Almoravides and Almohades harrying and tormenting your nation for five hundred years," the priest said. "These men have taken a vow of silence like their brethren the Cistercians. They pray, as we all do, and abstain from food for three, sometimes four, days of each week."

"It is a wonder anyone joins," Hanneke said, wishing for something to eat besides everlasting meat and mush. She longed for bread.

"The zeal is strong here," Father Bendicio said. She heard some wistfulness, as if he wished for zeal of his own. "They sleep in their armor, so they are ready at a moment's notice to fight."

He crossed himself. "Alas, their castle fortress was captured seventeen years ago by Almohades. They have temporary quarters not far from Las Claves, but they are always ready to ride anywhere, if needed."

She stood by the priest, mindful that her shoes were still in the ravine. Santiago and one of the knights rode toward the encampment, the others trailing along behind. "Ana, let me introduce you to our nearest neighbors," he called to her, and dismounted. "Wife, make yourself known to Don Ruy Díaz de Yanguas, grand master of Calatrava."

Barefoot or not, Hanneke gave him the same bow she had given King Alfonso.

"A graceful gesture before breakfast, Señora Gonzalez," he said, and she laughed. "You have a rare treasure, Santiago."

"I do. I left most of it in Toledo with Don Levi."

Hanneke tried not to show her disappointment at his words, but Santiago saw her dismay. After a tiny pause, he continued, "But I brought the best part south with me. Wouldn›t you agree, Don Díaz?"

"I do. I wish you joy and many children." He nodded to Hanneke, his eyes lively. "I cannot understand why the Gonzalez men are blessed with lovely ladies. They have nothing whatsoever to recommend them."

She heard the grand master's affection for her husband as he teased so gently, brothers of the sword. It relieved her heart as nothing else could have.

"Will you join us for breakfast, or must you travel?" Santiago asked.

"We will join you and share what we have. Then let us discuss this army you will raise." He put his hands on Santiago's shoulders and drew him close. "Is this to be our year at last?"

"I pray it is," Santiago replied simply.

The two armies parted before the sun was much higher, the Knights riding north, and Santiago leading his soldiers south. Hanneke turned in her saddle to watch the knights ride away.

"Women and uniforms," Antonio teased.

They traveled steadily for an hour or more, climbing toward a little break in the low hills ahead, the soldiers talking among themselves, no one wearing their helmets now. The whole column seemed relieved, thanks, in great measure, to the Knights of Calatrava. Hanneke felt it.

She studied the countryside, knowing it was to be her home, hoping she would like it. There were no houses about, but soon she saw shepherds and their flocks. Dogs dashed in and out, nipping the reluctant, but keeping a wary eye fixed on the older rams with formidable horns.

When Santiago called to her, she realized how far back she had strayed, in her eagerness to take in her surroundings. She rode to the head of column, placing herself between Santiago and Antonio, hoping she hadn't earned a scold.

Even Santiago seemed to relax. He gestured ahead. "When we are through that pass, you will see Las Claves. We are the key to this pass, hence the name."

"Las Claves," he said, when they were through the pass. Hanneke heard his relief. He leaned across her and spoke to Antonio. "Do you know, friend, I never come to this point without thinking, will it still be there? Have the Almohades burned it? I see they have not."

"What would you have done if they had?" she asked, curious.

"I would have taken you to the nuns in a convent south of Toledo for safekeeping first, then followed the raiders," he said decisively.

"Why? You said Las Claves can never be yours."

Had she overstepped herself? She watched Santiago's frown line deepen. She also watched it soften, then fade.

"Ana, that is a rather good question," he said finally. "What would I do? I am not certain I have an answer." He touched her leg. "Right now, I will give my horse the lead. See you at Las Claves."

With that, he dug his heels into his horse's sides. Soon he was far in advance of the others. She watched him turn into a speck on a vast plain, and there was the fortress of Las Claves before them all.

"What are you thinking?" Antonio asked.

"It's not what I expected." She frowned at her vague answer. How would she know what a fortress in *la frontera* should be? She wished it appeared more sturdy. Even in the heat of late summer, Las Claves looked cold and uninviting. She looked away, thoroughly unsettled.

"It was originally Moorish," Antonio said. "You can tell that by the stonework and arches. Santiago's grandfather captured it when he was a young man. All efforts since then have been to strengthen the walls. It may not even have had walls originally. I don't think the Moors gave much thought to the Christians ever regaining the smallest foothold."

Las Claves doesn't look safe, Hanneke thought, wishing the wall was higher. *But what do I know of warfare?* "It looks a little, well, shabby."

"It is beautiful to me," Antonio said simply. "When I first saw it, I was starving. They took me in."

"I have wondered what your story is."

"This winter, if I have time, I will tell you. Santiago is younger than I. Our friend Bendicio had just failed him as a squire. It was a time of desperate war and I became his squire."

"Now you are knight and friend?" She asked, wanting to know more.

"Probably no title that distinguished," he said. "All the same, war creates bonds that might not otherwise exist. You will see what I mean. Look there, he is motioning to me...to us, more likely. Shall we?"

Why should she feel reluctant? "I will come with the others. You go ahead."

He gave her a small salute and was soon galloping toward Santiago.

She rode at the head of the column, Pablo by her side. "We are nearly there," she said, hoping she sounded more confident than she felt.

"I don't know, *dama*," he said.

"I don't, either," she admitted. Giving herself a mental shake, she noted the harvest underway, with laborers in the field, and neat bundles of grain at the ends of rows. As they neared Las Claves, she saw houses huddled close to the walled fortress with the wide-open gates, massive gates with crisscrossed iron bands.

She waved to the children playing by the wall. They stared back. Shy, she turned her attention to Santiago and Antonio, dismounting in the courtyard. The soldiers rode past her, followed by Father Bendicio and Engracia, with Juana glaring at her as she hesitated. She felt foreign and alone, perhaps always the outsider.

Hanneke stared at the towering gates, squelching a moment of panic that made her want to turn and ride back the whole way she had come. "I can't," she said out loud, her courage gone. She looked around, hoping no one had heard her. She waited for her brain to tell her, "You must."

She waited. All she heard was her heart, her practical heart, reminding her that the deed was done.

She rode through the gates.

Chapter Twenty-two

She rode toward Santiago and Antonio, who stared above her at the gate's lintel, where Carlos stood. As she watched, stunned, he pulled a rotting head from the burlap sack that had been tied to his saddle, since the fight in the mountain pass.

"No," she said. "No."

She dismounted quickly, but not fast enough, as bits of rotting matter rained down on her. Every instinct in her body told her to leave this place, but where would she go? Her first thought was the Levis, but she banished that quickly, remembering a pogrom in Visslingen only two years ago, called down by an irate citizen who was certain Jews had killed his son as a Sabbath offering. It was all nonsense, but other innocents had died. No, she could never involve the Levis in her life here.

She had no choice but to move away from the shower of gore. She ran into the shadows, unable to take her eyes from the scene above. She watched in horror as Carlos jammed four heads down on four empty spikes, turning them around so the sightless eyes gazed across the valley.

She stood near a well, with a half-filled bucket resting beside it. She dabbed water on her face and raised her skirt to wipe it. What Carlos had done could only have been because that was what Santiago wanted. So much war was yet to come, and she was complicit, because her dowry financed it.

"God forgive me," she said. "God help me."

"He will, sister."

The words were softly spoken, kind, even, in this stark place now her home. She saw a small man standing in deeper shadows, leaning near inner stairs. He was short and dark, his head tilted to one side. Her second glance told her he wasn't so short, but hunched to one side, as if he stood on uneven legs.

"Manolo Gonzalez?" she asked, forgetting the others in the courtyard.

"*A vuestra servicio.*"

His smile lit up his whole face and glowed in his eyes. Hanneke bowed, then held out her hand. "You must know who I am."

He took her hand and pulled her closer. All his energy appeared to be centered in the brilliance of his dark eyes. He was as different in appearance from his younger brother as night from day. Hadn't Father Bendicio told her that Manuel Gonzalez resembled his slain mother?

"I know who you are, and I like what I see."

Who could not smile at that? "Thank you." Hanneke saw Carlos climb down from the catwalk, and Santiago start in her direction. "I can see that I have a lot to learn if I am to survive Las Claves," she said, hoping it wasn't too much to admit.

"We all had a lot to learn."

She wondered what to say to Santiago. Those heads! Santiago had been stopped by a several soldiers and appeared deep in conversation. With an effort, Manolo sat down on the third step. He patted the step beside him. "You'll have to help me up in a moment. Engracia will find me and fling herself on me soon enough. Ah, that is better. My dear Engracia. Did she mope and cry and complain?"

"Who wouldn't?" Hanneke asked in turn. "It was a ghastly journey."

"You are a diplomat." He took her hand in his. "She is nothing but silliness, but life without her would be even harder." His face lighted up. "I hear her. Help me up, please."

He winced when she helped him to his feet, but they both chose to ignore it. In the next moment, Engracia was in his arms, sobbing and kissing him at the same time, smoothing back his hair as she tried to encapsulate the whole, miserable journey into well-chosen words, none of which she possessed.

He patted her belly and spoke to his brother, who stood by Hanneke now.

"Brother, Engracia did not look like this when she left. Was there something in the water of Valladolid?"

Santiago put his arm around his brother, steadying him in Engracia's tumultuous embrace. "That must have been it. Manolo, how good to see you again. You have met Ana?"

"I have. Santiago, you are to be envied."

She didn't know what her husband would say and reminded herself to expect nothing. To her amazement, he rested his hand on her shoulder and gave it a little squeeze. "I know." He looked toward the gate. "Some might think Ana has other ideas. Do you?"

It was a question for the ages. All she wanted was to be left alone. The stairwell was suddenly too crowded, with Engracia clinging to Manolo, Juana frowning as usual, Pablo looking worried, and Carlos coming closer, gore spattered on himself. When she saw Antonio, she noticed something in his eyes that suggested he was aware of her desperation.

He could do nothing. No one could. "Other ideas?" she asked. "No. I am tired. That is all."

"I'll take you upstairs, wife," Santiago said.

He offered her his arm at the same time more soldiers joined them, arguing about swords or tents, or something she did not care about, but which she knew would demand her husband's attention.

"Antonio, take her to my room," he said, and left her there. He joined the soldiers and crossed the courtyard.

She turned blindly toward the stairs and started up, stumbling over her skirt, unsure where to go.

"Wait."

Antonio picked her up. He carried her up the stairs and down the hall, speaking softly to her. "The look in your eyes is a look I have seen in eyes of horses we have whipped to get a few more leagues out of them to escape the Almohades."

"It doesn't matter," she assured him. "I'll just sleep for fifty years."

She tried to make it sound like a joke, but he didn't laugh. Maybe he knew she meant it; maybe she didn't care. The bleakness of her life to come stretched ahead and she did not like what she saw.

He carried her to Santiago's room and put her on the bed. She turned away, too upset to open her eyes.

Antonio wouldn't leave her alone. He sat down next to her. "Until your husband releases me, you are my responsibility," he told her. "There are some things I can do nothing about, however."

Hanneke nodded. She understood.

"But those I can, I will. This is my pledge to you."

He looked like he had more to say, but he didn't. He found a light blanket and covered her. "Go to sleep, Ana."

She took him at his word and slept. In full darkness later, she heard someone moving around the room, a door opening and closing, hushed voices. At some point in the night, Santiago lay down beside her. He tugged on their shared pillow and pulled her close with a sigh.

"Do with me what you wish," she murmured, desperate for comfort, and he did.

"Thank you, Ana," he whispered into her shoulder later. "Someday when there is more time..."

She slept again, dreaming of knights in white with Greek crosses, and Carlos cramming heads onto spikes, and wind blowing hot and driving bits of gore into her hair, and Juana laughing at her discomfort. She sat up in fright, her heart racing, wishing for anything but Las Claves.

Santiago lay on his back, perfectly relaxed. She smiled in spite of herself, knowing she had much to do with his satisfaction. She watched him until her eyes started to close, and lay down again. She thought of winter coming eventually, and days with less for him to do. Perhaps he was right. Perhaps there would be time to get to know this man she was bound to for the rest of her mortal life.

When morning came, she knew it was long past the time she should have risen. As she sat up, wondering what to do, Santiago came into his room - their room, she reminded herself.

"You barely moved all night," he said. "Well, except for..."

Why blush? She had enjoyed herself. She sniffed. He must have bathed and washed his hair, which shone golden in the morning light. It was much shorter, too.

"Manolo is my barber," he said, touching his head where his hair used to curl around his ears. "Perhaps he should do his barbering when he is not more intent upon talking to me, eh?"

They laughed together. He touched her hair. "Don't let Manolo get near you with shears, chiquita." He kissed her. "Let me take you to a place much safer than Rio Tajo." He smiled. "At least for me! We have a bath house."

She stared at him. "Don't look so skeptical," he said. "It a legacy from previous Muslim owners that my grandfather displaced."

"I wish I had something better to wear than my woolen dresses and bridal clothes that don't fit," she began, then stopped, wary again. "I don't mean to complain."

"You don't complain."

"You told me not to ever complain," she said without thinking, then felt the familiar fear all over again, a reminder of their hard journey.

"I could have been kinder," he told her. "I wish there were not so much pressing on my mind."

"I'll make do with the clothing I have," she said, wanting to end this conversation.

"No need. Manolo found some dresses of our mother's. Here."

He tugged her from bed and led her to a Moorish chest on a carved wooden stand. She opened the trunk, breathing deep of the sandalwood lining. "How lovely," she said, pulling out a camisa, clean, delicate and lacy. Next came a blue cotton gown and a silk-plaited belt. She draped the lovely things over her arm. "What was your mother's name?"

"Liria," he said. "She was as pretty as her name. From what Manolo tells me, she was about your size. Just a little lady. Come with me."

They walked down the corridor, Santiago keeping step with her and not striding ahead, almost as if he wanted to spend a few moments with her. *I could like this*, she thought.

He stopped at the row of open windows. "*Mira, chiquita.*"

Hanneke leaned over the stone-worked railing and looked down on a garden. Bushes of orange blossoms and roses competed for the attention of bees, and was that a lemon tree? The garden had obviously been well-tended once, but not in recent months. She heard a fountain.

Santiago rested his elbows on the railing. "It is Engracia's special delight. Before she came, we used it for livestock." He shook his head. "You can tell she has been gone too long."

"I will help her tend it. I like to make things grow." She looked around and decided this was not a castle at all, to her way of thinking, but more like the inn at Toledo. She couldn't help wondering if the walls surrounding them were strong enough.

As they walked down the wide staircase, Santiago gestured to the great hall, with its Moorish and Almohad banners taken in battle and now hanging from smoke-blackened rafters. "Pray God we will add to our collection during the season of battle."

Outside, he pointed to the chapel, the soldiers' hall, and the bath house. "Many of my soldiers live in the village just beyond the gates," he told her, "but the single men live here. After the turn of the year, if I begin immediately, this hall will be full of more soldiers."

"Immediately?"

"I'm leaving with Antonio and a small guard as soon as they assemble. Go into the bath house. The water is warm."

She did as he said, wanting to obey and cry at the same time. So soon? Couldn't he stay a few days longer? Introduce her to Manolo's villagers? Tell her some stories about his childhood? Surely there were some happy ones.

Agitated, she hurried though the wonderful bath, washing her hair until she was satisfied, rubbing gingerly around her sunburned nose, wishing she were prettier. Not that it mattered. Who was there to notice? Santiago was going away.

The dress fit her as if Liria Gonzalez had told her seamstresses to make it thus and so for a small woman she would never meet. Hanneke smoothed down the soft folds, then tried to tug the bodice higher. Mama would never have approved, but Antje Aardema was far away in a Vlissingen cemetery, and her daughter was alone among strangers. And Santiago was going away.

She heard many horses in the courtyard. She paused at the bath house door, almost afraid to open it, certain that once Santiago rode away, no one would take any interest in her. She had never felt so alone in her life, and there was no remedy for it.

"You're braver than this," she said out loud, and opened the door upon an army ready to march.

Manolo sat in a chair beside the chapel with Father Bendicio standing near. As she watched, the soldiers knelt in the courtyard as the priest blessed them with success in finding more soldiers like them.

Her husband knelt beside Antonio, both men in their chain mail and helmets, with swords sheathed. She counted twenty soldiers, men she did not recognize. The men from their own journey stood and watched, too, among them ugly Carlos, with his scarred face and one eye missing, Carlos who took such delight in heads on pikes. She forced herself not to look up at the gate.

Manolo had told her that fresh troops were riding out, leaving the others behind to guard Las Claves and tend their own wounds from the journey. Only twenty? With difficulty, she tamped down an odd presentiment that there weren't enough. *Don't be silly*, she scolded herself. *What do you know of warfare?*

Here stood Santiago. She started forward, but no, he was embracing Manolo, who told him not to be away too long. "Remember, Santiago, there are those here who love you."

"Finding an army matters more," Santiago told him, then turned to his horse.

He saw Hanneke then. He nodded to her, but came no closer. He swung into the saddle and sat there as his soldiers mounted, his gloved hands resting lightly on the high pommel, completely at home on his big gray.

He barely knows I am here, Hanneke thought, and blinked her eyes to hold back the tears she knew would only embarrass her and irritate him.

"Ana?"

Antonio hurried from the chapel. "I wanted to say goodbye." He looked closer. "Why the tears?"

"I thought he might say goodbye to me," she said. "It would only have taken a moment."

"Right now, all he sees is an army," Antonio said. "There. I have said it."

She nodded, adding foolishness to her list of misdemeanors. "I know. I know. Someday when the Almohades are gone and he has land of his own, he will have time for me. Someday."

Antonio touched her arm. "I will look after Santiago for you and bring him home safe."

"How long will you be gone? One week? Two?"

He couldn't meet her eyes. "Several months. We will travel through Leon, Castile and Navarre, finding our army. Maybe even to Aragon in the east."

Months. She nodded, unwilling to speak what was in her heart, not to this kind man who had done nothing to deserve bitter words. Better leave them unsaid. "Go with God, Antonio," she said instead. "Don't worry about me."

The little army rode through the gate as wives and children waved to them, dogs barked, Father Bendicio swung his censer, and the dust rose.

After everyone returned to their homes and duties, Hanneke walked through the gate and watched the army until long after they disappeared in the pass.

She stayed there, alone, until mid-afternoon when Carlos tugged her away, because it was time to close the gates.

Chapter Twenty-three

That was August. When Carlos found her crying by the gate, he took her to Manolo, who put her to work. The first command went to Pablo, who was promoted from the kitchen to the patio and handed a scythe. "Don't kill anyone," Manolo said. A few rose bushes had near misses, but after a day the grass was manageable once more, and the fountain could be both heard and seen.

Now it was October. The days fell into a simple pattern of weeding through the morning and pruning rose bushes. The thorns tore at her hands until Hanneke found a pair of old gauntlets in Santiago's room – she never thought of it as their room – from his younger years.

She spent many afternoons in the chapel, sitting in the doorway to catch the light and mending old vestments that Father Bendicio claimed dated back to the days of the Visigoths, maybe even the Romans.

One rainy afternoon, as summer grudgingly yielded to autumn, she tackled Santiago's room. She worked her way through a mound of clothes, discovering that the deeper she dug, the smaller became the surcoats, tunics, hose and shoes.

She knew she would never forget the boy-sized tunic covered front and back with rust-colored stains and a gaping rip through the right shoulder. She remembered Father Bendicio's words about the battle where he ran away, and where Santiago's childhood ended.

"If you even had a childhood," she said out loud as she folded the garment and placed it in the bottom of the Moorish chest with Liria's dresses. She barely slept that night, thinking of the young boy who had no childhood, and whose father and servant blamed him because of another's mistake.

Other matters kept her awake. She dreaded early morning kitchen smells, especially the omnipresent odor of olive oil that came with every meal. Laying that aside, why could she not keep her eyes open after the evening meal? She was too young to be dozing like an old fishmonger at the docks, waiting to clean the evening's catch. If the kitchen odors drove away her appetite, why did her bodice stretch so tight across her breasts?

She wanted to talk to Engracia about the mystery of her disappearing monthly flow, but it was a private matter. How long had it been? Since the last time at sea?

She picked a moment when Pablo was off to the smith, sharpening the garden scythe, and Manolo was reading in his room. She stopped her assault on the purple weeds edging the fountain. Engracia sat close by, embroidering and humming to herself.

"Engracia, I have a question for you," she asked, trying to sound casual.

"Ask, my sister."

"I...I..." She could hedge around the matter, but why? It was just the two of them. "I want to throw up every morning, I can't stay awake at night, my bodice is too tight, and my breasts hurt."

Engracia's eyes widened. She put down her embroidery and patted the space beside her.

"And?" Engracia coaxed.

"There is also the matter of my missing monthly flow. It has vanished."

"When that happened to me I ran to Manolo, who told me I was with child. Men are so wise." Then it dawned. "Sister, when was *your* last flow? I think I know your ailment." She giggled.

"The ship at sea in June. That would make..." She counted on her fingers. "Four months."

"Stand up and turn sideways. Pull your gown tight across your middle."

Hanneke did, looking down, seeing the bump she was already familiar with, but which could be hidden from others still.

"Your waist is gone, and it appears that someone has taken up residence inside you," Engracia said. "I think you had better write to Santiago, if you can find him." She touched her forehead to Hanneke's. "I'm happy for you."

I am happy, too, she thought that night, comfortable in bed in her all-forgiving camisa, lying in the furrow Santiago had created through the years. *If you are too busy with battle to think much about me, no matter. In five months I will have someone to keep me company, no matter how long the war.* "Thank you, Santiago," she whispered into the darkness.

She woke earlier than usual, even before nausea struck. She tried to return to sleep, but she heard loud voices coming from the great hall. She wrapped a blanket around her and padded downstairs, hopeful. Perhaps Santiago had returned.

Manolo sat below, still in his nightclothes, Pablo beside him, Pablo who had decided by himself – after securing her permission – that he would include her brother-in-law in his duties. She hesitated on the stairs because two of the villagers stood with them. The local dialect was difficult to decipher, but she heard the word "Fire" more than once. She came closer.

The villagers hurried away. Manolo nodded to Pablo. "Summon Carlos from the soldiers' hall."

Hanneke came out of the shadows and put her hand on Manolo's shoulder. He smiled his approval at her presence, something he had done more and more lately. Perhaps he had decided she could be relied upon.

"Carlos worries me a little," she admitted, not wanting to say more.

"He is ugly, to be sure," Manolo said, "but I trust him as I would Santiago or Antonio. You should, too, sister."

"How is that? He watches me too much."

"Did you ever think that perhaps Antonio commanded him to watch *you*, now that he is gone? I know of Santiago's similar request to Antonio."

She hadn't considered that. The thought warmed her, even though her bare feet were cold.

"Never fear Carlos. His heart is large."

Here he came now, pulling a tunic over his nightshirt, his face a dark cloud of worry. "Trouble, señor?"

"Let me tell you of my early-morning visitors. You can decide."

With a glance at Hanneke, Carlos scratched his chest and sat.

"Two of my villagers tell me that their newly gathered haystacks burst into flames last night. And you know those two shepherds who only yesterday moved their sheep here from summer pastures?"

Carlos nodded. "One of them is the brother of my late wife."

"They are missing."

Carlos crossed himself, but it was no act of contrition, as far as Hanneke could tell. The ugly man looked irate that God Almighty would be so careless of Spanish lives. But that was Carlos. "Señor, I will take a few men, and we will see."

"That is what Santiago would have you do," Manolo said. Hanneke heard the relief.

Carlos exchanged a wry look with Hanneke. "*Dama*, he'd probably have my hide by now, because I wasn't already in the saddle."

"Go with God," she said, feeling more charitable toward him.

"If He can keep up."

After Carlos left on a run, Hanneke turned to go upstairs, her feet cold. Manolo held out his hand again, and she took it.

"Engracia tells me I am to be an uncle."

Hanneke nodded, too shy to speak, and hurried upstairs to change.

Manolo still sat in the great hall when she returned. He motioned her closer. "My dear, count the men gathering in the courtyard. If there are not at least ten, tell Carlos to add more."

She pulled her cloak tighter against the chill of wind trying to decide if it was autumn or winter. She looked first at the heads over the gate, as she always did, whether she wanted to or not. She squinted in the weak light, then looked again, wondering what was different. She remembered her task and counted ten riders; no need for more. Still, something was wrong.

"Carlos, please wait a moment."

"*Dama*, what?" he asked, trying to sound patient when she knew he was eager to be away.

"Look over the gate."

He looked where she pointed. He dismounted slowly, as if a weight had suddenly dropped on his shoulders. The mounted men groaned, but he cut them off with an oath. "We will wait here until the sun rises."

He stood close to Hanneke. For the first time, she welcomed his practical, profane presence. He stared into the dark space. As the sun rose, she saw twin streams of fresh blood dripping down the arch. She moved closer to Carlos.

"*Dios mio*," he said softly.

The four nearly skeletal heads were gone. In their place were two fresh heads that looked down on *them* through sightless eyes, and not across the plains.

His voice was small for a man so big. "We have found our shepherds."

They left, after the heads were removed and placed carefully in burlap. Hanneke stood at the gate, listening. There it came – wailing and screams from two houses. She walked slowly into the great hall to give Manolo the rest of the message, which meant a need for paper and pen and a letter to Santiago, once Manolo had control of himself.

Manolo directed his letter to the Knights of Calatrava. "I know he went there first. Perhaps they know his intentions. We can hope." He finished his message, sprinkled it with sand, then handed her the paper. "There is room at the bottom for your own news. I know you can write."

She picked up the quill, not certain how to say it. Manolo laughed at her. "So shy about something men and women have been doing since Adam and Eve! I would give much to see his face when he gets your message."

Before many minutes passed, a single rider raced toward the pass, message in his pouch. Rain began before he was out of sight. Hanneke stood at the entrance of the great hall and watched the rain sluice away fresh blood from empty spikes.

Carlos and his men returned in late afternoon, when purple and yellow clouds filled the sky.

"We saw nothing, señor," he said to Manolo, who had not left the great hall all day. "We will post a good guard. No fears. You can sleep in peace."

Who could sleep? Engracia cried and sobbed until Manolo ordered Juana to calm her, no matter what. Hanneke lay in bed, wondering if the Almohades would sneak up silently, or scream their terrifying, warbling war cry. *Please, Santiago, return to us,* became her prayer, hour after hour.

Carlos and his men rode out again with the dawn, to no success. Pablo said the cook and serving women told him it was a cat and mouse game. Engracia cried louder at this news, until even Manolo seemed to weary of her tears, rolling his eyes and shaking his head.

The game of cat and mouse continued one week, two weeks. One night, four fires blazed just far enough away to make a swift answering raid impossible. Another night, it was a flock of sheep, slaughtered between sundown and sunrise. Each afternoon, Carlos and his men returned grim and silent.

Every morning, disquiet dragged her from bed faster than nausea. Every morning she found Manolo sitting in the great hall, looking like a man who had spent the night with his eyes wide open, staring into the darkness. Every morning, she sat by him in silence. She knew he found her presence comforting, even if he said nothing.

One morning she woke with her usual start, certain she heard voices. She threw a blanket around her shoulders and ran downstairs, desperate to see Santiago.

Antonio sat with Manolo this time. He stood up, tired eyes lively, his hands held out to her. She reached for him, and he grasped her shoulders.

She looked beyond him, disappointed. "Santiago?"

"Manolo's letter reached us far to the north."

"He did not come?" Maybe she wasn't hearing him correctly.

"No, lady." He gave her that familiar half smile. "Remember, he is busy finding an army." He turned to Manolo. "Which we will have here by spring, God willing."

"I wish it were sooner," Manolo said in a low voice.

Antonio glanced at Hanneke, and Manolo waved away any concerns. "Ana know everything," he said. "In fact, she has turned into my rock."

"I am not surprised," Antonio said. He looked from one to the other, then nodded when Pablo brought in bread and cheese. He took a hunk of each. "Tell me what is going on."

Between the two of them, Hanneke and Manolo told him of death, and fire, and sudden raids. "Carlos looks and looks, but he finds nothing. They are toying with us, El Ghalib and his men," Manolo finished. "What can we do?"

"Carlos is a good man and reliable," Antonio said, "but I know the land where our fortresses end, and before the cities of the Almohades begin. I will ride and listen."

Hanneke clutched his arm. "What will happen to you?"

"Nothing." He shrugged. "I am from beyond the frontier, as you know. My Arabic is as good as El Ghalib's. I know what I look like, thanks to a raiding party on my village when my mother was caught outside city walls."

What could she say to that? "I will worry about you," seemed so feeble.

"No one has ever worried about me," he said, surprising her. "Yes, worry about me. I like that."

She laughed, in spite of deep misgiving. "I will! After all, you have loaned me Carlos, when you cannot be here to watch over me for Santiago."

"It's a fair trade." He looked at Manolo, who had listened to this whole exchange with amusement. "I will be gone within the hour. Get dressed, Ana. Aren't your feet cold?"

She hurried upstairs and dressed, her mind in a jumble. She ran downstairs, disappointed to see only Manolo. "He's gone already?" she asked.

"Only to the kitchen."

She remembered she was a matron and walked with some dignity to the kitchen. Antonio sat at the cook's table, cheese in one hand, as he drained a goblet of wine. He was dressed in a dirty robe, with an equally tattered scarf around his head. The cook piled food into a sack.

"Here I go," Antonio said. "I'll inquire here and there, see what I can learn." He regarded her. "For an early riser, you look uncommonly fine, *dama*. Something has changed. Care to tell me?"

Shy, she avoided his eyes. "Surely Santiago told you. I wrote it in the letter."

"He said nothing. What was he to tell me?"

She wondered why her husband had said nothing to his trusted friend about her baby. *There you go, Hanneke*, she scolded herself. *Santiago is too busy, even for good news.*

"I am with child," she said in a low voice.

"I thought there was something about you," he said with no hesitation. "This is good news."

"He never said anything?"

He regarded her thoughtfully. "We go from village to village, urging men to join us, promising them land of their own. I have seen Santiago so tired at night that he falls asleep with his spoon halfway to his mouth."

"He tells me things will be different, when the Almohades are pushed back," she said. "You know, when he has leisure time."

"Now there are two of you for me to protect, eh?"

She noticed he had neatly sidestepped her comment about leisure time, but chose to ignore it. "I suppose there are."

Antonio took the bag of food and stood a moment looking down at her. "Trust your instincts, Ana," he said. "Manolo can't really help and Carlos is busy."

Without a word, he kissed her forehead and left her there.

"I will, friend," she said to the empty room. "My instincts are all I have."

Chapter Twenty-four

El Ghalib's raid on Las Claves began in the quiet hour before sunset, when villagers were returning from their fields after preparing them for winter. All was silence, until that unforgettable sound, once heard never forgotten.

Hanneke sat back on her heels and dropped her pruning shears as the sound grew louder. She recognized it, and felt her breath come faster.

"Go inside, Engracia. Hurry," she ordered.

Then Engracia heard the war cry, too. She dropped her needlework and ran awkwardly for the great hall, holding onto her belly. Hanneke picked up the embroidery hoop, her first thoughts of Antonio. Pray God nothing had happened to him. She stopped and looked skyward. *Santiago, we need you here.*

She ran through the great hall and out the main door in time to watch the gates swing open and villagers pour inside, urged along by the guard left behind, which suddenly looked too small.

The villagers, some of whom she recognized by now, came carrying bundles hastily thrown together, dragging crying children, tugging animals' halters, coaxing donkeys and slow-moving cows that brayed and bawled. Through the gates she saw one of the distant huts burst into flames. One woman wailed and threw her apron over her head. Her lament was taken up by others, small babies joining in.

The war cries grew louder and the villagers moved faster, as Carlos roared to them that he was going to close the gates. Unsure of herself, wanting to help but not knowing how, Hanneke turned toward the entrance to the great hall. Maybe Manolo would agree to let some of his tenants with small children come inside.

The insistent braying of a mule stopped her. Hanneke watched as the animal, sitting on its haunches, protested at the top of its lungs as a woman and two little ones tugged at it. There they were, half in and half out of the gate, with Carlos breathing fire.

"I can help," Hanneke shouted. She grabbed the halter and tugged.

"Bite his ear, lady," one of the soldiers told her.

"Yes, my lady," urged the woman, who yanked her children away from the mule. "Yes! If the gates swing shut with us on the inside and the mule outside, my husband will beat me!"

Hanneke grabbed the closest ear and bit hard. The mule stopped in the middle of his own lament and leaped up, knocking Hanneke to the ground. She hurried to her feet and hung onto the rope as the animal flailed about, slamming her against the gate over and over, then crowding against her. She groaned as the metal bar dug into her back, but hung on.

"Let go, lady!"

She saw Carlos on horseback, his one eye full of worry, but sounding so far away. She dropped the rope and ducked as the irate mule swung around, then crawled away from the animal, only to have a dog trip over her and start growling. She put up her hands as Carlos kicked the dog and grabbed her. She clung to him, sobbing, as he carried her inside the great hall.

With tenderness she never could have imagined, the ugly man set her down next to Manolo and brushed the mud off her dress, then turned her head to look at the bruise near her ear. He shook his head as he would over a small child found dirty on the road.

"*Dama*, Antonio warned me about you. He told me you would save the world if you could. He will be angry with me!"

She touched his arm, grateful for his care, unhappy with herself for distracting him from more important duties. "It's not your fault, Carlos. I had to help that woman, don't you see? She had those little children." She touched her back where the mule had thrown her into the gate.

"I must return to my duty," Carlos said. "I have no choice."

"Go, and thank you," Hanneke told him. "Antonio will hear only a good report from me, sir knight."

He smiled at that, and touched his hand to his forehead.

"Is there anything else we should prepare?" Manolo asked. "What would Santiago do?"

"Just what we are doing," Carlos replied. Hanneke heard all the pride. "The gates are closed. El Ghalib will burn a few more houses." His voice trailed off. "The only thing is…"

"Tell me," Manolo demanded.

"We have never been attacked this late in the year. I will be glad to hear what Antonio has to tell us when he returns." Carlos rubbed his arm. "Getting cold too soon."

Manolo called for Pablo from the kitchen, and he helped her upstairs. By the time she assured him she was fine, and that he should see what good he could do in the courtyard, her whole body ached. She lay down with her shoes on. She dragged a blanket over her, and put her pillow over her head.

She woke up because the ache had concentrated itself in her belly. She wanted to drag herself to the door and call for help, but the pain was too great. She drew herself into a ball. *I will feel better in the morning*, she thought. *Won't I?*

She lay there as the pain came in cresting waves, minutes apart and then closer. She tried to rub her back, but any motion made her gasp. *I must get help*, she thought, at a loss because she could not stand. Maybe someone would miss her.

After what seemed like hours of agony, someone knocked. "Please help me," Hanneke called out in her loudest voice. Couldn't anyone hear her? Was everyone at Las Claves deaf? Or was her shout really only a whisper?

Engracia stood there, her eyes wide. "Ana, what is the matter?"

"Everything. Please get Juana. She…she doesn't like me, but I need someone," Hanneke pleaded. *Someone useful and not you*, she had the good sense not to say. "I think it's the baby."

She closed her eyes as Engracia hurried from Santiago's room – *gruss got*, where was he? – crying her way down the hall.

In mercifully few minutes, Juana stood beside her, her hand on her forehead. "You are sweating in this cold room."

Juana, don't scold me. I need help. "Never mind that," she managed to say. "Something is wrong."

She heard Juana's intake of breath. The servant rested her hand on Hanneke's belly. "There is trouble inside," Juana said. For a change, she didn't sound unkind.

"Please not that," she whispered. "A baby is all I want."

Time dragged by, but at least she was in her warmest nightgown with a blanket-covered iron pig at her feet. She could hear Manolo in the room, with his odd hitch as he walked. Engracia cried, until he said something soft to her and she left. In itself, that was a relief.

When he mentioned Santiago, she opened her eyes. "Santiago? You're here? I need you."

"No, child." She recognized Father Bendicio's voice. "We know where he is and Manolo is writing to him. He will come soon."

He didn't come. Not that night and not the next day. The cramps grew more insistent, rising and falling like breakers on a distantly remembered beach. Her body was a skiff, bobbing up and down, blown by the wind. Sweat poured from her, even as her teeth chattered with cold so deep she wondered why no one lit a fire. But there it was, glowing not that far away. Her misery grew as the pain increased and the tiny one twisted inside her.

As the room darkened to dusk, she heard the door open, bringing cold air with it. "Santiago?" she whispered. "Please be Santiago."

"I wish I were."

She was too weak to cry. Eyes closed, she felt warm hands cradle her face. "Antonio."

"Yes." He raised her sweaty head and put a towel under it. "I won't leave you."

"Promise?"

He couldn't have heard her. She hardly heard herself. She felt his lips nearly touching her ear. "Promise."

Comforted, she slept, crying out only when the pain was too great. During one of those awful moments, Antonio rubbed her back, then leaned across her and placed an orange where she could see it.

"It will taste so good soon, Ana. I have more of them."

Strange things happened to her body, forces over which she had no control. She heard a low-voiced but fierce argument, and the final words spoken so calmly. "She was left in my care. I won't leave her."

The bed creaked and someone sat behind her, pulling her onto his lap. She felt a rush of cold air as the blanket was lifted off her body and her nightshift raised to her waist. She gasped and tried not to scream as her body broke in two and a baby poured out in a gush of fluid. She struggled to touch her baby, then remembered nothing else.

When she woke hours later, she kept her eyes closed, not wanting to see the tiny, bloodied thing between her legs. The image brought a wail of grief she did not try to stifle. She heard the bed creak as Antonio settled himself next to her, holding her as she sobbed.

She woke much later. Antonio sat in the chair again, dressed in a black tunic. Too tired to speak, she nodded to him, and earned a smile. He picked up the orange lying on her bed and peeled it. He popped a section in her mouth. To chew and swallow was bliss. She ate the orange and looked around for more.

"You'll get another one tomorrow, after you eat some mush and eggs. Oh, don't look daggers! You're a ferocious woman, *dama*." He sighed. "And a brave one."

Better ask. Better get it over with. "My baby?"

He held out one cupped hand. "She was this small. So tiny, Ana, so perfect."

"What did you…" *I don't want to know, but if I do not know I will die.*

"Manolo found a carved box. Engracia lined it with velvet. Bendicio baptized her, and I buried her."

"A name? Please?"

"*Claro que si.* I named her Fermina, after my mother."

"Fermina. Thank you." She wanted to say more. Perhaps it was best she hadn't the strength.

Chapter Twenty-five

In the days that turned into weeks following the death of her daughter, she was aware of the smallest things – the crackling of a fire in the brazier that someone pushed close to the bed; the oranges; the wind howling around the patio.

She was more aware of Antonio Baltierra. He usually sat in the chair by the bed, busy sewing harness or fletching arrows. He would look up when she woke from the light sleep that was her closest companion. Whether it was the sleep of recuperation, as the body marshaled its forces, or the sleep of forgetfulness, she couldn't have said.

Others visited her, but Antonio was always there, especially during the longer nights. She tried not to cry – after all, women miscarried often enough – but when darkness closed in, she could not help herself. She would hear the scrape of Antonio's chair and his comforting presence as he bent over her to wipe her tears, or pull the blanket higher on her shoulders.

Her appetite gradually returned. She suspected a conspiracy between Pablo and the cook, who plotted to see what delicacies would tempt her. She could have told them that salt herring had the most appeal, but never bothered, because there was none. She tried their sweets and savories and shared them with Antonio.

Food made the quiet man more expansive. "You know, Ana, when I was a child, I never imagined such delights," he said, gesturing with his spoon at the burnt sugar and cream concoction she handed him, after a few bites.

"It's flan, and it's simple," she said.

"I never ate it before coming to Las Claves," he said. "My mother – Fermina – swept the tavern floor in our village." He paused to finish the flan. "She gleaned the scraps of food that fell there and made us a stew."

143

Hanneke stared at him. "How could you grow tall on such leavings?"

"It was a mystery to my mother." He leaned back in his chair, regarding her. "I was hungry all the time. Once I even bled the cow of my mother's master and drank that." He smiled at the distressed look on her face. "No frowns, Ana! Obviously it didn't kill me."

It didn't kill me. She thought about that as she half-dozed and rested. After a week or more of listening for Santiago's footsteps, listening so hard that she could almost think he was close by, but chose not to intrude on her mourning, she took Antonio's comment to heart. She had wanted Santiago, but he hadn't come and she was still alive. She faced the matter and survived it.

Her conviction in her own courage deepened one morning when she heard Antonio and Manolo outside her door.

"I wish you had not written to Santiago," Antonio said.

"Surely he needed to know," Manolo replied.

"Manuel, now he will know there is no need to return immediately, because there is nothing he could have done."

She listened for Manolo's response and sorrowed to hear it. "He would not be so hard of heart."

What do you say to that, Antonio, she thought. His reply was honest and perhaps what she needed to hear. "Manuel, I tell you, it has nothing to do with the heart. It has only to do with an army. He sees nothing else."

"Unkind. Unkind."

"So be it, señor. We are not standing in his boots. I for one am grateful not to be Santiago Gonzales. The price is high."

"I am grateful, too," she said quietly. "Poor man."

Then the day came when she was bored of lying in Santiago's bed, wondering about matters she could not change. The room whirled around as she stood up, but she remained on her feet, grasping the back of Antonio's chair until her head cleared. She pulled on her robe, and padded quietly into the corridor, happy to be upright.

The shutters of the balcony were closed. Winter had come. She opened one shutter and looked out on a garden at rest, bare branches clacking at each other, the fountain dry. The grass was green in places and brown in others. Moving slowly, she went down the stairs, and let herself out into Engracia's rose garden.

The cold grass felt good under her bare feet. *How glad I am to be alive*, she thought, wiggling her toes. She touched her belly where her daughter had been and felt brief sadness, sorrow like a sigh instead of a wound this time.

She was sitting on the bench when Antonio found her. He went inside and returned with her slippers. He knelt to put them on her feet.

"*Ay de mi*, Ana. Engracia and Juana are calling for you."

"Ignore them. Don't scold."

"I wasn't going to. Engracia thinks I am going to carry you inside. Do you want to go?" Antonio sat down next to her.

"Later. I'm thinking." She hesitated, wondering how to put tender thoughts into words. "If Fermina had lived, I would have brought her here next summer to sleep while I weeded the garden."

"I can see that."

"Fermina would have been beautiful."

"So was the woman I named her after," he said simply. "Let's both sit here and think."

When she finally rose to walk upstairs under her own power, she knew her healing had begun.

November passed into December with no grace and little comfort, everyone complaining about icy sleet coating the ground. Hanneke even found herself wishing for the hot breath of late summer that had heralded her arrival at Las Claves. She thought of the quiet Hanneke of August: hopeful, fearful, wishful, possibly almost in love. She knew the Hanneke of early December was still quiet, but there was more. Great sorrow had buffeted her, but with it had come acceptance and the understanding that she was still the mistress of small things. Not for her the grand emotions, apparently. Her life would be a quiet one.

There had been moments in early fall when she had yearned for the Netherlands. No more, not with her baby in Spanish soil. A part of her belonged to Spain. How much, she wasn't certain. Perhaps time would tell.

Engracia did not venture outdoors, even to attend Mass, fearful of slipping. There were others fears that Manolo cautioned them against mentioning to Engracia. No need for her to fear when Carlos and Antonio rode together, seeing nothing, but listening to the brave souls, shepherds mainly, who still lingered in pastures south of Las Claves, in that dangerous space between the Spaniards and the Almohades.

One day, two days of absence. Hanneke found it hard not to walk to the courtyard and stare at gates kept closed on Antonio's command. She knew it would be a good time for Santiago to return. She also knew better than to expect him.

Sometimes she visited Pablo in the armory. Manolo had put him to work sharpening knives and swords, but he never minded honing smaller items. This time she brought him her cloak pin, which he sharpened on a bit of pumice stone.

"You are now a master of many trades," she said, which made him beam.

"Mostly I am your true knight," he reminded her.

Engracia spent her time in bed, letting Juana bring her treats and give her back rubs. She demanded Manolo's presence, which he gave freely. Hanneke wondered at his supreme patience, not a trait she had noticed in his brother.

Tidying it as best she could, she happened to be in the great hall on the afternoon when everything changed. She had consigned weapons and chain mail to the armory, located a Turkish rug and cajoled the carpenter into making two benches close to the fire. No stretch of the imagination could call it homelike – with Moorish, Almoravide and Almohad flags captured in battle hanging from the rafters and two great swords crossed over the fireplace – but at least it comforted her.

She heard voices outside and the door opened on Carlos and Antonio. Carlos nodded to her and left for the soldiers' hall while Antonio removed his cloak. She smiled to herself as he looked around for a place to toss his cloak as he had in years past, considering the disheveled state of the great hall.

"I have become the martinet of Las Claves," she said. "You may hang your cloak on one of those iron hooks the smith so obligingly made for me while you were gone."

He laughed and did as she said. "Homelike," he joked, looking around at the high ceiling, battle flags and crossed swords.

The smile left his face as he walked closer. She saw all the exhaustion and worry.

"Something is wrong," she stated.

"We might have snow tonight," he said. "Now and then it snows."

"What else, Antonio?"

He took her hand, which startled her. She grasped it firmly. "Tell me."

He took a deep breath. "Can Engracia travel?"

"What are you asking?" She said it quietly because she saw servants out of the corner of her eye, bringing dishes to the table.

He pulled her closer and spoke in her ear. "It's only a feeling, Ana, but I pay attention to my feelings."

She felt the deep cold that must have seeped into the room when Antonio opened the door. "She can travel if she must. Should we...pack?"

He hesitated a long moment, as if weighing the consequences, then shook his head. "Not yet. Say nothing. I wish..."

"...Santiago would come," she finished.

He nodded, released her hand and headed for the soldiers' hall. He forgot his cloak, so she grabbed it and hurried after him, nearly bumping into him because he stood just outside the door, watching the gate swing open, his sword half drawn. Carlos stood at the door to the soldiers' hall, his sword already out of its scabbard.

"Go inside, Ana," he ordered. "Now."

She turned to obey, then heard a sigh of relief. "No, wait. I believe it is Santiago. God be thanked."

After weeks of waiting – no, months since he had left – Ana hurried down the steps into the courtyard, Antonio behind her.

She stopped because an army followed him, thirty soldiers at least, some wearing chain mail, others cloaked tight against the cold that had deepened in the last hour. They looked at her like predator to prey. When she stepped back, afraid, Antonio's hand went to her shoulder.

Santiago watched them, looking from one to the other. "And what is this?" he asked.

Antonio lifted his hand and came down the steps. "To say that we are glad to see you is an understatement. Come inside."

"You, the Arab bastard, are welcoming *me* to my home?"

What is he saying? Hanneke asked herself, stunned, as Antonio turned on his heel and walked toward the soldiers' hall. "We...we all welcome you, husband," she said, wanting to move closer, but fearful. "In half a moment, you will probably see Manolo. Engracia, no, because she is so big. Come in."

After a longer moment than she liked, Santiago dismounted. He stretched, then noticed Carlos still standing with his sword drawn. "Surely you haven't forgotten what I look like," he snapped.

"No, señor, no," Carlos said. He sheathed his sword. "Shall I show these...your..."

"The army I traveled Spain to recruit?" Santiago gestured to the mounted men. "There are more coming in a few weeks. Get your men here. Show them to the stables and the soldier's hall. Tell the cooks to get busy. Can you do that?"

What is wrong with you? Hanneke asked herself.

She knew Carlos well enough now to know he had been offended. She admired his restraint as he sketched a small bow to the man he had never bowed to before, as far as she knew, and gestured to the men to dismount. She watched them and did not like what she saw.

"What rough-looking men," she said, when Santiago came closer.

"Thieves, murderers, rapists - the best I could find," he said.

He clapped his own hand on her shoulder, a gesture so proprietary that she almost – not quite – feared him. She decided to lean into him, but his arms did not go around her.

They walked up the steps together. He looked around the great hall, with a smile. "I leave you alone and what do I see? Improvement. Thank you. Engracia never even thought to turn this hall into something grand. How have you been?" He peered closer. "You look a little fine drawn. Were you hoping for something better from our winters here on the plateau?"

She tried not to stare at him, but she couldn't help herself. "Santiago... husband... I miscarried."

"I know, I know," he said. "Manolo wrote. That was more than a month ago, wasn't it?"

"Five weeks, to be exact," Antonio said, coming out of the shadows. "It has been a long and painful time for your wife."

Santiago put his hand on her shoulder again, claiming her. What was he thinking?

"You're tired," she said, as her heart broke. "I am better."

"I buried your daughter next to your mother and father," Antonio said, coming closer, standing on Santiago's other side.

"Cold company," her husband said, "especially my father."

Hanneke told herself she was through with tears, but she cried anyway, trying to turn away to hide her weakness in front of this strong man she almost didn't recognize, but unable to move because Santiago's hand clamped down harder.

"Antonio, we passed two shepherds on our way here. They told us of raids in winter. How can this be?"

"I named your daughter Fermina. Ana was too ill."

"Please stop, both of you," Hanneke begged. "I can't bear it."

"Forgive me, Ana," Antonio said.

Silence. Somewhere above, Hanneke heard Manolo's halting gait. "Santiago, is that you at last?"

"Yes, brother! Listen to me, both of you," Santiago said, trying to keep his voice low, because he heard Manolo, too. "What could I have done, had I been here?" His whisper turned fierce. "I need an army! Don't either of you understand that? What could I have done?"

"You could have been a husband."

Santiago pushed Hanneke away and pulled out his dagger. Before Antonio could move, Santiago pressed the point against his neck. "Damn your impudence! What do I see when I ride in, hungry and weary, but your hand on her shoulder. Your hand! I am her husband. Not you. You forget who you are!"

As Hanneke held her breath, Antonio raised one finger and pushed the blade aside. "I do not forget who I am. I am Antonio Baltierra, a free man." He made no move to step back, but stared into Santiago's eyes.

Santiago lowered his dagger. He looked from Antonio to Hanneke. "What happened here while I was gone?"

Antonio's glance never wavered. "Beyond your wife's great sadness, nothing at all. Upon further consideration, I think Las Claves is not the place for me. I am not certain it is a place for anyone. Adios, Ana."

He was nearly at the door when Santiago called to him. "If you leave, do not return."

Antonio looked back. "Never fear. I will not. But you had better be very careful in the next few days."

"You're threatening me?"

"Never. I have too much regard for you, Señor Gonzalez. El Ghalib is threatening you. By all the saints, you couldn't have come at a better time, and with more fighting men."

Antonio left, closing the door quietly behind him. The dagger clattered to the floor. "Nothing happened between you and Antonio?" he asked, his back to her, his voice frosty.

"Nothing," she said, frightened of this obsessed man, even as she understood him better than she thought possible. She waited. She knew him.

When he turned around, his face was as wintry as the weather outside, the weather into which Antonio would soon be riding, going who knew where.

"Then I have done a terrible thing."

Chapter Twenty-six

"Sit down, husband," Hanneke said, her fear of him gone, or at least ushered into a dark corner. She saw a weary man, probably hungry, certainly dirty, who had traveled many leagues in the interest of his king and country. She sat down on the stairs, certain that her legs would never carry her to the inviting bench by the fire. She patted the tread beside her. *Do or don't*, she thought. *Our daughter is dead. My friend and yours is gone. I am afraid, but not of you.*

She only thought the words remained in her head. She put her hand to her mouth when she realized she had spoken out loud.

He sat down beside her and put his arm around her, but gently this time. "When the first letter came from Manolo, God help me, I knew where I should be." He bowed his head. "Right here with you."

She leaned against his arm, relieved.

"I also knew that if I stayed in that miserable village two or three days more, I could convince ten men to follow me. I chose, as it turns out, not wisely." He looked at the door. "I have lost a friend and a valuable ally." His glance settled on her. "And frightened you. Forgive me, if you can."

When she said nothing, he shook his head. "I hardly blame you. Please at least let me hold you close tonight, because I am tired of being alone."

"I am, too," she said, in a voice equally quiet. "You need to know something Antonio told me before he... before he left."

She felt his arm stiffen at Antonio's name, but continued, because he had to hear it. She took a deep breath to calm herself. "He asked me if I thought Engracia could travel. He said it was only a feeling, but he respects his feelings."

151

"I respect his feelings, too." He slapped his head and leaped to his feet. "*Dios mio*, Felipe! That rat!" He ran to the door, threw back the bolt and ran out, leaving the door open behind him.

Mystified, she stood in the doorway, trying to see into the deeper gloom that had settled on Las Claves. Felipe? Felipe. Surely not *that* Felipe.

It was that Felipe. Hanneke watched in growing discomfort as Felipe Palacios emerged out the gloom with Santiago, querulous as ever, eyes darting about seeking some misdemeanor or other, probably finding fault already, then staring at her with that hungry look she had feared in Valladolid and feared now at Las Claves.

"You were unkind to leave me in the soldiers' hall," Felipe Palacios said to her husband.

"I forgot you were with us," Santiago said, sounding not even slightly apologetic. "Manolo can find quarters for you here. Come with me."

Felipe shrugged and followed Santiago upstairs. He took a long look back at Hanneke, which made her hope this was only to be a short visit. *Stupid man*, she thought, glaring at him. *Las Claves is no place for a coward*.

She listened for Engracia's shout of delight, certain that noisy tears would follow. Ah yes, there they came. Hanneke went to Santiago's room and lay down, sore to her heart's core at the loss of a friend over nothing.

Santiago joined her quickly, probably as soon as he could extract himself from the noisy scene. Without asking, she helped him remove his surcoat, chain mail and doublet, then surprised herself by kissing his head when he sat down. He flashed her a tired smile that reached his eyes and took away a little of the sting of his arrival.

"A bath tonight?" she asked.

He shook his head. "All I want is to lie down and maybe kick myself for being unkind to a friend. I'll look for him tomorrow, although I doubt... Ana, forgive me."

"I forgive you," she told him, and sat close as his arm went around her shoulder. "Everyone is tired of the raids and wondering where the Almohades will strike next." She turned her head into his shoulder. "I wish I felt more strong."

"I wish you did, too. I can't think El Ghalib will continue his destruction so late in the season for fighting. I have soldiers now, and more are coming. So is winter. I do know this: no Arab likes snow."

He crawled in bed with a sigh and held up the covers for her. He fell asleep almost before she settled herself in his embrace, but not before she told him, "I feel safer when you are here."

"Thank you for that, Ana," he said. "You won't laugh at me if I tell you I feel the same way?"

"Only a little," she said, and felt his chuckle. She wanted to tell him she loved him, that she had been listening for him for weeks, that she had called out for him during her great distress. Before her mother died, she had asked her what love felt like. Mama had considered the matter in her thoughtful way. "Sometimes, when your father is out with his fishing fleet, I wish him home and safe with me. I feel uneasy when I cannot see him." Mama had laughed, until laughing made her cough. "If I had my wish, I would prefer that he always stay within hailing distance, right here with me. You know, in the next room. I almost told him that once, but I did not. He would only have teased me and said there would be no wealth without fishing."

She wanted to tell Santiago all of that, but he breathed slowly and evenly. Maybe there would be time in the morning. She thought of her mother, who had died not long after that conversation, probably with her words unsaid. *I will say something*, Hanneke thought, as she snuggled closer to her husband's warmth. *Mama would wish it.*

Santiago still slept beside her in the morning, and she hadn't the heart to disturb him. She dressed quickly and padded downstairs, looking around first to see that she was alone.

The air had a distinct chill. She sniffed the breeze, reminded of Decembers at home, and the anticipation of snow. She hurried into the kitchen and there was Pablo, kneeling by the fireplace, blowing on the coals and adding bits of lint. He gestured broadly.

"Welcome to my kitchen, fair lady, and God grant you a good day."

She curtsied playfully.

"Usually I am alone at this time of the morning, but you are my second visitor."

"Hopefully the cook wasn't first, and you didn't get a scold," Hanneke said.

"No." He pointed to his pallet on the other side of the fireplace, blanket neatly tucked and folded. "Who should wake me this morning but Antonio? He told me he did not sleep well, and I wasn't to pester him with questions."

"Is he still here?" Hanneke asked, not certain what response she wanted. Why did friends have to fall out over nothing? It was nothing, wasn't it?

"He left, but first he asked me for food. He sat right where you are sitting, looking sad, or maybe tired."

Hanneke stared at her hands in her lap. "Did he leave a message for me or for Santiago?"

Pablo added a larger log to the fireplace. "It was a strange message, but he said you would understand."

"Yes?" she prompted.

"Only this – if you were to find oranges in the courtyard by the well occasionally, you would know who they came from. Lady, do not cry!"

She stayed in the kitchen until all traces of tears were gone, wanting no one to pester her with questions. She ate bread and toasted cheese as the cook arrived, complaining about more mouths to feed in the soldiers' hall.

She yearned to visit Fermina's grave, but she did not, knowing in her heart that hers would be the second set of footprints there this morning. Better to wait here a bit, then go to Engracia. She could sit beside her sister-in-law, let her chatter, nodding or saying yes or no, as appropriate, with an *imagine that* thrown in occasionally.

Her plan to visit Engracia fell apart immediately, because there sat Felipe with her. For one day and then another, she stayed in the chapel with Father Bendicio, repairing old vestments, listening to the noise of soldiers in the courtyard and the constant rasp of sword blades on the grindstone.

The one good moment of the second day happened in the privacy of their chamber, when Santiago made love with her. She opened her heart as never before, grateful for his particular comfort. When they finished, he chuckled. "I did bathe," he whispered in her ear.

He was teasing her, a side of him she had not seen before. "So did I," she replied, and kissed him. She settled herself next to him, wanting to tell him that she was happy for the first time since Toledo. But no, he had other matters on his mind, even as he cuddled her close.

"I wish I knew what was going on," he said.

"I thought you had the matter of me and you well in hand just now," she murmured, pleased when he laughed.

He soon turned serious. "These last two days, nothing from El Ghalib," he said, and kissed her bare shoulder, moving aside the necklace.

Was this the moment to tell him about that necklace? He was mellow and still awake. Maybe another time. Yes, another time. His breathing became regular, far from the tumults of mere minutes ago. Another time.

Chapter Twenty-seven

Her eyes were closing when Santiago tensed beside her. She started to say something, but he put his hand over her mouth. Fearful where seconds before she had been so satisfied, Hanneke heard footsteps on the stairs. In one motion, Santiago rose from bed and grabbed the dagger he kept on the floor.

Naked, he opened the door slightly, dagger raised, then lowered it when Pablo ran in, breathing heavily.

"What?" he asked, as he reached for his tunic

"Antonio is below," Pablo managed to gasp.

"I did not expect this, Ana," Santiago said. She heard the hard edge in his voice return. "Is he alone?"

"Alone, señor."

"Tell him I will be right down. Dress yourself, Ana. I don't trust myself alone with Antonio because I do not know what he intends."

She threw on her tunic and found her slippers. She grabbed a blanket from the bed and ran down the stairs behind her husband into the great hall, where Antonio stood, his sword drawn.

He had left the door open, as if to guarantee himself a quick escape. Snow blew in and turned the hall into a wintry landscape.

Santiago pulled her behind him. "No one comes in here with a bare blade," he said quietly.

Antonio lowered it. "I did not know what reception I would find at Las Claves. We did not part well."

"No, we did not."

Silence, more silence. Hanneke watched the warriors measuring each other. *Antonio, for God's sake, tell him we are only friends*, she thought. *That's all. Isn't it?*

"You said Las Claves was not the place for you," Santiago said most formally. "What do you want?"

"To warn you." Antonio set his sword on the floor. "I traveled as far as the southern plain. You know the one I mean. El Ghalib has assembled a large army and they are coming here."

Hanneke had pressed herself against Santiago's back. She felt him tense. "Is this the truth?"

"I do not lie."

"Are you carrying this message to me from El Ghalib?"

Hanneke sucked in her breath as Antonio picked up his sword again and turned toward the door. "Why would you even think that?" he asked over his shoulder.

"Manolo told me you were never out of my room when Ana lay so ill. Could not Juana or one of the servants helped her?"

"We all helped her," Antonio said quickly. He turned around and Hanneke saw the hurt in his eyes. "Have I ever disobeyed a charge you have placed upon me?"

"Never."

"Did you not tell me to watch over her when you could not?"

More silence, then, "I did."

"I will always have her best interests at heart, Santiago, until you release me from your charge. Do you release me now?"

"No. I will later, when times are safer."

Antonio put down his sword again and came closer, his empty hands out in front of him. "I have never seen so many of the enemy all at once."

"Then we had better talk," Santiago said. "Pablo, bring food. Ana, leave us."

"No. She must stay. Don't look at me like that! Let me tell you why."

Hanneke sat next to her husband, as Antonio sat across from him at the table. He looked from her with a faint smile to Santiago, where he became all business. "Hear me, Santiago. Ana must remain with us because she will be in charge then we ride out of Las Claves with every soldier."

"That is too great a risk," Santiago argued.

"You haven't seen what I have seen," Antonio said simply. "Manolo will remain here, of course, but you know how easily he tires."

"There are that many?"

"There are that many." Antonio hunched closer, as if seeing El Ghalib's army. "If they attack us here, we haven't a chance. We can't withstand any kind of a siege. Las Claves is no fortress. The snow might slow them down, but for how long?"

Santiago sat in silence, reminding Hanneke of the night he sat so long and still on his horse as they approached the mountain pass, weighing the actions forced upon them, choosing. "Every man, you say?" he asked finally.

"Yes, even young lads without mothers. If I thought for a moment your priest would not make water and run, I would force him along, too. If we can't surprise them on the plain, the Almohades will pour through here like a river in thaw."

"Then we need not bother with an army for another hundred years."

"Sí, Santiago. Our dreams will be over."

Santiago stared at the Moorish battle flags hanging above them. Hanneke touched his hand, then held it. She felt him relax.

"Very well. Antonio, rouse the soldiers in the hall. Sound the alarm for the villagers and open the gates. Ana, let us dress."

Antonio was nearly at the door once more when he looked back. "Santiago, do you think our dear Felipe Palacios will be brave enough to join us?"

Santiago laughed for the first time, but with no mirth. "Possibly when hell freezes. As soon as the alarm sounds, he will disappear."

"Why is he here?"

"Antonio, I have no idea."

Should she interrupt them? Should she remind them of the connection between Jawhara and Felipe? So much had happened since then. No, no, this wasn't the time for the story of her necklace, but she had to say something. Ana cleared her throat. "My husband. Antonio."

They looked at her, Santiago with impatience. "Husband, do you not recall that Jawhara told us, or was it Engracia, that she was a gift to your sister-in-law from Felipe?"

"I had forgotten," Santiago said. He stared at the battle flags again. "Trust no one. It is a convenient credo, Ana. Be careful."

She wondered if this was the time to tell them that Jawhara and Yussef el Ghalib were brother and sister. But no. She would have to explain how she knew that, and about the necklace. *Trust no one*, she thought, dismayed with herself. *I should have said something much sooner.*

She opened her mouth to confess, but both men had already turned away, Antonio to rouse the soldiers, and Santiago upstairs to dress for battle. Deep in misgivings, Hanneke followed her husband. He threw on his tunic, then pulled on another one, feeling the padding of the two shirts. *Is it enough?* she thought in sudden alarm.

He must have seen the look in her eyes, because he kissed her cheek and added his winter doublet. "See here, I won't be able to move," he told her, then took her arm gently. "Don't worry, please. Follow me."

By now the entire household was awake. She put on her warmest dress over her camisa. Clad in his chain mail now, Santiago ran down the stairs and she ran, too.

He spoke to her over his shoulder. "The gate remains open until all the villagers and their animals are inside. Once that is done, do not open the gates again. Keep up, Ana! I mean that. All it takes is one Almohad warrior dressed like a beggar to throw the bar from inside." He stopped and she bumped into him. "Or Felipe. Let us pray my cowardly brother-in-law goes into hiding."

She ran with him across the icy courtyard to the armory, where Carlos distributed swords, lances, and also the battleaxes that made her shudder.

"Ana, pay attention." Santiago pulled her close for an intimate moment in a crowded place. "If we are defeated, I will see it coming. I will send someone…"

"Please don't talk like this," she whispered in his ear.

"…someone to bear tidings." He held her closer. "You must do as he says and flee. Follow the villagers and don't stop for anything."

"Abandon everything?"

"Yes, *chiquita*," he said, his arms tight around her. "Everything. Did we not come into this world naked?"

They hurried next to the kitchen, busy as noonday with the cook and his flunkies filling cloth bags with bread, cheese and sausage. Full of concentration, Pablo handed out the bags to soldiers. He stopped when he saw them.

"Señor Gonzalez, may I ride with you?"

Please no, Hanneke thought in sudden fear, *not my true knight*.

"*Sí o no*, Ana?" Santiago asked her. "He is yours to command." He spoke to Pablo alone, his eyes intense. "Only if you think you can kill a man. I won't have you hanging back."

"I would never do that," Pablo said and stood taller.

"Then go with Santiago," Hanneke said, wondering if her heart could break any more.

She resolved not to think about Pablo as they continued their circuit of Las Claves, Santiago pointing out the weak places, telling her where to place the old men and children for defense. The townspeople poured through the gate, carrying what possessions they could gather on short notice.

"How fast they will abandon their trinkets if El Ghalib comes knocking," Santiago murmured as he watched them. "Remember, Manolo will help as much as he can, but his concern is Engracia. Ana, these people will do as you say." He stopped his half trot and smiled. "Everyone tells me how kind you are."

"I am," she said practically. He laughed, then pushed her toward the kitchen. "Help the cook."

Hanneke returned to the kitchen, slicing sausage and cheese until her arms ached. Exhaustion hovered right behind her eyelids, but she shook it off and watched the sky for signs of daylight.

Finally, it was time. Santiago beckoned to her from the door. "We are leaving."

She wiped her hands on her dress and followed him, stopping to see the men on horseback. Surely it was enough, but why did they look so few in number? Maybe Antonio was wrong about the numbers. Please let him be wrong.

Santiago sucked in his breath. Manolo stood before them, clad in chain mail, ready for battle.

"No," Santiago said. "Not you."

"You need every man," Manolo said, his tone flat and final.

"Not this. Not you. I do not ask it." He took Manolo by the arm and tried to escort him back to the great hall.

Manolo twisted around to stare at his brother, one shoulder higher than the other. In his too-large armor, he almost seemed to be a caricature of a knight, but no one snickered. No one even moved. "Santiago, you are my younger brother. Do not order me about. I will ride with you."

"It should not be," Santiago said, but Hanneke heard in his voice that he knew he had already lost this argument.

Manolo's voice was firm. "It will be this time."

Hanneke turned away as her eyes filled with tears for Manolo and her husband, these brothers united and divided by a terrible incident years ago.

"I have no choice?"

"None, brother. Help me into the saddle."

Your heart is breaking, too, my husband, Hanneke thought, as Santiago and Carlos helped Manolo. "Tie me in," Manolo said, and Carlos did, his face a mask of worry.

When he was settled, Manolo beckoned to Hanneke. "Watch over Engracia for me. She does not understand." His voice hardened. "I do not know where her brother has hidden himself."

Out of the corner of her eye, she saw Antonio and Santiago exchange glances. They whispered, Santiago nodded, and Antonio took off a dagger at his belt. "I don't need two of these," he said to Hanneke. "Wear it on your belt. Use it on anyone who threatens you, Christian or Moslem." His voice softened. "Don't hesitate."

She took the dagger, then stepped back as Pablo led his horse to him. Antonio swung into the saddle. She turned to Santiago, her eyes blind with tears, as he reached for her, holding her close, then kissing her. He kept kissing her, even though his soldiers cheered and laughed. She heard, "Take her along, *señor*," then "Save it for later," followed by, "No fair. Where are our women?"

"I love you," he said, before he released her. "Someday we will have time." The soldiers of Las Claves were laughing as they rode away, the little army of Las Claves. Santiago rode at the head, with Carlos beside him and Pablo near, back straight and proud, her *caballero* kitchen boy. Antonio leaned down as he passed her. "I'll watch him for you," he said.

"Go with God, Antonio," she said, then stepped back, joining the women and children who had gathered by the gate.

When the last soldier passed through, three old men swung the gate shut. Hanneke joined the women and children as they lifted the crosspiece through the iron bars. Other women cried, raising their arms high, imploring the impersonal moon and stars.

Hanneke looked at the parapets, guarded now by boys and girls too young for the task, and *viejos* who should have been sitting before their breakfast fires, warming old bones. For a terrible moment, she wanted to scream at her father for welcoming those two priests more than a year ago to their manor in Vlissingen, ready to deal with money and herring for a royal connection. How stupid. How pointless. *And here I stand, you vain and foolish man*, she thought.

She re-entered the great hall and climbed the stairs, each one taller than the one before. She knew she should check on Engracia, even though she wanted to hide until the nightmare ended.

Looking around for Felipe, she tapped on Engracia's door, hoping he wouldn't open it and ogle her, now that her protectors were gone.

The room was silent. No Felipe. *Coward*, she thought, with all the scorn her tired brain could muster. *You have already found a good hiding place*.

"Ana? Ana? Please be Ana!"

"I'm here, Engracia. May I get you some breakfast?"

She came closer to the bed, then stopped, horrified, to see Engracia clutching at the bed curtain, her eyes wide with terror.

"Thank God! I thought everyone had run away," Engracia gasped. She grabbed Hanneke's hand. "Get Juana." Her breathing became labored. She panted and groaned, clutching her distended belly.

This, too? God spare us.

There was nowhere to run. Nowhere to hide. She thought of Manolo's bravery, Santiago's courage, and stalwart Antonio, felt shame, and took a deep breath. Hans Aardema had schemed and planned. Nothing could change that either. The time to blame and whine was long past. She was Santiago Gonzalez's wife, with the fate of many in her hands. At that moment, she realized that Santiago had no more choice in what he did than she.

She took a deep breath and remembered Pablo's calm acceptance of whatever life threw at him. "Dear Father in Heaven, make me equal to this small moment in Thine eyes," she said softly, as she knelt by Engracia, running her hand over her sister-in-law's arm. "All will be well, dear sister," she said. "I'll have Juana here in a moment. Don't worry. I am here."

Chapter Twenty-eight

Keeping a rein on her growing unease, Hanneke found Juana in the graveyard behind the chapel, staring down at the graves of Santiago's parents, Rodrigo and Liria. As much as she wanted to pluck at the servant's sleeve like an impatient child, she also knew better than to make demands of someone who hated Santiago. She remained silent.

Juana must have sensed her presence. She turned around, nodded to Hanneke and looked back at the two graves. "What is happening reminds me of another time, one I try not to think about." Her expression hardened. "But which I must think about, every time I see your husband."

"Santiago couldn't have been more than two or three," Hanneke said, not willing for the vindictive woman to scold a man doing his best to defend this place. *How can you blame a child like you do?* she wanted to ask, but knew this wasn't the time. "Engracia is in labor and I don't know what to do."

Juana stared at her then hurried away. *I should follow,* Hanneke thought, but knelt by Fermina's grave. *I would have loved you. Come to think of it, I already did.*

Father Bendicio intercepted her as she hurried beside the church. "Wait! Wait!"

Santiago was right about the animals. The noise of unhappy cows and sheep deafened her. *The Almohades don't have to sneak up on us,* she thought, as she shivered and waited for Father Bendicio. *We would never hear their loudest war cries over this din.*

She watched him pick his way through steaming cow piles, bracing herself for the worst. She knew that expression.

"Must these peasants camp in my church? Babies are making water all over the floor."

"Where would you have them go, Father?" she asked, raising her voice to be heard over a flock of sheep that thundered past, followed by a small boy with a stick. "The great hall?"

"No, wife of Santiago. You will need that for the wounded."

She turned and stared into the face of a woman no taller than she was, older by many years, bent nearly double.

"I hadn't thought of that," Hanneke admitted, happy to turn her attention from Father Bendicio, who fumed almost visibly.

"You have not been here when the men return. Save your hall for them."

"Thank you for good advice," Hanneke said. Was Father Bendicio worth placating? Why not? "Father, we can clean the chapel when the emergency passes."

"But, Ana, the Lord's house?" Father Bendicio could sound so plaintive, as if he was the only one in the world with challenges, while all around her loomed bigger problems.

Santiago, is this what leadership is like? I don't care for it, she thought. Temper, temper. She folded her hands at her waist, trying to look dignified. "Father, was He not a child once? Our Savior will understand."

The old woman chortled as the priest stalked past, then spit in the snow after him. "Worthless *fulano*," she grumbled, and backed away.

Hanneke stopped her. "V*ieja*, do not leave me now. I know nothing."

The woman squinted at her. "How old are you, *dama*?"

"Seventeen." It even sounded young to Hanneke, and she flinched.

"How could Santiago leave a baby in charge?"

"My husband had no choice. Please help me."

The old woman's eyes brightened. "You would take advice from me?"

"Only good advice." She smiled, despite her turmoil. "You certainly put Father Bendicio in his place."

"Child's play! I am almost ashamed I did it." The old woman took her hand. "Tell the children to spread hay and straw in the great hall."

"Very well. Why?"

"To absorb the blood."

Hanneke did not waste a moment. While children spread hay on the stone floor, she ran upstairs to Engracia and Juana. She stood there, hands clasped tight, as Engracia groaned through a contraction.

When Engracia relaxed, Hanneke touched her face. "I'm sorry I could not come sooner. There is so much to do."

No reply. Hanneke looked closer, startled by the coldness of Engracia's expression. "What?"

"How could you allow Santiago to drag Manolo away?"

Hanneke reeled back as though someone had shoved her. "You have that wrong!"

"I do not! Manolo would never leave me, not at a time like this. Juana said…"

Hanneke stared at Juana. She spoke to Engracia, but her gaze did not waver from the servant's face. "Juana knows nothing. Manolo *ordered* Santiago to take him. I was there. I heard him. If you don't believe me, ask any of the soldiers."

"Why would he do that to me? Is he a brother before he is a husband?"

Certainly he is, she wanted to say. *Everything comes before women. Don't you know that, you ninny?* She settled on, "The need is so great, Engracia. Please understand."

"I will never understand," Engracia managed to gasp, before another contraction battered her.

Hanneke gave Juana a measuring look, then left the room, angry with the servant, angry with herself, frightened. She wanted to go into Santiago's room and bolt the door. Instead, she walked down the stairs in time for Luis to start up the stairs and tell her that the gates were closing. They were locked in.

The snow had turned to sleet, then back into snow. Mindful of her footing, she crossed to the kitchen and ate bread and cheese that the cook bullied her to take.

She sat close to the fire and listened to Cook rage on about the inconvenience of war. A one-legged man, he pounded the bread dough with his fists as though it were the Almohades, then slammed it in pans to rise.

"Cook, how far away is this plain Santiago spoke of?"

"A morning's hard ride." Cook sat down. He looked at his wooden leg. "I used to be a soldier." He gazed past her into that distance she could not see. "They have met the enemy by now."

She tried not to appear frightened. At least she kept her mouth closed so she did not speak and remove all doubt. Cook smiled at her, exposing missing teeth. "Now we wait, *dama*."

"I need something to do," she said simply.

"Take this bread and cheese to those on the parapet," he said, and handed her a cloth bag. "You can climb ladders better than me."

Bag slung about her neck, draping her skirt over her arm, she clambered up the ladder, thankful that there were no heads on spikes, not after that awful morning of the shepherds' heads. One-armed Luis took the sack, setting it down as he continued to stare south.

"He told me to make sure you did not climb up here," he said, moving over to make room.

"Santiago?"

"Antonio. But here you are. I am honored."

She smiled at his incongruous courtliness, a Castilian trait she found endearing. "Tell me…Luis, is it? What do you see now?"

"Look for yourself."

He pointed south, where their valley funneled into another pass. She squinted, then rubbed her eyes. She leaned closer. "Two riders? That's all?"

"They will be a while," Luis said. Go back down. I will call you."

"No."

The armorer sighed. "He said you were stubborn."

"Antonio?"

"Santiago."

Luis called down for a blanket and a woman threw one up to him. He draped it around Hanneke's shoulders and the two of them leaned on the parapet's ledge. No conversationalist, Luis watched her out of the corner of his eye, as if measuring her. Everyone at Las Claves did that, so she paid no mind.

"Not our men," he said much later. "God damn." The wind seemed to blow colder at his words.

Silence again, until the two figures appeared at the edge of the now-deserted village of Las Claves. Luis grunted and spit over the parapet. "Jewish peddlers. God smite them."

Hanneke inched her way along the ice ledge back to the ladder. "They must be allowed to enter," she said to Luis as she started down.

"No!"

"What do you mean?"

He came closer with such a light in his eyes that she wondered if he was going to throw her from the ladder. "Santiago told us not to open the gates to anyone. You heard him. They could be spies. You cannot trust a Jew."

"They might have something to tell us. Suppose Santiago could not spare anyone with a message?" She continued down the ladder, fired up, angry. "Listen to me." She snapped off each word, liking the staccato of Castilian as never before. "He left me in charge and I am opening the gate."

"The consequence is on your head."

"It was from the moment everyone rode away this morning."

Hanneke stood by the gate when two peddlers rode in. "Welcome to Las Claves, *señores*," she said, extending her hands, then putting them together, petitioning them. "What can you tell us?"

The older man dismounted with a groan, as if he had not left the saddle for hours. "We did not expect the gates to open for us. We hoped, though. Jews always hope. "Moises Abravanal greets you, and my son Baruch."

"Come inside. If the gates don't shut quickly, that one-armed man on the parapet will spit on us."

Moises stepped forward quickly, belying his age. He looked around at the crowded courtyard. "We will not stay long." He gave her a look containing equal measures of sympathy and paternal advice. "You should not stay long either."

Hanneke knew she was cold. His words made her shiver in her heart. *Then the worst has happened*, she thought. *But I am the mistress of Las Claves now, as well as small things.* "Tell me all in the kitchen. Someone please grain these horses."

She dismissed the cook and handed the peddlers more bread and cheese. Moises shook his head at the sausage, but took a boiled egg. With impatience barely contained, she let them take the edge off their hunger, then sat down.

"I am Hanneke Gonzalez," she began, "Santiago's wife from the Netherlands."

"We have heard of you," Moises said. "All good, from Raquel Levi of Toledo."

Toledo seemed so calm, so safe. For one moment, Hanneke wanted to beg them to take her to Raquel.

Instead, she watched their eyes, certain they did not want to tell her what they knew. "We have to know, *señor*, so we can plan."

Moises did not hesitate. "We saw the armies from a distance around midday, *señora*. We dared not go closer to the fighting."

Hanneke let out her breath. "Did you...did you stay long enough to see..." She looked down at her hands. "I fear to ask you."

Moises Abravanal touched her hand lightly. "We did not see how they could win. They are vastly outnumbered."

She felt a sudden lift to her heart, relieved to know something, anything, proud of her brave men. "They knew that when they rode out before dawn."

"I am sorry, *señora*."

"Do you think...will my husband be here soon?"

Moises stood up and nodded to his son, who rose also, pulling on his cloak. "Those who are alive, if they can make it. I wish I bore good news."

She walked with them in silence to the open gate, standing close as the old peddler mounted. She looked toward the pass to the north, and suddenly knew what to ask.

"*Señor* Abravanal, please do this: get a message to Don Ruy Díaz of the Knights of Calatrava. Tell him we have dire need of him."

"I will. Farewell, and God keep you all."

Chapter Twenty-nine

Hanneke longed to run after the peddlers, begging them to take her along. "Help me," she whispered into the closed gate.

What kind of warrior would you say I am, Santiago – or you, Antonio – if you could see me now? she asked herself. She looked around at the animals and people in the courtyard, every one of them looking to her for guidance. They were her responsibility.

"When he gets back, you should slap your husband's head."

She looked around, startled, to see the old woman who had told her to spread straw and hay in the great hall. "I believe I will," she said, and felt better.

She knew she should go to Engracia, but her sister-in-law was only one person, and the courtyard contained many. Better to attempt to look like someone mature and reliable, even if she was far less capable than these hardy settlers along the *frontera* between Christian Spain and disaster.

Someone – perhaps it was the old woman – handed her a wonderful scrap of blanket, or perhaps a cloak that had seen better days. She wrapped it around her and climbed to the parapet again, where Luis stood. He pointed. She gasped to see the distant passage dark with the passage of horses and men.

"Why didn't you say something?" she asked.

"I don't know if they are ours or El Ghalib's." He shrugged. "If it is El Ghalib, it is already too late."

What could she say to that?

"*Dama*, even if it is Santiago, I will wait a moment more to see if they are being followed."

Dark began to settle over the land, the early dark of December, that wonderful time of year when no one in the Low Countries had anyone more on the brain than the coming of Christ's Mass, and feasting with *banketstaff*, pastry stuffed with almond paste, and *bischopswijn*, dark red wine, hot and flavored with oranges. There would be venison roasting and potatoes. She tried to remember when she had last eaten.

Here she was on the Castilian frontier, trying to see into the dark if anyone was alive from the little party that rode out this morning. She shivered in her scrap of a cloak, more from fear than cold. Luis might think she was brave; she knew she wasn't.

"No one is following them," Luis said finally, his voice full of relief. "Open the gates," he called down, then nodded to Hanneke. "Let us go down and see how bad things are."

"Should some of us ride out to meet them?" she asked.

"He said you would try to do that," Luis told her.

"Santiago?"

"Both of them," Luis said. "I promised them you would not."

Luis's promise didn't extend to her waiting beside the open gates as weary and wounded men rode slowly through them, some of them – the lucky ones lightly wounded – taken forcibly from their saddles by wives and mothers, scolded and led away. Other silent soldiers were wept over and taken, covered, to a quiet corner of the courtyard. Others, more dead than alive, were reached for gently, and taken into the great hall.

She saw the men of the shadows, the nearly spectral soldiers who had followed her husband into Las Claves only days ago. She had feared them then; now she saw them as they were, young soldiers with wide-eyed stares and gaping wounds that almost made her turn away.

One of them held out his hand to her and she grasped it, wondering why she had been afraid of them. *Why did I not notice how young you are?* she asked herself. With one-armed Luis's assistance, she helped him from his horse, then handed him over to a stout woman who half-dragged him toward the great hall.

But where… "Ana? Ana?"

She sighed with relief to hear Santiago, but it wasn't Santiago. She peered closer, reached up to clutch Santiago's gauntleted hand, but saw Manolo in front of her husband, his head sagging forward.

"*Gross got*, is he dead?" she asked. "Please no."

"He is wounded. Nearly everyone is wounded. Luis, is that you?"

"*Sí, señor, a su servicio.*"

"Get another to help me with Manolo. Find a horse and ride back to the pass. Tell Antonio and the others to stay as long as they dare, then ride fast."

"Master, may I stay there, too?"

"Please."

With a grunt of satisfaction, the one-armed man grabbed a slightly wounded soldier. The two of them managed to get Manolo from Santiago, who dismounted, then carried his brother toward the great hall. Santiago fell to his knees once, and others rushed to help.

She leaned close to her husband, wanting to tell him something – that she loved him, how worried she was, that Engracia was in labor – but unsure what to say. She looked deep into tired eyes and saw defeat. "Oh, Santiago," she whispered.

"Help me in the hall, then ... no. Engracia should not see him." He looked over her shoulder. "First help Luis mount."

She turned at his command, but Luis was already in the saddle. She wanted to remind Luis that he only had one arm, and to be careful. *He will think you silly,* she thought, then said it anyway, because they were stalwarts on the parapet who had watched together.

"Don't do anything rash," she concluded, which made him laugh. "I mean it! I would ride with you if I could," she added.

"They both said that about you," he told her, as he nodded to her and spurred his horse into darkness and death.

"Go with God," she whispered.

She stood a moment in the courtyard, watching as less-wounded soldiers took their dead comrades to the bath house, where they could be stripped, washed and shrouded for the long sleep. She turned at the sound of the gates closing. There would be no time to tend to the dead, not with El Ghalib out there.

All around her she saw need. She also saw women and older children helping the wounded inside, bringing food, finding blankets, pleading for Father Bendicio because it was nearly too late. The priest walked among them, his hand making the sign of the cross over and over.

The wounded in the great hall were strangely silent. Hanneke breathed in the terrible odor of blood, unwashed bodies, bowels, and something else that must be fear. Santiago laid Manolo down close to the fireplace and sat beside him.

"Husband, can you not take him to his room?" she begged.

He shook his head. "Ana, he is dying. I don't know what to tell Engracia."

"We daren't say anything," Hanneke said. "She's in labor."

He did something then that shocked her and delighted her heart. Amid the noise, the odors, the groans, he pulled her down and held her on his lap. A look and a word, and one of his soldiers drew Santiago's cape around them both. For a few blessed moments, silence enveloped them.

With a sigh of her own, Hanneke burrowed close to her husband. He told her quickly of the battle. "We wounded many of them and began a careful retreat. Here we are. Whether they come after us, I do not know."

"Doesn't matter," she whispered back, not wanting to leave their dark cocoon, that space for the two of them. "We're together and I like this."

He chuckled. "I have turned you into a woman of low expectations," he said. "Alas, we must move." Neither of them stirred. "I mean it." Still nothing. "Would anyone miss us if we just stayed like this?" he asked her finally.

"Eventually."

She heard Manolo stir, and groan, calling for his brother, and the idyll ended. The cloak came off, and Santiago leaned close to speak in Manolo's ear. "Ana tells me that Engracia is in labor."

"She doesn't need to see me this way."

His voice was barely a whisper. *Poor, poor Manolo*, Hanneke thought. *Why couldn't you have stayed here?*

"Santiago, forgive me," Manolo was saying. "I wanted to fight this once."

"You did, my brother, most valiantly. Let me send Ana upstairs to see if your baby is born."

"Yes, yes, before…"

…it's too late, she finished in her heart. She stood up. "I will bring your baby to you, dear brother."

"Lie. Tell Engracia I am busy," Manolo managed to say. "Don't tell her…"

…you are busy dying. She started for the stairs, picking her way among the wounded. She stopped at the foot of the stairs where Carlos sat, holding his hand to a great wound on his face. The blood had frozen on his face, and the patch was gone from his missing eye. She shuddered but did not look away, because Carlos was good to her.

"Carlos, have you a woman to help you?"

He shook his head. "Claudia is long gone. Who else would help this ugly man?"

"I would, but I am married," she teased gently, which made him try to smile, a ghastly endeavor. "Lie down. I will return."

She looked back as Manolo cried out when Santiago removed his brother's doublet, the leather front coming away with a great sucking sound. Father Bendicio ran over and stared down, aghast at what he saw. She hurried up the stairs, praying that Engracia had delivered the baby.

She stopped at the top of the stairs, then looked down at the misery below, an army defeated. Ringing through her mind were King Alfonso's words to her of a great winnowing that was no respecter of persons, indiscriminate in whom it harvested, as they attempted to reconquer Spain from an enemy entrenched for five hundred years.

"Are we *all* being winnowed here?" she asked no one.

She opened the door, relieved to hear a baby's cry. She thought of her own recent misadventure and touched her great emptiness. She had been the only one to cry then. This was better; Manolo's child lived.

Engracia lay curled around a little one with light hair still wet from birth. Juana and another woman clucked around her, tidying and soothing. Juana looked up and her face hardened. She took Hanneke by the arm and led her to a corner, giving her a shake for good measure.

"The army is back? Can you tear Manolo away from his precious brother and the soldiers to come here and meet his son?"

"Manolo is dying. The army was defeated," Hanneke said as calmly as she could, when she wanted to slap Juana.

The servant paled. "Then you must tell Engracia. I cannot."

"Manolo told me to lie to her and take the baby downstairs so he can see his son before he dies," Hanneke said, never taking her eyes from Juana. "Say nothing."

She brushed past the servant and sat on the edge of Engracia's bed, leaning forward to admire the tiny morsel in his mother's arms. "Engracia, he is wonderful."

"Where is Manolo? I want him here."

"Dearest, the army is back, and all did not go precisely well," Hanneke said, amazed at her own duplicity. "Manolo would come, but they are so concerned about the wounded – you know, there are always a few of them." She held out her arms. "Let me take your little one to Manolo. He wants to see you, too, but there is much to do at present. He will come as soon as he can."

Engracia nodded. "Very well. When I feel a little better, perhaps I can go downstairs to him and we can discuss names. I know the stairs are hard for him."

"Bless you, Engracia." Hanneke kissed her sister-in-law. *God forgive me for my lies.* "I'll bring him right back. I promise."

Juana's helper wrapped the infant – asleep now– in the blanket Hanneke embroidered in earlier, better days. She forced herself to walk slowly and carefully from the room, when she really wanted to dash down the stairs and hope she was in time for a dying father to see his child and heir to Las Claves.

The great hall reeked of death and that intangible odor she knew was the bitterness of defeat. She saw blood everywhere, soaking into the hay – *thank you again, old woman.*

Carlos lay in the hay, but a woman knelt beside him, wiping his face, scolding him gently, the way women do, who care. Hanneke saw a dead man beside her, and knew somehow that it was her son. "Bless you for tending this man, even in your hour of need," she said softly. "Bless you."

Manolo lay in Santiago's lap, raised up because breathing had become one long gasp. She knelt beside him and took his boneless hand.

"Engracia?" he managed, after several moments of gulping and swallowing his own blood.

"Manolo, here is your son," she said, speaking distinctly, unsure of how much he could hear. She held the baby out to Santiago, who had wrapped his arms around his brother.

Santiago held the infant close to his brother's battered chest. Manolo looked, his eyes going in and out of focus. He tried to raise his hand to touch his son, but he was too weak. Hanneke placed his hand on the child.

"Better," he murmured, his voice drowsy, but full of an emotion so close to contentment that she didn't try to stop her tears. He opened his eyes with the look of a man who wants to sleep, but knows he must be polite to his guests.

"A name, brother, a name," Santiago said. Hanneke saw tears filling his eyes and making a path through the dirt and blood on his face.

Manolo moved his finger across his son's cheek. "Rodrigo."

"Our father? But…"

"Rodrigo," Manolo said more firmly, almost sounding like Manolo of mere hours ago. "Promise."

"I promise."

Manolo turned his attention to his son at the same time the dam in his lungs broke loose and blood poured from his mouth. Santiago quickly lifted his nephew off Manolo's chest and held out the baby to Hanneke.

Manolo coughed, trying to clear his throat as the blood ran from his nose, too. He opened his eyes wide in terror and reached for Santiago, who held him close as he died.

Chapter Thirty

antiago lowered his brother to the blood-drenched hay. Not looking away from Manolo, he reached up and fingered the infant's wet hair. "Some would say I have now killed him twice," he said. "Once twenty-two years ago, and again tonight. Will it be enough, Ana?"

"You can't blame yourself," she said as she cuddled Rodrigo, breathing deep of his newborn fragrance. The gentle odor calmed her.

"Others will. I will take Rodrigo back to his mother. I will tell Engracia that her husband is dead." He shuddered and Hanneke put her arm around him.

"Let me come with you."

"No."

"Please, my love."

He looked up from his contemplation of Manolo. "Say that again."

"Please," she teased, which made him smile.

"Do you love me?" he asked.

Did she? She chose her words most carefully. In all the noise, tumult and raw emotion since the army's defeat, she decided to claim a little corner of peace for her husband, for herself. Whether they had years ahead or hours, she decided not to waste a moment. Their beginning had been something to forget, but it was only a beginning. She was married. She was here. She had saved his life at the river. Was he perfect? Who was?

In that moment, Hanneke Aardema Gonzalez forgave this man of the sin of being human, because she knew he was sublimely worth it. She also knew he had no more choice in the matter of their marriage than he did. The knowledge liberated her and gave her serenity, even in the middle of carnage and chaos.

"Love you? I know I do," she said, feeling oddly shy. "You speak to me of time later on, when the land to the south is conquered, but what about right now? I love you – I choose to love you – right now." She tucked her arm through his. "I am coming upstairs with you."

"It won't be good, I assure you," he said.

"I know that, my love. Why must you face it alone?"

"Come, then."

"One moment. Do you love *me*, Santiago?"

"I know I do," he echoed with no hesitation, and a half smile. She handed him the baby.

They walked upstairs in silence. Hanneke opened the door to Engracia's room. She walked beside her husband to the bed and knelt beside him. He laid Rodrigo in Engracia's arms, then quietly told her what happened.

Engracia stared at him, disbelieving, as her face turned to stone. In silence, she turned away from him. "I will never look upon you again," she whispered.

"As you wish, dear sister," he replied. "Only know that I will protect Las Claves with my last breath so Rodrigo will inherit."

"Liar," she said in that stone cold voice.

He flinched and Hanneke took his arm. He helped her to her feet and glanced at Juana. "Get her and Rodrigo ready to ride."

"She can't possibly ride," Juana snapped as she grabbed the baby from Engracia. "What are you saying?"

"I am telling you we have been defeated. One of my men will carry her. If Engracia remains, she will be captured. I will not pay a ransom, not if she willfully goes against sound advice."

Engracia began to weep. When Hanneke touched her shoulder, she shook off the friendly hand. "You are as evil as your husband. Leave me alone."

Hand in hand, without a backward glance, they left the room of mourning and spite. He walked Hanneke to their room, then stopped.

"Ana, in all this turmoil, I forgot about Felipe Palacios. Where in God's name *is* he?"

"I haven't seen him. He did as you thought he would – found a place to hide."

He looked around, indecisive. "I want to find him. I have questions now. Do you suppose he will magically appear when the choice comes to leave Las Claves or endure El Ghalib?"

"Perhaps," she said.

He leaned against the door, quiet and thoughtful. His silence was interrupted by shouts of "Antonio is here!" then "Santiago! Santiago!"

"There is no time to think." He held her close for a too-brief moment, then ushered her into their room. "I hope I do not regret... damn Felipe anyway. Dress warmly. Take only the necessities. I will go below, but please remain here until I call for you."

"I would rather be with you."

He started to reply, but Antonio, wrapped tight against the cold, started up the stairs, calling for him.

"What news?" Santiago demanded, as he ran down the stairs.

I'm not staying here, Hanneke thought, and hurried after him. Santiago turned around in exasperation, then managed a rueful smile. "Do you never listen to anyone? You can't fight this battle."

"She already has," Luis said at the foot of the stairs. "She didn't listen to me and opened the gates to Jewish peddlers."

"Ana, after I specifically told you..."

"What's more, she sent them on with a plea for help to the Knights of Calatrava," the one-armed man said. "She might be our salvation."

"How much time do we have, Antonio?"

"An hour at best. This gives us time to make the northern pass," Antonio replied. "We ten held them off as long as we could." He sighed. "Now we are five."

"Pablo?" Hanneke asked in sudden fear. "Please, please."

Antonio indicated with his head. She saw her faithful knight of the pots and pans squatting on his haunches by Carlos. "He was brave, and here he is." He returned his attention to Santiago. "Know this: Our little army mauled them, back on the plain. They are moving slowly."

Santiago pulled Hanneke to him and glanced around the hall at the wounded men. She saw Carlos with a bandage on his face, courtesy of the woman with the dead son. Other women, those with living husbands or sons, watched Santiago warily.

"I don't understand," she said. "Why are they looking at you that way? It's as if they fear you."

"They do. I hate this," he said softly. "Please go upstairs."

"No. I can help."

"You cannot." He held her off with hands on her shoulders. "You might not understand this. You will be my witness, if you will not leave."

His face impassive, he walked to the center of the now-silent hall. Even Father Bendicio stopped his prayers. Hanneke tried to follow Santiago, but Antonio pulled her back.

"This is a harsh thing, Ana," he said, keeping his voice low in the now-awful stillness. "We either stay and die or we run and fight another day."

"I don't understand."

"You will. Stay here. I mean it."

She retreated to the stairs and sat down. Santiago raised his hand. He took a deep breath and broke her heart.

"People of Las Claves, I cannot protect you any longer. We have lost. You men who can ride, find your mounts. Women, take your men who can walk, and your children. We will finish in here. Go now."

"Finish in here. What does he mean? Antonio?"

Antonio was already helping Carlos to his feet, directing Pablo to move him away from the hall. Hanneke braced herself against the wailing and clamor she knew would follow Santiago's words, but there was only silence. She watched as women and children sprang into action, prodding wounded men to their feet. They struggled toward the door of the great hall, urging and cajoling.

A few remained, tugging at their men, pleading with those who could not rise. Hanneke stood up to help, but Antonio held up his hand to stop her.

"Go upstairs, Ana," he ordered, his voice both urgent and adamant. "Put on your warmest clothing, but don't bother with anything else. Your mule will be ready in the courtyard."

She tried to reason with him. "These women need help. Can't you see that?" She looked over his shoulder to see these remaining women in tears, tugging at men who could not move. "Antonio, why are you stopping me?"

He startled her, grabbing her close to his body, as if to shield her from every bad thing. More gently than she would have imagined, he put his hand to her head and rested it against his chest. He whispered, "Ana, Ana, please. We can do no more for these men, and we will not leave them to be tortured."

"I don't understand!" she sobbed.

"You do. They cannot ride. If we leave them still alive, El Ghalib and his men will do terrible things to them." She felt his sigh. "I have seen what they can do. So have you."

She raised her head, not leaving the comfort of his arms, to watch Father Bendicio administer what she knew was Extreme Unction, not over one man, but over the remaining men. A woman tried to push him away, then screamed as another woman ran into the hall and dragged her away.

Clutching Antonio, Hanneke watched Santiago take out his knife and kneel by the dying man. He made the sign of the cross on the man's forehead, then slit his throat in one practiced stroke.

Antonio covered her eyes. "I must help Santiago. Go upstairs and do not look back."

She wiped her runny nose on her sleeve. "Is this day going to end?"

"They all do, eventually. Go, little one. You have already done more good here than you can possibly imagine."

She walked up the stairs as Santiago and Antonio killed the men too wounded to move. She heard the weeping, begging women, and knew she would hear them every time she closed her eyes.

Numb, she found a warmer dress and put it on, lacing it tight, then pulled on another one, and more hose. There was nothing more she wanted in the room. Her hand went to El Ghalib's gold necklace and she almost took it off, wanting nothing more to do with someone so terrible.

She jumped at screams coming from Engracia's room, but she was in no mood to cajole her sister-in-law or suffer Juana's paltry meanness. She couldn't go downstairs. She resigned herself to the inevitable and went to Engracia, finding her struggling to sit up, her eyes wide with terror.

"He will not leave me behind, will he?" she asked Hanneke.

Hanneke reeled back as if she had been slapped. "No! Never."

"Why not? It would be so easy for him to kill me and dispose of my baby. Las Claves would be his."

"Gracia, Gracia, I'm here to keep you and your child safe from Santiago Gonzalez."

Hanneke gasped as Felipe Palacios brushed past her, looking as tidy and clean as if he had come from the king's own tailor. "What are you saying?" she demanded. "Where have you been hiding?"

Felipe barely glanced at her. "Santiago Gonzalez will do anything to get

Las Claves for himself. He even married a fisherman's daughter for ready cash. I'll protect your interests, sister."

"How dare you even suggest such a thing," Hanneke said, appalled.

He sniffed. "At least you don't smell of herring."

There was so much Hanneke wanted to say, but the brave woman inside her counseled against wasted words, not with time at such a premium. She settled for, "Someone will smite you someday," in the language of the Netherlands.

She left the room without a backward glance and walked down the stairs, preferring the company of death.

Chapter Thirty-one

Hanneke did not hesitate in the great hall. One woman – a young girl, really – her belly big with child, tugged at her husband's corpse, pleading with him. His throat had been cut and his head had collapsed into his neck, but still she tried to lift him, stopping only to gasp for breath, and look around for help.

Hanneke did not hesitate. She grasped the dead man under his arms. "My sister," she began, her voice calm, "where should we take him?"

The girl stared at her, then sank to her knees, the spell of death broken. Hanneke lowered the body to the straw again and knelt beside the woman, who threw herself across her husband's body.

"Please help us," Hanneke begged of two soldiers who could walk, standing in the doorway. "Please help her outside. Find out if she has people here."

One of the men limped toward her. "I know her family. We will help her."

She remained by the body as one of the soldiers picked up the woman and carried her from the hall. Hanneke wanted to rise, but she felt the same exhaustion that had claimed her in the early days after her miscarriage. *When did I last sleep*, she asked herself, as she stared at the dead man.

Santiago squatted beside her and she leaned against him. "Is it done?" she asked.

"It is done. Now we must leave. Most of the villagers have already started for the pass," he said. He sat down and held her close.

She hated to burden him further. "Felipe is upstairs, convincing Engracia that he will protect her from you, who would leave her behind, kill her child and claim Las Claves for yourself."

"I wish I could say that surprised me," he said. "I have been thinking about Felipe in a different light, not very appealing. I think I know why he is here."

She started to speak, but he put bloody fingers to her lips. "Don't think this impossible, but he might be in league with El Ghalib." He searched her face. "Ah, you see that possibility, too?"

She nodded.

"Felipe knew our numbers here," Santiago said. "He must know the dowry terms. If I die in battle..."

"Please don't say that!" she begged

"Hush, hush, chiquita," he said, after a quick kiss. "If I die, who will rush in to marry you for that dowry? Felipe Palacios. Avoid the man, my love. I know he will never persuade you, but he could force you."

Could he be right? She touched his face, noting where the winter sun had scoured it. "We can have this discussion over a campfire tonight," she said, hopeful. She saw Engracia carried by Felipe, coming down the stairs, Juana with Rodrigo in her arms.

Santiago jumped to his feet. "No!" he shouted. "Anyone but Juana should be carrying Manolo's child."

Hanneke rose slowly, seeing the anguish on her husband's face. Was this how it was, all those years ago, when a baby was abandoned that Juana confused with another? When they reached the bottom of the stairs, she stepped between her husband and Juana.

"Husband, please." She spoke calmly, her hand against his chest.

"I will not allow her to carry Manolo's son in a retreat." His voice shook with more intensity than she could remember, even more than in the clearing with Jawhara.

Funny that she should mention Jawhara, with Felipe standing before her, his face bland. *What is your connection with El Ghalib? Good God, is Santiago right?* she asked herself, appalled. *I fear you far more than Juana carrying Manolo's baby.*

"My love, are you afraid that she will leave him, as Manolo was left, as you should have been?" Hanneke stood her ground. "Let's have this out right now."

Everyone else in the great hall hurried to gather up possessions, or wandered aimlessly, wondering what to do. They stood by the stairs, no one moving.

To her relief, Santiago took her hand. "My love, that is what I fear," he said, speaking only to her. "I have enough on my conscience. Not this, too."

He kissed her hand and she moved closer. "Then let it end here. Juana, will you protect the son of Manuel Gonzalez?"

"With my life," the servant declared.

"Please, husband," Hanneke said. "For your peace of mind, please."

"Very well," he said, after a long pause.

Hanneke turned to Juana. "You heard him. Now I exact a condition from you."

"Señora Gonzalez, you are wasting time," Felipe Palacios said.

"Be quiet," she snapped. "Juana?"

"Yes," Juana said, her voice louder. Whatever contrition she had felt seemed to retreat.

Hanneke took Santiago's bloody dagger from its sheath and pointed it at the servant, as Felipe gasped and took a step back, away from trouble, always away. "If you ever again speak ill of my husband, I will cut out your tongue. Do not think for a moment that I cannot." She looked around the hall of dead men. "I have been learning from masters and I will cut out your tongue if you utter any more evil."

"Bravo," Antonio said. "Bravo."

"Well?"

"I promise."

Trust no one, she thought, and glanced at Santiago. The look on his face told her he was thinking exactly the same thing. She leaned close to him. "I trust you alone," she whispered.

"And I, you."

"Let us ride," he said in a loud voice. "We haven't long."

He led her away from the others, his arm around her, then both arms, then she was as close to him as was humanly possible, fully clothed and standing in a drafty hall with dead people. "Whatever happens today, you can trust Antonio and Carlos." He looked at Felipe, nearly out the door now with Engracia in his arms. "I would not ever be alone in the same room with him, were I you."

"But you will be my great defender," she reminded him. "Won't you?" she added, when he was silent.

"Always," he said, but not quickly enough to calm the fear rising in her heart.

"Santiago…"

"We're wasting time."

Arm in arm, they walked to the open door. Pablo still scurried about the room, blowing out lamps and candles. He paused to straighten one of the bodies, folding the arms, lining up the head.

"Making all tidy, Pablo?" Santiago asked.

"Si, señor. Who knows when we will return?"

"Who indeed," Antonio said, joining them. He looked around the hall one last time. "We've drunk much wine and told innumerable lies in here, haven't we, Santiago?"

"That we have."

Crammed all day with people and livestock, the courtyard was empty, except for the few remaining soldiers. Santiago helped Carlos to his mount. Hanneke watched as he handed a folded piece of paper to the old soldier. "But I don't read," she heard, and Santiago's answering, "Get it to Antonio later. Promise me."

Santiago motioned Hanneke closer. "There wasn't time to find the sidesaddle, so ride your mule astride," he said, and started to lift her up.

She clung to him instead. "Kiss me," she whispered.

"In front of all these people?" he teased, or maybe he wasn't teasing. She knew how reserved Castilian men could be. As she stood in her husband's arms, she knew she had learned great lessons since the boat docked at Santander, principle among them that it was possible to fall in love with someone doubtful.

He kissed her, and all doubts fled. He kissed her again, and a third time, as if his need was as great as hers. He stepped back, took a long look at her, which made her wonder if he was memorizing her face.

"Up you get," he said, and lifted her into the saddle. "Ride beside Carlos, if you will. I'm worried about him."

She nodded. "You'll be at the head with Engracia?"

"Not this time. Antonio is leading the soldiers." He looked south through the open gates. "I'll make up the rear with a few choice men."

"Don't," she said. "Please don't."

He tugged on her booted foot. "I will see you when we are through the pass, Señora Gonzalez! Someday we will have another daughter and name her Liria after my mother."

He mounted his gray horse and made his way to Antonio, leaning close so as not to be heard. She watched Antonio's head go back in surprise, and then glance at her. Santiago shook Antonio's arm and demanded his attention. She couldn't hear him, but she knew this was no ordinary conversation.

And she worried. After another long look at her, Antonio nodded, and turned toward the head of the little battered army. Santiago went back into the great hall and came out with Manolo's body, which had been stitched into one of the Moorish battle flags. Engracia whimpered.

"I will not leave him for El Ghalib, sister," he said. "He comes with me."

He heaved the corpse onto the back of his horse and tied it down. Hanneke looked back to see Luis and Cook joining him in the rear, along with three of the new soldiers he had recruited through the length and breadth of the peninsula, promising them land to the south after victory.

There was no victory here. Luis asked if they should close the gates. "No!" Santiago shouted, loud enough for them all to hear. "I do not want El Ghalib to imagine for even one moment that he is getting something of value. It is a small measure of my contempt for him. Let us ride!"

Hanneke pulled the hood of her cloak tight around her face as the sleet bit into it. She wished she had remembered gloves, but there was no turning back to a fortress turned charnel house. Father Bendicio rode beside her, his black hood drawn so low over his face that he looked like a figure from a nightmare. She wondered how he was faring. She had not heard him speak for so long, except to hurry through Extreme Unction and then stand back as Santiago and Antonio murdered his parishioners out of kindness.

The army rode alone on the plain, traveling north toward the pass obscured by sleet. The villagers had fled with great speed, abandoning many of their possessions until the ground was littered with belongings that must have seemed indispensable only that morning. *How little things really matter*, Hanneke thought, as she passed barrels of clothing, broken goblets, bits of old armor, a mirror.

Animals were left behind in the headlong flight to the distant pass. Chickens roosted on discarded furniture, their heads tucked under their wings. A cat swung along steadily, a kitten dangling from her mouth. Pablo slid off his mule and picked up the pair, stuffing them in his doublet and flashing her a smile.

Hanneke looked back. There was no moon, but she fancied she could see an army moving toward Las Claves. She told herself she was imaging things, even as she watched Santiago drop back with his little force. They dismounted and waited there in the snow, walking around to keep warm, but always facing south.

She could barely see Antonio ahead, leading the remaining troops. She wanted to ride closer, but here were Father Bendicio and Pablo.

"Father?" she called, "Father?"

No answer. *We're all so tired*, she thought. *So tired.* Behind her Santiago grew smaller and smaller as she rode north to the pass she had entered in the height of summer, eager to see her new home, hopeful it would be the welcome end to a frightening journey. She touched her belly. Fermina had been inside her last summer, growing without her knowledge. "Santiago, we will name our next daughter Liria," she said, looking south for the last time. "Just as you wish."

Chapter Thirty-two

She must have fallen asleep, her chin touching her chest. She woke to find that her mule had decided, in that way of stubborn creatures, to head back to Las Claves and well-remembered hay. She looked around, disoriented and dismayed to see Antonio riding toward her. She tugged her mule back to the trail of the fleeing villagers, even as her eyes wanted to close again.

He had never spoken harshly to her before, but she knew she had earned a scold and waited for it. To her relief, she saw only concern, and something else – a certain unexpected shyness from the friend who had not left her during her miscarriage, comforting her through the blood and tears.

"Ana?"

She heard all the uncertainty in that one word – why could no one in this entire peninsula pronounce Hanneke? – and tried to make a joke. "Who else is the plague of your life?" she asked.

"You're no plague," he said. "I would do anything for you, but you must stay awake." He handed back the reins. "Santiago charged me with leading this retreat, and I cannot watch you as I usually do."

"I know. I'm sorry," she said, though, and rose up slightly in her saddle. "Call for Pablo."

"I will." He looked ahead to the retreating villagers. "We'll be at the pass soon. Santiago does not think they will follow us through the pass."

She heard more uncertainty. "What do you think?"

He shrugged. "I wouldn't have thought so, but then, I did not think they would attack this late in winter."

Maybe it was wishful thinking, but as she watched him gallop back to the head of the army, she thought she saw the pass. She clucked to her mule and urged some action, but the distance seemed not to shrink. Only by looking behind her and seeing Santiago and his little group of defenders turn into specks could she tell she had moved at all.

In the deepening gloom she thought Pablo waited for her. The mule gave her a reproachful look when she dug in with her heels, and stopped.

"This is no time for reluctance," she said, and slapped the reins against the beast's hide. "Blame King Alfonso for making you a gift to me."

The mule refused to budge. With growing panic, Hanneke realized how far behind Pablo she was. She dismounted and tried to tug the mule forward. Nothing. "Stay here then," she said and dropped the reins. "If you change your mind, you can catch up with me." She started walking toward Pablo.

To her further irritation, and then her terror, the mule shot past her, eating up the distance to the pass. She tried to run after her, but the snow was a hindrance, since it was only a layer covering mud underneath.

She looked back toward Santiago, hoping he hadn't been witness to her utter stupidity, and stopped. Was it her imagination, or were those distance figures growing larger? What trick was the snow playing on her exhausted mind? Antonio had commanded her to stay awake, but she was so tired.

Now Pablo seemed to be shouting at her and pointing. She even thought she heard Santiago calling her name. She shook her head to clear it, thinking for one moment that she could turn over in bed and curl up against her husband.

Her eyes half-closed, Hanneke watched the soldiers ride toward her. She looked to the south and east, and there they were, too. Were there that many men in Santiago's rear guard?

"Oh God, I am fortune's fool," she said out loud, when she realized the soldiers riding toward her were El Ghalib's men. Terrified, she saw Pablo coming in her direction now, but slowly, as if she dreamed him. Father Bendicio came no closer on his horse; in fact, the disgraceful man fled. She stood there, not knowing where to turn. As she felt the thunder of many horses under her feet, she touched her neck, knowing that before this night ended, her head would be on a pike at Las Claves.

There it came, that warbling war cry of the Almohades. She knew enough Arabic now to discern, "Allahu Akbar." She pulled her cloak tighter around her as she remembered the used and discarded women at the threshing floor. She would be lucky if all that happened was her head on a pike. In fact, it would be a blessing.

She stared in horror as Santiago and his read guard, mounted again, veered toward the Almohades, who must have circled Las Claves and kept going, determined to stop the headlong flight of the Christians.

"No," she said softly. "No." She started running toward Santiago, struggling through the snow and mud, even as Pablo behind her screamed her name. He was alone on the plain. Father Bendicio was a dot in the distance, riding away, abandoning her and Pablo. Who could blame him?

Soon she was close enough to see El Ghalib's warriors distinctly. Santiago lay on the ground, the Almohades standing over him until she attracted their attention by waving her arms and shouting. They whirled toward her, scimitars raised.

Frightened, overwhelmed, still she came, slower now because her side pained her. The soldiers were in no hurry and waited as she approached. She passed Luis, sprawled out and dead. Cook moaned as she passed by, her eyes on Santiago. El Ghalib's soldiers parted for her, some of them grinning at her, others reaching out to touch her cloak and tug on it, saying things to her that made Santiago swear. She shuddered and kept walking.

She forgot them all as she fell to her knees in the red snow beside Santiago. She could not see a wound, but when she put her arm under his back to raise him, her arm felt warm and wet.

He watched her, his expression oddly inscrutable for someone in so precarious a state. He did not seem to be in pain and this puzzled her. Perhaps the blood pouring over her arm and settling in her lap was in her imagination. She looked closer and sighed to see that his arms lay at odd angles, and his legs, too, as if all feeling was gone, as if they had already died and only his eyes lived.

"Santiago…" She didn't know what to say.

"*Chiquita*, didn't anyone ever tell you to ride away from danger and not toward it?"

It was a gentle reproach, almost a fond one, which broke her heart as nothing else could have. "But you were here," she whispered and pulled him closer.

She looked up at the soldiers of El Ghalib, wondering for one fanciful moment if they would help her. It seemed unlikely, so she decided not to give them another thought. Still, maybe they could be a little kind.

"Sirs, please back up a little," she asked them. "I'm already frightened enough, and I am certainly not going anywhere."

They looked at each other as if they couldn't believe someone would say something like that, but did as she said. They moved even farther back when Pablo rode toward them, his face white, his eyes huge.

"Pablo, you really should turn around," she said as kindly as she could. "Maybe they will let you go."

"Never," he told her. "A true knight would never do that, would he, Señor Gonzalez?"

"Certainly not. Besides, two sillies are better than one."

How can this man sound so conversational, so matter-of-fact? Hanneke asked herself. She removed his helmet and kissed his forehead. "That's better," she told him, although nothing was better or ever would be.

To her surprise and relief, the Almohades backed away, mounted their horses and rode off. "I didn't expect that," she said.

"They will be back. They will bring El Ghalib and he will have fun with us," Santiago said, the hard edge back in his voice. His rancor played out quickly. "Ah well. I will lie here with my head in your lap and think of better times we might have had."

He could have said anything but that. She bowed her head over her husband's ruined body. "This is my fault," she whispered.

"Hardly. They came on faster than I believed possible. I have a theory…"

He paused and smiled. "But I don't want to waste my time on theories. Ana, this dowry arrangement, signed and documented by lawyers and priests, was for one purpose only."

"I know," she said and kissed his forehead.

"Don't waste those," he said. "Kiss my mouth."

She kissed his mouth and he kissed her back with enough energy to almost fool her that if they could somehow get away from the Almohades, all would be right again.

"Something happened though," he continued, when her lips were still as close as a kiss away. "I fell in love with you." The frustration returned. "Damn me, but I had to raise an army! All I wanted to do was stay close to you."

She kissed him again, then stopped when she heard horses and men returning, many of them this time.

"Ana, Ana…"

She tried to swallow her fear and looked down. "Can I do anything for you?"

"No. Yes, you can. Pull away my chain mail – it's sliced through up the back – and just rest your head just below my neck. I can still feel that."

She swallowed and did as he said, then opened the front of his doublet and rested her head against him. She craved his warmth.

"That does feel good. Ana, you told me my cousin Alfonso spoke to you of this enterprise. He said that some of us would be winnowed out, before victory." He sighed. "I did not think it would be me. What a proud and foolish man you married."

She kissed his chest, which was wet with her tears. "I had no doubt that *I* would be winnowed, Santiago."

She felt his chuckle. "Don't be so certain of that. I…"

He must have heard the horses, too. Pablo pressed closer to her as they were now entirely surrounded by El Ghalib's army. She tightened her arms around her husband. "I hope they do not make that war cry. It scares me."

"You're probably afraid of thunder, too, aren't you, even though it is lightning that kills?" he asked, amused. He contemplated her. "There is so much about you I never knew."

"My love, you knew enough," she said, and rubbed her cheek against his neck.

"Pablo? Where are you?" he asked, staring directly at Pablo.

"Señor, I am right here. You are looking at me."

"Am I? Watch Ana for me, until you can get her to Antonio."

"Señor, I will do it."

There was so much she wanted to say. "Santiago, I …"

"Let me talk, my love," he told her. "Please. Somehow, some way, you will get to Antonio…"

"And the others?"

"I don't care about the others," he said, with a touch of his usual impatience. "I have told Antonio what he must do. Do not argue with him. Do what I have told him to do. It might keep you safe against…"

He looked up at the circle of horsemen. "…against El Ghalib, or perhaps Felipe," he finished. "Promise me, Ana. Do what Antonio says."

"I promise." It was an easy promise. She knew she was not going to leave this circle of death alive.

"Kiss me once more."

She kissed him and sat back, not releasing her husband, but ready to bargain now with Yussef el Ghalib. Her hand went to her necklace. She had grown used to it around her neck. She would miss it. She lifted it over her head.

"Pablo. Take this to El Ghalib. I am certain he is near."

"I am afraid."

"You are my true knight, and this is but a small moment in God's eyes. That is what you have always told me. Do you believe it?"

He nodded and took the necklace. "I should call his name?"

"Yes."

She gave him a reassuring pat and he stood up. The mother cat and kitten jumped out of his doublet, and the soldiers laughed.

"Ana, what…"

As calmly as she could manage, and as quickly, Ana told Santiago about the necklace, and El Ghalib's promise at the river, given in gratitude for doing what he could not do for a beloved sister. "Don't be angry with me, Santiago. I should have told you sooner," she told her husband, then looked away. "Perhaps we weren't on the best of terms then, you and I."

"We were not," he said. His breath came slower and slower. "Angry? Not now. You can bargain for your life with that necklace. I am grateful."

"That wasn't the bargain I had in mind, dear man. Here he is."

Pushing Pablo in front of him, Yussef el Ghalib stood beside them, looking down. He relieved her heart by kneeling in the snow. He was wrapped against the weather with only his eyes showing, but she recognized Jawhara's eyes.

He showed her the necklace, then put it around his neck, working it inside his tunic. "Tell me what you wish," he said. "Be quick. I trust no one."

But not too quick, she thought. *Let us give Antonio time to get everyone through the pass.* She decided to burst into tears, which wasn't hard, not at all. She wanted to weep for every moment lost, never to be, with this hard, obsessed, determined man she had been forced to marry, not of her choice. Things had changed. How was she going to manage without him?

"Come, come, Señora Gonzalez," El Ghalib said, his patience wearing thin. "Tell me. What is your wish?"

She dried her eyes, taking her time. "It is this, Yussef el Ghalib: Please allow my husband to die peacefully in my arms."

"No, Ana, no," Santiago said, his words starting to slur together. "Ask for safe passage for you and Pablo from this killing field."

"It is my wish, husband, and not yours," she reminded him. "This is what I choose."

"You might want to reconsider," el Ghalib told her.

"I don't care what happens to me," she said. "When this good man is dead, you may do with me as *you* choose."

"Ana, no."

"Hush, Santiago. And when he is dead, this enemy of yours, Yussef, please see that his body and that of his brother, tied to his horse over there, are buried at Las Claves in the graveyard."

"Nothing for yourself?"

"I would like one small thing." She smiled briefly. "I have decided I like small things."

"Speak then, wife of my enemy."

"Bury Santiago next to the little mound with a wooden marker that reads, 'Fermina.'"

"Who might that be?" el Ghalib asked, more softly.

"Our daughter, Santiago's and mine." she said. "She was four months in my womb, then no more. Please, sir."

El Ghalib sat back on his heels. "I didn't know." He stood up and looked down at Santiago, as if debating what to do.

"Please, señor," she said. "You promised me one favor."

"I did, but you have asked for more."

"So I have," she said. "Please."

Santiago opened his eyes. "I can't see anything," he whispered.

She cried, her tears dropping on his chest, but he didn't feel them. El Ghalib knelt once more by the dying man. "Santiago, what an enemy you have been! Las Claves is mine again, but you still have something better, damn you."

"I do, don't I? Ana, my heart, put your cheek against mine. I might feel that. Hard. To. Breathe."

She did as he said, and he sighed. "*Gracias.*"

"Adios, my enemy," el Ghalib said.

"Adios. Yussef?"

"What now?"

"Don't trust Felipe Palacios," Santiago said, straining to speak as the paralysis clawed higher at his lungs. "He wants Hanneke's dowry. He won't have it."

"You will prevent that from beyond the grave?"

"I will. I have."

"You can work a miracle? You are a dead man."

"I know."

What was left to say? El Ghalib bowed to Ana. "I will fulfill your wish."

In mere minutes they were alone except for Pablo, who stood apart, her true knight. Mama cat in his arms, her kitten hopped about in the snow.

Ana touched Santiago's face and kissed him. To her dismay, he was beyond kissing her back. She cradled him in her arms and rocked back and forth. He tried to open his eyes and failed. His lips moved. She put her ear close to his mouth.

"I love you, Ana."

"I love you, husband."

He may have died then, or it may have been later, when she finally realized he no longer gave her any warmth. She tried to rise, but her dress was frozen to Santiago by his blood. Sobbing, she yanked on her dress until she was free.

Pablo helped her arrange Santiago's cloak over his body, anchoring it down with snow. She hoped el Ghalib would fulfill the rest of her bargain with the necklace. The thought of leaving Santiago here with no protection from scavenging animals tore at her heart. In this, as in all other matters of her life since those two damnable priests arrived at Hans Aardema's house in Vlissingen, she had no choice.

She knelt one final time by her husband's body and rested her cheek on his chest. The silence within battered her own beating heart.

As the sun rose, Hanneke and Pablo started walking toward the pass, the kitten tucked safely in with its mother once more. They held hands, each looking back when they thought the other wasn't watching. The sky was clear now, almost painfully blue.

"Do you hear thunder, *dama*?"

They both looked back where they had last seen the Almohades and saw the riders. "What should we do?" Pablo asked.

Hanneke turned to face the army galloping toward them from the east. The worst had happened. She feared nothing.

"We will wait for them. I suppose El Ghalib changed his mind. If you want to run, Pablo, I can slow them down."

"Never! I promised Señor Gonzalez that I would protect you," he said, shocked.

"You did, my true knight." She covered her face with her hands, praying to *Padre Celestial* that she would remember every moment of her brief life with Santiago Gonzalez, praying that she would be brave, no matter what el Ghalib did to her.

They stood shoulder to shoulder, even when the army drew close enough for them to see it was the Knights of Calatrava, sent south on a rescue mission by peddlers, searching for survivors.

PART II

Chapter Thirty-three

Had she known a rescue would harrow up her heart, Hanneke would have sent Pablo ahead by himself and stayed with Santiago until she froze. Couldn't Don Ruy Díaz, master of the Knights of Calatrava, understand that she didn't want to speak of what happened? He expected answers and she had none, except that her husband had died in her arms and she was a stranger in a harsh land.

She covered her face with her hands and trembled as Don Diaz asked gentle question after question. She wanted to scream at him to stop, but her mother hadn't raised her to be so impolite. All she could do was shut out the sight of him and tremble.

"Let me try, Don Díaz."

She tensed when an arm went around her shoulders and someone smelling of both incense and the oil of chain mail pulled her close.

"It's too much, isn't it?"

Another question, but she could answer this one with a nod, her hands still covering her eyes. She heard this man with the quiet voice speaking softly to Don Díaz.

"We will take you to the others," the man said. "We stopped there first. Antonio Baltierra sent us on."

She took her hands away. "He lives?"

"They all do," Don Díaz said. "They made it through the pass and El Ghalib seemed disinclined to follow." He looked away. "That, I do not understand. Why would he not follow us. It would have been so easy."

"We kept him busy, Santiago and I," she said, as her heart broke some more. "He couldn't move and his chain mail was split up the back. They destroyed his spine with an ax."

"You stayed with him to the end," the more comforting man said. She heard the respect in his voice, and wondered if he was a priest.

"*Claro*," she said, then sagged against him. "I grieve for him. Please just let me grieve for him. It is a small thing I ask," was the last thing she remembered saying.

When she revived from her faint, she was sitting in front of the kind soldier on his warhorse, his cloak around them both. She looked around for Pablo. "Pablo?" she asked, alarmed.

"He's riding farther behind us. He has a mother cat and a kitten." He chuckled at that.

She nodded because it made perfect sense, even though nothing else did. The light was nearly gone from the sky, but the clouds had puffed away and the moon rose. The land was white and oddly uniform. How did they know which way to travel?

"Where are we?" she asked. Then, "Pardon me, but what is your name? Are you a priest?"

"Father Anselmo *a su servicio, señora*," he replied. "Some of us are priests, who ride with the Knights of Calatrava. We are about through the pass ourselves, nearly to the monastery of Santo Gilberto."

"Father, I don't remember a monastery there," she said, thinking of last summer, and warmth, and a newly aroused awareness of her husband who now lay dead under his cloak and a mound of snow. *Please, El Ghalib, take Santiago with you back to Las Claves. Do what I asked*, she begged in her mind and heart, knowing better than to mention El Ghalib, not to the Knights of Calatrava, who had suffered so much at the hands of the Almohades. In a curious way, she was now bound to El Ghalib, like it or not. He had honored her wish; he deserved her silence.

"It is an old ruin," Padre Anselmo told her, "destroyed five hundred years ago when the Moors began their conquest."

She vaguely remembered walls and rubble. How could anyone stay there? She thought back to their mad dash from Las Claves and knew even a ruin might offer some puny protection. She reminded herself that she lived in a world of low expectations. She had none, herself, but others might still have retained a few. Good for them. She sighed, dreading her arrival at Santo Gilberto and more questions. How many times would she have to tell her sad story? Once seemed too much.

She would tell Antonio. Before he could not talk, Santiago had urged her to speak to him; why, she did not know. The question was too large for her brain, so she closed her eyes and slept.

"Take her gently."

She woke to find herself in Antonio's arms. All she could do was burrow closer to him, relieved to her very soul that he lived. Carlos stood at his side, ugly, wounded Carlos, whose one remaining eye was a mere slit in his swollen face.

"I'll find you a place, Ana," Antonio said. "Thank God you are alive."

He turned his attention to Don Díaz, who had dismounted. "Before God and all the saints, I am more than grateful that you are here, sir knight," Antonio said. "We have great need of you, as you can see."

Don Gonzalo rested his hands on Antonio and Hanneke in his arms. "Strange are the ways of the Lord Almighty. How curious is His will, to send the message of your need through two Jewish peddlers." Hanneke saw his respect when his eyes rested on her. "They spoke of a brave woman at Las Claves."

"Santiago put her in charge when we rode out, and she did not fail us."

"Take good care of this one," the master of Calatrava said, making it more than a suggestion.

Antonio bowed his head, but his words relieved her heart. "Months ago, Santiago commended her to my watch, when he was elsewhere. He never rescinded it. Rest assured I will continue to fulfill that order, Don Díaz."

Followed by Pablo, Antonio carried her into a ruin with stone walls but no ceiling. Some of the villagers gathered around him, the women with questions. When they looked and did not see Santiago, they began to wail.

The mourning followed her through one room and another until he found a corner where a campfire burned. When he set her down, Hanneke drew herself into a ball and pulled her cloak over her head, shutting out everyone. She heard him talking to the women. "Give me a moment," she heard. "Please. I insist." The voices stopped.

Antonio sat down beside her, his hand on her head. "I have to know," he said finally. "Why are *you* still alive?"

Hanneke owed him the story. She pulled the cloak off her face and sat up. She looked around the cell-like room, which mercifully had three walls, even if no ceiling. The floor was broken tile, and cold.

How could she object when his arm went around her? They were comrades in suffering from her earlier heartache, which, terrible as it was, bore no resemblance to the yawning cavern of her new loss.

"I will only speak of it once," she said.

"That is all I ask. Then you need to know something else."

As she forced her tired mind to find words to describe the sight of her husband lying so twisted in snow turning red around him, she heard someone at the entrance to her pathetic sanctuary. She wanted to turn away when she saw Felipe Palacios, wretched coward. It was no figment of her imagination that Antonio's arm involuntarily tightened around her.

"I am glad to see you," Felipe said, coming closer, bowing a little, abasing himself in strange fashion. "I will take care of you, now that Santiago is no more."

"Go away," she said softly. "Leave me alone with Antonio Baltierra."

Like an irritating itch under her skin, he wouldn't quit. "You need to understand your situation. With Manolo dead, God rest his soul" – he crossed himself, the soul of piety – "and Rodrigo so tiny and Engracia, well, Engracia, I have put myself in charge of Las Claves."

"That in no way affects me," Hanneke said quietly. "I wish you well in your new acquisition."

She could have picked a kinder word than acquisition, but none came to mind in any language. Where had this coward been when Santiago needed every man? What venom had he fed into his silly sister's ear about Santiago sending Manolo to his death? She trusted him not even slightly.

Still he stood there, his hands together so piously. "Please leave me alone," she said. "What I have to say is for Antonio's ears only." Might as well assure Felipe where he stood in her estimation, not that it mattered. "Antonio was brave enough to fight for Las Claves, and I consider him the leader of the soldiers. If something changes that, then so be it. Please leave us."

What could he do? He left, but not without a backward glance that suggested the matter wasn't closed. His eyes narrowed when he glared at Antonio, and she felt great unease. Maybe she should apologize to Felipe for her plain speaking, blaming it on the shock of her husband's death. Later; it could wait.

"You have not made a friend there," Antonio said.

"He never was," she replied. "Not since Valladolid, when he tried to… to…insinuate himself into my life. I will never trust him."

"That is two of us." He relaxed his grip on her shoulders. "Tell me what you wish. I would like to give you space, time and comfort in which to grieve, but we have none of those luxuries at present."

She understood him completely. "Let me tell you this: El Ghalib and his army are retaking Las Claves now. I'm certain you are aware of that. It was his goal all along."

"I know. We are waiting for more soldiers here. When they arrive – if they arrive – we will march on Las Claves again." He held himself off from her to appraise her. "I am astounded that El Ghalib did not at the very least hold you for ransom."

"I thought as much." She rested her head against Antonio's chest. "My story begins when I killed Jawhara. Listen, please."

She took a deep breath, folded Santiago into her heart where he could give her courage, and began, leaving out nothing. She stopped when tears overwhelmed her. Antonio held her close and crooned to her in those moments. Several times, he looked up and spoke softly to someone in the door, who left.

"I gave the necklace back to El Ghalib and asked that he let me hold my husband until his death," she whispered.

"I cannot imagine that pleased your husband," Antonio said, with just a shred of humor.

"You know it didn't," she said, and felt her heart lift a little, but only a little. "He wanted me to ask for my own safe passage. Personally, I didn't care what became of me once he was gone."

"This is hard to hear, Ana," Antonio said. She thought she heard the pain of a man's loss of his friend. "I wish to God matters had fallen out differently."

Maybe someday she could look on this whole wretched turn of events with something approaching resigned philosophy, but now was not the time. "I pressed my luck and asked El Ghalib to see that Manolo and Santiago were buried at Las Claves, with Santiago next to Fermina. He said he would, because they were heading there."

"And not to attack us here," Antonio said, and she heard the relief. "With the Knights gathered, and other soldiers expected soon, we *will* retake Las Claves."

She was silent, wondering why anyone wanted Las Claves. Antonio seemed to sense what she was thinking. "We have been going back and forth with the Almohades for years," he told her. "The time has come to stand. Santiago and I felt it all over Spain, as we traveled and recruited this fall."

"But this winnowing," she said. "I hate it."

She smelled blood on her hands and clothing, and felt despair so overpowering that she could think of nothing beyond her husband's last look into her eyes. Santiago had showed her something worse than fear: regret. She knew now that last look was regret, as time ran out.

Chapter Thirty-four

Over her anguish, Hanneke heard Antonio speaking low to others. He eased his arm out from around her, even as she cried and clung to his comforting presence. "Later, Ana," he said in her ear. "We have a matter of considerable importance to discuss soon, but I am being actively threatened by the women of Las Claves. Take pity on me, *dama*."

He backed away and she found herself looking into the calm eyes of the old woman, *La Vieja*, from the great hall at Las Claves, who had told her to spread around the straw. Beside her knelt the young widow big with child that Hanneke had coaxed away from the body of her husband.

The widow held out a bowl of something hot. Hanneke swallowed down saliva and realized how hungry she was. How could she even think of food now? She tried to turn away, but the fragrance compelled her to pay attention.

"That's better, *dama*," *La Vieja* said. "No one needs to starve, even if she is sad. Here is a spoon."

Hanneke sat up and took the bowl on her lap, relishing the warmth to her hands. She took a bite and it was bliss. Another bite confirmed her belief that wheat porridge was the finest delicacy found in Spain. She ate and cried at the same time, until the level was half down in bowl, then looked around.

She saw familiar faces, kind ones, the women she had helped in the courtyard after the gate was shut, the women she had smiled at during visits to the village. Some had lost their husbands, like her; others, their sons. She saw great pity in their eyes and she felt their sorrow at her loss, which, in the scheme of things, was no more than their own.

A little boy crouched nearby, his eyes following her spoon from bowl to mouth. He said nothing, but he watched, dignified in that manner she had learned to recognize as Spanish. She knew he was hungry. They all were, but the women hid it better. She could hide it, too.

"Here, *niño*. I can't possibly eat another bite." She held out the bowl to him. He took it without a word. Hanneke watched him eat, wondering who his mother was, because no one sat close by him.

"Where is his mother?" she whispered to the old woman.

"Dead many years," *La Vieja* whispered back. "His father died this morning in the retreat from the battle."

"But who will…"

"All of us," *La Vieja* said proudly.

Tears filled Hanneke's eyes, more tears. She let them flow as she watched the child. *We have all lost our dear ones*, she thought and wept.

Soon they were all crying, some silently, some with great gasping sobs. Two of the women swayed from side to side in their misery. Another raked sharp fingernails down her face, leaving bloody tracks. Others raised pleading hands to the cold, impersonal heaven overhead. As the business of sorrow filled every empty space in her heart, Hanneke wept in sadness and unity.

The great storm of lamentation finally tapered off and Hanneke was left drained from the terrible exertion of mourning. She leaned against the cold stones, tired down to the marrow of her bones. She made no objection when *La Vieja* covered her with a blanket that smelled of mice droppings and horses. She felt a firm hand on her shoulder, then more gentle fingers making the sign of the cross on her forehead.

She was nearly asleep when she heard many horses. She gasped and tried to leap to her feet, but the old woman held her there.

"It isn't El Ghalib," La Vieja assured her. "Listen."

She listened, and it was worse. "Santiago! Santiago!" she heard.

"I have to go to him," Hanneke begged. "Let me go!"

"No, no, señora, do you not remember that Santiago is the great victory cry of Spain?"

She put her hands over her ears. "I can't bear it," she said. "There is no victory tonight."

"There is! We are still alive. Stay here. I mean it." The old woman left her side and spoke to someone standing there. Time inched along, until she heard another shout. She sat up quickly, her heart hammering in her breast, when Pablo ran into the room.

He took her hand, and she felt his excitement. "*Dama!* Thirty more soldiers."

"See there, señora?" La Vieja said. "Go to sleep. We are safe enough."

She slept, whether they were safe or not. As in all things, she had no choice, because her grief had rendered her unable to do anything but sleep. Was this what Antonio had planned when he left her with the women? She did not doubt it.

Hanneke woke hours later, sensing that she was not alone in the little room, probably a cell used five hundred years ago by a monk of Santo Gilberto, back when the monastery had a roof and the Rule of Benedict regulated their orderly lives.

She sat up slowly, quietly, letting her eyes accustom themselves to the gloom. The fire had burned itself down to glowing coals, even as the cold deepened

"Ana. We must talk."

"Antonio?"

He shifted then, and she saw him leaning against the wall, his sword drawn and resting on his lap. *I have another true knight*, she thought, touched.

Another form stirred. Antonio reached over and patted the form. "Sleep, boy."

Both my knights, she thought, allowing in a small measure of contentment. She held out her hand to Antonio. "I can share this blanket, you know."

He was beside her in a moment, then under the blanket she held out. "My feet are freezing," he whispered. "Pardon my poor manners."

He seemed suddenly shy, and she thought she understood why. An hour ago, he had left her with the village women, and he probably wondered what she thought of his dereliction. As their noisy mourning filled her mind again, she felt only gratitude.

"Thank you for what you did," she said. "I needed them, didn't I?"

"You did. How do women mourn in your Netherlands?" he asked.

"Quietly. No one says anything." She thought of silent funerals, and hollow-eyed women, grieving inside. "Could this be better?"

"I think it must be." He found her hand. "We are marching against Las Claves as soon as it is light," he told her. "We are moving out with every man and boy who can fight, and we will win this time. I know it."

"I believe you," she said, wishing the Knights of Calatrava and thirty more soldiers had taken to the southern plain yesterday with Santiago and his men. She shook herself mentally. What good came of wishing for what would never be?

"I wanted to put you in charge of the women and children here, as you were before, but Felipe Palacios assured me he was better suited than any mere female." He gave a snort of disgust. "Have you ever met someone you hated on sight?"

"Only here," she said, "and it is the man you speak of. I doubt you will find Felipe *el Cobarde* before you ride out tomorrow."

"Without a doubt. *El Cobarde*. You've already given him a title?"

She managed a slight smile. "The village women did that. I'd rather even see Father Bendicio in charge than Felipe Palacios."

"What happened to Bendicio?" he asked. "Is he dead, too?"

"Is he not here?" Hanneke asked, startled. She thought of her last view of the priest as he fled, leaving her and Pablo behind as her husband lay dying in the snow.

"He is not here. Like *El Cobarde*, our priest vanishes when a challenge comes."

The room grew lighter. She didn't hear anyone stirring yet, but she remembered Antonio had something to tell her, something that Santiago stressed as he lay dying. *You told me you had given Antonio an order and I must obey, whatever the consequences*, she thought. *I hope it is not onerous, for I do not feel brave, either.*

"Antonio?"

He had dropped into slumber, propped up against the stone wall, his breath coming and going evenly. *Poor man*, she thought. *You shoulder so many burdens. I am one more.*

She touched his arm and he opened his eyes. "My apologies," he said. "Where was I?"

"Sleeping," she teased. The light-hearted moment passed quickly. Another breath and she was back on the snowy plain with her husband dying in her lap. "Before he...Antonio, he said I was to do what you said. What did he mean?"

"Yes. I came in here for a reason."

"You are tired. I understand. Can it wait until daylight?"

"No." He was awake now, and decisive. "Is there enough light for you to read this?" Antonio reached into his doublet and pulled out a parchment fragment. "He gave this to Carlos before he left to protect our rear. And... and he told me the same thing."

"I was watching you both. You seemed surprised."

"Read the note."

Full of misgivings, she took the note and stood close to the single window high on the stone wall. She read it, gasped, and read it again, after looking back at Antonio, who was on his feet now, too, his eyes on hers. She sank down, her legs unable to keep her upright.

Antonio crouched by her, never taking his eyes from her face. "In all the turmoil, I have thought of nothing but that note and you. Ana, what do you think? Was he right or wrong?"

She looked at the note again, seeing the purpose in every word, as well as the desperation. "I didn't think he loved me," she said softly, "certainly not at first. Neither did I love him." She felt the tears gather, even though there wasn't time to weep. "That changed. His last words to me were of love and regret."

She said it quietly, her feelings so intimate, so bound up in the man who either lay dead under a shroud of snow at the mercy of winter, or was now interred in the cemetery at Las Claves next to his daughter. Everything depended on the kindness of his enemy.

"He was right about the dowry," she said finally, even as her heart broke over and over, like waves on the shore. "I fear that Felipe Palacios will go after my dowry by forcing me to marry him."

"Should we do this thing, Santiago's dying wish?"

"Do you think my husband knew he was going to his death?" she asked. It was one more hard question among many, but she wanted to know, had to know.

Antonio nodded. "Five men were never enough to hold off El Ghalib. We all knew it. I told him I would go. You heard me."

"I did." She put her hand on his arm. This time he turned his hand over and clasped hers. "Why did he insist?"

"I wish I knew. To expiate Manolo's death? To prove one more time to his dead father that he was worthy?" Antonio leaned closer until they were nearly nose to nose. "I believe it was more than that. He wanted to give you every opportunity to escape."

Hanneke knew he was right. She had seen it in Santiago's eyes, and felt it in their last embrace. "This is hard," she whispered.

"I know." His cheek rested against hers. It was wet. "Will you, Ana?"

There was only one answer. She had no choice. "Yes. I will marry you."

Chapter Thirty-five

Hanneke Gonzalez, widow of one day, became the wife of Antonio Baltierra, free man, at dawn in the ruined chapel of Santo Gilberto, in the company of Don Ruy Díaz de Yanguas, and Carlos, as witnesses. Father Anselmo married them, this day of the birth of Our Lord, 1211. Don Díaz nodded his approval, kissed the bride, and told Antonio to get the men of Las Claves ready to retake Manolo Gonzalez' domain. The matter had consumed one half hour, at a time when every second mattered.

Don Díaz had been easy to find. He and the Knights had bedded down in the ruined chapel of the old monastery. She paused in the doorway, fearing the all-seeing eye of God etched in stone high on the back wall. Should they do this? Antonio took her hand and she followed after him.

The Master of the Order of Calatrava made the sign of the cross over them both, then led them aside. "What can I do for you children, or can I imagine?"

You're a shrewd one, Hanneke thought, *or has Antonio already spoken to you?*

"I spoke to Don Díaz, Ana, but here is Santiago's message." Antonio took his own deep breath. "I suppose it was his last will and testament." Antonio handed him the note and stepped back, watching his expression. Don Díaz read it and handed it back.

"You are right, Antonio. His final thought was of his wife. It is his will."

Don Díaz turned to Hanneke. "Do you see the necessity for this drastic maneuver on the part of your late husband?"

Would there ever be a time when the mere thought of Santiago's final moments would not harrow her heart? She swallowed, grateful Antonio

209

had not released her hand. "Nearly his last words to me were that I should agree with what he had already ordered Antonio to do," she said. "I see the necessity. He does not trust Felipe Palacios to look after my interests."

"I believe that worm would do nearly anything to gain control of Ana's dowry," Antonio said. He stepped closer. "Don Díaz, there might even be a connection between Felipe and El Ghalib. With your permission, Ana?" Antonio asked.

"Tell him."

With an admirable economy of words, Antonio told the Master that Felipe had brought forward Jawhara, El Ghalib's sister, as a servant for Engracia Gonzalez when they passed through Valladolid in summer. "We were betrayed by that servant, as we journeyed to Toledo," he concluded. "Felipe plays a deep game, and I fear for our Christian cause."

Don Díaz sat in silence. Hanneke edged closed to Antonio. "We live in chaotic times," the Master of Calatrava said finally. "We cannot take the chance that if Felipe forces Ana to marry him, her dowry would end up favoring the Almohades." Ana saw his sympathy for her. "How crass is money, when we are looking at a broken heart."

Hanneke held her head high. "I will do what Antonio says, because my dead husband – God rest his soul – would not wish to see the people of Las Claves ruined and the conquest set back for years. Do what you must."

"Very well, child." Don Díaz turned his penetrating gaze on Antonio. "You will defend and protect this widow?"

"With my life," he said, his voice firm.

"I will summon Father Anselmo." He put his hands on their shoulders. "There is no time to cry banns for three weeks or indulge in the niceties. Have no fear, though. This will be a marriage most legal. An earlier pope stated in an edict that Spain under the thumb of the caliphs has certain latitudes allowed to none else."

He nodded to them. "Give me thirty minutes. Señora Gonzalez, find a better dress and a comb. Antonio, find me two witnesses of your choosing."

"You, Master, for one," he said promptly.

"Thank you."

Antonio walked Ana back to where the villagers were stirring. Hanneke smelled wheat mush boiling. He tugged on her hand and pulled her into an unoccupied cell.

"Should this marriage be common knowledge for all? What do you think?" he whispered, his lips close to her ear.

Surprised that someone wanted her opinion, Hanneke considered the matter. "Not yet. There are those who would not understand such unseemly haste" – *am I one of them?* she asked herself – "and we have no concrete evidence to tie Felipe to such evil." Another thought struck her with some force. "And you, señor, do not need to be in more danger from such a duplicitous man, if you are announced as my husband."

"That's another thought," he said. He gave a light-hearted bow that did wonders to her heart. "Antonio Baltierra, free man with a bullseye on his back. Not for me, thank you."

"No. You are too kind for that," she said quietly.

"Very well. I will inform Carlos and Pablo, if you agree," he said. "I want Carlos as a witness, too."

When did that ugly, vulgar man become so important to her? Carlos was precisely right. "Yes, please."

Antonio hesitated, until she nudged him and gave him a questioning look. "There is this, too, Ana, as challenging as it might seem: When we retake Las Claves, I am duty bound by Santiago to fulfill *his* last order. Just north of Toledo, he has arranged for a number of soldiers to join us. I must gather them. When I leave you, Carlos will be your protector."

She nodded, aware of Carlos' courage in the fight, and his uncomplaining suffering in the great hall, all to serve Santiago Gonzalez. "He will be a good protector."

Still, the fear remained. She could not shake it. "Please assure me that you will not be gone long."

"It is a matter of two or three weeks," he said. "After I return, we can tell the villagers of our marriage." He chuckled, but she heard no humor. "Spain is a land of hard choices. Everyone understands that."

There was nothing more to say, and time was passing. "We should find you a dress and a comb," he said.

Impulsively, Hanneke clutched Antonio. His arms went around her as he pulled her close in consolation. "This is one of those events I would rather look back on, than go through," she said. "Adventures are not reassuring when they are in progress, are they?"

"I think not," he said, and pressed her head to his chest. "Maybe someday we will be old and wise and have brave stories to tell of how we reconquered Spain. Right now, it's frightening, isn't it?"

They embraced another moment for strength, then went about the business of a wedding, and preparing a battered army to march.

The dress was easily obtained, to Hanneke's surprise. She also knew she could trust La Vieja. She found the old woman humming as she stirred a kettle of wheat. *I don't even know your name*, Hanneke thought, *but I trust you.*

No one else stood by. Hanneke helped her take the kettle from its tripod, and sat down with her. With an economy of words she knew she was learning from Antonio Baltierra, Hanneke explained the wedding, the reason for it, and the need for secrecy. La Vieja nodded, taking it all in without a qualm. "Between you and me, *dama*, I would not trust Felipe with a fart," she said. "Antonio is a wise and good man. He will keep you safe."

Hanneke felt her heart lift to hear La Vieja's assessment of the quiet man who had stood by her in other trying times. "And the dowry, too," she added. "Isn't that what is most important?"

"If you insist," La Vieja said, then moved to more practical matters. "I will find a black dress for you, *dama*, and a comb."

Hanneke waited, dipping a spoon into the wheat mush. Santiago had told her once that when food is available, you eat. She ate. La Vieja returned with a black dress and a comb. She helped Hanneke take off her bloodstained garment, shaking her head and sniffing back tears. "Señor Gonzalez deserved a longer life," she said, which made Hanneke weep.

She dried her tears and combed her hair until it was straight. La Vieja plaited it into two intertwined braids. "What is your name?" Hanneke asked. "I am remiss in not knowing. You have been so kind to me."

"Teresa Gomez," La Vieja said. "My old fellow, God rest his soul, was a shepherd." She paused in her weaving of Hanneke's hair. "He would like to have seen this land free of caliphs and Almohades." She patted Hanneke's head and secured the braid with a leather string. "He liked Señor Gonzalez." Her hands went to Hanneke's shoulders. "We all did."

Hanneke rested her cheek on Teresa's hand. "And I."

Time was passing. She stood up, happy that the dress was short enough for her, even if it was black. But then, she was a widow, at least for another few minutes. Even then, the matter must be kept silent.

"I can trust you, Teresa Gomez?" she asked quietly.

"With my life, *dama*," La Vieja replied. "We villagers will help you all we can. Go. Marry another good man."

Hanneke easily found her way back to the nearly empty chapel. Antonio stood there, flanked by Carlos and Pablo, her true knight.

One small matter slowed the proceedings, which, as she thought about it later, meant more than she knew at the time. Father Anselmo asked her full name. She nearly said Hanneke, then changed her mind. "It is Ana now," she said firmly. "Just Ana. None of you Spaniards can say Hanneke, and for some reason, I don't mind anymore." She didn't. It was one more small thing to discard.

Father Anselmo chuckled. "Forgive us of our linguistic sins, daughter."

Hanneke knelt close to Antonio, her eyes closed. Tearless now, she mourned a good man, and begged his spirit, if it lingered nearby as the deceased were rumored to do, to know she was doing what he commanded. Then again, if it were anyone but Antonio, she would never have agreed to this startling turn of events.

Antonio, you watched over me in my saddest moment, she thought, as Father Anselmo blessed them with long life and many children. *I will be true and kind, and we will see what happens, once Spain is reconquered. I can promise no more.*

She felt it was enough. She opened her eyes to see Antonio watching her. "Are you well?" he whispered.

She nodded. She was.

They left by separate doors, the men to their horses. Soon she stood in the chapel with only Father Anselmo.

"That was a serious morning's work," he commented, "and here it is, barely dawn."

"Did I do the right thing, Father?" she asked.

"You did the only thing," he replied firmly. "Now, my dear Señora Baltierra – I will still call you Señora Gonzalez because of secrecy – I will give you a copy of the marriage document soon. Keep it safe. There will be one for Antonio, as well, and Don Ruy Díaz."

"I will go to the women and see how I can be of use," she told him. She took the priest's hand and kissed it. "Thank you," she said simply.

Chapter Thirty-six

Hanneke knew she needed to see Engracia, needed to make some awkward truce with her. She had heard a newborn baby several times that morning, but her courage failed her. She remembered Engracia's last words to her at Las Claves. *You may not want to see me,* Hanneke thought, as she walked toward the sound of a baby crying. *All the same, we have to make some peace with each other, if we are to endure Las Claves.*

She waited in the courtyard first, hands clasped together, shivering in the cold, as the men mounted their horses, gathered their reins and filed out of the monastery, Las Claves on their minds.

She waved to Pablo and Antonio, who edged his black horse out of the line. "Whether it is victory or defeat, I will send Pablo and Carlos back with news," he said, bending down from his saddle, his words for her alone. "If it is victory, come on." He looked at her in that all-encompassing way of his. "If it is defeat, ride to safety in Toledo. Don't wait for anyone here, especially if *El Cobarde* tells you what to do. Never hesitate."

She watched his expression harden as he looked beyond her. "Felipe stands behind you in the shadows. Try not to be alone with him."

"The women will help me," she said. "Don't worry about me. Go with God." *Husband, please don't be upset with me if I make a mistake and call you Santiago, on occasion,* she thought. *How does one forget?*

Antonio gave her a small salute and rejoined the line of march. She felt her courage dribble away as he rode out with the others. When Pablo looked back, she blew a kiss to him and waved, wondering if she would see any of them again. Her smile lasted until the army was out of sight.

It might have lasted longer, but here came Felipe.

"Señora Gonzalez, perhaps you and I can have some conversation," he said.

He stood too close to her. She stepped back. "Later. For now, I will go to the women and see if I can help anyone."

He dismissed them with a casual wave. "Oh, them."

"Yes, them," she said, her irritation growing. "The wives of shepherds and muleteers, weavers and blacksmiths."

"Come with me to Engracia," he said.

He had her. She needed to see if there were any good feelings to salvage. "Very well."

She wouldn't have minded his oily unctuousness as much if he hadn't been joined by two men taller than he was, and scarred, one by smallpox and the other by knives. Hanneke shivered involuntarily, wishing they would move away, and not practically tread in her footsteps.

"Amador and Baltazar," Felipe said, with a casual wave of his hand. "They look out for my... interests."

"How fortunate for you," she managed to say, hoping her voice didn't quaver.

"Here we are," Felipe said, as she fought the urge to break into a run.

There was no door on this cell, either, but it had more of a roof, at least some protection for a new mother and baby.

She turned to Felipe and his thugs. "You all can wait outside. I would speak to Engracia alone."

Felipe turned sorrowful eyes on her, eerie in a disconcerting way because there was nothing in his face that indicated compassion. He might have been discussing his favorite hound. "They will be in the hall as you wish, *dama. I* will remain here with my dear sister. We would hate to upset Engracia, wouldn't we?"

"That is never my intention, Felipe."

He bowed to her, and she felt all the mockery. "I will sit over here out of the way, Señora Gonzalez. Oh, and look, here is Juana."

Hanneke nodded to the servant, who glared back. She tried to throw off a basketful of misgivings as she approached Engracia's pallet, a far cry from the comfort of her bed at Las Claves. "May I join you, sister?"

"If you must," Engracia said, nothing in her voice of welcome.

This will be a short visit, Hanneke thought. She leaned forward to look at Rodrigo, and couldn't help a smile. "He's beautiful, Engracia."

"What a pity his father will never know him," Felipe said.

How could Felipe be so quiet? He stood right behind her. There was nowhere she could move without pushing him aside.

"Yes, it is a pity," Hanneke said, reaching down deep for courage, even as the hairs on her neck rose. "We know sorrow, do we not, Engracia?"

"It wouldn't have happened to me if your husband had not insisted that Manolo ride with the army!" she burst out, holding Rodrigo closer, as if fearing contamination.

What did she dare say, with Felipe looming there and thugs in the hall? She remembered a brave man. "Engracia, I was there when Manolo came into the Great Hall in his armor, defying my husband to stop him."

"Santiago could have tried!" Engracia said.

"He did try," Hanneke said, determined not to raise her voice. "Manolo would not listen to reason."

Engracia burst into tears. She wailed until the baby in her arms began to move restlessly. "Felipe said Santiago forced him to ride! How dare he?"

Enough was enough. Hanneke rose, sidestepping Felipe. She looked directly at the man, who could not maintain her eye contact, a small victory for her after days of defeat. "Felipe was not there. He was already hiding somewhere at Las Claves so he would not be forced to join the soldiers."

She could have said anything else, but she chose the truth. In the painful silence, Engracia stopped crying. "Felipe would never lie to me," she said, but Hanneke heard no certainty in her voice.

"I was there in the great hall," Hanneke said, biting off each syllable. "I heard everything that happened. Believe what you will."

Borrowing courage from both of her husbands, one dead and the other riding to battle, she turned on her heel, skirted around Felipe and made for the hall.

She wasn't quick enough. Felipe grabbed her elbow. "Watch what you say, Señora Gonzalez."

Where was her courage coming from? "It is the truth, and you know it," she replied. "Let go of me or I will…"

"Will what? You have no champions here," he said.

No, I do not, she thought in fear. In that split second before she bolted and ran, she remembered something her father had told her once, when she came home in tears after a dog chased her. "Stand your ground, daughter," was all he said. "Convince yourself and others will be convinced."

Very well, Papa, she thought. She jerked away from Felipe's grasp and stared at him, not blinking. "You would be surprised about my champions," she said. To her satisfaction, she realized that Castilian was a good language for defiance.

She left the room just as she heard a welcome voice. "*Dama?* We have been looking for you! We have made the most wonderful stew. There are too many goats underfoot in this palace of ours. Come with us."

She sighed with relief to see La Vieja and two equally formidable-looking villagers bearing down on her. With a glare at the thugs watching them, Teresa Gomez took her by the arm and pulled her away, talking all the while about the treat waiting for them. "Smell that aroma? Today is Christmas!"

She had forgotten. She had forgotten everything except Santiago dead in her arms, a cold ride to this ruin, a wedding as dawn was breaking, and the backs of all the soldiers riding away. "Christmas?"

"Yes!"

Hurried along by the women, they turned the corner and slowed to a walk. La Vieja did not loosen her grip on Hanneke, but she glanced over her shoulder and whispered, "One of the children saw you being led away by those men. We were worried."

"I wanted to see Engracia," Hanneke said. Her relief was so great that her legs felt loose and disjointed. "They frighten me."

"You'll stay close to us, *dama*, just as Antonio would want." La Vieja's eyes filled with tears. "And Santiago, as well. Come now. Let us feast. It's a modest feast, but we have all seen lean times, have we not?"

The women led her into a larger room. She looked around her at fading murals, wondering if this was the chapter house, where monks gathered to discuss the business of the monastery, sing, and mete out punishment. Now there were children, babies, goats and chickens. Her heart turned over to see Mama Cat and kitten who had accompanied Pablo and her to the killing grounds. The kitten kneaded her mama with little paws and sucked, while Mama blinked her eyes a few times at Hanneke in greeting.

For all the noise, there was order, and warmth and friendship. She put her hands over her eyes and stood there until La Vieja led her to an overturned pail and sat her down. "In time, in time," she crooned. "The pain changes, *dama*. It becomes easier to bear, I promise."

Other village women came close. She knew them – the worried mother with two little ones and the mule that refused to come in the gate, causing

Hanneke all her trouble. Who in this gathering had not suffered? There was the young widow, and look, she had an infant in her arms. Hanneke nodded to her, "When?"

"After midnight, *dama*, on Our Lord's birthday," the widow said. "I have named him Jesús, of course."

She saw kitchen children, and the widowed sister of Carlos. *These are my friends*, she thought, grateful.

The stew filled her belly. The cooks felt charitable enough to give some stew to Felipe and his thugs when they stormed in, ready to demand. *La Vieja* held out a pail of stew for them. "You needn't thank us," the old woman said in her kindest voice. "Go, but please return the bucket."

They were kinder to Juana, who came in, asking for food for Engracia, and much kinder to Father Anselmo, inviting him to sit down and stay awhile. He ate a companionable bowl, then took Hanneke aside to give her two marriage documents, mere scraps of the formal document of her wedding to Santiago. "Keep these close. Make sure Antonio keeps one on his person, as should you."

She nodded and took the pages, written in a courtly hand that seemed not to belong in their rough and tumble setting. "Better times ahead, father?" she asked, and he nodded.

"We are most optimistic people in Spain, because we have to be, daughter."

Who could deny that, especially on Christmas? Hanneke looked around her at friends and villagers. Her smile froze to see Juana watching the transfer of documents, a question in her eyes.

Once Amador and Baltazar left, they sat all afternoon in warmth and friendship, some singing, the little ones dancing, and Father Anselmo clapping out a rhythm. When dusk came near, they heard a horse and the shouts of a rider.

Everyone leaped up and crowded into the ruined courtyard, where snow fell lightly, covering many of the defects of their surroundings.

"What news, Pablo?" Father Anselmo called. His arm was firmly clamped on Hanneke's shoulders.

Pablo sat tall in his saddle, even though his arm was bandaged and blood seeped through. "It is a victory. We have driven off El Ghalib," he declared, his voice strong. In his confidence, Hanneke could see little of the kitchen boy from Santander who had been pushed from the dock, bullied by King Alfonso's son, championed her when no one else dared, and never failed her, much like Antonio.

"Is there a message?" Father Anselmo asked, as he helped Pablo dismount.

"We are to leave in the morning and return home," the boy said. "Las Claves is ours again." His tired eyes brightened. "Not a man among us died."

Younger boys led away his horse to be grained and wiped down, while Pablo ate his way through one bowl of goat stew and another. When the others returned to their own corners to begin planning, Hanneke came closer.

"Pablo, please tell me: Did El Ghalib keep his promise?"

He nodded. "Once the Almohades were gone, that was the first place Antonio and I went. Señor Gonzalez lies next to Fermina, and Manolo also."

Hanneke bowed her head in gratitude and love. *Thank you, Yussef El Ghalib*, she prayed silently. *I asked for far more than my necklace promise. You will be my friend forever.*

Chapter Thirty-seven

Carlos joined them shortly after dark, riding more slowly, his wounded face obviously paining him. It was a ghastly attempt, but he managed to smile as a woman helped him from his saddle, supporting him and scolding him in that way of women who care deeply.

Hanneke smiled to see it was the woman about his age who had tended him in the great hall, after she could do no more for her son. "We will find you a bed after you eat," she told him, as she tried to tug him into the monastery.

He stopped her. "Señora, I need a moment with the widow of Santiago Gonzalez."

Hanneke knew mutiny when she saw it. She put a placating hand on the woman's arm. "I will make him tell me quickly. I promise."

The woman backed away a few paces – but only a few – as Hanneke led Carlos to a bench outside the entrance. "Pablo told me that Santiago and Manolo were buried where I had asked," she began. "Tell me of your victory."

"The older I get, the more I realize that nobody ever wins," he said.

"I am not that old yet," she said, which made Carlos smile as much as his wound allowed. "You won. I am grateful."

He nodded, and winced from the pain of that alone. She heard the quiet triumph in his voice. "We surprised them and drove them out, *dama*. We chased them as far south as we dared. Antonio does not think we will see them again this winter." He leaned back in sheer exhaustion.

"You, my friend, are going to eat something and lie down," Hanneke said firmly. "You will sleep. Tomorrow, if this kind lady and I feel like it, we will see that you return to Las Claves in a wagon."

He started to protest, then gave up. "This is no way to treat a warrior," he grumbled. "Who am I trying to fool? You are a warrior, too, *dama*."

Hanneke sucked in her breath at the compliment, wishing with all her heart that Santiago could have heard this. "Thank you, Carlos. Isn't it time you started called me Ana?"

"Such a liberty!" he exclaimed, shocked.

"Carlos! Besides that, I wish you had remained at Las Claves. You're in no condition to travel," Hanneke said, but gently. "Antonio can't have agreed to this."

"I wore him down," Carlos said, and she heard his pride. "I reminded him that I should be where you are, when he is not. What could he do then?"

"Carlos," she said again, touched. She nodded to the woman who waited to help him.

"You have your champions, Señora Gonzalez," she heard from the shadows when Carlos left.

Not them. Why them? She turned around to see Felipe, flanked by Baltazar and Amador. *I will be safe at Las Claves tomorrow,* she thought, and reminded herself that Carlos thought she was a warrior. "My champions? Yes. I am grateful," she said, hoping she sounded serene, the last thing she felt. "Excuse me."

They didn't move until Carlos roused himself at the doorway to growl at them to respect a widow in mourning. As she joined the women and children, she prayed that Engracia would see the need for her brother to escort her and her infant son home to Valladolid for a lengthy stay, the sooner the better.

Pablo was the center of attention in the hall, as the women made sure his bowl of stew was full, and there was wine. She sat close, listening to his story of a battle quickly won, with no more loss of life.

True to her practical self, La Vieja wanted to know what the village looked like, and Las Claves itself. "The enemy rampaged a bit and threw things around," Pablo said.

The widow with the new baby asked the question on everyone's mind. "The dead in the great hall? What of them?"

"Buried, all of them," he said. "We saw to it."

He hesitated. Hanneke knew there was more, but she took him by the arm. "We are grateful for what you have told us, Pablo. Rest now, while we prepare for tomorrow."

She took him aside when the others left to pack. "What else happened?"

"*Dama*, the Almohades had put their own wounded in the hall, and thrown our people into a pile outside," he whispered. "Antonio and the others had just finished sorting them out and burying them, when I rode out."

"And the Moslem wounded?" she asked. "Did they…suffer the same fate as our wounded?"

He nodded. "The worst wounded were killed before we could retake Las Claves."

She put her arm around her true knight. Hanneke heard Engracia's baby wailing in the distant cell, as her mind went back to the terrible sight of Manolo breathing his last as he drowned in his blood. She thought about the Christmas before this one at home with Papa and her stepmother, and Father Bendicio, teaching her Castilian.

"Next year, Pablo, next year," she said, keeping him close. "We will have a peaceful Christmas with our loved ones around us." She looked at him, wondering why she had never asked. "Do you have family?"

"Only you," he replied with a grin, his usual optimism resurfacing.

"The honor is mine, dear one," she told him.

With Pablo as everyone's true knight and guide, the villagers left the ruined monastery at daybreak, moving slowly because many were on foot. The little ones rode in the wagons. Pablo had tucked the mother cat and kitten inside his doublet again, which made the children laugh to hear protesting meows, then loud purrs.

Hanneke rode beside him on Carlos's big horse, feeling her first measure of contentment in days to hear the women's laughter and excited murmurings, eager to see their husbands again, and their sons. Carlos had protested his incarceration in one of the wagons, but it wasn't much of an objection. His kind villager had worked her own miracle on him, cleaning his face and applying a better bandage.

Felipe rode alongside the wagon carrying his sister, nephew and Juana, but his henchmen, probably at his command, rode beside her. *Don't look at them*, she told herself. *You will be in Antonio's protection soon.*

La Vieja had no qualms about offering her opinion of them as she kept up the slow but steady journey on her mule, close to Hanneke. "I wonder why two big, strapping fellows like you didn't ride with the army to retake

Las Claves?" she asked Baltazar, who swore at her, and told her to mind her own business.

"The safety of the village of Las Claves is the business of everyone around you," La Vieja insisted. Hanneke admired her persistence, even as she feared for her. "Was your master afraid to be alone?"

That's enough, Hanneke thought in sudden alarm. To her surprise and relief, Baltazar sawed on his reins and pulled his horse out of the line. Amador followed him as they retreated back to Felipe like querulous children eager to tattle and whine about their treatment.

"Teresa, be careful with those two," Hanneke warned. "I trust them not in the least."

La Vieja smiled at her. "Señora, when you reach the advanced age of fifty years, you may say what you want." She spat in the mud, which had followed the snow. "Worthless ones."

Fifty years. As they jogged along slowly, she thought about her own seventeen years, wondering why she felt even older than La Vieja. To her dismay, her five months with Santiago Gonzalez had already begun to shrink into mere seconds, when measured against a lifetime like La Vieja's. How soon would it be before she forgot what Santiago looked like? Hanneke turned her head, not wishing to exhibit the weakness of tears.

La Vieja understood. "*Dama*, you will know joy again," the woman said, keeping her voice low, because this was their conversation only. "Joy and woe go hand in glove in Spain. Joy always comes around."

Hanneke wiped her eyes with her dirty sleeve, longing for a bath and clean clothing, and a fireplace. She looked around her again at the women and children, the old men, the animals. *Here I am*, she thought, *hoping for luxuries, and you are wondering if there is still a roof on your house or a well unpolluted.*

The journey was not a long one, in terms of distance. Hanneke rode back and forth among the villagers, seeing their serious faces and long gazes at nothing. In terms of emotional toll, she saw the strain on young and old faces alike. *How much can people take?* she asked herself. *How much can I take?*

Restless, longing for Antonio's protection, she continued circling among the travelers, ignoring the pointed animosity of Felipe and his thugs, and the fierce dislike of Juana, as she held Rodrigo. Engracia looked as beaten down as a horse whipped to continue a journey, and trying to decide whether to bear it or collapse under the weight. In spite of herself, she felt her heart go out to the bewildered woman.

Her balm was the kindness of her fellow travelers. La Vieja touched her in particular when she said, "*Dama*, you are doing what Señor Gonzalez would have done if he were here. God rest his soul and make short his time in Purgatory."

Hanneke looked back at her little train of stragglers. "Señora Gomez, you have all been so good to me, a foreigner."

La Vieja shrugged. "*Una extranjera*? You are one of us. Never forget that."

I am, she thought. *I belong here*. And so she was smiling when they arrived at Las Claves, where the massive gate was under repair. She motioned for the villagers to gather around. "Let us all go first inside the gate and see what Antonio and the others would like us to do."

No one objected except Felipe Palacios. She should have thought he might. He shouldered his horse past the little ones and old women, scattering them, and held up his hand. "*I* will tell you what to do," he ordered. His withering glance at Hanneke went nowhere, because La Vieja spit on the ground by his horse's front legs.

Hanneke tensed when his hand went to his dagger. He kept the weapon sheathed when the old men crowded close in front of Teresa Gomez and Hanneke. She could hardly imagine a less menacing group, but Felipe seemed to fear them. He looked about for Baltazar and Amador, who had already ridden through the gate. He followed them.

"Such a pup," La Vieja said. She pointed. *Mira, dama*! Here is Antonio!"

Thank God, she thought, *thank God. I am so tired*.

Chapter Thirty-eight

Antonio walked to the gate, his arms outstretched. "You are a welcome sight," he told everyone, who gathered around him. He looked at the young widow with the new baby. "Here we have another villager?"

He put his arm around the widow and admired the sleeping baby. Hanneke stood close enough to hear what he whispered to her. "Your man is buried in a good place, among the other defenders of Las Claves. We have all paid a terrible price."

"None more than the wife of Santiago Gonzalez," the widow said. She blew a kiss to Hanneke. "We are in this struggle together. She is one of us."

Hanneke fought to control her emotions. Antonio helped her from the horse, saying nothing because he didn't have to. His eyes spoke volumes.

It comes down to this, Hanneke thought, *as sorrow and joy warred inside her*. She looked around and pushed sorrow farther away. "You honor me, señora," she said. "And you, Antonio."

"You honor all of us, Señora…" Antonio hesitated. "Gonzalez." He spoke to them all. "El Ghalib was surprisingly kind to us," he said, which made them chuckle. "He didn't burn us out. I know! Who can understand an Almohad? Go to your homes. I believe you will find matters much as you left them."

He nodded to one older man who looked to Hanneke as if he had been a soldier in his youth. "Señor Rubio, you are in charge in the village. Let me know tonight what people need, and we will see how we can work together to provide it." He put his hand to his heart. "Go now and God bless you all."

In a matter of a few minutes, the villagers left. Soon it was just the two of them, as Pablo followed the wagon carrying Engracia and Juana through the gate.

"Well done, Ana," Antonio said. "Come inside."

She looked up from habit, relieved to see no Almohad heads on spikes. "Were there...did they?"

"No, and neither will I do that," he said, "not ever again."

"Why didn't El Ghalib destroy the village?" she asked.

"I don't know. The great hall is a mess, but nothing upstairs was touched, either. You will find your room as you left it."

Except there will be no Santiago, she thought. "I don't think I can go up there."

"I'll go with you," he said. "Actually, there is something in the room you need to see."

They started to cross the courtyard though the surviving soldiers Santiago had recruited, and the Knights of Calatrava, but were stopped by Felipe Palacios, who stood beside an uncomfortable-looking Don Ruy Díaz of the Knights of Calatrava.

"Stop, Antonio," Felipe ordered.

Antonio waited. Almost without being aware of it, Hanneke moved slightly behind the man at her side.

"What is it you wish, Señor Palacios?" he asked most formally. "There is much to do."

"I am relieving you of any leadership you think you might exercise here at Las Claves," Felipe said.

"By whose authority?" Antonio asked kindly enough. "I was the close companion in battle to Santiago Gonzalez, and these good soldiers are used to me. We never saw *you* riding out to save Las Claves."

Felipe took a step forward, flanked by his goons Amador and Baltazar. Hanneke held her breath, then let it out slowly. "Someone had to remain behind to protect the women and children."

"Señora Gonzalez did that quite well, didn't she?" Antonio countered. Hanneke heard all his wariness. "Before the warriors rode out" – he emphasized warriors – "the three of us circled Las Claves. Santiago told his wife precisely what to do, and she did it. You were nowhere in sight."

The soldiers chuckled and nudged one another, which brought out angry red spots in Felipe's face. The villagers remaining inside laughed.

"She did, Antonio," Don Díaz said, after a withering glance at Felipe. "She also had the wisdom to get a message through to me and the Knights.

In a struggle where every sword and lance counted, you were among the missing, Señor Palacios."

"It is my right to take charge here!" Felipe declared.

"By whose authority?" Antonio asked again. The courtyard was so quiet that his voice carried.

Felipe pointed a shaking finger to the wagon carrying Engracia and her son Rodrigo. "*My sister* Engracia told me that since Rodrigo Gonzalez is an infant, and she a mere woman, I am in charge here at Las Claves. Damn you, Antonio, you, the son of a woman who whored with the Almohades."

"No, no," Hanneke whispered. There was nothing to lose. She took a deep breath and walked toward Felipe, a man she knew she now feared above all others. She looked around her at men tested in battle.

She heard murmurs at the gate and turned to see the villagers had returned. She saw widows too young and mothers who had lost sons. She saw her friends.

"Be careful, Ana," Antonio told her. "His words don't wound me. People know the truth about my mother."

She nodded, but this was her fight, too. "Felipe, you would lead the people of Las Claves?" she asked. "Are you strong enough?"

He flinched, but moved closer to her. She stood her ground, hands clasped in front of her to keep them from shaking. When he stood too close to her for comfort, he spoke so everyone could hear.

"I am also determined to protect your dowry, Señora Gonzalez," he said. "Who knows what would happen to you if you fell into unscrupulous hands? Women cannot think for themselves in these matters."

"So that is it?" she said, speaking clearly. "Does everything in the universe revolve around gold?"

"I am only thinking of you," Felipe said. "Engracia has already signed papers declaring me regent. You have no say, not you, and not that bastard Antonio Baltierra. You are only the widow of the second son."

She knew he was right. She bowed to him, even as she seethed. "And you sir, must learn how to lead men who know what you really are. I wish you joy in your victory."

Hanneke turned her back on him and walked into the house of Manolo Gonzalez. She passed a stony-faced Engracia and a triumphant Juana holding Rodrigo, who would never know his good father. She looked around the ruin of the great hall with the blood-covered straw and buckets of water, bloody and filmy now. Overhead, the battle banners of the Moors and other tribes of North Africa who had conquered this peninsula in the name of Allah still hung, moving slowly, oddly alive.

It grated her very soul that she knew Felipe had the upper hand. Engracia had every right to confer upon her brother all power over Las Claves, to protect her son's interests. Now Felipe eyed her dowry. It was precisely as Santiago had predicted, even as he lay dying. Everyone in the courtyard had heard him.

She knew she could never reveal to anyone that Antonio had married her. Even the slightest whisper, the smallest suspicion would mean his death, to clear the way for Felipe. She had no doubt that Amador and Baltazar were capable of relieving the world of a good and loyal man, even if their master was not.

She would have to go, and soon, but where? How? It could wait, it *had* to wait for a day. Exhaustion claimed her. All she wanted to do was lie down on the bed she had shared with her husband, close her eyes, and wake to find that the whole matter had been merely a peculiar dream. She walked up the stairs by herself, grateful to be alone, certain it wouldn't last.

Antonio was right; the room was untouched. "Yussef el Ghalib, you are a complicated man," she said out loud. "What am I to make of you?"

"My question precisely."

She gasped and whirled around, then sighed to see only Antonio in the doorway. "Don't do that!" she scolded, her voice shaky.

He closed the door behind him. She must have had the same thought he did, because they met in the middle of the room in a fierce embrace. "I'm terrified," she blubbered into his shoulder.

"So am I," he said. He held her off to see her better. His eyes bored into hers, commanding her total attention. "There is a massive shouting match going on in the courtyard. Don Díaz is completely out of patience with Felipe, even though he must agree the *foul* little fellow holds the winning cards. That's the only reason I managed to get past the crowd. Felipe will miss me soon, when the argument ends."

"I must leave," she said, grabbing his surcoat.

"I know he will find some subterfuge to prevent it," he replied, loosening her grip, but keeping his hands over hers. "I will ride out tomorrow with the Knights as my escort, at least as far as their holdings. Another day or two will see me to Toledo, where I will, God willing, still find those additional mercenaries. I will be back here before two weeks have elapsed. I must."

"Take me with you."

"It is too dangerous. When I return, we'll find a way to get you to that convent south of Toledo. I have no idea where El Ghalib is. It pains me to say it, but you're probably safer here for the moment."

She hoped he was right. She sat down on the bed, defeated.

That was when she noticed the bracelet. She looked at Antonio, a question in her eyes. "This is what you wanted me to see, isn't it?

He nodded and sat beside her. He picked up the pretty thing, turning it over in his hand. Hanneke sucked in her breath when she recognized the links of the chain. "Yussef left this here, didn't he?"

"We can only guess."

Wordless, she held out her arm. He worked the little clasp and the bracelet was hers.

"What game is he playing?" she asked. "I used up more than my share of the bargain. I can't think he is the sort of man to mock me."

"I can't, either. It may be that we are not done with him yet, but not in a bad way. I wish I knew."

He stood up and looked down on her, then kissed the top of her head. "Don't worry about your personal safety. Carlos is here."

"Carlos is wounded," she reminded him.

"I would never discount him for so slight a reason," he replied with a half smile. "He is a most dogged, loyal man. And there is Pablo, your true knight. Stay close to them. Visit the village."

He walked to the door, looked out and listened. "It's quieter now. I will stay tonight in Don Díaz's camp. Right now, I had better make my careful way to the soldiers' hall."

"What is careful about that?" she asked, half in exasperation, half in amusement. "Can you become invisible? There is only one way downstairs."

"Not quite. Two doors down is an unused room with a window I can barely squeeze through. There is a vine from roof to ground. I believe it will hold my weight."

"Antonio, you amaze me."

He hugged her again, gentler this time. *Don't let me go*, she wanted to say, but knew better. "The last thing I will ever do is whisper any suspicion that we are married," she assured him. "It may have seemed like a precaution, but the game has changed, hasn't it?"

"I fear so." His exasperation was probably visible to the distant moon and stars. "I should have known Felipe would worm his way in through Engracia."

"I will be watched closely enough, but there is no reason to draw a target on *your* back, Antonio Baltierra."

"I appreciate that, believe me I do."

She remembered the marriage lines Father Anselmo had given her at Santo Gilberto, and drew them from the front of her dress. "You are to keep this," she directed. "I have a copy. So does Father Anselmo."

"What a strange venture this is," he said, looking at the little paper. He kissed her cheek this time. "I will see you in two weeks."

She watched him stand so silent in the darkening hall, then sidle two doors down. The door closed quietly behind him and she returned to her room. She closed her own door, wished it had a bolt and a crossbar, in addition to the key. She turned the bracelet around and around on her wrist.

Two weeks. Fourteen days. Twenty-four hours in a day. And one bracelet.

Chapter Thirty-nine

That first night alone in the bed she had shared for too few nights with Santiago left her tossing and turning, seeking for a warm spot, and in tears because the warm spot was cold and lying in a grave. She considered Antonio Baltierra and wondered at his thoughts. She knew he held her in high regard – a woman has a way of knowing things even *she* can't explain – but was he regretting their sudden marriage?

No matter the outcome of the next few weeks, and even the coming season of war, she knew better than to mention the marriage to anyone. She knew enough about her world to know life could be brutally short, woefully unfair, generally both. Santiago's plan to protect her and the dowry might appear unseemly, provided Felipe turned out to be a thoughtful and wise regent for Manolo's infant son. Was Santiago too distrustful? She knew all signs didn't point that way.

She finally rose from her tangled sheets, dissatisfied with herself and sensing all was not well, and never would be, not while Felipe and his henchmen roamed about Las Claves. She dressed warmly and threw one of Santiago's short cloaks around her shoulders, even as she wondered how long the garment would smell of woodsmoke, and around the neck, the odor of the man she married in reluctance, and came to love.

The hall was not entirely dark because the moon shown through the Moorish latticework that opened onto the garden below. She could see her breath, but at least there was no snow. The stairs were stone and silent, the great hall partially cleared of the debris of death and suffering. The battle flags hung there still. She sniffed the remnants of the fire and breathed in the fragrance of coal and ash.

231

She took a side door, one she knew Santiago had to stoop to get through, but which allowed her simple passage standing up. She closed it quietly behind her and walked along the path leading to the cemetery, shaking her head over the new graves. Before she went to bed, she had heard Felipe arguing with Antonio about the burial of ordinary soldiers and villagers among the family dead.

"Where else do those good men deserve to lie?" Antonio had said. "They gave everything for Las Claves. What have you given?"

That had ended the argument, to Hanneke's relief, but she worried. Felipe had a long memory. She counted on him not having the courage to do anything about men dead and buried.

She knew there would be sentries and guards, because Antonio had placed them in and around Las Claves. She recognized the first one, a shepherd who had marched with Santiago.

"Dear lady, what are you doing out here at this hour?" he asked so kindly.

"I want to see Santiago's grave and that of our daughter," she said.

He bowed and reminded her that it was a raw night and she mustn't catch a cold, then continued on his steady way. Finding Santiago's grave took her a moment, because of all the new mounds, some twenty lives gone.

There it was, raw and new, with Santiago's shield stuck at the head. A cross would come later, when spring arrived and there might be time for niceties. She looked to his left to see Manolo's eternal piece of Spanish ground, wishing he had not forced Santiago to take him into battle. "You have set off a dreadful turn of events, brother-in-law," she said out loud. "There is now a usurper who I do not doubt will find a way to wrest your land from little Rodrigo, something your brother never would have done."

She looked to Santiago's right to see Fermina's little mound. "I wanted you so much," she said softly. "Now your father will keep you company." In another moment she lay prostrate on Santiago's grave, her hand reaching out to Fermina.

"Ana, you'll turn into an icicle."

She had no idea how long she lain there, but Antonio's arms were around her now. She let him sit her up and leaned against him when he knelt beside her.

"I have so many regrets," she said, then, "By the saints, why are you here, too?"

"My sentry is the father of a daughter about your age. He apologized to me for not scolding you himself, but that didn't stop him from waking me." His arm went around her. "We little people all look out for each other at Las Claves. Please remember that."

They sat in silence as the stars turned overhead and the faint light of dawn made tentative motions to do something. Still saying nothing, Antonio got to his feet, stretched, and held his hand out to her. "Up you get, *dama*. Don Díaz must be away today, and those soldiers waiting for me north of Toledo are probably wondering where San… someone from Las Claves is."

"It never ends, does it?"

"It will. Come with me. I want to see Carlos. I want him to understand what needs to be done here while I am gone."

"Please let me ride with you," she asked again.

She could tell he hesitated this time. *Please, please*, she thought, wondering what he would do if she ran alongside his horse as the Knights left Las Claves.

"I should, I know I should," he told her, his arm around her shoulder. "If I knew with any certainty where El Ghalib and his army are right now, I might, but I do not know that. You have a gallant defender in Carlos."

"I wish you would change your mind," she said, unwilling to yield, as he led her to the soldiers' hall.

She drew back at the door. "I should not be here."

"Carlos is in the infirmary. You won't be troubled by any of the men."

He opened the door and she saw two beds, Carlos in one and a man with no left hand in the other. She took a closer look at the other man, sighed, and covered his face with the blanket. She pulled back the blanket for another look, then covered him again, thoughtful.

"Was this Almohad here and alive after you retook Las Claves?" she asked Antonio.

"Yes. We did what we could for him," Antonio replied.

"Would El Ghalib have done as much for you?" she asked, curious. She had her own opinion on the matter.

"Well, *dama*, you are still alive, aren't you?" He took her by the shoulders and pulled her close for a brief moment. "Now is not too early to decide how to treat our wounded, and theirs. How is this madness ever to end if we continue thinking of each other as less than human?"

She gave him a quick hug before he could release her. "Antonio, you are a good man."

Carlos sat up and watched them both, his face less swollen, his eyes certainly brighter. "I will keep a good eye on this one, Antonio," he promised.

"It is your only eye!" Antonio teased, then turned serious, a man in charge, even though Felipe Palacios had decreed he wasn't. "See that you do, my friend. Between you and Pablo, keep her in your sight." He came closer to Carlos. "I truly trust only the villagers. Are you well enough to get up?"

"*Claro*, Antonio. I am not wearing any pants, so I will wait until you leave. Watch for me, *dama*, after the soldiers leave. I'll be in your sight."

"You relieve my heart," she said, wondering why she had thought him so uncouth and rude earlier. "I will be in good hands," she told the man by her side, even as doubt assailed her.

It was easy to say, in the company of two brave men, but harder to believe when, after Mass and bread and meat, the Knights of Calatrava and many of Santiago's soldiers left Las Claves, Santiago's men to rendezvous with other troops from Castile and Navarre. Enough men remained behind for protection, but many of them, like Carlos, were recovering from injuries.

With Pablo at her side, she watched them leave, her hands pressed tight together. Out of the corner of her eye, she noticed Felipe and his thugs. None of them looked sorry to see the warriors ride away. Was Felipe actually gloating?

Suddenly it was too much. She ran alongside the soldiers until she came to Antonio. To her relief, he reached down and pulled her onto his saddle. "I'll take you to La Vieja," he said, "but no farther. I want a word with her."

She had to be content with that. "I am uneasy, too," he said, "but how much damage can a coward do in two weeks or so? He might try ingratiate himself with the villagers, but they are no fools."

She knew he was right. This part of the fight was not hers.

Antonio left the line of march and rode closer to the grand master Knight. Head to head, they conferred quietly, then he took her down a side road. "I'll catch up with them."

He stopped before a house barely elevated beyond a hovel, handed her down, and then dismounted. La Vieja opened the door immediately.

"Come in! Antonio, you are not thinking about stealing away this little one?"

"I would if I could," he replied seriously.

La Vieja's face grew solemn. "Do you not trust El Cobarde either?"

"I do not. If Carlos were not here, and Pablo, I would be more afraid."

"Then why are *you* here?" Teresa Gomez asked, sensible as always.

They seated themselves at La Vieja's rickety table. Hanneke smiled to see chickens pecking about. One had laid an egg in a saucer.

"Should I tell her?" Antonio asked Hanneke.

"I already did," she said, "but please strengthen my words."

"I thought you might," he replied.

Hanneke watched La Vieja's face as he quickly described their early-morning wedding and the reason for it. "I trust Felipe not at all – neither did Santiago – and thought that might be a prudent precaution," he finished, glancing out the door as the last of the soldiers passed. "Now that Felipe has proclaimed himself Rodrigo's regent and made it perfectly clear that he is interested in Ana, this kind lady fears for *my* safety."

"As well she might," La Vieja said with a nod. She covered Antonio's gauntleted hand with her hand. "Be careful! We'll keep an eye on *la dama*, too."

"That's all I ask," he told her. "I must leave. See me out, Ana."

She followed him from the hut. His arm went around her again. "I can do no more than this," he told her as they walked to his black horse. "I won't be long."

She knew she should feel better. At least she could pretend. "I know. I have two brave knights to protect me." *But what if they can't*, she wanted to ask. *Pablo is a boy and Carlos is wounded.*

He stood beside his horse for another long moment. "Try to put a thought into Engracia's otherwise empty head that she and her baby might be more comfortable in Valladolid with her parents." He chuckled. "You should have heard her so sweetly browbeat Manolo last summer. I am certain he let her go to Valladolid to maintain his sanity. You will, of course, insist that Felipe El Cobarde must escort her there."

"I can try."

"Good." He patted his leather pouch under his surcoat. "I have our marriage lines secure. Where are yours?"

"In a chest in San... my room."

"Wear it around your neck. Do it when you get back to your room," he said, in a voice of command that told her he had learned much from Santiago.

"I will."

She waited for him to mount his horse. Instead, he held her close and kissed her. "Don't forget me, *dama*," he whispered in her ear. "I have already assured you that once this matter is settled, you are free to do what is right for you. All the same, don't forget me."

He mounted his horse and gathered the reins, started out, then turned back. "One thing more. If matters go terribly wrong, do not hesitate even a moment to leave. I have observed that most women like to make certain all is in place before they act. Don't be that woman."

"I won't," she said, trying not to show her fear. He had to leave, after all.

She watched until he was out of sight, then squared her shoulders and returned to Las Claves. It was a short walk. She stopped several times to visit with villagers who had become infinitely dear to her, now that she had fled with them, worried, suffered and returned. She knew Antonio was right. She could trust them.

But what was this? The carpenters from the village had finished repairing the gate. They had clustered together, talking and gesturing, looking over their shoulders. As she approached, her heart dropped into her shoes to see Baltazar cramming a freshly cut Almohad head onto a spike.

"*Dios mio*," she whispered. It was the man from the infirmary, the one she had covered in death.

Shocked, she looked away. "Be careful," one of the villagers told her as she passed.

Don't look back. Don't look back, she told herself. She forced herself to walk across the courtyard and enter the manor where Santiago and Manolo no longer lived and offered her protection.

Felipe sat inside the great hall, booted feet propped on the low table near the fireplace, a wine bottle in one hand. He gave her his most unctuous smile.

"You didn't need to put that head on a spike," she said, not caring if she offended him, angry with herself for not demanding that Antonio take her with him, no matter the hardship of the journey. She knew hard journeys.

"Yes, I did, widow of Santiago Gonzalez," he countered. "You will see some changes here. Are you ready for them? I am." He laughed and turned his attention to the wine.

Her every thought now centered on getting to her room, where she could at least turn the key in the lock. She hurried up the stairs, praying to God and all the saints that Felipe was not behind her. She ran to her room, relieved to lock the door. She knew it was puny protection, but better than nothing.

She made herself relax when she heard no sounds. She knew Santiago had a small pouch where he kept odds and ends. She pulled it from his chest, dumped it out and opened the smaller chest that had belonged to his mother.

Her heart nearly stopped beating to see the marriage document resting on top of everything. "Mother Mary protect me," she said in Dutch. Her knees failed her and she sat on the floor. She was certain she had left the parchment folded at the bottom of the chest, out of sight. There it lay, visible to all. Someone had searched and found it. Numb, she plucked the document from the chest, and stuffed it in the pouch, which went around her neck.

She was too late. Someone knew.

Chapter Forty

By the end of the week, Hanneke took Antonio's parting advice. She ran for her life.

In the days that followed her discovery of her out-of-place marriage document, she did what Antonio had warned her against at first: nothing. *I know I hid the paper* waged fierce battle with, *I probably left it carelessly on top*, until she couldn't decide which was right.

Nothing happened of an alarming nature, which calmed her. Servants from the village continued to clean the great hall. She and Pablo helped, shoveling the mounds of bloody straw onto a single-wheeled cart, which others dumped outside the walls and burned. The day spent in that labor had led to a nightmare of prodigious proportions that left her wide awake and staring into the dark, terrified she would see Father Bendicio walking from pallet to pallet, offering absolution then Extreme Unction, or Santiago kissing his mortally wounded soldiers' foreheads then knifing them, rather than risk torture. She found herself fearful of every noise.

There were sounds no nightmare could explain, mostly footsteps in the upper hall near her room. *It must be Carlos*, she told herself. *It has to be.* He was up now and watching out for her when Pablo worked in the kitchen. When life at Las Claves started to resume its usual course, Hanneke began to relax.

She feared Juana was the light-fingered person who had pawed through her belongings. Perhaps she was wrong, because Juana had not changed. She continued to mete out her usual scowls and sour comments, no more, no less.

To Hanneke's relief, Engracia seemed to be gentling her stony unkindness. A surprisingly mild Juana had knocked on her chamber door one afternoon to urge Hanneke to visit Engracia.

Making sure she had her key, Hanneke locked her door behind her and followed the servant around the upper hall to Engracia's room, where Rodrigo was napping and her sister-in-law contemplated a half-finished sampler in its frame.

"Threads seems to knot themselves of their own accord," she said with a smile.

"You're braver than I am to even attempt such a task," Hanneke said, pleased to hear Engracia sounding more like herself. "I would run screaming from the room."

They laughed together, which soothed Hanneke as nothing else could have. Engracia glanced at Juana, who stood attentively by. "Juana, you can find something to do downstairs, I am certain."

Juana bowed and left the room, but Hanneke didn't hear a door open and close. She hoped there was another door, because she wearied of being fearful of all sounds and no sounds. Antonio had wanted her to suggest that Engracia might feel more comfortable in Valladolid with her family. Maybe this was the opportunity.

Engracia had her own complaint. "Hanneke, why is it that only Juana comes to see me now? My particular servant Dolores says she is afraid to come to Las Claves unless she is in the kitchen. She won't attend on me. I don't know why."

"Nor I," Hanneke said, although she had a perfectly good idea. Even *she* felt uneasy in the great hall if Baltazar or Amador were about. Even if they said nothing or did not move, their eyes seemed to follow her. She understood Dolores's reticence. At least in the kitchen there were other people at work.

This was a good opening. "Dearest, isn't it time for you to return to Valladolid and your family?" Hanneke asked, keeping her voice low, as she wondered where Juana was. "Your mother would love to see Rodrigo, and you have more willing servants there."

"I want to. I asked my brother, but he won't hear of it," Engracia said. Hanneke heard all of her frustration. "This is silly, but Felipe claims that… that Antonio has designs on Las Claves and I must be here to protect Rodrigo's interests."

"No," she said quietly. "Remember when I was so ill, well, you know… It's still hard to talk about."

Engracia patted her hand. "I can imagine. And here I am with my lovely boy."

"He told me then that both he and Santiago were counting on land of their own farther south, once El Ghalib and the other Almohades were defeated. No. Antonio does not covet Las Claves. He is from farther south. He wants to return there."

"You tell Felipe," Engracia urged. "He doesn't listen to me."

He terrifies me, Hanneke thought. *Why am I still here?* She patted Engracia's hand. "My dear, believe me when I say that Santiago never encouraged Manolo to join the battle. I was there and I heard every word."

"And Felipe was...who knows where?" Engracia said. "Sometimes I wonder."

"You knew Santiago's heart," Hanneke said, as her own broke again. "He loved his brother."

Engracia squeezed her hand. "Ana, I have wanted to believe this, even though Felipe tells me I am wrong."

"Believe it," Hanneke said firmly. "Felipe never knew Santiago, did he?"

"Not really. Hanneke, thank you for your comfort."

They parted as friends. Her peace of mind lasted less than a minute. As she went to the door, Juana came out of the alcove with the altar and saints, where she must have heard every word. She opened the door for Hanneke. "Be very careful, Señora Baltierra," she whispered.

Show no fear, Hanneke thought, her mind in a panic. Remember what Papa said. *Show no fear*. She turned to face Juana, letting her eyes bore into the servant's eyes. She stared in silence, then turned on her heel and left, not to return to her room and cower there, but to find Carlos.

To her relief, he was no farther than the gate, where the blacksmith was reattaching the final large hinge. Never mind that she knew Amador watched her from his perpetual perch by the entrance to the great hall. She linked her arm through Carlos's arm and tugged him to the side for a moment's conversation.

"Listen," she said tersely but softly, and told him of finding her marriage lines out of place, and being called Señora Baltierra by Juana only moments ago. "I have to leave *now*," she said. "If Juana knows, then Felipe must know, too. Antonio is in terrible danger. Felipe will send one of his thugs to kill him, and pave the way for forcing me to marry him. I know such coercion happens. It mustn't happen to me."

"Yes, yes," Carlos soothed. "Write a letter. I'll find someone to carry it north to Toledo."

"I need to leave *now*," she repeated, tugging on his arm for emphasis.

"The day after tomorrow will do," Carlos told her. "I'll make sure Pablo knows. We'll leave before sunup then. I can arrange for horses."

"No, now!" Hanneke insisted. "Not tomorrow!"

Carlos smiled at her. "They both told me how forceful you can be, little one. Trust me to do the right thing here." He chuckled. "I am the expert at skulking about."

She had to be content. The man would not budge. He returned to his work and she stayed close to the gate, rubbing her arms, cold because it was January and she had run outside without a cloak, panicking like a chicken who sees the *huisvrouw* approaching with an ax. She thought of her father again and tried to show no fear.

When she thought she could move without falling to her knees in fear, she crossed the courtyard, ignored Amador leering at her by the entrance to the great hall. Up the stairs to her own room she went, head high, eyes ahead. Were they closing in on her? Had they waited a few days, toying with her, letting her think they knew nothing, to lull her into carelessness? It had nearly worked. It might work yet. Until it did, she wasn't ready to surrender to anything Felipe had in mind, and she knew it was her dowry.

She unlocked the door. Felipe appeared out of the afternoon gloom and slid in right after her. She gasped and stepped back, but there was Baltazar, ready to stop her.

"What would you have with me?" she asked Felipe quietly, calmly.

He seemed surprised at her serenity.

"Well?" she asked, her voice still calm. "My husband is dead, and you obviously know that Señor Baltierra and I were married in an attempt to prevent any challenge from you to claim me and therefore the dowry."

More silence. She gathered together a little more courage from that quiet place in her heart that had been through so much. Santiago had said once, in anger, that she was a terrible liar. *I'll test that*, she told herself, *because I have no other resource.*

"Don't even think you can kill Antonio," she said, looking Felipe in the eye, which she knew he never cared for. "The Knights of Calatrava are well-informed of the danger to that good man. He will have an escort all the way to Toledo." She folded her arms to prevent them from shaking, and waited.

"I will find a way," he snapped. "Don't try to leave this place."

She had satisfaction, a puny one, when he looked away. "Where would I go?" she asked. "I am going downstairs in a few minutes to the kitchen because the cook is expecting me. You may leave now."

"I've won, you know," Felipe told her.

To her astonishment, Felipe left. She locked the door behind him. She wrote a note to Don Levi, *La Judería*, Toledo, and in a few words spelled out the danger to her dowry and to Antonio. *I will run and hide*, she concluded, then blew gently on the ink to dry it. She folded the note and stuck it between her breasts.

When she left the room, she locked the door behind her, well aware that Baltazar watched her every move in the hall. She put the key back in the pouch around her neck and descended the stairs, Felipe's henchman right behind her, practically on the same tread. She closed her eyes in terror when he touched her hip.

"Never do that again," she said, with all the venom in her body.

He stepped back, startled. Head high, she went to the kitchen, hoping beyond hope that someone would help her. Cook had died with Santiago's little forlorn-hope army of five, and Dolores's father had reluctantly assumed his duties. To her relief, Dolores was kneading bread. Pablo turned the meat slowly on the spit, his eyes troubled.

"Here I am to help," she sang out. "I am sorry I am late."

Please pretend I do this every night, she begged in her heart. "Wouldn't you know it, Baltazar wants to help, too, don't you?"

"I hadn't..."

"Señor Martinez, Baltazar can fetch you some water."

She had no idea what the new cook's name was. She stared at him through desperate eyes and he understood.

"I do need water," he said, as he stopped stirring whatever awful concoction he had dreamed up, because he was no cook. "Just around the corner you'll find a pail. Thank you!"

No one said Baltazar was bright. He snatched up the pail and left. Hanneke motioned Dolores, Pablo, and her father closer. "I am in dreadful danger from Felipe Palacios," she whispered. "Dolores, take this note to *La Vieja*. Señor, do you have a small knife?"

Dolores grabbed the note and ran to the door. "Walk slowly and calmly,"

Hanneke said, as she took over the bread. "If she gives you a message for me, come back quickly."

"I am Julio Villa," the cook said. He handed her a knife, which she put in the pouch around her neck with the marriage lines. "We will alert Carlos."

"And me, *dama*?" Pablo asked.

"When it is full dark, make your way to La Vieja. I have no more plan than that."

Baltazar returned with water and looked around suspiciously. "Where is the servant girl?" he demanded, grabbing Hanneke's arm.

She shook him off. "She is with child, and the smell of roasting meat troubles her. She will return when her stomach settles." *I am turning into quite the liar*, she thought. "Hand me those pans. The bread is ready."

She deftly shaped the dough into loaves, placed it in the pans, and handed Baltazar the baker's peel. "Until Dolores returns, you are to put these in the oven over there and for heaven's sake watch them! I will tell Engracia that dinner will be ready soon."

Please be as stupid as I think you are, if only for a few moments, she thought, as she slowly washed her hands, then rolled down her sleeves, taking her time when she wanted to run. She slipped out the kitchen door, hurried up the stairs, and locked herself in her room.

She knew Baltazar wouldn't stay long in the kitchen. She has no idea where Amador was. She snatched up Santiago's short cloak, leaned against the locked door and willed herself to think. Antonio had traveled down the vine from the room two doors away, but she needed to keep this door locked.

She opened the window, breathing deep of cold air only getting more frigid. There was just enough light to assure her that there really was a ledge. Whether it would hold her weight, she had no idea. If she climbed out and fell to her death, so be it. She had tried and she had been winnowed, too. Hanneke looked around the room for the last time. "Santiago, help me," she whispered. She touched her marriage lines. "And you, Antonio, you. God keep you safe."

Chapter Forty-one

The ledge was icy, but it creaked and held. She gasped when the vine bowed out as she climbed down, but it did not snap. The dry leaves rattled and protested even her slight weight, but no one appeared on this side of the fortress to check out the noise, which sounded to Hanneke like a full-throated tenor singing with a hurdy-gurdy accompaniment.

She closed her eyes in gratitude when she stood on firm ground again, firm enough at least, with snow and mud mingling. Her heart stopped when she heard a low laugh, all the worse because she knew that laugh. She looked up, barely breathing, knowing who she would see, nearly unwilling to look. *Help me, Santiago,* she thought, bypassing all the saints and Father Eternal.

"Why did you not think Manolo had a key to your room?"

"Juana, what a pleasure to see you," Hanneke said, as she stared at the window she had just vacated. "Are the goons there with you?"

Juana laughed once more. "Them? *Them?* What fools. No, I locked the door behind me, like you did. Santiago should have died years ago, but I did my best to kill him with words. You are a different matter. You are weak where he was strong."

A knife flashed in the moonlight. Hanneke stood there, waiting for the servant to throw it and end her life. Instead, she watched as Juana climbed out on the ledge, too, Juana who was taller and weighed more.

"You did him fearful damage," Hanneke said, unafraid. "Nothing you do to me will equal that."

"We shall see, widow of the man I hated as no other, and now the whore of Antonio Baltierra."

"Santiago, the child *you* wronged," Hanneke said, not caring what happened.

"He ruined my life!"

"You did that to yourself, Juana. There will be a judgment someday..."

This time, the vine was less forgiving. When Juana leaned from the ledge and grabbed the vine, it fell away after her first step and threw her to the ground in a judgment much quicker.

Hanneke leaped back as the servant landed on both feet. She heard bones break and grind sideways as Juana suddenly became much shorter. She crashed to the ground beside Hanneke with a shriek and a groan.

Juana held out her hands in supplication. "Help me," she whispered. "The pain!"

"After all you have done to Santiago?" Hanneke said. "Why should I?"

She wanted to do nothing, but another woman suffered. Almost against her will, Hanneke took a step closer and knelt down, only to see the light go out of Juana's eyes.

Hanneke turned away. "It is over, Santiago," she said. "Juana goes to her own torment now."

She knew she dared not waste another moment, but Antonio hadn't mentioned a gate so tall, and with a padlock. She stood in front of it, alarmed about this impediment to her escape, only just begun. She ran her hand over the padlock and let out her breath when she realized the hasp was free of the lock. She pushed and the gate swung wide.

She let her eyes adjust to the gloom, wishing she had fled in sturdier shoes. Hopefully, no one would be looking for her, because she couldn't be missed yet. Who would miss Juana? Only Engracia.

There was nothing to do but stroll into the courtyard then edge toward the gate, where the carpenter was putting away his tools. She could stop and chat, but when Felipe eventually began to search for her, the carpenter might say something. She didn't know the man well enough to beg him to lie for her or hide her. If he did lie for her, she did not think Felipe would treat him kindly, when found out.

His back was to her. She picked up a shard of roofing tile that had somehow ended up by the gate and heaved it as far as she could. The carpenter looked up. "Marco, you naughty boy, is that you?" he asked into the growing darkness. "Marco? Mama will scold, if you are teasing me."

She held her breath until he set down his tools and walked toward the sound, calling for his son. She passed through the gate before he turned around, hoping to reach the shelter of the huts and houses before anyone took notice of her.

"La Vieja? Please open your door," she whispered into wood so old and dried out that she saw into the single room through the gaps. A shadow passed in front of the gaps and the door opened. Teresa Moreno grabbed Hanneke's hand and pulled her inside. "What happened?"

Hanneke deep a deep breath and another, then told the old woman how Juana must have searched through her belongings and found the marriage lines. "Felipe knows. I locked myself in my room and escaped out the window. Juana is dead. She tried to follow me and fell from the window."

La Vieja clapped her hands. "No loss at all."

"I don't know where Carlos is. Did Pablo..."

La Vieja nodded and held out the scrap of paper her true knight had taken to her. "Felipe thinks you are in your room?"

"I pray he does."

La Vieja nodded with satisfaction. "He hasn't the imagination to think you would escape out of a second story window. This is good. You have bought us time."

Hanneke nodded, relieved to her soul to hear *us* instead of *you*. "You will help Pablo and me?"

"How could we not?" La Vieja said. "You became one of us when you bit that donkey's ear."

"It seems so long ago," Hanneke said, remembering the confusion, the pain, and the sorrow of what followed.

La Vieja took her hand and ran with her down the row of huts to one slightly larger, more house than hovel, and opened the door without knocking. The room was dark, but Hanneke saw people. Pablo ran to her and grabbed her around the waist. She hugged him.

"Where am I?"

"In my house, Señora Baltierra, the house of the potter. Pablo and Teresa have told me everything. My house is now your house. I am Francisco Ferrar, and I am at your service."

"I have put you and everyone in the village in danger, Señor Ferrar," Hanneke said.

"There is nothing we would not do for you, brave lady," he said, with a slight bow. "Had you not sent those peddlers to the Knight of Calatrava, we would all be dead. I have your note that must go to Antonio. One of us will leave immediately. I…"

He stopped and listened. Hanneke held her breath and heard it, too, a weak call for help. She knew the voice.

"Carlos?" she whispered. "What are they doing to him?"

Señor Ferrar spoke to two of the shadowy figures, who left in silence. Another word, and a third man took the note she had written. "We cannot waste a moment. Ride to Toledo, Chato." Señor Ferrar touched Hanneke's arm. "Come with me. You and Pablo will have to hide and be very quiet. I know a place."

Hanneke grabbed La Vieja's hand and kissed it, then followed Señor Ferrar from the house. There was more noise from Las Claves, shouts and a summons for more soldiers, then torches.

"Don't look at them," the potter said. "It will only frighten you more. Follow me. This will not be pleasant, but it will be safe."

She felt Pablo's hand in hers as they threaded their way through one alley and another. Soon they stood beside a fence. She sniffed, then looked closer at the dark shapes moving about and grunting.

"Who checks a pig sty?" Señor Ferrar asked. "There is a small shed here with a surprise in it." He looked back. "Let's hurry. Those torches…"

They skirted the pig sty, Hanneke hanging on tight to Pablo. The potter stopped before a shed that looked no larger than a dog shelter. Hanneke's heart dropped. There was no safety in such a place. She doubted the two of them could squeeze inside. "Señor Ferrar…" she began.

"Trust me." He knelt down and opened the door. "Years ago, when things were really dangerous along the frontier" – Hanneke rolled her eyes at that, but was wise enough to remain silent – "my father built this."

He disappeared inside. Pablo sidled closer to her. "Dama, is this a good idea?" he whispered.

"I am out of ideas," she whispered back. "We must trust others."

The potter reappeared, brushing off his cloak. "Just as I remember! Pablo, you go first. Crawl inside and feel for the hole. You'll find the ladder. Hurry."

He gave the boy a little shove. Hanneke listened to hear the creak of wood and then silence. "Excellent!" Señor Ferrar said. "Your turn, señora. Don't be afraid."

She crawled inside the tiny shed, past cobwebbed bottles and a rusty pail, feeling carefully until she found the open space. She patted around and felt the ladder. In a moment she sat beside Pablo in a small, well-timbered room.

"See there?" she heard Señor Ferrar say above them. "I will cover this just so. I think you will be here several days. We will bring food when we come to slop the hogs in the morning. No noise."

"What will we do? Where will we go?" she asked, already dreading the moment when the potter left them alone. She heard the hogs nosing around the wall of the shed closest to the fence. The stench overwhelmed her, but she knew Señor Ferrar had done his best.

"I have something in mind," he said, "something no one will think of. For now, huddle close. It will be a cold night. Don't leave this hole, no matter what you hear. *Adiós*."

Hanneke listened as the potter settled a board in place, then spread dirt around, some of which dropped through onto them. She leaned back against the earthen wall and closed her eyes.

"I'm afraid," Pablo whispered.

"I am, too," she replied. "What have they done to Carlos?"

She knew he was probably dead. She closed her eyes and prayed for his soul. *Please, please, be far away, Antonio*, she thought, adding him to her petition to *Padre Celestial*, who seemed so distant from a pig sty in Spain.

"Do you think we will die here, *dama*?"

Did she? Did it even matter what she thought? Her heart went out to the villagers who were putting themselves in terrible danger. "Not if our friends here can help us, Pablo," she said. "Rest your head on my shoulder. It's been a long and terrible day."

He did as she said. "How will this make it better?" he asked, ever the practical one, her true knight.

"I don't know, except that it will," she said, and closed her eyes.

Did she sleep? She must have, because much later she heard the door open, and someone brush away the dirt, which meant more of it rained down through the cracks. She tensed, praying it was Señor Ferrar, and not Baltazar or Amador coming to stare down at them and do unspeakable things. She knew it would not be Felipe. He wasn't a man to venture near a pig sty.

Señor Ferrar's cheerful voice greeted them. "*Buenos dias*, my dears!" he said, but softly. "Reach up and hold out your hand."

She did, and she closed her hand around soft bread and something that felt like sausage. Whatever it was, the hogs still clustered close to the back wall of the shed smelled it and started squealing in anticipation. *Cannibals,* she thought. *This is your brethren, wretched beasts.* She handed the food to Pablo, and held her hand up for a wineskin.

"I will try to return tonight," he whispered. "Ration the food out for the entire day, in case I cannot."

Hanneke reached up for a touch, just a touch of someone above ground, who could come and go and not stink of hogs. "What of Carlos?"

His reply was slow in coming, so she prepared herself for the loss of her other true knight, the man she knew would protect her until death. It must have come to that.

"He was stabbed by Amador and left outside the walls of Las Claves," Señor Ferrar said. Hanneke heard all the weariness and disgust in his few words. "Carlos is a hard man to kill. We have spirited him away. He might live." She heard all the doubt. "Bad times have come to Las Claves. Perhaps it would have been better if we had left this place to El Ghalib."

He had already done so much. Was it too much of her to ask about her future? "Señor, I..."

"Oh, there is one thing more. Who did Felipe Palacios find last night but the servant Juana," he said, his voice almost cheerful this time. "She must have fallen out of Santiago's window, although why she was there, I dare not surmise."

"Juana?" Pablo asked.

"The very woman," Señor Ferrar said. He spoke more quietly, as if he feared the hogs restless above them would tell tales. "Felipe and his thugs summoned all of us to the courtyard, to tell us the bad news and warn us to be careful." He turned conspiratorial. "He knew we would be sad to know that Juana had died a most terrible death." He chuckled. "He told us to hurry home." Another laugh. "He thought we would be sad. We rejoiced that Santiago's tormentor was gone – out of El Cobarde's earshot, mind you."

"She tried to follow me out the window and fell," Hanneke said.

"Excellent!" Señor Ferrar said.

"I am putting you in such danger," Hanneke said.

"Never fear, *dama*. We have not given up. As I stand here, we are expecting an answer to our petition to find a safer place for you."

"Where? Who?"

"In good time, child." He replaced the boards, moved dirt, and closed the door.

They were four days in the hole by the pig sty, days of cold and snow that left them itching and burning with chilblains. The rain was worse. Mud from the pig sty made its way into their hideout. The itching might have been fleas. At least they had gotten over the awkwardness of having to relieve themselves in a not-too-distant corner of their underground shelter. What was another fragrance at a pig sty? At least there wasn't any danger of being betrayed by body odors. And lately, it seemed they were breathing the same air in and out, which made her lightheaded.

Each visit by Señor Ferrar assured them that Carlos still lived. "We have hidden him in an abandoned hut belonging to our late *compadre* Luis, who died with Santiago. Carlos asked about you, but we were vague. If he should be captured and start to rave in a delirium of fever, we wouldn't want him to tell our secret."

Finally, four days after she had run in terror, the game changed. By now, they sat mostly silent, because others had searched the area, someone even opening the door to the shed, sticking his head inside, and swearing at the stench. As small as she was, she could not stand upright in the tight space. An enemy with mischief on his mind would have to haul them out.

The day's meal was skimpier than usual. Apology in his voice, Señor Ferrar had reminded her gently that January and February were the months of scarcity, never more than now, when El Ghalib's army, while not destroying their houses, had made off with what precious little sustained them.

"This is when my wife starts to dream of March, when the grass returns, bringing with it dandelions," Señor Ferrar told them. "She makes a wonderful soup."

He returned after full dark, something he never did. She held hands with Pablo, praying it wasn't Amador or Baltazar, hoping that Señor Ferrar had a little more food, wishing he would tell them that Antonio had received her hasty note and was safe.

Señor Ferrar didn't hand down food. He held his hand out to her. "Take my hand and let me help you up," he said quietly. "We have found a safer place."

She took his hand and tried not to cry out when she stood straight for the first time in days. But first, Carlos. "How is my champion?" she asked simply.

"He yet lives." Señor Ferrar chuckled. "La Vieja swears it is hard to kill an ugly man."

He opened the door to the shed and looked both ways, then ushered Hanneke and Pablo through. "Follow me."

It was on her lips to beg to see Carlos, but she said nothing, trusting in this kind man who had risked so much. He led them to a man dressed like an Almohad, which made her draw back.

"Never fear, *dama*. Sometimes the safest thing is to travel in an unexpected direction. For all that he has lived among us for years, Mansour has connections that I know better than to question. He will take you to some people who move back and forth from the Arab world to the Christian world."

"I didn't know anyone could do that," Hanneke said, still unwilling to move a step closer to Mansour, with his Arabian headdress, wicked-looking scimitar and desert robes.

"Gypsies can," Señor Ferrar said. "Go with God and Los Gitanos."

Chapter Forty-two

Hanneke and Pablo traveled south for two days in silence with Mansour. They walked as he rode, eating nothing because they had nothing, and their silent guide was not inclined to share what little he had brought for himself. At least by the end of the second day he was not spitting in their direction. As a woman with no expectations, Hanneke counted it good; she had no choice.

They traveled by night, struggling through a cold and barren land, and slept by day, curled up close to each other for warmth, while Mansour wrapped himself in his voluminous robe and snored. Hanneke thought about stabbing him with her little kitchen knife, but changed her mind. It was foolish notion to begin with, and she doubted the knife was sharp enough. At least Mansour seemed to know where he was going, wherever that was. She put her trust in the villagers who had appointed Mansour to ferret them to safety.

One incident gave her hope, during those days of walking and starving. Mansour at least did not begrudge them water. One evening, when she reached for the hide water bag he held out, he suddenly grasped her wrist. She knew better than to pull away. She knew better than to do anything.

She took a calming breath when Mansour fingered the chain bracelet, a copy of her necklace from Yussef el Ghalib. She saw something besides hostility in Mansour's perusal; she saw recognition.

"El Ghalib?" he asked.

She nodded.

Mansour gave them something to eat that night. She curled up close to Pablo again, tired of walking, wishing and praying that Mansour would move in some other direction besides south, to the land of his own kind.

To her further distress, she discovered she was praying and wishing with the same weariness.

She woke early on that third day because she was starving and her stomach seemed to bore through to her spine. She pulled her legs close and rested her chin on her knees. She thought of her home in Vlissingen, and buttery cookies, and even those scraps of herring that the fishmongers gave away to the poor folk who clustered around the dock. With a little fat, she could take those scraps and fry a delicious meal she would have scorned only a year ago.

I want this to end, she thought, and pressed her forehead against her knees. *I don't care how.*

"Señora."

Mansour never spoke to her. She looked into the early-morning darkness and saw Yussef el Ghalib. Her heart lifted for a moment, then sank back to the depths. She rested her forehead against her knees again. What possible good could come from even acknowledging his presence? "I wish you would go away," she murmured. "I am miserable and so hungry."

He didn't say anything. She wanted him to leave, but she didn't need to be rude to this enemy, this friend, this...what was he? "You have your necklace, Yussef," she said. "I like the bracelet you left, but I don't understand it. You allowed me what I asked for, with the necklace; even more. I can expect nothing else."

"I know," he said. "You have come so far and received so little."

"All I want is for Antonio to be warned about Felipe Palacios." She turned to him, keeping her voice low. "I don't know what devil's bargain you struck with that evil man, but it has ruined all of us, hasn't it?"

"Not yet," he said. "Antonio has been warned."

"Good. That is all I wanted."

"Nothing more for you?"

"No. I have no expectations. I suppose you wanted the dowry, too." Might as well air that dirty linen. "Were you going to divide it with Felipe?"

"That was the initial idea – to steal you away and hold you for ransom, if somehow he did not marry you."

Hanneke knew she had to give him at least grudging approval for honesty. "What changed?"

"I came to know you." She could have sworn she heard him chuckle.

"There is nothing funny about what is happening, Yussef."

"No, there is not. Ana, has anyone ever asked you what *you* want? We greedy men want your dowry. We want land." Another low laugh. "My side wants you Infidels to bow to the true religion. Your side says Christ this and Christ that."

"No one ever asks a woman what she wants."

"Think a moment, then. What do *you* want?"

Why not humor the man? Some small wisdom told her she had nothing to fear from Yussef el Ghalib. He might even be a friend.

"I wish…oh, you will laugh."

"No, I won't," he assured her.

"Well then, I wish that when Father Bendicio and that other priest arrived at my father's house…I wish they had brought along Santiago." She stopped. So much kindness to a woman really was laughable. "I told you it was foolish." El Ghalib was silent. "Are you asleep?" she asked.

"No, Ana. I'm thinking about what you said. You would like to have met Santiago Gonzalez first?"

Since the whole business was preposterous, she relaxed and considered it. "I wish he had introduced himself, told me about his life in Spain, and maybe even his fears and worries. We would talk and I would tell him about myself."

"After that, he would ask you to marry him?" To Hanneke's ears, El Ghalib sounded genuinely interested.

"Yes, if he decided he wanted to." Another thought struck her. "If he wanted to," she repeated. "Yussef, I don't think he had a choice, either. I had not considered that." She looked at him. "Do you have choices?"

Silence.

Are we all pawns in a dangerous game? Hanneke asked herself. She looked toward the east, where the sun was rising, suddenly, deeply aware that there were two sides to this matter of choice. "He… he would ask me and I would say yes or no. If it was yes, I would follow him with my whole heart. If it was no, he would leave and we would both find others." She laughed then, but softly. "I told you it was improbable, but that is all I want: a choice. I suppose I don't care about money, or land, or even religion." She crossed herself at that. "Maybe I *do* care about religion a little." She smiled when he laughed. "I want to choose my husband, bear his children, be a good wife and mother and do kind things. That's all. These are small and simple things, but I ask too much, don't I?"

"It shouldn't be too much," el Ghalib said. "None of us live in a world that good, however."

"I wish we did." She reached across yawning chasm separating them and touched the hand of her husband's enemy, noting in her heart that is wasn't such a wide space.

The sun was nearly up. "I must leave," Yussef said. "Thank you."

"For what? For wasting your time?" she asked, in charity with this man.

"No. For sharing your whole heart," he told her. He moved closer, closing that huge gap. "You did choose once. You handed me the necklace and you chose to stay with your husband as he lay dying. You didn't know what I would do to you. You could have chosen your own safety, but you didn't."

"Don't remind me," she said as tears came.

She was in his arms then, his comforting arms, as she struggled with fresh sorrow. "He wanted me to choose safety. Begged me. You were there. You heard him."

"I remember. You chose love, instead," he said, caressing her cheek with his. "He was a man most fortunate. You chose then."

"I would choose the same."

She closed her eyes when he kissed one cheek, then the other. "Don't give up, habiba," he said. "I wished I dared help you more, but you see my position. Santiago was my enemy. I have pledged my allegiance to Caliph Muhammad al-Nasir."

"I understand, Yussef. I truly do. Thank you for what you have done for me right here, right now."

Then he was gone. She heard a horse's harness jingle, hoofbeats and silence. Perhaps she had imagined the whole thing. Hunger could do that to a body.

Santiago had called her habiba once, after a moment of tenderness in bed before armies beckoned. "It means beloved," he had told her. "Be careful, Yussef," she said softly, even as Pablo sat up and stretched.

Mansour's food ran out that afternoon as they arrived at the camp of Nito and Florinda. Pablo and Hanneke's breakfast had been more water. She didn't tell Pablo or Mansour about her early-morning visitor, knowing the danger El Ghalib had put himself in. She and Pablo stayed back in the clearing, letting Mansour go first.

She realized she had not imagined El Ghalib's early visit when an older fellow, shabby in a cloak chewed by moths, ignored Mansour and came toward her, holding out his arms. "Señora Gonzalez?" he asked, making an elaborate bow. "I was told this morning by our mutual friend that you would be arriving today. Welcome to the caravan of Nito and Florinda! I am Nito, *un gitano muy fuerzo*." He pounded his chest with pride.

Who would not smile at that? He didn't look like a man with bad intentions, so she made a bow of her own. "Thank you, señor. Did our mutual friend acquaint you with my troubles?"

Nito's eyes grew sad. "*Oye*, such troubles! We will keep you safe in our caravan." He gestured at shabby wagons with strange markings, horses that didn't look strong enough to pull either one, and two dogs even skinnier. "Perhaps some might think that caravan is too grandiose a word for what you see before you," he admitted. "I have discovered in life that if you do not trumpet your worth, no one else will."

Nito and Florinda's enterprise seemed to have fallen on hard times. Granted, January was not the month in which to look around and see greatness. Perhaps she should be charitable, especially since this caravan seemed to be her lot for now.

Pablo edged closer and whispered, "*Dama*, we are going to get lice here."

"We probably are," she agreed, following Nito's gestures toward the fire. "Another small moment in God's eyes?"

From the look of the empty pot, they had just missed a meal. As she went closer to warm her hands over glowing bits of charcoal, one of the younger men gave her a hard look and scuffed dirt on the fire. She stepped back, disappointed.

Nito watched her. "Señor, we are so hungry," she said, pawning away the last of her dignity, if she even had any remaining. "Is there anything left?"

"Alas, no," he said, again with that sorrowful look that was supposed to explain their predicament. Very well. There would be no food.

"What would you have us do for you?" she asked simply.

The old fellow gestured to Pablo. "You. What is your name?"

Pablo told him. Nito pointed beyond the wagons. "Do you see Fatima my love over there?"

Pablo squinted. "I see an old camel."

Nito took Pablo by the arm. "Let me introduce you to Fatima. But not too close."

The animal had been resting on the ground, looking like a mildewed carpet. As man and boy approached, she rose slowly, grunting and passing gas. Hanneke stared in fascination at a monkey on the camel's back as it ran up and down, chittering and scolding.

"Pablo, your unhappy task is to walk beside Fatima and keep her moving," Nito said. He handed Pablo a long stick. "Poke her if she tries to sit down, but don't get too close! Can you do this?"

Pablo gulped and nodded. Hanneke took a step back when Fatima bared her yellow teeth at the world in general.

"Good! Remember this, Pablo: If I point to that wagon, run and jump in."

Hanneke looked where he pointed to the wagon that dipped dramatically to one side. "What is inside that wagon?" she asked.

Nito took her hand and tugged her after him. "You are about to find out. This is where *you* will be, señora." He put his fingers to his lips and kissed them. "You are the lucky one!"

Pardon my skepticism, she thought, as they walked to the crazy-tilting wagon. Nito climbed the steps like an agile lover, and not an old man of at least forty. "Florinda, my sweet! Look what we have here! A fortune teller, I think."

A what? Hanneke asked herself in amazement as he tugged her inside. He parted the beaded curtain and she stared at the largest woman she had ever seen. Florinda, Nito's sweetheart, seemed to go on forever, settled there in her corner of the wagon, spreading out like a greasy pudding. She was dressed in yards and yards of black wool, with silver bangles like barrel hoops marching up and down her arms.

"Florinda, my little love, let me introduce you to Señora Ana Gonzalez. Yussef wants us to watch out for her. Come closer, señora, and meet my bountiful bride."

Hanneke edged closed, afraid that if she moved too fast, she would slide into that human mountain and disappear forever. She leaned backward in involuntary self-protection, then moved cautiously ahead.

Not only was love blind; it was also without a sense of smell. Wave after wave of foul odors rose from the mound of flesh before her.

Florinda smiled at her, until her eyes disappeared into rolls of fat. Hanneke held out her hand and watched it disappear into the warmth and softness that was Florinda, Nito's gypsy queen, *la gitana*. Hanneke should have been repulsed, but she wasn't.

Nito looked from one to the other, his eyes shining with pleasure, as if he had introduced a queen to an equal. "You will be friends," he said. "We are leaving now."

"As you think best, husband," Florinda said. Her voice was deep and rich, as it resonated through her gigantic body.

Nito leaned close and kissed her. "My treasure, I will come to you later," he said. He tweaked one of his wife's massive breasts. "When this little one is long asleep."

They giggled together. Nito leaped from the wagon, called to the driver, and they joined the caravan with a great creak of the wheels that alarmed Hanneke.

"Is he not a pearl?" Florinda said as she settled herself.

"Yes, a pearl," Hanneke agreed, amazed at her traveling companion.

Florinda smiled to herself, sighed with happiness, then gave Hanneke her attention. "Yes, you will be a fortune teller. The last one ran away with one of her customers." She giggled like a maiden behind her massive hands. "She convinced him he was handsome and virile."

"He wasn't?" Hanneke asked.

Florinda shrugged. "Skinny and small. He believed her because people like to believe a fortune teller." Her gaze turned serious, business-like. "I need someone who can charm money out of priests and old women. You must be able to understand the sorrows and joys of young virgins. Someone who…"

The barely moving wagon ground to a halt. Hanneke held her breath, waiting for the axle to snap under the weight of Nito's lovely bride. She pulled back a dirty curtain and saw Pablo running toward them. She opened the door and pulled him inside.

He grabbed her arm. "Nito says it is a strange man with a big, tattooed man beside him!"

"Amador," Hanneke said. "He wasted no time." She looked again, only pulling back the curtain a little as her heart began to race. "And Felipe. Florinda, save us."

Chapter Forty-three

Florinda wasted not a moment. Her eyes bored into Hanneke's. "Do you fear small places?"

The filthy shed by the pig sty had been bad, but she endured. "I have hidden in small places before."

"*Dama*, it is Felipe!" Pablo exclaimed.

Hanneke put her finger to her lips. "Shh. We know. Be calm."

"He will do bad things!"

"Silence," Florinda hissed. She pointed to an impossibly small chest. "Empty my medicine chest. Hurry!"

Please, not that one, Hanneke thought in a panic. "It's so small. I cannot possibly fit."

"You can if you want to," Nito's delicate dainty said. "Would you rather Felipe won?"

Pablo had already pulled up the lid. Hanneke threw herself on her knees by the chest. She yanked out strange marked packets of earth, coils of hair and snake skins, and objects she could not name and didn't want to. When it was empty, Florinda ordered Pablo to take a rock with odd markings on it and bash out a little hole near the bottom.

He worked faster as they heard the monkey on Fatima's back shrieking, and the jingle of Spanish harness. Sweat sprang up on Hanneke's forehead, even though the wagon was cold and she could see her breath.

"Climb in," Florinda ordered, her rich voice hard with an edge that even Nito had probably never heard before. "You will fit if you take off your dress."

Hanneke threw off her dress, which Pablo folded and handed to Florinda. Hanneke sat down in the chest and wedged herself sideways, her face close to the hole Pablo had hacked. She fought down her panic as

Pablo tossed in the charms, the earth, the hair, magic bones, mystic vials of liquid, curious stuffed creature only visible in nightmares. Hanneke shut her eyes as gypsy treasures rained down on her.

Florinda spoke softly. "Pablo will close the trunk and lock it."

The monkey screamed and the dogs barked. Even in the trunk, Hanneke heard a sword pulled from a scabbard. One dog stopped, the other whimpered.

As she fought down her panic, Hanneke heard the lock turn. "What of me, lady?" she heard Pablo say.

Hanneke felt the wagon heave as the woman must have shifted herself. "When I raise my skirts, crawl behind my legs."

"But lady, what would a priest say?"

"He would envy you," Florinda snapped, all shred of calm gone. "Do it!"

"Sí, señora."

Florinda called out, "Nito, why have we stopped?"

Hanneke heard his reply. "My jewel, my pet, look here, we have welcomed Señor Palacios from Las Claves. Sir, will you stay for our evening meal, as poor as it is? Do you want your palm read?"

Hanneke heard no reply. All she could think of was the lock on the trunk. *I can't get out*, reverberated in her brain. Her nearly naked body itched from the debris in the trunk, but she could not move to scratch.

"We will look around, old man," she heard Felipe say. "If I find that woman and boy, after you have assured me they are not here, Amador will slit your throat."

You could never do it, Hanneke thought, in spite of her own terror. *El Cobarde, I promise you, someday someone will do worse to you.*

Hanneke steeled herself when she heard boxes and barrels thrown from the other wagon. A woman swore then screamed in terror, after the sound of a slap. More boxes tumbled out. Hanneke gulped back her sobs. If someone threw out the magic chest, her neck would break.

She closed her eyes and waited, desperate to move, unable to budge. When the wagon creaked and shifted, she knew Felipe or Amador – maybe both – were inside.

The men rummaged through boxes and the smaller chest of charms, which made Felipe scream and leap back. He must have seen the shrunken head that Florinda claimed was good to ward off evil. Perhaps it *was* good; Felipe slammed the trunk shut.

Despite her terror, Hanneke could not deny that Florinda was equal to these men ransacking her belongings. The woman hummed to herself as they thrashed about, then passed wind. "A thousand pardons, señor," she said serenely. "Some things cannot be helped."

It had to happen. Felipe knelt by her trunk and jiggled the lock. "Open it, fat woman," he demanded.

To her horror, Hanneke heard a great rattling of keys. Felipe snatched them from her. "Which key?" he demanded.

"I do not remember, señor. It has been so long since I have opened that trunk. Try that one. No, no, the one next to it."

Hanneke heard a key crammed in the lock, then another and another. The keys hit the wagon floor and Felipe sat on the trunk. "That miserable Arab we stopped not far from here told us you were harboring a woman and a boy. Before he died, he insisted! Where are they? Answer me!"

Florinda broke wind again, impressively louder this time. Felipe swore and left the wagon. Hanneke felt the wagon shake and knew Florinda was laughing softly to herself. Hanneke clawed on the inside of the trunk.

"No, child," Florinda said under her breath. "He is right outside."

Hanneke struggled to move as panic took over. Bits of bone and fur slid down her neck, then something slithered past her ear and nestled against her cheek. She bit down hard on her wrist to keep from screaming. Her mouth filled with blood and she fainted.

When she opened her eyes, she was lying stretched out on a pile of rags as noisome and odorous as Florinda. She immediately drew herself into a ball, terrified because she couldn't see anything. Was it possible to go blind from terror? Perhaps she was dead. She felt her face, then realized it was night.

"*Dama?*"

Thank God no one had found Pablo. How could they? He had wedged himself behind Florinda's legs, where no man was brave enough to venture, unless it was Nito, her amorous husband.

She wanted to laugh, but she ordered herself not to, knowing that if she started to laugh, she would never stop.

"Child? They are gone."

For how long? she asked herself.

Pablo helped her sit up, and she realized she was wearing her black dress again. Her shoes were on her feet. Only the greatest force of will kept her from leaping up and running away, if she had any place to run.

As she sat there, numb and stupefied at the same time, Pablo brought her a cup of soup. She warmed her hands on it, then sniffed, hoping not to smell anything that resembled the trunk and its belongings.

"One dog is dead," Florinda commented. "Eat."

Surely not, she thought, and held off the cup. She sniffed again, knowing how hungry she was. Poor dog.

She looked around in alarm when the wagon creaked, but it was only Nito. He squeezed himself beside his mountain of a wife. She saw no jocularity this time, and her heart went out to him. "Pablo and I can leave tomorrow," Hanneke said quietly.

"Where would you go?" he asked. "Who do you know? Your Castilian is remarkably good, but your accent…" He shrugged. "I have made a promise to Yussef el Ghalib. I would fear to disappoint him."

"Can you get me north to… Toledo? Antonio Baltierra mentioned a convent just south of the Rio Tajo."

"Santa Catarina. Perhaps, but not now. If we turn north too soon, Señor Palacios will be on us." He stirred. From the sudden stench that grew worse and the clatter of arm bangles, Hanneke knew Florinda must have put her arm around him. "Yes, yes, my love, we will manage. I sent one of my men to follow Felipe, just to make sure he wasn't waiting close by."

"And?"

"They are moving north, but slowly. There are six men."

In the dark, she heard Nito slap his knees. "Here we are. Señora Gonzalez, you will have to help us get by for a while." Hanneke heard a loud smacking kiss. "My lovely bride will teach you how to tell fortunes."

"Señor, all that fortune that follows me is bad luck," Hanneke said.

"That will change, once you know the secret."

"But sir, suppose someone recognizes me?"

He tipped his head as he scrutinized her. "That will change, too."

Chapter Forty-four

They woke to snow, which changed to icy rain, which meant no one traveled that day. The others woke; Hanneke had never slept. As soon as she closed her eyes, she was back in the trunk again, fighting down panic, trying to breathe.

She wanted to sleep. Staying awake at night meant she could not escape the hunger that drilled more deeply into her middle with each passing hour. Also, she could not ignore the sound of Nito and Florinda making improbable love. The wagon tipped alarmingly and she grew dizzy, then nauseous.

Then lonely. She thought of Santiago, who had admitted to her one time that there weren't enough hours in the day for all the love he wanted to give her. He always promised that after the coming season of battle, there would be more time. Time ran out and the winnowing began.

She hoped Antonio Baltierra still lived, wondering if he would make extravagant promises to her that he could not keep, either, no matter how heartfelt his intentions. That was another life, another Hanneke. Now she must learn to tell fortunes, she who believed in nothing and no one, she who had no hope.

She must have slept. When she woke, the weak light of the winter sun would have shone through the wagon's one window, if someone had ever cleaned it. She was alone in the wagon, alone in the sense that no one who could move about was in there with her. She doubted Florinda had left the wagon in years; she was nearly a fixture, not a person.

Ah, but that was unkind. Florinda indicated a bowl on the ledge by her and Hanneke picked it up, wisely knowing not to be hopeful, because she would only be disappointed. It was a watery soup flavored with spices and odd things that must have come out of the magic trunk, with some meat floating on top, and a few brindle hairs. She drank it, chewed, and would have given the earth for more.

Now for the lessons, she thought, dreading them, but Florinda had other ideas. She held out a large fabric pad. "Unlace your bodice. Slip off your dress. See if this will do."

After a glance around, Hanneke did as Florinda commanded. Shivering in the cold, she followed the woman's directions and draped the hump over her shoulder. She wiggled it into place and tied it across her stomach. She pulled on her dress again.

Florinda tucked and adjusted the hump, then sniffed and dabbed at dry eyes. *"Qué lástima!* How sad for one so young and lovely to be a cripple!" She winked at Hanneke. "Women great with child will touch your hump for luck," she said, her tone businesslike. "You will bring them easy labor. When they touch your hump, you must say, 'God bless you, mistress.'"

"'God bless you, mistress,'" Hanneke repeated.

Florinda appraised her a moment, then clapped her hands. "I know! Hand me my sewing kit."

In a few minutes she crafted a patch for Hanneke's eye. She tied it on. "That will do. You needn't wear this all the time, but you should get used to the hump." She clapped her hands again. "Now you will learn to tell fortunes."

Hanneke didn't learn, not when Florinda pulled out a dusty book with illustrated hands and lines, in some strange script. As the afternoon wore on, all the lines and their meanings blended into one tangled web. She wanted to learn, but she could not concentrate, not with her stomach aching continually.

She admitted defeat when Nito came into the wagon late in the afternoon to light the lamp and flirt with Florinda. "What have you learned, little one?" he asked, then tsk tsked. "Poor child to bear such an infirmity as a hunchback."

She stared at her hands with their traitor lines. "I can't, Nito," she whispered. "People will lay down coins they cannot afford, and I will be exposed as a fraud."

Nito was silent, much as Florinda had been. Shame covered Hanneke because she had failed these people who had already suffered indignities for her.

Before the silence became too great, Nito sat beside her and took her hand, which he rested on his knee, palm up. His fingers were feather-soft as he traced the lines. "I see a long lifeline, little one, as well as much love and many children." He traced another line. "The line of Mars is long, too." He smiled at her so kindly that she wanted to weep. "I did not think we could turn you into a gypsy overnight."

She pulled her hand away. "Perhaps I could do whatever that woman in the other wagon does, and she could tell fortunes."

He shook his head at that. "Never! Yussef el Ghalib would slit *my* throat. She dances when the mood is on her, and spreads her legs for men." He shrugged. "Her husband isn't too happy about that, but even *he* has to eat."

"I...I couldn't."

"No, you couldn't," he said, and took her hand again. "Let us try this: pretend you are a young girl with no dowry and no hope."

"I had a dowry and it brought me no hope," she said.

"So Yussef told me," he said. "No hope?"

"None."

"Not even a little?"

She thought about that. What did she hope for? Nothing. What did she want? Even less. Still, Nito expected some sort of answer. She hoped Antonio would not die because of her. She wanted warm weather. "Nothing grand." She sighed. "I can pretend."

"That is enough." He looked at her hand a long time, studying it, then passing his other hand over her palm in a circular motion.

She knew it was foolishness, but she watched and waited. His fingers stopped and he pointed to one of the lines.

"There it is," he said, his voice low, meant only for the two of them. "The line of Venus is long. You will be lucky in love. Remember, Ana, you are a poor girl who has *not* lost all hope."

She opened her mouth to speak, then closed it, as she understood what he was doing. *I have not lost all hope yet*, she thought, as she felt a tiny spark inside her. A more skeptical Hanneke might argue that the spark was the twinge of her stomach contracting, but was it? She cleared her throat.

"How can this be, sir? I am a poor girl with no dowry. I am fit only to be a servant."

Nito continued, his voice dreamy. "This line tells me that you will soon meet a man of large fortune. He will be so captivated by your beauty that he will carry you away to a lifetime of riches. I see a different dress for Sundays, and food when you are hungry, and new shoes." He pressed his hand down on her palm. "Do you understand, Ana?"

"Yes," she said quietly. "When you have only one dress, two dresses is heaven. Bread and olive oil when you are hungry sound like a banquet."

"Exactly! When soldiers come for their fortunes, you will tell them of Almohades they will kill, and land that will be theirs to the south, once they are victorious."

"And orange groves," she murmured, thinking of Antonio and his gift of oranges when she needed them most.

He kissed her cheek. "Yes. The fortune is not lines in the hand, but whether you can look inside someone and see the longing there." His eyes softened. "Do you think it is all a hoax, Ana? Tell me truly."

She hesitated, then nodded. He took her hand again, and retraced the lines. "The part about much love and many children?" He gently curled her hand, as if to keep the future inside. "I really do see that in your hand, Ana."

Her test came three days later, when they were all at the point of starvation, but moving again because sleet yielded to mud and then sunshine. Everyone except Florinda was forced to walk, pushing and tugging at the wagons mired in mud. Pablo had become adept at urging Fatima along, staying just out of reach of those yellow teeth. By now, the monkey curled around her true knight's shoulders and picked at his lice.

As she struggled through the mud, Hanneke practiced her fortunes, scrutinizing other travelers on the muddy road that seemed to lead slightly north, but more east. That woman there – did she need to know she was loved? That man dressed for a pilgrimage – does he yearn to know that God loves him? "What do I say?" she whispered as she walked. "What can I promise?"

They arrived in the village of Santa Luisa, a bedraggled town that looked as though it had been picked over by Moors and Christians for centuries. Nito seemed to see a different place, one where there might be money.

"What are you thinking?" she asked.

He shrugged. "We will camp at the edge of town, here, in fact. Some will come to see the monkey, some to listen to me play. Some might watch

Magdalena dance. Some will lay down a coin to hear their fortunes. It won't be much, but we never need much, do we?"

The dog meat was gone. Supper was hot water with chicken bones tossed in, then removed when the tiniest skim formed on the water. The woman from the other tent threw down her bowl in disgust.

"How will I have the strength to dance?" she groused.

"You seem to have the strength to lie on your back and moan for strange men," came Florinda's deep voice through the curtains of her wagon.

The woman swore and darted toward the wagon as Pablo huddled closer to Hanneke. Her husband grabbed her by the hair and shook her like a dog. "Bide your time, Magdalena," he warned.

Hanneke looked away. Nito cleared his throat more loudly than he needed to and reached for his guitar. He seated himself on the wagon tongue, made himself comfortable, and began to play.

Magdalena stood up, turning her back to Nito and the cascades of sound that rippled from his guitar. She began to move her feet slowly back and forth, almost as if against her will. She swayed to the music and then stopped. She spat on the ground and walked to her wagon.

The sound followed her. After a moment, she returned to the campfire and looked at Nito for a long, hard moment. "Damn you," she said, then raised her arms and danced.

From her seat in the shadow of Florinda's wagon, Hanneke watched as the villagers of Santa Luisa came close, women with small children who stared at the dancer, their eyes wide. When Magdalena's husband whistled and the monkey ran into the circle, the little ones gasped with delight.

Hanneke watched the mothers. *It has been a long winter for all of us*, she thought. *Hard for them, hard for me.* How often did Santa Luisa see a monkey or a dancer? And there was nasty old Fatima, a vile beast, but exotic.

Nito finished and Magdalena posed with her head gracefully lowered, as if she danced for the Caliph of Al-Andalus. Small coins dropped in the dirt around her, but she did not stoop to retrieve them. The monkey scurried from coin to coin, putting each piece in its mouth, then depositing them at Nito's feet, to more applause.

"What news?" asked a man in the shadows.

Nito rested his guitar across his lap. "News? I bring you news of battles to the south. The Almohades have been beaten back." He gave Hanneke a sidelong glance, as if to say, *I can stretch the truth.* "There is plague in parts of Cádiz, caused, according to the holy fathers, by Christians who do not tithe. The Blessed Virgin appeared to a child in an olive grove near San Lucar." He leaned closer to his rapt audience and lowered his voice. "The Jews of Algeciras have been carrying off small children for use in sacrificial rituals."

The mothers of Santa Luisa gathered their *niños* close and looked about them in defiance of the Jews of Algeciras, wherever that was. Nito strummed a single chord and gestured toward Hanneke. "I will play for you gladly, but behold La Joroba Morena, the dark hunchback. She will tell your fortune."

Her heart thumping, Hanneke walked with that rolling gait Florinda had made her practice to the tent between the wagons that Pablo had erected. She sat inside and waited.

The first to enter was a woman with a small boy. She coaxed her son forward until he sat on the stool in front of La Joroba. "I have only a small copper, but please, tell my son's fortune. His father is away with an army, preparing to fight the Almohades."

Hanneke took the boy's hand in here, praying that she would not tremble, even as she wondered if the boy's father waited to join Antonio Baltierra. Perhaps he had died in the snow before Las Claves. She stared intently at the grubby palm and passed her hand over and under it. She looked at the child's thin cloak, the shoes shabby but neatly mended, the patched tunic. His fingers were red and swollen with chilblains.

She touched his cheek and he smiled at her. The peace and dignity on his young face humbled her, reminding her again, if she needed reminding, of the endurance of these people she had been thrust among.

"I see war," she began, "war in this season to come. It will be followed by peace." She found the longest line in his palm and traced it to his wrist. "You will live long in the land to the south, where it is warm even in winter. The birds never fly away. Your fingers will not itch and burn, because the winds blow warm."

"I dream of such a place," his mother said.

"It is there for you and your son," Hanneke assured her. "There is someone else…"

"José," the woman breathed more than said. "Please, by the saints."

"Ah, yes, José. Surely it is he. I can say no more."

The women wiped her tears and reached for the purse at her waist. Hanneke put out her hand. "No, no. My first look into the future each evening is always free." She saw resistance on the honest woman's face. "It must be so. This is how I plead with the saints to bless me."

"Then I will not argue," the mother said. "Go with God, Joroba Morena."

"May you find orange groves," Hanneke whispered, as they left her tent.

A young girl followed, then an old woman with the side of her face swollen, and another woman and child. Hanneke told their fortunes and took their coins, pleading with God not to smite her on the spot as she lied, play acted, and lied once more.

She thought about the matter as the customers dwindled then stopped. Everyone left her tent happier than they came in. Was that so wrong? Spain was a land of hardship. What was the harm in smoothing away a sorrow or opening a window on hope?

She had one last client, a soldier, from the looks of him. She squinted closer in the gloom, then sat back, trying to distance herself. She had seen the man before. Was he one of Santiago's last gathering of soldiers before the battle in the snow with El Ghalib? Was he one of the young men who had clung to her hand and told her he was afraid?

She motioned for him to sit. He studied her, and she was grateful for the eye patch and hump. She saw the question on his face.

"Your fortune, señor?" she managed to ask.

"I know you from somewhere."

"Me? A poor hunchback?" She was breathing too fast. She willed herself into calm and took his hand. She passed her hand over his, praying she wouldn't tremble, and promised victory in battle and land to the south.

He said nothing. She released his hand and she sat back. He rose without speaking, put down not a single coin, and left the tent in silence. When she thought he was gone, he opened the tent flap. "I will remember where I know you," he said.

She remained still, barely breathing, until she heard someone mount a horse and ride away. When she stood up, she felt older than Nito and Florinda combined. Should she say something to Nito? What would she say? Better to say nothing than to worry him needlessly.

She left the tent and watched the monkey gather the last of the coins. Magdalena had finished dancing. She stood at her wagon, arguing with her husband, who turned away finally, his hands clenched. Nito played on, his eyes closed, playing for himself now, because the villagers had retired.

She sat beside him. When he opened his eyes, she placed the coins between them. "It isn't much," she said. "I did my best, though."

"It will buy us food, Joroba Morena," he said. "What did you promise?"

"Hope, just as you said," she told him, her heart full for the first time in a long time, maybe even since Santiago died in her arms.

For all that he was stupidly silly about his giant mound of a wife, Nito was a wise man. "For them or for you?" he asked.

"Both."

He already knew her too well. "Something is troubling you."

"No, no." she lied. "I am tired, is all."

He nodded, then helped her to her feet. "Tell me when you feel like it."

Never, she thought. *Never*.

Chapter Forty-five

Everything changed at Rincón.

After Santa Luisa, there was another little village and another, all of them shabby, with people fearful until they saw the monkey and heard Nito's beautiful playing.

"I haven't the heart to argue about the few coins they toss our way," Nito said one night after everyone had crept away in silence to their homes. "No one has much, do they?"

"So they say," Magdalena snapped. "It's hidden somewhere, I know it."

Nito ignored her. "Ana, what are your thoughts?" he asked. "You don't say much."

There isn't much to say, she told herself. *Lately, thought takes more effort than I possess.* "I suppose I am grateful to be alive."

That wasn't good enough for Magdalena. "Even though you put us all in danger? Tell me why we must be burdened with you?"

"Because Nito is kind and El Ghalib insisted," Hanneke said, tired of the dancer's endless sniping. "Pablo and I can leave now, if we must."

"Not now," Nito said, after a lengthy, measuring look at Magdalena. "He wants me to get you closer to Toledo and..."

"Closer? Closer?" Magdalena spit out the words. "We are going farther away!"

"Caution," was all Nito said, then, "Do something with your wife!" to Magdalena's husband. "Listen, all of you: I do not wish to provoke a quarrel with El Ghalib, or Felipe Palacios of Las Claves. We tread a fine line. Don't forget that, Magdalena."

Hanneke spent more time walking and less time in the wagon, with its fearful stench. They moved slowly enough. From Fatima, to the horses, to

271

the entertainers, exertion became more difficult as they grew more hungry in a land with little to spare. She found herself thinking about herring, and the chewy black bread that the Aardemas had abandoned when Papa became wealthy enough for white bread. Hanneke longed for black bread smeared with honey. She woke up one night licking her fingers, almost tasting honey.

They traveled in company with others, taking no chances. They tried to blend in with the merchants and ordinary folk on foot, journeying through a bleak January and into February.

Blending in with a camel and a monkey was not an easy matter. Hanneke found herself looking over her shoulder, wondering when Felipe and Amador would ride up unheralded, see her and snatch her away. She thought she saw Amador once, riding beside her as she walked, then spurring his horse and galloping ahead, only to look back and leer at her. Impossible.

Another time she was certain she saw Antonio, bending over in his saddle, tracking her as he had looked for her after Jawhara and the funeral pyre. *I am losing my mind*, she thought. *No. I am just hungry.* She knew that her strength was leaving her faster each day she traveled and starved. Her monthly flow that had returned after Fermina's death had dried up again. Her breasts were turning into empty sacks. Her hair lost its shine. She idly twisted a few strands around her finger one night and they fell off in her hand.

It wasn't just her. Pablo moved more slowly. When she asked him questions, he answered slowly, as though his brain starved, too. Even during the difficult days of their journey from Santander to Las Claves, Santiago had remarked on Pablo's good cheer. Now Pablo walked with his head down, as if needing to look at his feet to make certain they were moving, or if they were even his.

This couldn't continue. Tonight she would ask Nito to point her north toward the Rio Tajo. That is, she would, if she could remember.

That afternoon, they came to Rincón.

It was a town like the others, with a row of spectral windmills and stone buildings that seemed to lean away from the wind. If anything, Rincón looked more prosperous than most, with sturdy walls and groves of bare trees. Perhaps there would be food in this town, and people with money. Hanneke glanced at Magdalena in her wagon, plaiting her hair and arranging it carefully, her eyes on Rincón, too.

Something about Rincón made the hairs on Hanneke's arms stand up. In another moment, she would have shrugged off her feelings, but Pablo came to her side, his expression uncertain, as if he wondered whether his words would make any sense.

"*Dama*, perhaps it is time you and I left this caravan," he said, keeping his voice low. "We could strike off toward Toledo, if someone could tell us where it is."

"Pablo, what is the matter with Rincón?"

"I don't know." He shrugged. "Do you feel it?"

She did, but how could she explain? "We will follow Nito." She touched his arm. "I, too, have been thinking about leaving. We can talk tonight."

What was this? As they approached the village, she saw people hurrying up a rocky path that seemed to slope down to a chasm. The men were in an odd festive mood, nudging each other, some making throwing motions. Another one staggered and fell, as if struck by something, which made everyone howl with laughter. Women and children came, too, so Hanneke reasoned there was no foul intent.

"Where have they been?" she asked Nito.

Nito called to a priest hurrying along. "Father, we are strangers. May I ask, is something happening of a festive nature? We are entertainers and…"

The priest stopped. "This is Rincón." He spoke impatiently, as if to say, *Why do you need more explanation?*

"You have me there, father," Nito said, with apology and deference. "What happened?"

The priest leaned closer. "It was just a stoning." He spoke conversationally, as if discussing ordinary things. "A woman was found to have congress with the devil." He lowered his voice. "She tried to knife her husband after the birth of her two-headed baby, or so he told us." He wrung his hands like Pontius Pilate. "The matter is over and Rincón is safe from evil. Excuse me." He hurried on.

Nito took Hanneke's arm. "Rincón is not for us," he said, his eyes troubled. "I have seen villages where people have their blood up. Not for us."

"Nito? Are we leaving?" Florinda asked from inside her wagon.

"Yes, my sweet," Nito said, trying to calm his voice. "This is not a place for gypsies."

Magdalena eyed the people flowing by the wagons, laughing and calling to each other. She turned on Nito. "Look at them," she demanded, waving a finger in his face. "They are in the mood for entertainment. This could be an evening where we finally make some money!"

"You don't understand," Nito said. "What we heard…"

"I don't care what you heard," she snapped. "I want to dance!"

She leaped off the wagon and began to whirl about and snap her fingers, throwing out her breasts, thrusting her hips. The crowd gathered, and soon the ground was speckled with more coins than the monkey could gather quickly.

When Magdalena stopped, the men howled for more. Nito held up his hand. He tried to clear his throat, but his words sounded faint. "Kind people of Rincón," he began, then tried again. "Kind people, we will sing and dance for you later, after we have rested from our journey. There will also be fortunes told, and camel rides. Go to your homes. Let us prepare."

Hanneke held her breath when no one moved. The crowd seemed to breathe together like an enormous, restless animal. A fetid, musky odor permeated the air.

Nito sensed the danger. He reached inside the wagon for his guitar, which be played softly, slowly. He played until the spell was broken and they were alone.

"Nito, we can't stay here," Hanneke pleaded.

"We dare not leave," he said. "They would tear us apart. We must perform for them tonight."

Chapter Forty-six

No one spoke as they prepared for the evening's entertainment. Magdalena looked around in triumph. She had won; they were staying.

Pablo wasn't certain anyone in their right mind would pay to ride Fatima. "*I* wouldn't," he assured Hanneke. "Even if I had money."

"Pablo and I have been thinking it is time for us to leave you," she said to Nito, as he started to walk away. "You have been so kind, but..."

"You are feeling some danger, too?" Nito asked, rubbing his arms. "I have seen places like this before, but we must stay tonight. We dare not leave until we give them what they want."

"Tomorrow then?" she persisted.

"Tomorrow." Nito tried to laugh and failed. "Once we are gone from Rincón, you may change your mind."

She shook her head, but he pressed his argument. "Ana, Yussef el Ghalib dictated that I should shelter you, at some risk to myself I might add." He drove the point home with something close to triumph. "I could turn you out here in Rincón, but I need your fortune telling."

You are a wily one, Nito, she thought, *to remind me that I am in your debt*. "Very well, since you have made the matter clear to me."

"I knew you would understand." He sweetened the extortion. "Do you know, I have come to like you, Señora Gonzalez. Cheer up! Eventually we will turn toward Toledo. Until then, think of the money we can make with your fortunes."

Deep in thought, hungry, tired, she ducked into Florinda's wagon, wondering if Nito would ever freely let her go. She put on her hump, distracted and irritated with herself for not standing up to Nito. Maybe in another town she might dare hold back some coins from him and take a bath at an inn.

She had to smile when Pablo came toward her riding Fatima. "I did not think you would willingly get on her back," she said.

"I wasn't willing," he replied. "Nito's helper picked me up and put me here."

"How is the view?" she asked, happy, even if for a small moment, to think about something silly.

"Good. I rode to the edge of the clearing. I saw a small camp in the distance." He sighed and looked down at her. "I wish we were over there and not in Rincón." He raised up. "People are coming here, but I still don't think anyone will want to ride Fatima."

She went inside her tent, ready to tell the people whatever she thought they wanted to hear. She lit her lamp and pulled it closer. "Come in," she called. "La Joroba Morena is ready."

La Joroba Morena promised the people of Rincón everything. She discovered mystical lifelines in the hands of men, women and children that assured health, wealth and victory over the Almohades. She told them they would find lost coins and lost love, and endless vigor. She let pregnant women touch her hump and endured the stares of old men.

She stopped once to take most of the money to Florinda and then carry a drink to Nito, who had been playing and singing for hours.

"Thank you," he said, and set down his guitar, even though his audience howled for more. "I wish the good citizens would tire, but they grow rowdier."

"I have promised everything in the world, and it is not enough," she whispered back.

He picked up his guitar. "Still, it has been a profitable evening. Perhaps we should not complain."

Someone was already seated at her table when she returned. She sighed, wising to be done, longing for sleep even more than food. She hurried around the man, sat down and looked at him.

If he noticed how she sucked in her breath and widened her eyes, he did not make any mention. It was the soldier again, the one from Santa Luisa. She started to rise, then noticed someone outside the tent. As she sat down and tried to stifle her rising fear, she suddenly knew who Pablo had seen camping outside of Rincón.

"I have come again for my fortune, Joroba," he said, holding out his hand.

"I told your fortune in Santa Luisa," she said quietly.

He leaned closer. "Then let me tell yours. Obviously there has been a miracle since Santa Luisa."

"What? How?"

"You wore an eye patch in Santa Luisa," he said. He reached up and grabbed her shoulder. "And even more of a miracle, your hump has changed sides."

She shook off his hand, and tried to rise, but he forced her down. "You can come with me and Amador back to Las Claves, or I can tell the people of Rincón, who know a witch when they see one."

"Please, no," she begged.

"Señor Palacios told us how anxious he is to keep you safe from scum who would squander your dowry." He stood up, towering over her. "Amador!"

"No!"

Ignoring the heat, she grabbed the lamp and threw it at the soldier, who ducked and moved closer as she tipped up the table. The lamp struck Amador as he came inside the tent. As he shrieked, the fire on his sleeve leaped to the tent and set it ablaze, too.

The soldier beat out the flames on Amador, giving Hanneke time to duck under the back of the tent and run. Another man – dear God please not Baltazar – grabbed her cloak, which she untied and left in his hands as he roared his displeasure. She scrambled under Florinda's wagon and out and nearly ran into the camel, who tried to bite her. She tugged at Pablo, who was helping someone down from Fatima.

"Run!" she said. "Don't look back!"

They darted behind the wagons. When the music stopped, people roared their displeasure then screamed to see flames. She gasped as Magdalena's wagon began to burn. "What have I done?" she said, then ran faster, grabbing Pablo's hand.

She didn't realize where they were heading until the path became stony and steep. She couldn't turn around because there were others on the path, some with torches. She heard swords clanging in their scabbards.

They stood staring down at what had to be the stoning ground. "This is a mistake," Pablo said, bent over and gasping for breath.

My entire life since I left the Netherlands has been a mistake, she thought. She thought about leaping to her death. Who would care? She looked up at the stars. That tiny spark within her that Nito had told her to search for when telling fortunes still burned. *Antonio would care. I care*, she reminded herself. She stepped back from the edge and forced herself to think.

She ran to the edge and looked down on bones and a body. The moon had not yet risen, but there was enough starlight to indicate a path to the bottom. She looked back and saw pinpricks of light.

"Pablo, my true knight, follow me," she said, and picked her way along the sloping ledge.

"I'm afraid," he said.

"So am I. Do it anyway."

Scarcely breathing, Hanneke made her way from one rocky shelf to another, moving carefully and slowly, even though every fiber in her body screamed at her to hurry. Over one rocky shelf, down to another, over and down, they zigzagged to the bottom of the chasm, careful not to dislodge any stones and disrupt the eerie calm of the pit.

Maybe hell is silent, dark and cold, she thought, as she waited out a small rock fall and prayed that no one heard it, no one living, at least.

She doubted that many minutes had passed since she left the stoning ground and finally, finally stepped onto the chasm's floor. The moon had risen, so she flattened herself against the stones and looked around her new prison.

Despite her fear, her heart went out to the woman who must have gone over the edge only hours ago. *I do not think you ever coupled with the devil*, she thought, her mind amazingly clear. *I doubt you had a two-headed baby. I think your husband tired of you for some reason. God grant you peace.*

She heard the men above and moved closer to the stony wall. She saw Pablo, and then she didn't see him. Panicked, she looked closer, then saw the cave. Grateful for a black dress, she inched along the wall then crawled inside.

They huddled there, arms around each other, and listened to the men overhead. They heard arguments, and recrimination, and dares from one to another to go down and check. One or two tried, then stopped.

"Will they go away?" Pablo whispered.

"I don't know."

She held Pablo close when he started to cry. "I think we had better find out where this cave goes," she whispered.

Chapter Forty-seven

The cave proved to be their salvation, if salvation meant trading the worst for something not quite so bad. Gradually, Pablo felt heavy against her side and she knew he slept.

The tiny spark that had given Hanneke the courage to find a way down to the pit flickered out as she listened to the bonfire above and grew colder with each passing moment. How far could she run and hide, with no knowledge of where she was going and how to get there? Did Antonio even live anymore?

Back at the caravan she had burned the tent and Magdalena's wagon. She doubted Nito wanted anything more to do with her. El Ghalib had told her plainly that he dared not help her anymore, not with his own caliph demanding total loyalty.

There was no one. Sitting there in a cave of bones, Hanneke accepted the reality that she was alone. When Pablo sighed in his sleep, she knew only one thing: she had to get Pablo to a place of refuge, where others could see him safely back to Santander and the monastery. Sometimes even a true knight is only a kitchen boy.

The hours passed. She strained to hear what was going on above her on the stoning ground. She had no way to know if anyone remained there, or if they had given up. Perhaps they assumed she had gone elsewhere, because no one seemed willing to climb down and find out. She needed light to find her way in the cave, but she didn't know if the sun penetrated to this depth.

How can one wait impatiently for the sun to rise? It happens every day, she reminded herself, in its own due time. When the sun finally rose, after a darkness so profound that she doubted her very soul, she bowed her head in gratitude. One more day was hers.

She opened her eyes, reminding herself that what she saw might frighten her, and looked around. As sunlight filtered into the cave, she saw bones, to be sure, but there in the corner was a cloak.

Her eyes on the cloak, she gently shook Pablo awake, careful to keep her hand over his mouth in case he called out in surprise. "It is morning," she whispered. "We made it through the night."

When he sat up and rubbed his eyes, Hanneke shoved back all her fear and walked to the cloak. She touched it, then lifted it from the skeleton it covered, shook it out, and draped it around her shoulders. The cloak smelled of mildew and death, but her gratitude was unlimited. "Whoever you were, thank you," she whispered to the skeleton, a fellow sufferer. She lacked the courage to peer outside the cave and see the poor woman who had died yesterday.

Hanneke sat with Pablo, sharing the cloak, until the sun's rays moved farther into the cave. Eyes wide, Pablo looked around. "*Dama*, I think we should leave this place."

"So do I. It is time to put Rincón behind us."

He asked no questions, which was good, because she had no answers. He didn't ask for food, because there was none. He followed her farther into the cave, mindful of his steps, trusting her.

They walked until the sun ran out, moving slower, picking their way as the cave floor sloped. Too soon they stood in total darkness. Hanneke closed her eyes, resigning herself to death because she could not imagine surrendering to Baltazar or Amador who would no doubt use her cruelly before they brought her to Felipe. *This is the end of it*, she thought. *I was winnowed, too.*

She wished the Lord God Almighty, in His kindness, would smite her right then, but He didn't. When she opened her eyes and heard distant running water, she understood why.

As she looked toward the sound, she saw light, just a pin prick, but daylight. She grabbed Pablo's arm. "Do you see that?"

"Yes!"

She knew he wanted to dart ahead, but she held him back. "We will go slowly," she told him. "We cannot see the ground. Someone might be waiting for us outside."

Their sedate pace picked up when enough sunlight began to guide them. When she could see her feet, she let go of Pablo's hand. "Do not leave the shelter of the cave," she warned. "We do not know what lies ahead."

When she reached the cave mouth, a low opening she had to crawl under, she saw Pablo squatting by a stream. As she watched, eyes wide, he reached down and pulled up a fish, and then another, tossing them in her direction. Two more fish and he stopped.

She crouched on all fours beside him to scoop water down her parched throat. When she finished, she leaned back against the safety of the cave's wall and looked at the stream, watching it flow beside the cave, then widen a little.

"*Dama*, do you have a knife?"

She reached into the pouch around her neck, feeling her marriage document and the little knife of no consequence. "Will you scale and gut them?" she asked, swallowing down saliva as she handed him the knife.

He went to work, deftly slicing off heads, then opening their bellies. "We don't have a way to cook them."

"Never mind. I don't want a fire to alert anyone."

Neither of them hung back. The only sound was chewing and swallowing. The raw fish slid down easily; she only wished there were more. She licked the scales off her hands.

"Maybe I can catch another," Pablo said.

"Please try."

He caught three fish, and they downed those quickly, wanting more. When the weak winter sun was overhead, Hanneke took a good look at their surroundings. It was the same terrain they had traveled over for the past two weeks – hilly and stony, with bare trees here and there, the endless plain of Castile.

"I don't even know which way is Toledo," she admitted. "Do you?"

Pablo shook his head, then pointed to the stream. "I do know that little streams flow toward bigger streams, and then to rivers. Let us follow the stream."

At her urging, he caught three more fish and prepared them, but put them inside his doublet. "We can eat them later, *dama*. Should we start walking?"

She nodded. "Little streams to bigger streams."

Fed and somehow fortified, they traveled with extreme caution, looking behind as often as they looked ahead. Rain came, then sleet, then rain. The flinty soil turned slippery, compounding their misery

Shivering, even in the wonderful cloak, Hanneke decided the weather was a blessing. Even wolves like Amador and that soldier must prefer a warm fire. She hoped they would assume she had died, and carry that fable back to Las Claves, where Felipe Palacios was master.

In the whole day, they heard horsemen only once and hid themselves in a clump of brush, flattening low and hoping for the best. Hanneke looked up after they passed, seeing two riders, and she wondered.

They ate the fish when they could wait no longer. She knew Pablo was not one to complain. Like most Spaniards, he took life as it came. He matched her step for step.

Sure enough, the small stream they followed poured itself into a larger one. The trouble came when the larger stream dumped into something wider and deeper, and flowing faster.

"If we cross this, I think we will be on the right side, when the stream gets wider," Pablo said. "I'll go first."

He gasped when he stepped into the cold water, wobbled and waved his arms about for balance, then righted himself. Hanneke followed, gasping too, then holding the cloak tighter so it would not billow out and drag her too fast.

Even though the water came no higher than her knees, the current pulled Hanneke down. She scrambled to her feet and cried out in frustration when her sopping cloak tugged her down again.

Pablo reached for the cloak, tripped and fell against the slippery stones. His face went white and he groaned, reaching for his leg. Hanneke lumbered toward him, and grabbed him when he sagged.

"Can you stand if I help you?" she asked.

He nodded, biting his lips as she hauled him to his feet. He sucked in his breath from the pain as she half-carried, half dragged him to the opposite side, where she sat him down as gently as she could. Bracing herself against the current, she swung his legs onto firm ground, then sat beside him.

In silence he clutched his ankle and rocked back and forth. Hanneke knelt over him, touching the spot he held, feeling the break. She breathed a prayer of thanks that no bones protruded, even as she knew Pablo's journey had ended.

"We have to find help," she said, her arms around him.

"Who is here to help us? Look around."

She didn't need to look to know that they were alone in midafternoon on a cold day somewhere in Spain. They would sit here, soaked through, starved and shivering, until they died.

"Let me see what I can do." She wrapped her borrowed cloak around the boy and stood up, moving away from the stream, seeing no one, not even an enemy. She stood still, listening, then shook her head. She thought she heard bells, but how could that be? The shelter of trees was no shelter because the branches were bare. No birds sang. There were no churches. How could she hear bells?

She heard them again, and closer, then stepped back in surprise when a child in rags and carrying a bucket came slowly toward her.

The bucket looked too big for one so small. Upon seeing Hanneke, she hesitated, then shook the bells more vigorously. Hanneke watched as realization dawned. The bells warned her to come no closer. Lepers.

The child stopped, dropped the bucket, and turned as if to run. Hanneke raised her hand. "Please don't run. I need your help."

"No one needs us," the child said, but she did not run.

"I do. My friend Pablo – he's at the river – broke his leg crossing the stream. Could you go back to your…your village? Your camp? Please send someone." She came forward slowly, her hand out. "See here. I will fill your bucket while you get help." She grabbed the bucket, knowing the girl would bring help, because she needed her bucket back. "I'll fetch water for you."

The girl ran, her bells setting up a clamor. Hanneke watched her go, wondering if she had done the right thing. *You don't even know what the right thing is,* she scolded herself. *After all, your turn to be winnowed is long overdue.*

She returned to the stream and carefully filled the bucket, balancing herself on the rocks. When she told Pablo what had happened, he shook his head. She saw all his despair. She took the bucket up the slope. She waited.

To her infinite relief, she heard a few bells, then many, and then she saw them – all of them cloaked in mountains of rags and looking like walking haystacks. As she watched in grateful appreciation, she saw one among them that made her draw in her breath.

"It cannot be," she said. Tears came to her eyes and she started walking, then running, which frightened the lepers.

"No, no," the man said. "She will not hurt you. Far from it."

She wasn't mistaken. She slowed to a walk, then sighed with relief as Father Bendicio embraced her.

Chapter Forty-eight

She had last seen the priest galloping away from her, fleeing in fear from approaching Almohades, her husband near death. He held her off, filled with his own questions. "Why are you here? Where is Santiago? What of Antonio?"

Break my heart, coward priest, she thought, then dismissed her sudden anger. Other matters pressed more on her heart. "I will tell you everything, but first you must help me. Pablo's leg is broken, and we are freezing."

She gave him a push that seemed to recall him to his duties. "Yes, certainly. Ernesto!" he shouted. "I need you."

A giant of a man came forward, rag-covered like the others. He picked up Pablo, who had lapsed into unconsciousness, and draped him gently around his shoulders, as a shepherd carries a lamb. When he raised Pablo, his cloak fell away and Hanneke saw open sores.

Father Bendicio touched her hand. "Do not fear. This is my little parish. Ana, I have found my flock."

She followed him without another word. She turned once to speak her thanks with her eyes when a woman with half a face wrapped her own cloak around Hanneke's shoulders, murmuring words that fell half-formed from her ruined mouth.

The child with the bucket walked next to her. "This is my mother," she said, as she held the woman's hand.

"You are lucky, child," Hanneke said, "for she is kind."

Not far from the stream they came to a huddle of shelters made of twigs and straw, not even approaching the dignified title of hovel, or even shack. Ernesto the leper carried Pablo into one of the shelters, followed by Bendicio.

"Go with the woman," Bendicio said. "She will find you something dry to wear." He must have noticed her hesitation. "Fear not, my dear. Trust me."

"I do not know why I should, Father," she said simply.

"I don't either," he replied. "We will talk later."

She followed the mother and child into another shelter, ducking in the low doorway. She did as the child said, and removed her soaking dress and camisa, then wrapped herself in the blanket the mother held out to her.

Eyes lively, the young girl ran her hand down Hanneke's arm. "Your skin is like mine," she said, then ducked her head in her mother's embrace, embarrassed.

Hanneke and the woman with the ravaged face smiled at each other. "Your daughter is a treasure beyond price," Hanneke said. "I envy you."

The woman hugged her daughter speaking low words that only the child understood. *I am envying a leper*, Hanneke thought, touched to her heart. She wrapped herself in the blanket and slept.

When she woke, Father Bendicio sat beside her. She sat up carefully, making sure the blanket covered her.

"I wanted to be here when you woke up," he said, with no preamble. "These people, good as they are, can be" – he searched for the word – "disconcerting."

"Pablo?" As much as she owed him now, Hanneke didn't know if she wanted to talk to Father Bendicio.

"He sleeps. I did what I could for his ankle, and wrapped it tight." He sighed and looked away. "All he is concerned about is that he knows he will slow you down. I didn't have the heart to tell him he isn't going anywhere for many weeks."

What could she say to that? She could have said, "You never have had the courage for anything, have you?" She saw the face of a penitent sinner, and she could not. Better to say nothing. She looked away, sick at heart because she had to leave her true knight with this unworthy man.

He wouldn't let her ignore him. "Ana, I must know what happened! Why are you here in such a state? Where is Santiago? Antonio?"

In that miserable hut, with other lepers gathering, she told Father Bendicio, Las Claves' coward priest and the man who taught her Spanish, about Santiago's death first of all. If she could get through that, then the story was hers. "You rode away when you saw the Almohades. I stayed with Santiago until he died." He didn't need to know about the necklace. "Why they did not kill me, too? I was ready to die, even as I am now."

"Ana, I..."

"Let me finish. Felipe Palacios and a few of his thugs are now in charge of Las Claves. He wants to force me to marry him and get the dowry. I refused him and ran." He didn't need to know about Antonio, either. Suppose Felipe should ride in here tomorrow and force an even greater coward to blurt out more? "Pablo and I are being hunted. Carlos is likely dead. Antonio is trying to gather in the rest of the soldiers that my dowry has bought, if he still lives. There you have it, Father Bendicio. Make of it what you will."

"I know I am a coward," was all he said as he left. "I need to tell you what I have learned." He managed a smile. "It will keep."

The others left, too, until only the woman and child remained. The girl returned her black dress. "I held it over the fire to dry it and scorched it a little," she said. "Your camisa, too."

"At least they are dry and warm," Hanneke said. She looked closer. "My dear, did you burn your fingers doing this?"

She nodded. "Father Bendicio has some salve. He brought some wonderful salve with him." Her face clouded. "The trouble is, no one gets better with it except me."

Hanneke took a good look. "You're not a leper, are you?"

"No. Only my mother."

"What is your name?"

She shrugged. "We are not sure. Mama calls me something, and I answer to it, but we cannot tell."

The mother said something, and held out her hand to her daughter, who told Hanneke, "Our meal is ready."

Hanneke gathered with the lepers around the iron pot under a shelter. Father Bendicio raised the lid. "Meat," he said, his eyes lighting on Ernesto. "Thanks be to God."

Ernesto beamed at him, then lowered his gaze and murmured, "Some people are more careless with their early lambs than others."

"You know that is wrong," Father Bendicio chided, but gently.

"We're hungry," Ernesto said.

"Thus is every theological argument I ever learned at Salamanca rebutted," Father Bendicio said. He raised his voice in prayer, then handed Hanneke a spoon.

"We have no bowls. It would be better if you went first. I have set some aside for Pablo, when he wakes."

She took the spoon, mindful that everyone watched her. She ate quickly, holding her hand under her chin so she did not lose a drop. She could have wolfed down the entire stew, for it was only a small lamb. She handed the spoon back to Bendicio.

The girl ate next, then all those who could feed themselves. When they finished, Bendicio motioned the others forward, the ones with mouth and throat lesions. As she watched, Father Bendicio put a piece of meat in his mouth, chewed thoroughly, then leaned toward an old man with no lower jaw. The man tipped his head back like a fledging in a nest as Bendicio spread the meat in his ulcerated throat and added a little broth.

"Very good sir," Bendicio said, when the man swallowed as best he could. "A little more?"

He fed the same leper more, then another. By this time, the girl had chewed meat for her mother. Others who could chew helped those who could not.

Bendicio glanced at Hanneke. "It took me some time to get used to that, but now..." He shrugged. "I am learning, Ana. Please believe me."

"I believe you, Father," she replied, as her heart began to soften toward this imperfect man. What if he was only doing the best he could?

The first old man grunted for more food. Bendicio fished another piece of lamb from the pot and handed it to Hanneke. She chewed it soft for the leper and despite everything felt kinder, wiser and more grateful. What an odd journey this had become.

Soon the pot was empty. Father Bendicio handed it to the little girl, who scampered away with it to the stream.

"Father, you didn't get any," Hanneke said.

"I swallow every now and then."

"It isn't enough."

"It is," he assured her. He picked up a tin with the remaining stew. "Let us take this to Pablo."

They walked slowly from the campfire. "I fled north, after that dreadful night," Bendicio said, picking up his narrative of that awful night she craved to remember less relentlessly. "There is a monastery in Toledo. The abbot took me in and did not question me until I was ready."

The child returned with the pot. He motioned for her to fill it with water and return it to the campfire.

They went into another shelter. Pablo lay on his back, staring at the fading sky through the hay and twig awning. Hanneke fed him the stew as Father Bendicio held up his head. When he finished, Pablo closed his eyes and returned to sleep.

As Pablo slept, Father Bendicio continued his narrative, his voice lower. "I told the abbot I didn't want to be a priest anymore, but he wouldn't hear of that." Father Bendicio's voice took on a wondering tone. "He told me, 'You will always be a priest, so you need to start learning how.'"

"And then?" she prompted, when he fell silent.

"He gave me that pot and told me to find the lepers. 'Let them teach you,' he said. "Here I am."

Pablo stirred and cried out. He tried to sit up, but Hanneke held him, brushing the hair from his forehead.

"When do we leave?" he asked, his eyes anxious. "Felipe might even be at Rincón now."

"I know, I know," Hanneke said, soothing him. "We will discuss it tomorrow. Sleep, my true knight."

"I cannot," he said as he closed his eyes and slept.

"You will sleep with my little friend Luz and her mother," Bendicio said, as he helped her from the shelter.

"Luz?"

"That is what I call her. Everyone should have a name." He smiled into the unknown distance. "She is everyone's light, so it is the perfect name."

They stopped at the women's shelter. She leaned close and whispered, "Father, how much longer will Luz's mother live?"

He shrugged. "How much longer do any of us have in this vale of tears? The ulcers in her throat will dig deeper and deeper. One day she will not be able to swallow at all." He hunched his shoulders against the cold. "We will pray, and she will starve to death before our eyes. Then we will praise God for something or other."

"Father," she chided gently.

"I have a little way to go before I am a perfectly reconciled priest."

They paused before the shelter. "I am leaving tomorrow, Father," she said.

"Where will you go?"

"I do not know. Antonio said there is a convent south of Toledo."

"Santa Catarina. Yes, go there." He became all business, and not the floundering man she was more familiar with. Poor Father Bendicio: not for him the bold stroke, the chance circumstance. "It is directly north from here. Let us say, two days. Someone will help you."

Hanneke doubted she had two days, not with Felipe determined to find her, and Amador and Baltazar thirsty for revenge. She had to ask the hard question. "Father, I do not doubt that Felipe will be on my trail soon, if not already. If he shows up, what will you tell him? If he only sends Amador and Baltazar, they are even worse."

He could not look at her, which chilled her heart. *Worthless priest*, she thought, then reconsidered. "At least hide Pablo among the lepers, before you tell them where I am heading."

"Ana ..."

She couldn't leave him so despondent. She owed him little, but even that little could not be ignored. "Father, your courage is of a different kind," she told him, wondering if this was true, but determined not to ruin an already fragile creature. "Tend your little flock. Hide Pablo."

"Very well. That I will do. Go with God, Ana, bravest of women."

Chapter Forty-nine

Hanneke left at first light, after accepting a handful of wheat from Luz, shyly given, and two coppers from Father Bendicio, who regretted he could not give her more. She didn't check on Pablo, knowing that if he was awake, her departure would overset him. Ernesto the leper gave her a walking stick, telling her not to hesitate to use it. "Beat any scoundrels soundly, *dama*," he told her.

Too exhausted and hungry to beat anything, Hanneke assured him she would be vigilant. Her cloak from the death cave was returned cleaner. She gathered its warmth around her, dismayed how heavy it was. Could she even wear it?

Father Bendicio blessed her and walked a little distance beside her, either to assure himself that she was someone else's problem soon, or to pretend to put a brave face on the matter. Or perhaps he was only doing the best he could.

He pointed her north. "Two days to Santa Catarina. You are nearly there."

The handful of wheat was gone before the sun struggled through the clouds resting, as though exhausted, on the horizon. The kernels clumped into a ball that sank to the bottom of her shrunken stomach; she wished she had never eaten them.

Relying on Ernesto's walking stick, she walked through a wintry landscape – devoid of trees, fences, animals and houses. She hoped the slight undulation of the land would be a refuge from detection, but no one rode this way. The flinty soil cut into what remained of her shoes and the wind threw bits of sleet at her that cut her face. Perhaps Spain was beautiful in springtime, the only season she had not witnessed. Would she live that long?

She hunched herself against the weather, wondering at the growing ache in her shoulders that began to spread down her back. She hoped she was walking north, and not traveling in a circle that would take her back to Rincón and the stoning ground.

She had only one fear. She saw no place to hide in this wide and open land. What if she topped a rise and found herself staring at Baltazar or Amador? What if she turned around to see Felipe ready to snatch her back to Las Claves for his own purposes? She knew she was being winnowed out like Santiago. It was only a matter of time.

Prayer seemed a useless tease, but it cost her nothing to pray for Antonio, to pray that he was alive. She prayed he had not taken whatever soldiers he could gather back to Las Claves and into Felipe's dangerous orbit. She prayed he had headed to Valladolid, where Santiago had told her King Alfonso resided most often and was gathering his own troops for war in summer.

Even worse than hunger was the fear that Antonio had not been alerted to Felipe's misdeeds. Perhaps he thought she was still safe at Las Claves, Carlos protecting her. Yussef el Ghalib had told her he dared not stay in Christian lands to assist her, not with the danger of betrayal hanging over him, a most loyal Almohad. Maybe Yussef had never planned to warn Antonio at all, even though he said he had. Her thoughts made awful companions for a journey.

She came to a village as the winter sun surrendered to night without a struggle. Dogs announced her presence, growling and sniffing. Even they turned away, uninterested in a woman with hair matted, and her clothes in tatters.

She passed quietly through the village's single street, searching for an inn. She had no money for lodging. Perhaps there would be a small fire where she could warm her hands. If only her back didn't ache so much.

Through a haze of exhaustion, she saw what looked like an inn, where a woman swept the entrance. She raised her broom at Hanneke.

"Shoo! Take your rags and stink somewhere else!" She pushed Hanneke back into the street.

Hanneke fumbled for one of Father Bendicio's coppers and held it out. "Have you any bread?"

The woman snatched the coin and scrutinized it, then returned it. "I might. What more do you want?"

"May I come in? Is there a fire?" Hanneke asked, as she felt a growing need to sit down.

The woman barred the door with her broom. "Go around back. I have paying customers inside who don't want lice dropping in their soup. What would they think of me?"

Perhaps that you are a charitable Christian, Hanneke thought. *Lepers gave me food and a bed for the night.*

She found the back door and knocked. The woman opened it and held out her hand for the coin. "Over there," she directed. "Not near the main room. You're filthy."

Hanneke sat on the floor by the fireplace and the woman held out a small loaf of bread. Hanneke reached for it, but the woman pulled back. *Please don't tease me*, she thought in agony.

As Hanneke watched in despair and then relief, the woman slapped a bit of fat meat on the bread. She thrust it at Hanneke, as if angry at herself for being charitable. "Here! You're so thin. You should be ashamed."

Hanneke ate quickly, before the woman changed her mind. She saved half the meat, tucking it inside her dress. She leaned her aching back against the wall. Eyes half closed, knowing she would be evicted soon, she watched the woman hurrying back and forth between the fireplace and the high counter to the main room, muttering to herself.

"They come riding in here from Rincón, demanding this and that, talking to the villagers. As if Rincón is someplace special…."

Hanneke winced and sat up, every tired nerve humming. She rose slowly and peered around the counter. To her horror, Amador and Baltazar sat hunched over their food, their backs to her. "Th…those men?" she whispered to the woman.

"Yes, yes! They're looking for someone, a murderer, I think, and asking around." She sighed with exasperation, and looked toward the fireplace, where hunks of beef Hanneke could only dream about roasted. "I'll get the meat off the hooks and see what they want. You're in the way."

Hanneke moved aside as the woman hurried to lift the meat from its spit in the cavernous fireplace. She made rapid trips from fireplace to table, muttering, moving aside other food. She stopped in mid stride, picked up another small loaf and threw it at Hanneke. "Take it before you starve to death!"

Hanneke grabbed the loaf and stuffed it inside her bodice. When the woman's back was turned, she let herself out the back way. To her relief, the town gate was still open. Hand to her back, pressing against the ache, she hurried toward the gate. Another bit of good fortune came her way when several travelers on horseback, accompanied by a large wagon and muleteer, came through the gate. She walked out as they walked in, talking and laughing, no one the wiser. The gate swung shut behind her.

She hurried as fast as she could, pausing too often for the simple act of breathing, which made her cough up brown froth. After a few miles, or more probably mere steps – she couldn't tell anymore – she stopped to listen for horses. Nothing. The woman in the inn must have been too busy to talk to Amador and Baltazar. Small favors. Small blessings. Small chances. Small woman. Small hope.

When the moon rose, she saw a hut on the edge of a stand of trees. She saw a sudden gleam of light when the door opened, and waited for the growl of dogs. Nothing. She came closer, her hand to her mouth to quiet her cough, and knocked.

A wisp of a fellow with a shock of white hair and milky eyes peered at her. He clapped his hands and announced over his shoulder, "Milagra, we have a guest for the evening."

Hanneke couldn't help herself. She looked behind her. No one stood there; she must be the guest.

A woman even smaller than she was stood up by the fire pit. "This is no night for a young thing like you to be out. Sit."

Hanneke looked around. There was nothing to sit on. Milagra put her hands to her face and laughed. "Silly me! Such a cold winter. We have burned our stools. Please sit on God's good earth."

Hanneke sat, and wrapped her cloak tighter around her. The old man came toward her, waving his hands in the air until he touched her hair. "I am Velardo," he said.

"I am Ana Gonzalez," Hanneke said. "Thank you for your kindness."

Velardo motioned to Milagra. "Wife, bring food." He turned toward Hanneke. "She is quite the cook. You will see."

Hanneke sniffed and smelled nothing. Milagra handed her a bowl and a spoon. Hanneke tasted the contents. It was hot water. She looked up, mystified.

The old couple sat close together sharing one bowl between them. Milagra caught her glance. "My Velardo is such a provider," she said, her voice so tender. "He brings me this and that, and I can make a wonderful stew."

Hanneke sipped the hot water as Velardo drank, uttering little cries of approval. She watched the old couple, amazed, then continued sipping the hot water. "This is wonderful," she said. "You must tell me your secret for such a soup."

Milagra turned her head into Velardo's shoulder like a young bride. Hanneke watched their joy. Crazy they might be, but they had shared everything with her. She could return the favor.

"Here," she said, reaching insider her bodice for the small loaf and remaining bit of fat meat. "Let me add to your feast."

Milagra took the food from her with shining eyes and gave the fat to Velardo, who sucked on the morsel and smacked his lips. The three of them finished the soup with little bites of bread until it all came out even. When they knelt to pray, Hanneke knelt with them, her heart full. Were they crazy? She didn't care; they were also kind.

Velardo prayed for their nonexistent flocks, their invisible children, and the Christian kings of Castille, Navarre, Leon, Aragon and Galicia, plus the pope in distant Rome. Hanneke prayed that she would survive the night.

Milagra motioned for her to take the part of the mattress closest to the wall. She lay down and wrapped her cloak about her, because she could see her breath. Milagra settled in next to her with a sigh. Velardo followed, after he circled the room a few times, checking the door and the firepit.

"He is a careful man, is my Velardo," Milagra whispered. "May you find a good man just like him someday."

I did, Hanneke thought, not with sadness this time, but remembrance. She thought about Antonio, too. *Maybe I found another. Please God, let my fortunes change.*

Was it minutes later? Hours? Hanneke felt the whole hut shake with the reverberation of someone banging on the door. Alarmed, she burrowed deeper in the straw.

Milagra sat up first. She said something quiet to Velardo, then tossed her blanket over Hanneke. She padded to the door. "Yes? Yes? It is late."

"Open this door."

Hanneke lay perfectly still at the sound of Baltazar's voice. There was no mistaking that deep rasp. She closed her eyes, all the terror returning. *Please, Milagra and Velardo*, was all she could think. Then, *No coughing*.

Milagra fumbled with the bar on the door, taking her time. Velardo started to snore. Hanneke turned slightly to see, keeping the blanket over her head, peering through wisps of straw. Baltazar came in quickly, followed by Amador. The men filled the little room, towering over Milagra, but the old woman did not step back.

Baltazar squatted by the fire pit and held out his hands. "How do you even stay alive here?" he asked in utter disdain. "There's no fire."

Milagra drew herself up. "My man provides very well," she said. "Don't wake him."

Amador laughed. "You don't even have furniture!"

If she ever needed to know what dignity looked like, all Hanneke had to do was remember Milagra, so tiny and yet standing tall. "We manage, *señores*," she said calmly, as though poor blind Velardo were the king of Castile. "What is it you want?"

"We are looking for a pretty woman, small with dark hair. She speaks good Castilian, but with a strong accent. She was seen begging in the village nearby. She is dangerous. Is she here?" Hanneke heard coins rattling. "This purse is yours. Did someone visit you tonight? We have searched the village. Someone saw her leave. You're the only house for miles around. We have already searched your shed. *Dios mio*, what do you live on?" He shook the pouch again. "Here it is, for what you know. You need money."

Hanneke closed her eyes, thinking of want and poverty relieved in an instant. All Milagra had to do was point to the far side of the bed.

Milagra sat down on the bed. "The only one who came here tonight was *La Virgen Maria*. She brought us a loaf of bread and some fat meat."

Milagra, no, Hanneke thought in terror. *What are you saying?*

Amador swore, and Milagra gasped. "*Señor*, she will never visit you, if that is how you speak of her! Say a prayer and do an honest act of contrition."

"Are you crazy, old woman?" Amador asked.

"Perhaps I am," Milagra said with considerable dignity. "If La Virgen returns with more food, what would you like me to ask her?"

Baltazar muttered something that made Milagra suck in her breath. "*Señor*, *not* in my house. San Pedro will shake you good if you think to enter into eternal rest, after what I think will be a lengthy time for you in Purgatory."

Hanneke heard Amador and Baltazar talking softly, then laughing. She waited, her eyes closed, desperate to cough. To her infinite relief, she heard the door slam. Milagra threw the bolt. All was silent until they heard the sound of horses. Hanneke pulled back the blanket.

Blind Velardo spoke up, quite awake. "I should have taken my sword and run them both through! Imagine, wife, they thought we would betray a guest for money."

"We would never," Milagra said, "not with La Virgen Maria, San Pedro and any number of saints to protect us here in our fine dwelling. I am relieved you controlled your ferocious temper, husband. How could we ever have explained two men cut into small pieces? We don't even have any pigs to help with disposal." She patted Hanneke. "Go in peace tomorrow, daughter."

Chapter Fifty

"I have heard that the convent of Santa Catarina is a fine place," Milagra told her in the morning, after their breakfast of water scrambled in a pan with a touch of salt. "I wish you would stay here, because you are not well."

"Since we are wishing," Hanneke said, "I wish I had food to leave with you."

Milagra kissed her cheek. "The Virgin Mary will return in a day or so and we will be fed. Did you know she visited us last night? If she does not return, Velardo is quite the hunter."

"A morning's walk," Velardo told her as he escorted her to the door – three steps – and opened it with a flourish.

She paused, remembering. El Ghalib's bracelet slipped off her wrist with ease, not even requiring her to work the clasp. She looked past Velardo to Milagra, because the old woman could see.

"Please take this," she said. "It is gold and you can trade it for food."

Milagra held it up to the light. "Beautiful! I will treasure it always." She patted Hanneke. "Velardo will hunt. I cannot part with this."

How have you old dears stayed alive this long? Hanneke asked herself. "Do this then: If a tall warrior – a Christian named Antonio – very handsome and with black hair, should ask about me, please tell him I am walking to Santa Catarina." She leaned against the doorframe and coughed. When she had the strength, she continued. "There might also be an Almohad warrior named Yussef. He has three blue stripes on his chin. Tell him the same, please."

"Ana, how many lovers do you have?" Milagra said, her eyes bright. "My handsome Velardo had to fight for me, too!" She cast her eyes down modestly. "I was a great beauty."

297

"Milagra, I do not doubt that for a moment," Hanneke said, touched and grateful for hot water meals and a safe bed for the night.

"Go with God," Velardo said, as he bowed and ushered her out of the hovel.

Santa Catarina might have been a morning's walk for someone in strength, but not her. After less than a field and a slope, Hanneke dropped her walking stick. It took too much effort to bend down, so the stick remained behind.

In spite of sleet that alternated with rain, she discarded her cloak when she started to sweat, dragging it behind her first, until even that was too much effort. She thought it must be the end of February. March was coming, and spring. Did she need a cloak?

She found herself resting more than she walked, and coughing until brown froth spilled from her mouth. She did notice that the land began to slope gently. *Small streams flow down to larger streams*, she thought, remembering Pablo, missing him. *Larger streams to a river. Pray to God it is the Rio Tajo, then Santa Catarina soon.*

She saw occasional houses no grander than the hovel where Milagra and Velardo lived, but knew better than to seek help. Amador and Baltazar had probably visited each of them last night.

A few steps, then rest, a few steps more. As the sun struggled overhead, flirting with clouds and gusts that threatened to topple her, she entertained visitors. The first guest was the hardest, when Santiago pranced past her on his gray stallion. She begged him to stay, but he shook his head, blew her a kiss, and cantered away, back straight, eyes ahead. She teetered between anger and utter despair, until she reminded herself that he was only a trick of her imagination, *una fantasma.*

Engracia and Juana hurried past, only stopping to scold her for losing her cloak. Juana gave her the usual frosty glare that changed in a blink to blank eyes staring at mud. Hanneke shuddered.

Antonio passed her once after the sun gave up entirely and hid behind clouds. He held out his hand to her, and she to him, then he disappeared. Of all the apparitions, this was the hardest to bear. He had never abandoned her before; why now, when she needed him the most?

His visit brought her to her senses. She shivered and looked around, seeing bare trees, and then, to her relief, something grander. She saw the

Rio Tajo stretching before her in the distance. She started walking again, no faster than before, but with purpose.

To her dismay, the apparitions – two horsemen this time – were not done with her, even though she could see the river. She looked closer, her heart in her mouth when Amador and Baltazar came toward her at a slow walk. She stood still and waited for them to pass, like all the others. Instead, they turned about and rode on each side of her, matching their horses' gait to her halting walk.

When Baltazar leaned over and prodded her with his boot, she knew she had lost. "Don't stop," he chided her and prodded her again, harder this time. "Walk, damn you."

"Leave me alone," she said, which only brought laughter.

She kept walking, wishing she could outrun them, knowing she could barely move. When they fell back, she wondered if they were real, or merely vivid phantoms brought on by her failing body.

She sighed with relief when she heard a horse ride away, but Baltazar remained. He continued his horse's slow walk beside her.

"Amador has gone for Señor Palacios and the others," he said. She heard all the triumph in his voice, and then his mock concern. "Felipe is *so* deeply devoted to your welfare, señora. He cannot understand why you have been running from him. All he means to do is keep you safe."

"He wants my dowry, now that Santiago is no more," she said, not looking at Baltazar because he frightened her.

He pushed her harder with his foot and she fell down. "He especially wants to know how you fooled us at Rincón."

She struggled to her feet. "It's easy to fool idiots," she snapped.

He struck her with his quirt again and again as she crumpled to the ground and tried to cover her head. *Get up*, she told herself, *get up*. She rose to her knees, but he pushed her down.

She made it to her knees in time to see the cruelest apparition of all. None of the other ghosts had revisited her, but here was Antonio, accompanied this time by Carlos. If it had only been Antonio, she might have hoped for a tiny moment that he had searched and found her. But no, not with Carlos this time, Carlos who had died at Las Claves.

She fumbled with the pouch around her neck, trying to work out the little knife, wondering if she was strong enough to kill herself, provided the blade wasn't dull. There was nothing to live for, not with two phantoms riding toward her. At least Baltazar had stopped beating her. In fact, he had stepped back.

To her further aggravation, Baltazar grabbed her around the waist and hauled her to her feet, holding her close. "You can't have her," he screamed at the ghosts. "Amador is coming with Felipe and others. We are taking her back to Las Claves."

"I'll fight you for Ana," Antonio said. "You will lose. Let her go."

Hanneke stared at the two men riding toward her. "Carlos lives?" she called. "You are not phantoms?"

"No, Ana, we are not," Antonio said. "Hang on a few minutes more."

Carlos grinned at her. "Señora, you know I am a hard person to kill. How should we do this, Antonio? Do you want to take him or may I? He nearly killed me at Las Claves. Please, may I? I've been good."

Baltazar shrieked and pulled Hanneke in front of him. She tried to take a deep breath and another, but ended up draped over his arm, coughing more bubbly saliva.

Baltazar jerked her up by her hair to shield him, as other horsemen thundered up behind him. He looked over his shoulder and laughed. "Señor Palacios, look what we have for you." He pushed Hanneke toward Felipe Palacios as Engracia's brother leaped from his horse.

"No, no." She tried to scream, but it came out in a whisper and another rush of froth.

Felipe yanked her from Baltazar as Antonio and Carlos backed up, moving closer together, all expression gone from their faces. She sobbed to see Amador, too, and four soldiers, men of Las Claves, one of them the soldier from Rincón. Felipe pinned her arms at her side, holding her in front of him, shielding himself, a coward to the end, even though they were seven against two.

"Kill them," Felipe said. "It is two men to your six. Why are you waiting?"

No one moved. Felipe swore when Hanneke coughed and turned her head to dribble froth from sorely tried lungs onto his surcoat. He let go of her to wipe his hands, fastidious to a fault, except this was not the time or place.

She sank to her knees as Antonio and Carlos backed their horses closer to the trees. "Don't leave me," she whispered.

She sank lower until she sat in front of Felipe, unable to rise. Out of weary eyes, she watched as Amador and Baltazar led the four soldiers toward Antonio and Carlos, the horses in a line, moving slowly as if in a nightmare. Still they waited.

"Please, Antonio, please," she said, then noticed something remarkable. He was smiling. So was Carlos.

"Felipe, she is my wife," Antonio said, sounding most conversational and reasonable. "Santiago ordered me to marry her, just to keep her from you and your greediness."

"No ecclesiastical court in all of Spain will honor such a marriage. No betrothal was announced. No banns were called. It was done in secret," Felipe spit out. "You have lost, Antonio, you bastard of many Almohad warriors who had their fun with your mother! Kill them, you men of Las Claves! What are you worthless soldiers waiting for?"

How could Antonio smile like that? Hanneke pleaded with her eyes.

Antonio motioned with his hand. "Don't rise, Ana. Not an inch." He crouched lower in his saddle, and she did the same. "Stay there. Hold still." He straightened up.

She heard sudden hoofbeats behind her, a warbling cry, and a whoosh as a blade swept by, ruffling her hair. She glanced behind her, horrified, in time to see Felipe's head drop and roll down the slope toward his startled soldiers.

She crawled away from the carnage, looking back once to see Felipe Palacios lying on the slope slightly above her, minus his head. Behind him on horseback sat the man who had gone far beyond the bargain they made last summer. "Yussef," she whispered. "Yussef."

El Ghalib dismounted and picked her up. She rested her head against his chest, his arms tight around her. "Help them," she whispered. "Please help Antonio."

"Antonio and Carlos don't need my help," he said. He turned slightly so she could watch, as Antonio, moving fast, kneed his horse forward and sped an arrow directly into the middle of Baltazar's forehead. Amador turned to flee. His hands flew up and he fell from his horse, a knife in his back.

With all the calm of a professional killer, Carlos surveyed the bloody wreckage before him. To Hanneke's horror, Amador still moved.

"Antonio, a little more to the left would have been perfect." Carlos rubbed his shoulder and winced. "A few more weeks will see me in better form."

"You were good enough," Hanneke heard Antonio say. "Amador will writhe and suffer, *ojalá*. I have no objection to that."

Hanneke turned her attention to the great-hearted man who held her. There was so much to ask him, but all she wanted to do was close her eyes and sleep, if her lungs would let her. She patted him to get his attention. "Why? You have already exceeded all the bargains for the necklace."

"I thought I had, but I can put no price on your humanity to my sister Jawhara." He gave her a brief smile. "I started following you, after I learned of Rincón. Before Allah, you were hard to find." He sighed and held her closer. "I must turn you over to another because he has a prior claim. Let us wait a moment and see what happens." An interested spectator, Yussef watched the remaining soldiers. "If they are wise…"

Antonio sat with his bow and arrow in his lap, his eyes on the soldiers before him. Carlos tapped another wicked-looking knife against the pommel of his saddle.

"*Soldados*, it is your choice," Antonio said. "Do not doubt that Carlos and I can and will kill you." He looked each man in the eye.

"Señor Baltierra, do not be hasty," said one. "He…he gave us no choice."

"As I said, Marco, the choice is yours. If you wish to live another day, throw down your weapons. Return to Las Claves. Tell whomever Señor Palacios left in charge what has happened here."

"What then, Antonio?" another one asked.

"We need an army, Salvador," Antonio said simply, after a glance at the Almohad who held Hanneke in his arms. "I will never speak of this day again, if you join us in the cause of Spain. As for now, go to Las Claves. I am done with you."

Salvador looked down. "These corpses?"

"Leave them. It's been a harsh winter. Perhaps the wolves and wild boars aren't too particular."

The soldiers rode away with no backward glance. Antonio dismounted and in a breathtaking move, prostrated himself before the great enemy of Spain. "I will never be out of your debt," he said. He stood up. "May I have her?"

El Ghalib kissed Hanneke on the forehead. "If you do not treat her well, I will know."

"I imagine you will. Farewell."

Hanneke wanted to pat El Ghalib's cheek, but her arm didn't seem to belong to her. She tried to thank him, but nothing came out.

"She is fading fast," Yussef said. "Mount your horse. I will hold her up."

"You're so light," Antonio said, when she was in his arms. "Too light. *Dios mio*, Ana."

El Ghalib mounted his Arabian and put his hand to his head and chest. "If we meet in battle, Antonio Baltierra, you have no promise. As for you, Ana, well, no man wins everything." He smiled. "Choose wisely, *habiba*."

Hanneke remembered nothing more.

Chapter Fifty-one

The bells of Santa Catarina raised her from the dead.

When she was coherent weeks later, she considered her survival as she lay peacefully on her back in a quiet room. She watched the play of sunlight across the coverlets, and knew the credit really belonged to Antonio Baltierra, the man who never left her side through the great trials of her life.

She didn't make things easy, forcing him to pummel her shoulders, then lean her over the bed with his finger down her throat until she vomited gluey matter from somewhere inside her. The black-robed women who glided around trying gentler cures had objected. Dimly, as if from some other room, she heard him snap at them in a voice unfamiliar to her. They let him alone to continue his torture.

The hot wheat poultice covering her breasts came as a relief, because then he left her alone to allow the heat to work its particular magic on her lungs. She wanted to kick him when he rubbed her legs and declared her how scrawny she was. She tried to tell him about Milagra and Velardo who only fed her hot water, and how could a woman to be anything but thin on such a diet, but the words weren't there.

With no control over whether she lived, Hanneke had vague memory of watching from a curious distance while a priest touched oil to her forehead and hands and Antonio cried. It had taken an age, but she managed to put her hand on his head, which stopped his tears. Maybe it even gave her hope, because she didn't die after all.

She couldn't die, not with someone working so hard to keep her among the living. Antonio didn't seem to understand how weary she was, how exhausted. Never really strong since the death of her daughter, living was simply one more torture. She tried to explain this to him, until she became aware that she was speaking in her native language. No wonder he wouldn't let her go; he didn't understand. In that case, what could she do but live?

Perhaps she wanted to live, after all. The moment came after a day of struggling to breathe, when Antonio lay down beside her, gathered her close, and made her breathe along with him. That must have been his last resort, with his arms around her. She felt his heartbeat as his chest lifted and fell. She compelled herself to breathe with him, in and out, steady. She never looked back after that moment.

Now she lay in peace, enjoying the sun, as she listened to the bells of Santa Catarina. As a sunbeam played across the coverlet, she raised her hand to catch it.

"Ana?"

She turned her head to the sound of Antonio's voice, pleased that nothing ached. There he sat, watching her so intently, the steadfast man who refused to let her surrender to death. He needed a shave and his hair was long and curling over his shoulders. He had obviously not taken care of himself. As she looked at him, she realized he had been taking care of her, to the exclusion of all else.

"Antonio, you need to shave and get your hair cut. Must I insist upon something so basic?" she asked, teasing him because she had decided to live.

To her consternation, tears streamed down his face. To her relief, he rested his head on her stomach. She fingered his hair, enjoying the feel of his black curls, certain he was the most handsome man in all of Spain's kingdoms.

"I'll cut my hair for you," he said finally, and looked toward the door when someone knocked. "Sister Filomena, look who has decided to speak to us. In fact, she is nagging me. Such a wife."

Was there something in the water at Santa Catarina that made everyone cry? Hanneke looked from one to the other, and then another sister glided into the room, with the same result. Soon the room was full of weeping people.

"Really, all of you," she murmured. She looked to the door and saw Carlos, battered and crude and possessing more lives than most cats. "Well now, here is someone I *know* is too tough to cry and carry on, simply because I feel like scolding my...my husband. Oh, Carlos, not you, too?"

By the end of the week, she sat up. She was learning everyone's names, these dear people who had all worked so hard to tug her away from the land of the dead, some of them cajoling, if memory served her right, and others demanding her survival, Antonio doing both.

Sister Filomena consoled Hanneke when she finally noticed she had very little hair. "Child, it was so badly tangled, brittle, and full of lice," the nun said. "Dry your tears. It will grow."

"What must Antonio think?" she wailed. "It barely covers my ears!"

"He told me you are the most beautiful woman in the world," Sister Filomena said, and she had to be satisfied with that.

Sister Filomena must have been right. Hanneke loved each night when Antonio stayed with her, getting between the covers and doing nothing more than holding her. She laughed, her face warm, when he hefted one breast and then the other, and whispered in her ear. "They're improving, Ana. Keep eating."

She ate, the nuns bathed her, and she started to walk again, holding onto Antonio, appalled at her weakness. Stairs were beyond her, but she sat in a chair for most of one morning, pleased with something so simple. "Little steps," Sister Filomena cautioned. "Death banged on the door for you, and who knows if he still lurks about?"

She laughed at that notion, until the awful morning when it seemed entirely possible.

Antonio was late coming upstairs with her breakfast. He had fallen into the habit of going to the kitchen to eat his fill and then bringing a tray upstairs for her. She was able to feed herself now, so he propped his slippered feet on the bed and watched her, commandeering a bit of bread or cheese for himself if he felt like it.

He came into the room this morning, tray in hand, but she turned away in shock.

"Ana, I..."

From chain mail and surcoat, booted and with his broadsword clanking against his leg, he was dressed for war. He set the tray on the table beside the bed, then sat down next to her.

"Ana, I received a letter early this morning from King Alfonso. We are to meet with our armies in a week's time. I must think of Spain, now."

She sank down in the bed and turned her face to the wall.

"I have no choice, dear heart," he said. "I nearly left without telling you, but I am not a coward."

"No. You are a warrior," she said, still not looking at him.

"I will be back within the week, once all my men are gathered, and before we ride south as an army. Ana, look at me."

He spoke so gently she had no choice but to give him her attention. He put his hands on either side of her body, leaning so close she smelled the oil on his chain mail. "It comes down to this, as you knew it would. Be honest with yourself." His voice was soft and deceptively tender, as if he could convince her that he sat with her as usual in his long tunic and soft shoes.

"Send Carlos. Send anyone else," she said. "I have already lost one husband to war. I cannot do this again."

"I have delayed and delayed until I am nearly in Alfonso's black book, Ana. Carlos has gathered the troops and we must join with the other armies. I'll find a way to return before we move south in earnest. I promise I will."

"Then you will ride out no matter what I say or feel." Her words sounded toneless to her ears, spoken by someone she did not know or even like.

"I must." He stood up and she turned away again. He closed the door quietly behind him.

Chapter Fifty-two

She left her food untouched that day and the next. She ate something on the third day because Sister Filomena burst into tears, knelt and begged her to eat. When the sisters pleaded with her to at least sit up and dangle her feet over the edge of the bed, she closed her eyes, tired of people telling her what to do, when she wanted to die. She shook her head over anything more than a scrap of bread and a sip of wine. Finally it was too much trouble to open her eyes. She heard the nuns clustered around her bed, praying and whispering among themselves, but she was too tired to shoo them away.

She was in her now-familiar stupor when Antonio returned. She roused herself slightly, but it was too hard to open her eyes. She heard nuns in the room, and snatches of conversation – "Pining for you." "She will die without you." "We are ready to summon the priest again."

Leave Antonio alone, she wanted to say. *He is busy with war. Just go. Don't tease me.*

He was speaking too loud. She heard, too close to her ear, "When have any of us done anything except disappoint her? What choice does she have but to do everyone else's bidding?"

Husband, don't try so hard, she thought. *Life is cheap in Spain. So is mine. This I know.*

Antonio patted her hip. "Ana, I have an idea."

Good for you. Can't you see I am almost dead? Leave me alone.

When he left the room, she felt only relief.

She had no idea how long he was gone. One day? Five hours? Time meant nothing to her anymore. She had started to cough again and her lungs hurt. Antonio was gone. Why bother?

That day or the next – who knew? – she heard the door open. She sniffed leather and campfire, but she was too tired to open her eyes.

"No. Not there. Put down a blanket. Yes, over there."

The room was quiet again. Hanneke prepared to sink into deeper sleep when she heard a mewing sound, the noise kittens make when they are hungry or lonely. *These people of Spain are so inconsiderate*, she thought, startled at her anger. *Can they not drown unwanted kittens?*

The crying became more insistent. She opened her eyes, but saw no kittens. With an effort that made her sweat, Hanneke raised herself up on one elbow and stared in the direction of the noise. She sucked in her breath. Was she dreaming?

Antonio stood in the doorway, making no move to come closer. He watched her, ignoring the baby crying. His eyes challenged her, daring her to do something.

She could tell from the cry that it was a young one. The naked baby kicked out with its legs, punctuating each wail with a wild movement of the arms. She looked closer; it was a girl. Her hair was dark like Antonio's, like hers.

Antonio stared off into space. He glanced her way, then turned on his heel and left her alone.

She lay down, covering her ears as the baby cried. The afternoon wore on as shadows changed places with each other, and still the baby cried. When she started to whimper, Hanneke pulled back the blanket and hauled herself upright.

The floor looked so far away. She stretched out her toes, feeling for the cold stone. She slid closer to the edge and pulled herself to her feet.

The room whirled around and she sat down. Two or three deep breaths, and she tried again. "Hush, little one," she crooned. "You must be cold and hungry. How could someone leave you like this?"

She felt ten feet tall and only inches wide, but she put one foot in front of the other, grasping the nearest chair until she could move, then dropping to her knees and crawling until the baby was in her arms. She curled herself around it, shivering more from exertion than cold.

She heard footsteps. Antonio covered them both with another blanket. She rested her cheek against the dark curls and closed her eyes, content.

She woke in her bed. She cried out, feeling in the bedclothes, searching for the baby.

"Over here, Ana."

Antonio sat holding the sleeping baby. Someone had dressed her in a gown and she was loosely wrapped in a blanket, sound asleep.

"There is a serving woman in the kitchen with a new baby," he said. "She assured me she has enough milk for this little morsel, too."

He answered the question in her eyes. "When Carlos and I were returning only yesterday, we came across a village in ruins." He settled the little one closer to him. "No, it was not the Almohades. Maybe a family vendetta. She was crying in a dead woman's arms. I left, of course. It was not my fight."

He brought the baby to her, settling her in Hanneke's arms. The child stirred, then made herself comfortable.

"I thought about her all the way here." He propped his legs on the bed. "I have...we have all seen children like this. They die quickly. Perhaps it is better."

"Surely not," she murmured. She breathed deep of the baby's milky fragrance.

"I rode back for her. Sister Filomena wonders if you would care for this *niñita* until other arrangements can be made. She thinks she can find a family to raise her as a servant." He shrugged. "I don't know. Are you strong enough? I have to leave again. Perhaps I should not have assumed..."

"I will manage, Toño," she said, seeing his smile at her little nickname. "It's probably the least I can do, you know, to repay the sisters."

"Of course. It's only for a little while."

"Does she have a name?"

"I wouldn't know it. And look at her. She must have some Almohad blood." He sighed. "I know the look. It is mine, too. Do you care? It's an imposition."

She kept her voice calm, offhand. "I said I didn't mind. We should name her."

"You choose."

She pulled back the blanket and ran her thumb gently across the baby's toes. They curled against her hand and she smiled at a good memory. "Santiago told me that we would have another baby, and she should be named Liria, after his mother. Liria?"

He smiled into her eyes. "I would like to do that honor for my friend. Yes. Liria. It's a small enough name for a little scrap."

They sat together, at peace. He told her about the armies assembling, led by King Alfonso, in the mountains to the west. "All the kingdoms have united for this fight," he told her. "I believe we will succeed."

"And women wait," she said softly, smiling inside now, because Antonio was running a finger down Liria's arm, then down hers as well.

He nodded. "They do. Will you?"

"We'll see."

"It's only fair. I'm certain Sister Filomena will find someone soon for Liria." He stood up. "Now I will take her to the kitchen. No, no, don't worry. The woman feeding her wants her close by at night. I'll bring her back tomorrow." He wagged his finger at her. "After you have eaten a substantial breakfast and not a moment sooner. Agreed?"

"Agreed."

The pleasant pattern continued for two days, days when she cuddled Liria and walked carefully around her room, regaining her strength. Antonio spent more time at the window, looking across the plains to the south, as if planning the coming battle. He took Liria to the window once, pointing out the distant mountains and telling the baby how many soldiers were here to protect her. "And your mama...I mean, Ana, too. She will watch you," he said.

You transparent man, she thought, amused. *You think you're so clever.*

"I have to leave tomorrow," he told her that afternoon.

Hanneke waited for the chill to wrap around her heart again, but it was different this time. She knew he had work to do, and so did she. Someone had to take care of Liria until the nuns of Santa Catarina could find her a home. "Be very careful, Toño," she said.

"Careful doesn't win battles," he said cheerfully.

"I mean it," she told him, her eyes unwavering on his.

"I will be, *dama*, for you," he said. "I'll take Liria. Come with me to the kitchen so you can meet the wet nurse."

"Just point me toward the kitchen. I will be fine tomorrow."

Antonio tucked Liria under one arm and put his other arm around Hanneke. "You've never been to the kitchen. I will just walk along with you. You know, for company."

Even though they walked slowly, Hanneke was ashamed at her weakness. Antonio appeared not to notice, keeping up a steady conversation as they moved at a snail's pace.

The stairs were a particular trial. She stopped before they reached the bottom. "Toño, I cannot,'" she said, dismayed and in tears.

He held her up. "You can. Wife, you have come this far. You can walk the rest of the way. After all, I looked for you all over Castile."

Liria began to wail as they neared the kitchen, Hanneke barely moving, leaning on Antonio. The wet nurse came toward them, her arms outstretched. Her own child slumbered in a box by the great fireplace. "I heard her and my milk started flowing! Come, little pet."

She took Liria and opened her bodice, standing right by them. "This is your lady, Señor Baltierra? She is as pretty as you said."

"Yes, this is my lady."

Antonio picked her up, over her protests and tears. "She is tired. I'll take her back upstairs. She wanted to find the kitchen. You will see…" He stopped, as if the name was new to him, but welcome. "You will see Señora Baltierra again quite soon, now that she knows the way."

Antonio put Hanneke back in bed and wiped her tears. "You'll be downstairs again before you know it." He tucked the covers around her, hesitated a moment, then sat down and took her in his arms. He kissed her soundly, held her off briefly, then kissed her again. A third time seemed like a good idea, too.

"*Vaya con dios,*" she told him, when he stood in the doorway for a long moment.

"*Y tu, esposa,*" he replied. "Until we meet again."

Chapter Fifty-three

The next afternoon, Hanneke made her way to the kitchen without stopping, holding Liria tight and clinging to the wall. As delightful as watching Liria was the pleasure of watching Hernana, who ruled the kitchen. With Liria or her own baby clinging to her nipple like a barnacle on a ship's hull, Hernana cut up vegetables, shredded meat, and strained milk, talking all the while.

Since Hanneke was now a fixture in the kitchen, Sister Filomena put her to work. "You can scrub vegetables sitting down," the nun said. "When you feel stronger, Hernana will show you how to make butter."

"I already know how," Hanneke said, pleased what her mother had taught her, back when they both thought she would marry a Dutch merchant.

"You don't mind?"

"Not at all. I was beginning to feel useless," Hanneke replied, when what she really meant was "lonely."

"We need your help. The spring planting is on us and we are laboring in the fields. Hernana will instruct you in here."

As the weather grew warmer, Hanneke found herself on her knees by the flowerbed around the statue of Santa Catarina, plucking weeds while Liria lay beside her on a blanket, waving her arms at the leaves overhead. Hanneke yearned to share each little milestone in Liria's life with her patient husband who knew, better than anyone, what would bring his wife back from the dead.

"You, who have seen me at my worst, you knew, didn't you?" she whispered out loud one night after Liria fell asleep in her arms. "Please may you return soon." She thought of her long-ago conversation with Yussef el Ghalib. "Toño, I choose you."

She knew she was growing stronger, her body filling out as the signs of starvation vanished. She smiled to think that Antonio would appreciate the heft of her breasts now. When her monthly flow returned, gone since her days of hunger, she rejoiced in this homely sign of her womanhood. She was whole once more.

Or nearly whole. This wasn't a matter to discuss with the chaste brides of Christ who prayed and worked for the greater glory of God, but she wanted Antonio Baltierra in other ways than for his help and good humor. She had to content herself with remembering how truly impressive he looked, wearing only his smallclothes, when he went into the Rio Tajo to help her rescue Santiago.

The only remedy for this new, most-pleasant hunger was work in the gardens and fields, the kind of work that wore her out and kept her thoughts more seemly. The fields soon drew her for another reason, one that set her heart pounding.

The armies from the kingdoms of Spain marched south, some passing by the convent. At first they were little streams of soldiers from the kingdoms of Castile, Aragon, Navarre, Leon and even Portugal and France. Many paused at noon for a drink from the well, or a moment in the shade of the convent walls. One soldier from far away Portugal fell sick and was left with them by his comrades. The sisters tended him until he died, then buried him within their walls without ever knowing his name.

The little streams of soldiers flowed into bigger streams and then a river of men as spring passed into summer. At night, the lights of their campfires winked all about the convent like fireflies announcing summer, the season of war.

"In all my lifetime, I have never seen so many armed men," Sister Filomena said one afternoon as they stood by the convent gate, watching soldiers ride past, eyes to the south. "They fly so many different flags, but they are united in this effort as never before."

Liria in her arms, Hanneke watched them, wishing Antonio were among them, wishing he would swing out of line for at least a kiss. Sleep never came easy on those nights.

One afternoon, the terrible beauty of Spain came home to her, forcing her to admit that to leave Spain would tear the heart from her body.

A knight and his son had stopped for water, as many had before. Stiff from long hours in the saddle, they dismounted and shared the dipper of water Hanneke offered them.

"Where are you from, *señores*?" she asked. Dressed in chain mail like his father, the boy fingered Liria's curls as Hanneke held her.

"Salamanca," the knight said. He touched his son's shoulder. "We must ride, *hijo*."

They were reserved and reticent like so many Spanish men, with a certain sadness that humbled her. Out of curiosity, she asked, "Why do you ride, señor? So many have marched south already. Surely it is enough."

He smiled at her and touched Liria, too, as if for good luck. "We have confessed. We have left our affairs in order. We are not afraid of what is before us."

She understood at last. The expression she assumed was sadness was that particular dignity of brave people who knew their destiny and did not tremble before it. Tears came to her eyes, so she shifted Liria to hide her weakness. Some had called her brave, but as she watched the knight and his son, Hanneke knew that their brand of bravery was bred in the bone. This was their country and they wanted it back, all of it.

Standing by the well, holding Liria close, Hanneke knew she would never again yearn for Vlissingen. Compared to the exaltation that was Spain, everything else paled into insignificance. As the horsemen rode by, she realized with stunning ferocity that that she wanted this strength for her children, waiting to be born if their father returned.

Summer arrived, hot, fierce, and windy. Liria grew fretful, crying for no reason. Desperate to know what was wrong, Hanneke despaired until Hernana pointed out the little tooth that was about to break through her swollen gums. "She is already starting to chew on my nipples," Hernana said with a laugh. She nudged Hanneke. "When your man returns, Ana, you will have babies to gnaw on you!"

"Antonio, it is a tooth. Nothing to worry about," she said out loud as she prepared this child who was now her daughter for bed. "We have heard that soon there will be a battle. I know you are busy, but I thought you should know."

No one answered. She nestled against Liria and prayed that the battle, when it came, would be swift.

News of what the soldiers called the battle of Navas de Tolosa seemed to come to them on the wind that blew hot from the south. The sisters did not know where Navas de Tolosa was, beyond the speculation that it might be in Andalucia, the mighty stronghold of Caliph Muhamad al-Nasir of the Almohades. *That* news sent Hanneke into the flower bed where the statue of Santa Catarina stood. She weeded with ferocity, remembering Antonio's cheerful words that battles weren't won by being careful.

News trickled north, a word here, a whisper there, and all the words and whispers spoke of victory. Official news came in late July from a courier heading to Valladolid. He came walking up the road because his horse limped.

"Have you nothing I can ride?" he asked Mother Abbess.

"My son, we have not," the gentle lady told him. "Our animals are plow horses. A little further on toward Toledo, there is an *estancia* of fair size. You will have better luck there."

Mother Abbess motioned to Hanneke and Sister Filomena, who joined her at the well, where the courier poured dippers of water over his head, matted down by his helmet in all this heat.

"But tell us, sir, please, what news?"

He stared at Mother Abbess. "Everyone knows!"

"We do not," she apologized. "The official traffic around here usually takes the closer Toledo road. We know there was a victory, but that is all we know."

"It was a great victory," he said. "We fought deep in Almohad country. I do not think they will recover."

Hanneke propped Liria on the well's lip. "Tell us, señor, were there many wounded and killed?"

"It was war, señora," he said. He whistled to his lame horse. "Some died, some were wounded. On the whole, we were fortunate. I must go now."

"Please, señor, what of Antonio Baltierra of…of Las Claves?"

"I have heard the name. A big tall fellow? Brown hair and one arm?"

"No."

He gathered the reins in his hands, ready to move on, then looked back and noticed her tears. "Señora, there were many at Navas. You will hear soon. Why, any day now, your man will return. *Adiós.*"

But she did not hear. While the nuns spend their free moments praying in the chapel, she watched the road.

The armies returned finally, borne in like the tide, carrying in triumph the battle flags like ones in the great hall of Las Claves. Smaller flags and scimitars bristled from their saddles. The soldiers rubbed down their horses with prayer rugs.

Hanneke feared at first to venture among their campfires to ask of Antonio. Clutching Liria to her like a talisman, she finally gathered her courage to face the dirty, bearded men.

"He was killed." "He is wounded." "He is missing." "I do not know." "Antonio Baltierra?" "A tall man?" "A man with no teeth?" "*Dama*, you may come with me. I have land now." "Come with me." "Or me." "Or me."

Some of the soldiers rode directly to the convent, bearing their wounded. In a fever, she ran among the injured as they lay on pallets in the chapel. They all looked like Antonio, every one of them.

Mother Abbess and Sister Filomena forced her to leave the chapel and forbade her from entering until the wounded were dead or gone. "Ana, you cannot do this to yourself," Sister Filomena said, her own eyes filled with anguish.

She knew she could not. Hanneke plopped Liria on her hip and hurried down to the kitchen, where she scrubbed pots and hauled water and muttered to herself.

Through the rest of the long summer, the Christian warriors, the Knights of Calatrava and Salvatierra, and even adventurers from France returned from war. Hanneke questioned knights and vassals, hearing so many stories that she was convinced that if someone actually told her about Antonio, she would not know it.

She endured their boasting of land to the south, theirs now, granted from the rulers of their kingdoms. They had only come north again to gather their boldest villagers to follow them south, where life, while hard, meant property that many of them, as younger sons, would never have had without Navas.

She spent a quiet time that evening after Vespers in the field where the grain was ready to harvest, remembering Santiago's promise to her that he would have land for their children to come, and orange groves. She made herself stay awake long into the night, unwilling to dream of their final moments together in the snow, and cry because time ran out. Others owned his promised land now.

Gradually, the armies vanished. August passed and September came and still she stood by the convent gate, shading her eyes and watching to the south for more soldiers. She stood there until one evening Sister Filomena linked arms with her and pulled her away to walk through the wheat field that was now partly harvested.

Sister Filomena said nothing as they circled the field, watching the sun go down, listening for the night birds. They stood close together for the sunset, their arms around each other. The nun raised her face to puffs of wind that carried the scent of grain. "Autumn is in that breeze, Ana, my dear."

"Yes, sister." Tears slid down Ana's face.

"Will you...will you return to the Low Countries?" Sister Filomena asked quietly.

"No. Somehow it isn't right anymore. And there is Liria." She made herself smile. "Sister, you and Mother Abbess made a poor attempt at finding a home for Liria."

"I thought we did rather well," Sister Filomena said. They laughed together, as Ana sniffed back more tears.

"You may stay with us. You know you are welcome."

"I know, sister," Hanneke said, "and I am grateful. I will decide soon."

As they circled the field again, Hanneke stopped. The dowry. "Sister, I need to go to Toledo," she said. "Immediately."

"I don't understand."

Hanneke started in motion, moving faster, thinking ahead. "The condition of my dowry was that I had to live until...let me think...late July, I believe."

"You've done that," Sister Filomena said with a smile.

"And...and if I outlived Santiago, someone else could claim me and the dowry," Hanneke explained. She took several deep breaths, thinking of Antonio Baltierra, wondering where he lay in death. "Antonio did that and now...it's so hard to say."

"Then don't," the nun replied.

"The dowry, what's left of it after interest is paid, is mine now to do with as I choose. I need to speak to Don Levi in Toledo. I need to go tomorrow."

Chapter Fifty-four

In two days Hanneke stood before the house of Don Levi, dropped off by a pious farmer near Santa Catarina who crossed himself several times before he chirruped two Christian horses past the entrance to La Judería.

After promising the old fellow not to worry, Hanneke assured him that she would find a conveyance to an inn in the Christian part of Toledo. She promised to return with him tomorrow by noon, when he finished other business transacted for Mother Abbess, his sister.

She paused on the steps, knowing what she looked like – her hair too short (in some weird way it had come in curly), her skin tanned from working in the fields at Santa Catarina, and her body not quite so thin as to frighten the Levis, but not as abundant as when she had met them a year ago. Her clothes were plain this time, not the genteel style of the dress she wore a year ago to impress the Jewish banker and get a better monetary arrangement for her husband Santiago Gonzalez.

Other things about her had changed, the things a person couldn't see. Perhaps Don Levi would notice; perhaps he wouldn't. Hanneke doubted she could fool Raquel Levi. She touched the leather pouch she still wore about her neck, the one containing the lines declaring her married to Antonio Baltierra now.

She took a deep breath and lifted the door knocker. A few brief words of explanation to the servant found her sitting again in Don Levi's office. He came into the room with his wife, which eased her heart. She bent a knee to him, then to Raquel, who seemed to see right into her heart and its sorrow.

"We have heard, Señora," Don Levi said.

"All of it?" she asked.

319

"All of it. Word travels. Please be seated. Raquel, will there be wine?"

"The best." Raquel sat beside her.

The door opened with a servant bearing wine and *dulces*. Hanneke was almost embarrassed to reach for anything. She had forgotten how rough her hands had become, pulling weeds, and later swinging a scythe not too well, but at least in earnest.

Neither Levi seemed to notice, or at least to care. She saw that Raquel was with child, and found herself missing Liria with all her heart. A child as young as Liria doesn't understand when her mother assures her that she will return tomorrow. Liria was also too young to know that sometimes people want to return and cannot.

Gentle questions from the banker, along with excellent wine, loosened her tongue. She told the Levis the entire story of the struggle in the snow for Las Claves, the necklace she bargained, Santiago's death – Raquel held her hand through that harrowing memory – and her sudden marriage to Antonio Baltierra, Santiago's dying request.

She took out the marriage lines Father Anselmo had rushed onto a scrap of parchment in the long-unused chapel of Santo Gilberto. Don Levi nodded. "What a trying time for all of you," he said. "Please tell us the rest."

Hanneke thought Raquel Levi had a tender spot in her own heart for Antonio and was not surprised to hear her sniff and reach for a handkerchief when Hanneke told her about Liria, and how he had gently bullied her into folding that little one to her empty heart.

"That is my tale, Señor Levi," Hanneke concluded. "It is October, and Antonio did not return from Navas de Tolosa. I have no word of him, or of Carlos, either. I can only conclude that…that…" She closed her eyes.

The silence in the room gave her comfort because she felt the goodwill of the husband and wife. "I have survived, and I suppose what is left of the dowry is mine," she said finally. "I have presented myself to tell you this story and ask what happens now."

"It won't be difficult, Señora Baltierra," Don Levi assured her with a courtly bow from where he sat. "I have gone over the numbers and subtracted what portion is due to the House of Levi. I knew you would come to us in good time."

He rummaged in a box on his desk and spread out the original document of marriage, beckoning her to move her chair closer. She looked at the parchment, seeing again her father's bold signature and her smaller one, signed under duress and with tears. Her eyes followed the additional clauses that came next, the ones that so frustrated Santiago and amused King Alfonso.

"It seems so long ago," she said. "A different person signed that document." She looked at the little man seated across from her. "Does Spain change everyone?"

"I don't know," he said. "I have always lived here. So has Raquel. What have you learned from all of this turmoil, chaos and war?"

"That I don't belong in The Netherlands any longer," she said promptly. "I have Liria, and there is this new woman who looks back at me when I pass a mirror. She is a little battered and heart sore, but she gets up every morning and cannot imagine herself anywhere else. I choose Spain."

"You won't regret it." He handed her a smaller sheet with numbers in columns. "There is still a substantial sum, now in your sole charge. You can live where you choose for the rest of your life, if not in luxury, at least in definite comfort." He smiled at Raquel. "My wife hopes you choose Toledo. So do I."

Hanneke leaned toward Raquel until their shoulders touched. "I might do that," she said. "I like Toledo. Right now, if I may, I would like to take out a small sum to repay the nuns for their kindness, plus a little more to use here tonight for lodging. I'll leave the rest as it is, and return to Santa Catarina."

"Very well." He jangled a bell and a clerk appeared. The two conferred quietly, then the clerk left and returned with another document. Don Levi held it out to Hanneke. "For several months, I have had this ready for you to sign. I knew you would come eventually. Look it over."

She did, seeing everything in order, pleased to know there would be money enough for her needs, and then some. She ran her hand over her Dutch name on this new document and held out the parchment to the banker. "Don Levi, please cross through *Hanneke* and replace it with Ana. Everyone calls me that, and I have begun to think in those terms, myself."

There. She had put voice to what had been in her heart, probably since Antonio had left her to join the armies moving south, perhaps longer. She waited for some regret, some sadness, but there was none. She knew who she was - Ana Aardema Baltierra, widow, and as Toño would probably have added with a smile, free woman.

"Wise choice," Don Levi said. He scratched through, added, and initialed, then handed it back for her signature. "What will you do now?"

"I will watch the road from the south until winter returns, then I will decide what to do."

They must understand because they knew Antonio Baltierra. A person couldn't abandon the idea of his return until all possible hope was gone.

When Don Levi leaned forward again with a document for her to sign, Ana noticed *his* necklace, remembered from her first visit to La Judería. Her hand went automatically to her throat, recalling *her* necklace, made by the same goldsmith, but bartered in a desperate place for the peace of her dying husband. Should she say something to Don Levi? She smiled inside, knowing it was another small thing; she could ask.

"Don Levi, I had necklace like yours once, given to me by Yussef el Ghalib. May I ask: How did you get yours?"

If the banker was surprised, he masked it well. He fingered the chain. "Here in Spain, many people owe us favors." He shrugged. "Let us say, my friendship with Yussef is … complicated."

"So is mine," she said. "You have heard my necklace story. I am less complicated."

When he laughed, she joined in his laughter, certain she would learn no more from him, and equally certain he did not need to know more from her. Even an uncomplicated woman needs a little mystery around her to treasure as years passed.

Her requested funds given to her in another leather pouch, Don Levi's personal servant took Ana to that inn on the quiet street near the cathedral. When the driver passed the cathedral, she asked him to stop. She handed out coins to the few women who begged in near darkness, and wished she had asked for more coins from her banker.

She thought of a much younger woman riding between two warriors in the heat of summer, with no idea what was to come, as she loved one, then later, the other. *I wish matters had been different, Santiago, oh how I wish it*, she thought, as dusk gathered. *Antonio, we never had time either, did we? Or you, Fermina? Dear God, why was everyone winnowed except me?*

Ana didn't request the same room. She shook her head over dinner, until she remembered Antonio's firmness that she not neglect her health. She agreed to bread and soup when she returned from a last excursion. In the process of all this, she noted with some amusement that the man who ran the inn didn't know what to make of a woman who traveled so boldly without a male escort. She wanted to assure him it wasn't by choice, as nothing had ever been by choice. She doubted he would understand, when she barely did.

She wrapped herself against the autumn chill in one of Sister Filomena's older cloaks and walked to the place, silent now, where a brother and his little sister had played, sang and danced for her. It was too late in the season for the pleasures of summer; no one danced.

In her mind – no, in her heart – she danced with the girl, learning the steps, feeling again all the awkwardness of an outsider. Antonio had joined her and then Santiago, the three of them dancing, freed for a moment from heavy cares and deep responsibilities. She decided to bring Liria to this magical place someday, when she thought she could bear it.

As for now, Ana stood in quiet contemplation, humbled at what difference a year could make in three lives. She blew three kisses to the wind and left Hanneke Aardema behind.

Chapter Fifty-five

Ana returned to Santa Catarina and grieved in silence, working hard at all tasks assigned her. The brightest moment came with the arrival from Toledo of Pablo and a girl she remembered as Luz, of the leper colony. They were brought by a clerk sent from Don Levi. She hugged Pablo and included Luz in her embrace.

Over bread and cheese, his story tumbled out, how Father Bendicio had sent the two of them walking to Toledo after the death of Luz's mother. "He remembered Don Levi, and gave me a letter for him," Pablo said.

"How did you get to Toledo?" she asked.

He grinned, her kitchen boy, her knight. "Little streams flow into big streams, and into the Rio Tajo."

Mother Abbess welcomed them into the community, and sent Pablo to help her brother, the farmer who had braved La Judería with Ana. She found Luz a quiet place in the kitchen, watching two babies when Hernana was busy.

Ana sent the clerk on his way in the morning, with a letter of gratitude to Don Levi, and the request that ten gold pieces make their way through a reliable source to Father Bendicio. Winter was nearly here and shelters of branches would never do. With quiet satisfaction, she watched the clerk leave, confident she had fulfilled any remaining obligation to a complex priest who would never be brave in the eyes of the hard society he inhabited, but who possessed another kind of courage few could match.

A week of rain followed Pablo's arrival, drenching the fields and pleasing farmers in a dry land. Ana joined the others in the kitchen, filling bins and barrels with provender for winter. Even with all the sisters in one room, there was no idle chatter. Mother Abbess read to them from St. Benedict's Rule.

The morning the fields were dry enough, some returned for the light work of gleaning. No one minded, because the air was crisp with the fragrance of balsam from nearby foothills.

No matter the day or the hour, Ana found herself looking to the south, watching for soldiers who came no more. She had told the Levis she would make a decision when winter came. As the season closed in, she wondered if she would ever not turn south and watch, no matter where she was or how long she lived.

What was the harm in one more look before she went inside to help with the nooning? She looked, then looked again. "Sister Filomena, I see soldiers."

"Child, it is farmers. We have seen them all month."

"Soldiers. I am certain."

The nun looked where Hanneke pointed. "Yes, soldiers. One of them carries a lance. Hopefully they do not bring news of more trouble to the south already."

"They would come faster, I suppose."

Ana bent to her work again, gathering the stray wisps of sheaved wheat. She meant to save some of it for herself. One of the sisters said she would show her this winter how to make Liria a summer hat out of wheat.

The soldiers passed by in the distance. Idly she looked once more, mindful this time that Sister Filomena watched her with sadness. Ana knew the nun was a tender soul. Maybe it was time to stop looking so hard for what would never happen. At least it would spare Sister Filomena.

As she watched, one of them glanced back at her.

"*Dios mio*," Ana said, startled. There could not be two men with the face of Carlos. "Sister...I....I must go." She dropped the wheat and started toward the convent gate.

Sister Filomena called after her, but Ana only picked up her pace. She saw the men admitted through the gate and walked faster. As she reached the edge of the field, one of the novices burst out of the gate, running toward her and waving her hands.

"Ana!" she called. "Mother Abbess says you are to come at once."

Ana ran into the courtyard, calling out to Carlos, who stood beside a roan as ugly as he was, and a strange bay, not Antonio's black stallion. She stopped, suddenly shy, until Carlos opened his arms to her. She ran to him and he held her tight.

The novice sent to fetch her from the field gaped in wide-eyed amazement. "Lady, these are rough men! Mother Abbess said...."

Ana extricated herself from Carlos' embrace. "You don't understand. This is Carlos and...and..."

"Lady, no tears," Carlos said. "They unman me."

She took one deep breath and another, until she could speak. "Where did you come from? Where have you *been* for the last three months?"

"We have been below the old *frontera*," he said. "It is a long story."

"We? We? Antonio, too? Please tell me yes!"

He nodded, his eyes wary.

"All this time I have been waiting...." She shook her head. "Carlos, *why*?"

"Antonio would not be here today, except that I forced him to come."

Forced him? The man who saved her life, time and again? The man who told her he loved her? Her husband? Aghast at this strange turn of events, she stared at Carlos. "Wha... what game is this?"

He put his hands on her shoulders. "It is no game. You will see. Antonio is back."

"Carlos, he... he... we parted in such accord," she stammered. "Why would he not..."

"Go to him," he said most tenderly, considering that this was Carlos, indestructible man, a warrior down to his toenails, someone she had feared until she knew his heart.

She looked down in dismay at her muddy dress, then put her hand to her head. She brushed at the chaff in her wildly curly hair. "Not like this. What will he think?"

He smiled for the first time. "Whatever you do will be the right thing, *dama*, whether you are tidy or not. Prove me right. That's all I ask."

She kissed his cheek and ran into the convent.

Hernana was nursing Liria when Ana burst into the kitchen, pulling off her dress and rushing naked to the water barrel, where she scrubbed herself. There was no hope for her dress, so she shook it out, scraped at the most obvious muddy spots and pulled it back on, all in the space of a few minutes while Hernana watched, open-mouthed. Even Liria turned to stare at her, distracted from Hernana's nipple. Milk dripped on her cheek.

Ana looked at her baby and laughed. "Silly girl! You are so wasteful. Hernana, please tell me that you have a comb?"

"Of course I do not have a comb in the kitchen."

Ana ran her fingers through her tangled curls. She smoothed down her dress. "How do I look?"

"Like a wild woman," Hernana said. "Sit down. Tell me."

"But I want to look pretty," Ana exclaimed. "Something is wrong." She burst into tears.

Hernana coaxed Liria back to the business at hand while Ana Baltierra sobbed in the kitchen. She cried until she felt a hand on her should, but she refused to look around.

It was Mother Abbess. "Ana, you are wanted upstairs. He told me right where you would be. If I do not return with you, I know he will come down here and see you in such a state. Dry your eyes. I do not want you to see him and weep."

Ana wiped her eyes on her apron. "Mother, what is wrong?"

"Promise me."

"Very well."

Mother Abbess left. Ana sat dry-eyed, staring at Hernana, who touched her knee. "It is never as bad as you imagine. Go, Ana, and take Liria with you."

Ana took Liria on her lap, running her hands over the familiar little body, breathing in the fragrance of her until she felt, if not serene, then at least calm.

She propped Liria on her hip and took her time on the stairs. She paused in the doorway of the audience room to draw a deep breath.

"You will not know her, Señor Baltierra," Mother Abbess was saying. "She is strong now, and well."

"I know her already. I saw her in the field as we rode by. Carlos wanted me to stop then, but I could not. I don't even know why I am here."

His back was to the door. She entered quietly for a look before he heard her and turned around. His hair was cut short as always. He sat straight in the chair as always. His was the posture of a horseman, so familiar to her, but something was different. Maybe it was the way he hunched a little to one side.

"Antonio."

He rose, but he did not move toward her. She came forward. "Antonio, I had given up," she said simply.

He still did not move, his hands together in their long sleeves. She saw the strain in his eyes, as if in pain, the skin stretched thin across his face.

She could tell he lived with pain now, and her heart went out to him. What had happened?

"We all work in the field," she said. "I wish I had time to tidy myself better, but nothing matters, because you have returned to me."

His eyes softened at her words. If only he would come closer. *Stubborn man*, she thought, torn between fear and irritation. *Whatever this is, you think I am not equal to it?*

She stood close to him, her back straight, too, realizing that he had said nothing to her. "Antonio, speak to me."

He avoided her eyes and watched Liria, who gazed back at him, wide-eyed. He fingered her black curls. "Liria, have you taken good care of your mother?"

Liria put her finger in her mouth, and nestled closer to Ana, wary. *Very well*, she thought, *you have a voice*. "She will become accustomed to you," she said. "She was so tiny when you left. It's been many months."

"Sit, you two," Mother Abbess said. "Right next to each other."

It was a small bench. Ana did not hesitate. She sat with Liria, then sighed with inward relief when he sat, too, their hips touching.

Mother Abbess offered Antonio a goblet of wine. He seemed to relax then. "This is as good as I remember," he said, after a long drink.

"Our grape harvest begins next week," Mother Abbess said. "Tell us of Navas de Tolosa."

He looked at Ana. "Do you want to hear?"

"You know I do, my love," she replied.

He made a sound deep in his throat. She examined him at close range, seeing the pain, the ravaged look. She could make him eat better, once they were together, as he had once coaxed her. *Patience, patience,* she told herself.

Liria surprised her, leaning toward Antonio. When he set down the goblet and reached for the baby, Ana saw the cause of his suffering.

His right hand, his sword hand, was missing fingers, muscle and bone. "Antonio, I am so sorry," she whispered. "What pain you must be in."

He settled Liria on his lap. To Ana's relief, she leaned back and snuggled in. When the little one was secure against his good arm and hip, he held up the maimed hand. When he spoke, Ana heard the bitterness and all the regret.

"Ana, I have become the person I feared the most: a one-handed man in a dangerous, two-handed world. What can I possibly offer you now?"

Chapter Fifty-six

In the silence, Ana became aware that Mother Abbess had left the room and closed the door behind her.

She made herself look at Antonio's hand. Two fingers and part of his palm had been scooped away as if by the curved blade of a scimitar. A scar from the bottom of what remained of his hand disappeared into his sleeve. The silence stretched on as she let the ugly sight register in her mind and make itself comfortable there. Some wisdom beyond her own – maybe it was more love than wisdom – cautioned her not to say anything until what she said would be right and true.

His head was bowed; he was a man defeated. She touched his cheek and turned him to look at her. When she did that, she knew what to say, because she loved him. Whether he believed her was his business. "Antonio, you are telling me that for all these months, you have been wondering if I would love you any less? Please assure me that you have more faith in me than that."

He held her gaze, which gave her hope. "Ana, do you remember when the three of us rode into Toledo past the cathedral?"

Surprised, she thought back to that first visit, which had seemed to be part of someone else's life, not hers. She remembered the delight of riding between two warriors, Spaniards in their absolute prime. Now one was dead and the other wounded in a way that left more than a scar.

"I remember," she said softly, wanting to treasure that moment in her heart. "I was so proud to ride between the two of you."

"Santiago said something that haunts me," he said. He fingered Liria's curls with his thumb and remaining two fingers. "I made some remark about seeing the beggars on the cathedral steps, and asked him if he ever thought about the old soldiers there."

She remembered her shock at seeing the beggars. "Yes. Santiago said it would be better to die in battle than to have to fight each day at the cathedral for food."

"And here I am." He managed a slight smile. "After the battle, King Alfonso granted me what would have been Santiago's land – an extensive holding near Úbeda, which is quite far to the south."

"Dangerous?" she asked, understanding with perfect clarity his dilemma.

"*Claro que si*," he replied. "I cannot even defend *myself* yet, let alone a wife and child and followers." He gave that offhand laugh she was familiar with, the one that told her he was settling into their friendship again, if nothing more. "I rely most heavily on Carlos."

"You can manage. I have infinite faith in you and Carlos."

She said it calmly, treading carefully, not wishing to wound him further. Her quiet words seemed to sink in, because he sat back and eyed her in that measuring way she had missed.

"Ana, I wasn't going to say this, but perhaps, just perhaps, in a few years when the frontier is more settled, we will have this conversation again. You know, when it is safer."

"Why wait?" she asked, her voice even softer, so he had to lean closer. "I love you now. What could I possibly fear, with you beside me?"

She put deeds to words. With her hands on either side of his face, Ana kissed him. She didn't stop with anything perfunctory, not with this man she adored. She kissed him slowly and thoroughly. Her whole heart rejoiced when he kissed her back the same way.

She wanted to continue, but Liria protested, squashed between them. Ana pulled away. "Liria! I am doing something so important with your father. How soon can I get you to sleep?"

Antonio laughed. "Ana, I hate to remind you, but it's not even noon yet."

She pulled her dignity together and whispered in his ear. "She takes a two-hour nap after the noon meal." Without question, this was a good time to run her tongue in his ear, the ear of a silly man who thought she would ever let him go. If the way he shifted about was any indication, Antonio Baltierra was highly susceptible to that sort of merriment. She stored that knowledge away for further embellishment.

"You know this is impractical," he told her, even as he breathed more heavily.

"Certainly," she agreed. "I should wait patiently and grow cobwebs while you and Carlos and your followers settle in. I can embroider and sing pious *canciones*! I am past patience. If you and Carlos ride out of here without me and Liria, I will run after you. Don't think for a moment that I won't."

"I believe you." He held out his left hand this time. "I have been practicing with this hand. I'm clumsy still, but I'm learning."

"Very well," she said, hoping, hoping. "Tomorrow let us ride to Toledo to the Jewish Quarter and Don Levi." She laughed, leaning against his shoulder. "I was there two weeks ago, arranging my affairs since I had survived two husbands. We will change what needs to be changed."

"Changed? I am the second husband… ah, I see. You went there and declared me dead, which gives you sole control of your remaining dowry."

"I thought you *were* dead," she said.

"Don't change anything," he told her. "We will let the Levis know I am alive, but I trust you to manage our affairs."

"That makes you a rare man," she said. His confidence in her touched her heart.

"I am a man with doubts and worries." He looked at his maimed hand. "Make sure you have thought this through, Ana."

"I have," she assured him. "I can tell you there is enough remaining of my dowry to build our lives in a new place." She took a deep breath, knowing this was the clinching argument, the one that mattered. "Toño, you never left me in *my* hours of need. How could I possibly desert you in yours?"

This time, she saw the fondness in his eyes, but it was more than fondness and more than relief. Ana knew love when she saw it. As she gazed at her husband, she knew she had been seeing this same more-than-fondness in his eyes almost since they met at the dock in Santander. The reality of his silent constancy humbled her. With a jolt, she knew if nothing had happened to Santiago, Antonio would have remained silent and constant all his life.

"Carlos told me that if I did not stop here today, he would leave me to my own devices. I agreed – what could I do? I was determined to tell you I do not hold you to this admittedly strange marriage of ours, as I promised when we were wed in such haste." He paused. When he continued, the words seemed to be dragged out of him with reluctance. "I can release you now, or I can make you wait a few years. Choose."

"I don't like those choices," she said, her hands in her lap, her eyes lively, because she knew she had won. "Dissolve this marriage? Wait a few years?"

"I don't like them, either," he told her. She heard confidence this time. "I knew that when I saw you in the door, tanned and healthy."

"My hair is stupid looking and I am muddy."

"Those are matters easily remedied," he joked. He turned serious, raising his right hand. "I'll need to draw on your strength, *esposa mia.*"

"It is yours for the asking."

"Then I ask, Ana Baltierra."

Thoughtful, overjoyed, Ana returned Liria to the kitchen and Hernana, with Luz eager to help. She washed herself thoroughly in the bath house, leaving Antonio with Mother Abbess and Sister Filomena. She passed Carlos in the courtyard and nodded to him, which made him grin and show off his missing teeth. "You're to eat the noon meal in the refectory with us," she told him.

"*Dama,* I am not a fine sort of man," he protested.

"You're the best sort of man," she assured him. "You are my husband's right hand, Carlos, and I bow before you."

She lowered herself into the same graceful bow she had given to King Alfonso what seemed like years ago, when she didn't know what she was capable of, or who her true friends were, when small things felt like large things.

"*Dama,* no," he protested.

"Too late," she said when she rose. "I am ever in your debt for getting Antonio here. Just remember – no swearing in the refectory. Mother Abbess takes a dim view."

Clean and dressed in her shabby best – her hair was going to be hopeless until it grew long – they dined in the refectory of Santa Catarina. Antonio Baltierra told them of Navas de Tolosa, how a shepherd had led the armies of the Spanish kingdoms through a mountain pass marked by the head of a cow.

"There were more of them than us, but we had surprise on our side. Thank you," he said, as Ana passed him the grapes. She watched with love as he carefully grasped a handful with his remaining digits and palm and ate them. "I…I was out of the fight not long after, but the armies pushed the Almohades back to the area close to Granada." He smiled at Ana. "Spain is nearly ours, and fairly won."

Mother Abbess crossed herself. "We heard so many stories from the returning soldiers. You have land?"

"Yes, Mother Abbess, I do, more than I ever dreamed."

"An orange grove?" Ana asked.

"No. I have olive groves and cattle," he said. She heard no regret. "We'll leave more conquest to our children."

Liria cooperated beautifully after noon in the refectory, pulling at her eyelids and leaning against Ana, who returned her to Hernana. "Keep her here until I come for her," Ana said.

"You're planning an afternoon romp in a convent," Hernana teased, keeping her voice low because Luz was listening. "He's still recovering. Don't wear him out!"

She didn't wear him out. After a few moments of awkwardness – he admitted he didn't have enough strength in his right arm to perform as he would have liked – Señor and Señora Baltierra figured it out, then figured it out again.

When she was settled comfortably beside him, Antonio closed his eyes, a smile on his face. "I'll admit to you that I have wanted to do that ever since we rescued Santiago from drowning."

She decided she would *never* tell him that the sight of his impressive near-nakedness during that same event had kept her going through recent long months. She settled on, "I didn't know you cared then," because she didn't know.

"Good! Santiago would have run me through." He ruffled her hair. "I like curly hair. How did this happen?"

"God only knows. You really like it?"

"*Si, esposa mia*. Stay awake for a few minutes. There is more to my story of Navas, but for your ears alone."

"El Ghalib," she said and he nodded.

"Surely he didn't…do that to you?" she asked, alert where moments ago she had been ready to sink into the mattress.

"No. He kissed her shoulder. "The Almohades were at breakfast. We poured out of the mountain pass and rode at them full tilt. One of them killed my horse …"

"Your beautiful black," she murmured. "I am so sorry."

"It was battle," he said simply. She heard his sorrow at the loss of his horse.

"Where was I? Ah, yes. I went down right at the beginning of the fight. My bad luck. I must have been knocked unconscious. When I came around, our soldiers and the Almohades were practically fighting on top of me. I don't remember much, but I remember the noise."

She thought of the ambush in the mountain pass before Toledo, and the warbling war cry. *I remember, too*, she thought.

"Carlos went running after another horse – you will admit that my new Arabian is a magnificent animal."

"I will," she said with a kiss.

"I hunted around for my shield. An Almohad warrior seemed to rise up out of the ground. I honestly did not see him before he struck my sword hand." She watched Antonio's eyes stare into that unknown distance. "Then El Ghalib was there. As he ran toward me, I hope to help me, one of King Alfonso's men stabbed him with a lance."

"No, no," she said.

"It was a free for all," he said. "An Almohad killed the soldier, then Carlos dispatched the warrior." He put his hand over his eyes.

Ana moved his hand and kissed each eye. "Don't see it," she whispered.

They clung together until Antonio's breathing returned to normal. "I am glad you will share my bed to help me through the dreams," he said, then smiled, because he was Antonio. "And for other matters."

She wanted him to finish, to tell her if Yussef el Ghalib, her great champion, still lived. She had to know.

"I know this is hard, my love. Please tell me…tell me he lives."

"I don't know, really," he said. "We were both bleeding so badly. Carlos wrapped my hand, and he looked at me, as if wondering whether to kill El Ghalib – such an honor *that* would be, probably worth his own lands." He settled her closer. "That was when Yussef worked the necklace out of his tunic and held it out to me."

"You let him live." She closed her eyes in relief.

"I was honor bound to do so," Antonio said. "He said something most curious. 'Do this, Antonio: Let your wife choose. Don't assume anything. Let her choose you or someone else. Abide by her choice. That is what I ask from you, not my life.'"

Ana kissed his bare chest, thinking of that good man, never her enemy. "My love, it seems that anyone with the necklace makes several bargains."

"It does," he agreed. He sat up, his eyes so serious. "Choose again, Ana, now that you know this. You are free to choose, even if it means you choose Yussef el Ghalib. He loves you."

"I suspected that," she said, knowing her gratitude to El Ghalib would always be in her heart. "Toño, I still choose you," she told him with no hesitation.

He kissed her, twining her together with him. "We left him there on the field. In these last few months, I have prayed that his own men found him and he is alive."

"I will pray, too," she said. "Now the necklace is yours."

He reached into his pile of clothing by the bed and took out the necklace. "Yours to wear again, my love."

She put it on. "No woman is well dressed without jewelry."

"You might want to add a camisa and gown. You know, when it isn't just us."

She laughed and settled beside him again, lifting up the necklace for another look. She knew the cost of the necklace in blood and tears, every drop. This necklace would go with her to the grave. It meant choice.

"After the battle, Carlos took me to Almadén, where he knew of a Muslim physician," Antonio continued. He closed his eyes, signaling to her that this part of the story was hard. "The old man did not care who he tended, Muslim or Christian. He removed splintered bone and torn muscle, and stitched me together."

"How brave you must have been."

"Carlos said you could hear me scream all over Almadén." He raised up on his good side. "I have heard much good of Muslim physicians. It is all true."

He slept then, this husband, lover and constant friend who had returned to her. Ana dressed quickly, knowing she was overdue in the kitchen, and that Hernana would tease her unmercifully. Her hand was on the door latch when she remembered something. She shook Antonio awake, but gently, then sat beside him.

"How is a man to recover strength to repeat his magnificent efforts if his wife wakes him?" he asked, but he was smiling.

"Oh, hush. I have to know. You say you have followers? Who?"

"All the villagers at Las Claves. Every one. I rode there a month ago.

Engracia and Rodrigo left for Valladolid earlier, but installed an uncle at Las Claves. How one woman can have so many useless relatives is beyond me. I give him six months to stay alive." He laughed. "Soon he will have no villagers to work fields, tend cattle or shepherd flocks."

"*All* of the villagers? How? Didn't he object?"

"I simply asked them. What could he do? They are under no fiat to remain, but free men like me." He held out his good hand and she took it in hers. "We will go to Las Claves after Toledo."

"And pick up Pablo at the first farm across the Tajo," Ana said. "He will be so pleased to see you."

"Your true knight will accompany us," he assured her. "The villagers of Las Claves – even *La Vieja* – will be ready to travel south." He kissed her hand. "Before we leave, we will go to the cemetery and pay our respects to a brave man and his daughter."

"I will always miss them both," she admitted.

"I would be disappointed in you if you didn't." He nudged her. "But don't miss Yussef el Ghalib too much, wife."

"No fears, Toño," she said.

"Ana, tomorrow in Toledo let us find that musician and his little sister. You and I will dance outside the gate, as we did once. The hope of us dancing there, even now as winter comes, pulled me through these months of pain in Almadén."

She kissed him. "See there, Toño, you never gave up."

"You have found me out, wife," he admitted. "I will be such an easy mark, a compliant husband."

Ana smiled inside. Hardly, not this man of hers.

"It's a small thing, I suppose, but will you dance with me in Toledo?"

"I was there at the gate two weeks ago," she said, tracing the lines of his face. "I will always dance with you."

After another kiss, Ana left the room and stood in the hall long enough to calm her mind and heart. She smiled to think of Hernana's awful tease coming, and clothing to pack for Liria. She had nothing of value to pack for herself, really, except the necklace.

Ana raised the necklace, wondering if it was good luck or bad luck. She decided it was good luck, though painful in the extreme, that she had the wrenching agony of staying with Santiago until he died, holding him in her arms, wishing for more time. Sometimes love hurts.

The necklace also kept Yussef el Ghalib alive, if alive he was. If the Almohad caliphate crumbled now, perhaps Yussef could use his considerable talent and undeniable charm to find a place for himself in a different Spain. She knew he would be welcome wherever she and Antonio settled. Sometimes love had no resolution.

She opened the door to her bedchamber again, more quietly this time, for another look at the man who had most definitely rumpled the sheets on a bed where she had slept alone and in tears. She admired the peace of his sleep, well aware that she had been responsible for at least some of that. As she leaned against the door frame, loving with her eyes the husband in her bed, Ana remembered the day Nito the gypsy taught her to read the lines in people's palms. Sometimes love teaches us.

You were a rascal, Nito, but you told me I had a long lifeline and could look forward to much love and many children, she thought. Maybe fortunetelling was all a hoax; maybe Nito knew something. She studied her palm and smiled at the lifeline.

Ana blew a kiss to the sleeping man then closed the door. There was much to do, if she and Liria were traveling tomorrow, first to Toledo, then Las Claves, then south to land promising more hard work and danger. She knew this moment in the corridor was probably her last peaceful time for days, maybe months.

Ana looked down at the necklace, knowing what it represented now: hard-earned, well-deserved love and the promise of more, never to be bargained away again, because the winnowing was over. "Certainly I will dance with you, Toño," she said softly. "I will always dance with you."

End

About the Author

A well-known veteran of the romance writing field, Carla Kelly is the author of forty-three novels and three non-fiction works, as well as numerous short stories and articles for various publications. She is the recipient of two RITA Awards from Romance Writers of America for Best Regency of the Year; two Spur Awards from Western Writers of America; three Whitney Awards, 2011, 2012, and 2014; and a Lifetime Achievement Award from *Romantic Times*.

Carla's interest in historical fiction is a byproduct of her lifelong study of history. She's held a variety of jobs, including medical public relations work, feature writer and columnist for a North Dakota daily newspaper, and ranger in the National Park Service (her favorite job) at Fort Laramie National Historic Site and Fort Union Trading Post National Historic Site. She has worked for the North Dakota Historical Society as a contract researcher.

Interest in the Napoleonic Wars at sea led to numerous novels about the Royal Navy, including the continuing St. Brendan Series. Carla has also written novels set in Wyoming during the Indian wars, and in the early twentieth century that focus on her interest in Rocky Mountain ranching.

Readers might also enjoy her Spanish Brand Series, set against the background of 18th century New Mexico, where ranchers struggle to thrive in a dangerous place as Spanish power declines.

CPSIA information can be obtained
at www.ICGtesting.com
Printed in the USA
LVHW041927290921
699032LV00013B/557